Praise for *Invaders*

★"In this very fine reprint anthology, Weisman has brought together 22 SF stories by authors who, although not generally associated with the genre, are clearly fellow travelers (not the ominous invaders suggested by the title). Among the major names are Pulitzer Prize–winner Junot Díaz, George Sanders, Katherine Dunn, Jonathan Lethem, Amiri Baraka, W.P. Kinsella, Steven Millhauser, Robert Olen Butler, and Molly Gloss. Among the best of the consistently strong stories are Díaz's "Monstro," the horrifying tale of a disease outbreak in Haiti; Gloss's near-perfect first-contact story, "Lambing Season"; Kinsella's totally bizarre "Reports Concerning the Death of the Seattle Albatross Are Somewhat Exaggerated"; Ben Loory's fable-like "The Squid Who Fell in Love with the Sun"; and Saunders's "Escape from Spiderhead," a deeply sexy tale of wild experimental science. In general, the stories tend toward satire and emphasize fine writing more than hitting genre beats—technology is usually a means to an end rather than the center of the story—but most of them could easily have found homes in SF magazines. This volume is a treasure trove of stories that draw equally from SF and literary fiction, and they are superlative in either context."
—*Publishers Weekly*, starred review

"Well, damn. From the first page to the last, *Invaders* surprised and intoxicated me, offering one stirring, visionary, warm-hearted, funny, probing story after another. Reading them in quick succession made me feel as if the world was flickering before my eyes, ricocheting from one possible reality to another, beneath a dozen different suns. It would be hard to devise a better survey of those contemporary short fiction writers, both celebrated and undersung, who have worked to smuggle the methods of science fiction into the mainstream."
—Kevin Brockmeier, bestselling author of *The Brief History of the Dead*

"For almost forty years I've believed and practiced and preached that there's no necessary distance between 'high literature' and 'science fiction.' *Invaders*

is convincing proof.   Funny, absurd, frightening, streetwise, probing, heartbreaking—the fiction collected here touches all registers."
—Carter Scholz, Hugo and Nebula Award–winning author of *Radiance* and *The Amount to Carry*

Praise for the anthologies of Jacob Weisman, editor

The Treasury of the Fantastic **(with David Sandner)**

"From the evocative images of Samuel Taylor Coleridge's 'Kubla Khan' and Lord Byron's 'Darkness' to Mark Twain's devil tale, 'The Mysterious Stranger,' and Max Beerbohm's devil plus time travel fantasy, 'Enoch Soames,' the 44 stories and poems in this compilation of fantastic literature provides a solid grounding in the development of the genre. Because most of the writers are 'mainstream' rather than genre authors, this collection also makes a good case for fantasy as literature, while the presence of Edgar Allan Poe, H. G. Wells, and Lord Dunsany alongside Edith Wharton, Emily Dickinson, and E. M. Forster breaks down the barrier between literary and genre fiction. VERDICT: This is an important collection for all lovers of fantasy and literature."
—*Library Journal*

"*The Treasury of the Fantastic* truly is a treasury of wonderful stories. . . . Turns out there's not a dud to be found."
—*Fantasy and Science Fiction*

"A marvelous mix of classics and rarely seen works, bibliophile's finds and old favorites . . . a treasury in every sense and a treasure!"
—Connie Willis, author of *Doomsday Book* and *To Say Nothing of the Dog*

"The fantasy tradition in English and American literature is rich and varied and strange. This is the book to read to find out what you never knew you needed to know."
—David G. Hartwell, editor of the Year's Best Fantasy series

"It was an absolute delight to see so [many] of these authors collected here and finding new treasures I hadn't realized really fell into the realm of fantasy."
—*My Shelf Confessions*

"*The Treasury of the Fantastic* is truly that, a comprehensive collection of fantastical literature from throughout the many years covering the romanticism era to the early twentieth century . . . an exquisitely curated collection. . . ."
The Arched Doorway

The Sword & Sorcery Anthology (with David G. Hartwell)

★"Heroes and their mighty deeds populate the pages of this delightfully kitschy yet absorbing anthology of sword and sorcery short stories from the 1930s onward. Hartwell and Weisman have selected some of the best short-form work in the genre, starting with the originator, Robert E. Howard, and his tales of Conan the Barbarian. The heroes are tough, savvy, and willing to knock a few heads in to get the job done. The soldier of Glen Cook's Dread Empire and Fritz Leiber's Grey Mouser make strong appearances, as does Michael Moorcock's Elric of Melniboné and his dread sword, Stormbringer. Female heroes are as ruthless as their male counterparts: C. L. Moore's Jirel of Joiry walks through Hell and back to get her revenge, while George R. R. Martin's Daenerys Stormborn becomes a true queen by outmaneuvering an entire city of slavers. This is an unbeatable selection from classic to modern, and each story brings its A game."
—*Publishers Weekly*, starred review

"The 19 stories in this volume span a time period from 1933 to 2012 and provide a strong introduction to this fantasy subgenre."
—*Library Journal*

"Awesome collection, very highly recommended."
—*Nerds in Babeland*

"Superbly presented . . . reignited this reader's interest."
—*SF Site*

"A big, meaty collection of genre highlights that runs the gamut from old-school classics to new interpretations, it serves as an excellent introduction and primer in one."
—*Green Man Review*

"Hard and fast-paced fantasy that's strong from the first piece right through to the last."
—*Shades of Sentience*

"Hartwell and Weisman's choices are top-notch and provide both an excellent introduction to the subgenre for new readers and exciting reading for long-time fans."
—*Grasping for the Wind*

"This engaging anthology is a terrific way to meet some of the best fantasists for those unfamiliar with their works and for returning vets a chance to enjoy fun short stories."
—*Midwest Book Review*

INVADERS

22 TALES FROM THE OUTER LIMITS OF LITERATURE

EDITED BY JACOB WEISMAN

TACHYON || SAN FRANCISCO

Tachyon Publications LLC
1459 18th Street #139
San Francisco, CA 94107
(415) 285-5615
www.tachyonpublications.com
tachyon@tachyonpublications.com

Series Editor: Jacob Weisman
Project Editor: James DeMaiolo

ISBN: 978-1-61696-210-4

Printed in the United States by Worzalla
First Edition: 2016
9 8 7 6 5 4 3 2 1

For Sheila Williams, friend and mentor since the beginning.

Special thanks to James Patrick Kelly & John Kessel, James DeMaiolo, Ellen Datlow, Gordon Van Gelder, Lettie Prell & John Domini, and Bernie Goodman for their help in assembling this anthology.

CONTENTS

JACOB WEISMAN

Introduction

Jacob Weisman is the editor and publisher at Tachyon Publications, which he founded in 1995. He has been nominated for the World Fantasy Award three times and is the series editor of Tachyon's Hugo, Nebula, Sturgeon, and Shirley Jackson award–winning novella line, including original fiction by Nancy Kress, James Morrow, Brandon Sanderson, Alastair Reynolds, and Daryl Gregory. Weisman is also the co-editor of *The Sword & Sorcery Anthology* (with David G. Hartwell) and *The Treasury of the Fantastic* (with David Sandner). Weisman lives in San Francisco, where he runs Tachyon Publications in the same neighborhood in which he grew up.

There's a long tradition of writers with serious literary credentials who have occasionally written works of science fiction: Kingsley Amis, Margaret Atwood, Angela Carter, Pat Frank, Russell Hoban, Aldous Huxley, Doris Lessing, George Orwell, Marge Piercy, Kurt Vonnegut, and Bernard Wolfe among others.

In recent years, however, as the barriers between science fiction and literature have begun to crumble, the crossovers are becoming even more commonplace. In 2014 a trio of very accomplished sf novels were published and shelved outside the science fiction section.

The Martian by Andy Weir is the straight up science-fiction story of a NASA scientist marooned on Mars, which harkens back to the works of Hal

Clement and Arthur C. Clarke. It made all of the bestseller lists and is now a motion picture starring Matt Damon. *The Martian* won the Seiun Award for the best long sf story translated into Japanese, but did not garner any nominations for the larger sf awards.

Emily St. John Mandel's beautifully evocative *Station Eleven* is a post-apocalyptic novel following the exploits of a troupe of Shakespearean actors. Like *The Martian*, *Station Eleven* won a single science fiction award, the Arthur C. Clarke Award for the best science fiction novel published in the United Kingdom. It received no nominations from any of the other sf awards, but did manage nominations for the PEN/Faulkner Award for Fiction and the National Book Award.

The final novel in this trio is *Nigerians in Space* by Deji Bryce Olukotun. *Nigerians in Space* is a taut thriller about a fictional Nigerian space program. The space program turns out to be something of a MacGuffin, but there are other elements that will make the book very appealing to fans of sf. However, so far *Nigerians in Space* has not received a wider audience.

Olukotun was the last author selected for this anthology. I'd not heard of him when I began work on this book, nor even really when I sat down to read his story, "We Are the Olfanauts." I was impressed by the story (hopefully you will be too) and intrigued enough by the title of his lone novel that I immediately tracked down a copy of *Nigerians in Space*. Once the book arrived, I read through most of it that evening and finished it later the next morning. *Nigerians in Space* deserves not only to be rediscovered (or perhaps discovered), but should rightfully garner a seat at the table with *The Martian* and *Station Eleven*.

My own interest in these types of writers began with a book I commissioned in 2009, *The Secret History of Science Fiction*, which was edited by James Patrick Kelly and John Kessel. *Secret History* wasn't originally conceived as a throwing down of the gauntlet, as the challenge to the very fabric of science fiction that it was taken to be in some circles. It was intended to be a serious investigation of the intersection between literary writers who occasionally dabbled in science fiction and science fiction writers who occasionally dabbled in something resembling literary fiction. In *Secret History*, literary writers including Margaret Atwood, T. C. Boyle, and Don DeLillo were found hobnobbing with the likes of sf legends such as Ursula K. Le Guin, Connie Willis, and Gene Wolfe.

The reviews were mostly positive, except when they weren't. Then they tended to be angry, defensive, and sometimes bewildering. "This is another book," the critic John J. Pierce said to me and John Kessel on a panel that we were all on together at Readercon, "telling us how we should write."

Well no, not really. *The Secret History of Science Fiction* does show how certain types of writers might tackle somewhat similarly themed subject matter. But I don't think John Kessel (or I) would ever tell anybody that they should write like Don DeLillo (if only it were that easily accomplished). The book was much more about facilitating a reconciliation between two branches of literature as opposed to issuing a challenge.

But Pierce was genuinely upset. And it is plainly easy to see how science fiction writers and critics might bridle after toiling in one of the poorest of literary ghettos for decades upon decades. "Thanks for all your hard work," they are worried they will hear from the literary establishment, "but we'll take it from here." It becomes a very real concern when science fiction is reduced to what is shelved over in science fiction and "serious" literature is what is not, whether a book is about marooned astronauts or about a plague that wipes out the majority of the human race.

The most consistent thread of criticism received by *Secret History* is that somehow the work by the bona fide science fiction writers in the book was somehow superior to the other stories. Or, as the critic Paul Kincaid put it in a (mostly positive) review on the *Strange Horizons* website, "the stories written by the science fiction writers are almost invariably stories written in the knowledge of science fiction, written as a way of exploring what it is that makes the story science fiction." But the implication here, and stated explicitly in other reviews, is that these other writers, writing without the necessary knowledge of the history of the genre, were somehow off the mark or ignorantly reinventing old tropes.

This concept of science fiction exceptionalism is, in fact, a long held belief of the science fiction genre. In the earliest days of the science fiction pulps, fiction was mostly a vehicle to expound upon the advances in technology that would lead to a more exciting, and perhaps better, or even utopian, future. Science fiction readers were true believers in a shared vision of the world(s) to come, who found each other through letters columns of the various magazines and fanzines (the Internet of the early twentieth century). They formed social clubs, held conventions, and communicated vigorously among themselves. The majority of science fiction's writers came from within its own ranks.

In his collection of essays *The Jewel-Hinged Jaw*, Samuel R. Delany lays out what he now famously calls "the protocols of science fiction," arguing that there is not only a set of rules and skills that is required of the reader to decode a work of science fiction, but also a necessary knowledge of themes and concepts that science fiction writers have been building on for years. Delany posits that a phrase like "the door dilated," as employed by Heinlein in one of his novels, will only baffle a reader unfamiliar with the concept of iris doors or the technology that they imply. Delany goes on to suggest that due to the added burden of the continual dialogue between its writers and readers, it is not only wrong to judge science fiction against the standards of literary fiction, it is also irrelevant to do so.

Delany's eloquent defense of sf exceptionalism may have been slightly exaggerated at the time but is almost certainly no longer true. *The Jewel-Hinged Jaw* was published in 1977, the same year that *Star Wars* set new box office records. Much has changed since then. *Locus*, the trade magazine of the science fiction field, estimated that in 1977 there were just 315 sf titles published. In comparison, they estimated that there were 2,177 sf titles brought out by traditional print publishers in 2014. Add in the many thousands of self-published books and it becomes clear that it's no longer possible for anyone to keep up with everything published in science fiction, or even with very much of it. At the same time, the general public's knowledge of science fiction tropes has also increased exponentially, with film after film borrowing heavily from the most successful sf novels. Add in a renaissance of television shows that began years ago with *Firefly*, *Farscape*, *Battlestar Galactica*, and several generations of *Doctor Who*, and was followed by countless others.

Whether it's time travel, iris doors, or an Internet that jacks directly into the brain of the user, we've all seen it, probably more than once. To find something truly new, we have to turn to the works of Hannu Rajaniemi, Kameron Hurley, and other writers further out on the cutting edge, where there are fewer road maps to follow than before.

What I set out to discover in *Invaders* was the answer to a simple question, posed indirectly by the critics of *The Secret History of Science Fiction*: If non-genre writers are indeed writing something different from the rest of the science fiction field, what are they actually writing? The answer is that it can indeed be different, or not so different at all. Mostly it depends on the writer.

Let's say a writer grows up watching sci-fi movies and TV and reading science fiction novels, but then gets an MFA in literature and writes mainstream fiction in commercial markets as diverse as *The New Yorker* or *Tin House*. Could that person be considered a science fiction writer at all, even if he or she only publishes something like sf from time to time? What if the story appears in a science fiction magazine, like a couple of the stories published in this book?

Gordon Van Gelder, the publisher and former editor of *Fantasy & Science Fiction*, suggests that the difference between stories published in mainstream outlets and his magazine is mostly one of markets and reader expectations. In *Invaders* you'll find a lot more stories about sex and relationships because that's what you'll find in mainstream magazines. But you'll also find squids, spaceships, zombies, plagues, time travel, alternate dimensions, and aliens. You'll find a myriad of authors tackling the very essence of science fiction, whether the authors consider themselves to be writing science fiction or not. Or whether or not they're aware that they are writing in a tradition that goes back over a century—or ninety years if one dates science fiction publishing back to the first issue of Hugo Gernsback's *Amazing Stories*.

Most of the writers collected here are still actively publishing. Some of them are young writers who grew up surrounded by the science fiction tropes pervasive in popular culture. Many of them are older writers intrigued by the possibilities of exploring a new medium. All of them are extremely talented writers who refuse to limit their ability to tell a good story because of arbitrary restrictions of genre. And that cross-pollination is ultimately a positive and important step for both literature and for science fiction.

—San Francisco, 2016

J. ROBERT LENNON
Portal

J. Robert Lennon is the author of two story collections, *Pieces for the Left Hand* und *See You in Paradise*, and seven novels, including *Mailman*, *Familiar*, and *Happyland*. He teaches writing at Cornell University.

In "Portal," Lennon explores the familiar trope of a doorway to other dimensions without much concern toward the device's origins. "Portal" was first published as the lead story in Lennon's most recent collection, *See You in Paradise*.

It's been a few years since we last used the magic portal in our back garden, and it has fallen into disrepair. To be perfectly honest, when we bought this place, we had no idea what kind of work would be involved, and tasks like keeping the garden weeded, repairing the fence, maintaining the portal, etc., quickly fell to the bottom of the priority list while we got busy dealing with the roof and the floor joists. I guess there are probably people with full-time jobs out there who can keep an old house in great shape without breaking their backs, but if there are, I've never met them.

My point is, we've developed kind of a blind spot about that whole back acre. The kids are older now and don't spend so much time wandering around in the woods and the clearing the way they used to—Luann is all about the boys these days, and you can't get Chester's mind away from the Xbox for more than five minutes—and Gretchen and I hardly ever even look in that direction. I think one time last summer we got a little drunk and sneaked out there to have sex under the crabapple tree, but weeds and stones kept poking up through the blanket and the bugs were eating us alive, so we gave up, came back inside, and did it in the bed like normal people.

I know, too much information, right? Anyway, it was the kids who discovered the portal back when we first moved in. They were into all that magic stuff at the time—*Harry Potter*, *Lord of the Rings*, that kind of thing—and while Gretchen and I steamed off old wallpaper and sanded the floorboards inside the house, they had this whole crazy fantasy world invented back there, complete with various kingdoms, wizards, evil forces, orcs, trolls, and what have you. They made paths, buried treasures, drew maps, and basically had a grand old time. We didn't even have to send them to summer camp, they were so . . . tolerable. They didn't fight, didn't complain—I hope someday, when the teen years are over with, they'll remember all that and have some kind of relationship again. Maybe when they're in college. Fingers crossed.

One afternoon, I guess it was in July, they came running into the house, tracking mud everywhere and breathlessly shouting about something they'd found. "It's a portal, it's a portal to another world!" I got pretty bent out of shape about the mud, but the kids were seriously over the moon about this thing, and their enthusiasm was infectious. So Gretchen and I followed them out across the yard and into the woods, then down the little footpath that led to the clearing.

It's unclear what used to be there, back in the day—the land behind our house was once farmland, and the remains of old dirt roads run everywhere—but at this time, a few years ago, the clearing was pretty overgrown, thick with shrubs and brambles and the like. We figured there'd just been a grain silo or something, something big that would have resulted in this perfectly circular area, but the kids had uncovered a couple of stone benches and a little fire pit, so clearly somebody used to hang around here in the past, you know, lighting a fire and sitting on the benches to look at it.

When we reached the clearing, we were quite impressed with the progress the kids had made. They'd managed to clear a lot of brush and the place had the feel of some kind of private room—the sun coming down through the clouds, and the wall of trees surrounding the space, and all that. It was really nice. So the kids had stopped at the edge, and we came up behind them and they were like, do you see it? And we were like, see what? And they said look, and we said, where?, and they said, Mom, Dad, just look!

And sure enough, off to the left, kind of hovering above what had looked like another bench but now appeared more like a short, curved little staircase, was this oval, sort of man-sized, shimmering thing that honestly just screamed "magic portal." I mean, it was totally obvious what it was—nothing else gives the air that quality, that kind of electrical distortion, like heat or whatever is bending space itself.

This was a real surprise to us, because there had been nothing about it in the real estate ad. You'd think the former owners would have mentioned it. I mean, the dry rot, I understand why they left that out, but even if this portal was busted, it's still a neat thing to have (or so I thought at the time), and could have added a few thou to the asking price, easy. But this was during the economic slump, so maybe not, and maybe the previous owners never bothered to come back here and didn't know what they had. They looked like indoor types, frankly. Not that Gretchen and I look like backcountry survivalists or anything. But I digress.

The fact is, this portal was definitely not busted, it was working, and the kids had taken special care uncovering the steps that led to it, tugging out all the weeds from between the stones and unearthing the little flagstone patio that surrounded the whole thing. In retrospect, if I had been an expert, or even a well-informed amateur, I would probably have been able to tell the portal was really just puttering along on its last legs and would soon go on the fritz. But of course I was, and I guess still am, an idiot.

We all went over there and walked around it and looked through it—had a laugh making faces at one another through the space and watching each other go all fun-house mirror. But obviously the unspoken question was, do we go through? I was actually really proud of the kids right then because they'd come and gotten us instead of just diving headfirst through the thing like a lot of kids would have done. Who knows, maybe this stellar judgment will return to them someday. A guy can dream! But at this moment we all were just kind of looking at each other, wondering who was going to test it out.

Since I'm the father, this task fell to me. I bent over and pried a stone up out of the dirt and stood in front of the portal, with the kids looking on from behind. (Gretchen stood off to the side with her arms folded over her chest, doing that slightly disapproving stance she does pretty much all the time now.) And after a dramatic pause, I raised my arm and tossed the stone at the portal.

Nothing dramatic—the stone just disappeared. "It works!" Chester cried, and Luann hopped up and down, trying to suppress her excitement.

"Now hold on," I said, and picked up a twig. I braced my foot on the bottom step and poked the twig through the portal. This close, you could hear a low hum from the power the thing was giving off. In retrospect, this was probably an indication that the portal was out of whack—I mean, if my TV did that, I'd call a guy. But then, I figured, what did I know?

Besides, when I pulled the twig out, it looked okay. Not burned or frozen or turned into a snake or anything—it was just itself. I handed it to Gretchen and she gave it a cursory examination. "Jerry," she said, "I'm not sure—"

"Don't worry, don't worry." I knew the drill—she's the mom, she has to be skeptical, and it's my job to tell her not to worry. Which is harder to do nowadays, let me tell you. I got up nice and close to the portal, until the little hairs on my arms were standing up, and I stuck out my index finger and moved it slowly toward the shimmering air.

Chester's eyes were wide. Luann covered her mouth with her fists. Gretchen sighed.

Well, what can I say, it went in, and I barely felt a thing. It was weird seeing my pointer finger chopped off at the knuckle like that, but when I pulled it out again, voilà, there it was, unharmed. My family still silent, I took the bull by the horns and just shoved my whole arm in. The kids screamed. I pulled it out.

"What," I said, "what!!"

"We could see your blood and stuff!" This was Chester.

Luann said, "Daddy, that was so gross."

"Like an X-ray?" I said.

Chester was laughing hysterically now. "Like it got chopped off!"

"Oh my God, Jerry," Gretchen said, her hand on her heart.

My arm was fine, though. In fact, it felt kind of good—wherever the arm had just been, it was about five degrees warmer than this breezy little glade.

"Kids," I said, "stand behind me." Because I didn't want them to see what I was about to do. Eventually we'd get over this little taboo and enjoy watching each other walk super slowly through the portal, revealing our pulsing innards, but for now I didn't want to freak anyone out, myself least of all. When the kids were safely behind me, Gretchen holding them close, I stuck my head through.

I don't know what I was expecting—Middle-earth, or Jupiter, or Tuscany, or what. But I could never in a million years have guessed the truth. I pulled my head out.

"It's the vacant lot behind the public library," I said.

I think that even then, that very day, we knew the portal was screwed up. It was only later, after it was obvious, that Gretchen and I started saying out loud the strange things we noticed on the family trip downtown. For one thing, the books we got at the library—obviously that's the first place we went—weren't quite right. The plots were all convoluted and the paper felt funny. The bus lines were not the way we remembered, with our usual bus, the 54, called the 24; and the local transit authority color scheme had been changed to crimson and ochre. Several restaurants had different names, and the one guy we bumped into whom we knew—my old college pal Andy—recoiled in apparent horror when he saw us. It was just, you know, off.

But the really creepy thing was what Chester said that night as we were tucking him in to bed—and how I miss those days now, when Chester was still practically a baby and needed us to hug and kiss him goodnight—he just started laughing there in the dark, and Gretchen said what is it, honey, and he said that guy with the dog head.

Dog head? we asked him.

Yeah, that guy, remember him? He walked past us on the sidewalk. He didn't have a regular head, he had a dog head.

Well, you know, Chester was always saying crazy nonsense back then. He still does, of course, but that's different—it used to be cute and funny. So we convinced ourselves he was kidding. But later, when we remembered that—hell, we got chills. Everything from there on in would only get weirder, but it's that dog head, Chester remembering the dog head, that freaks me out. I guess the things that scare you are the things that are almost normal.

Anyway, that first time, everything seemed to go off more or less without a hitch. After the library we walked in the park, went out for dinner, enjoyed the summer weather. Then we went back to the vacant lot, found the portal, and went home. It's tricky to make out the return portal when you're not looking for it; the shimmering is fainter and of course there's no set of stone steps leading up to it or anything. Anybody watching would just have seen us disappearing one by one. In an old Disney live-action movie (you know, like *Flubber* or *Witch Mountain*) there would be a hobo peering at us from the gutter, and then, when we vanished, looking askance at his bottle of moonshine and resolvedly tossing it over his shoulder.

So that night, we felt fine. We all felt fine. We felt pretty great, in fact; it had been an exciting day. Gretchen and I didn't get it on, it was that time of the month; but we snuggled a lot. We decided to make it a weekend tradition, at least on nice days—get up, read the paper, get dressed, then out to the portal for a little adventure.

Because by the third time it was obvious that it would be an adventure; it turns out the portal wasn't permanently tied to the vacant lot downtown. I don't know if this was usual or what. But I pictured it flapping in the currents of space and time, sort of like a windsock, stuck fast at one end and whipping randomly around at the other. I still have no idea why it dropped us off so close to home (or so apparently close to home) that first time—I suppose it was still trying to be normal. Like an old guy in denial about the onset of dementia.

The second time we went through, we thought we were in old-time England, on some heath or something—in fact, after I put my head in to check, I sent Gretchen back to the house to fill a basket with bread and fruit and the like, for a picnic, and I told Luann to go to the garage to get the flag off her bike, to mark the site of the return portal. Clever, right? The weather was fine, and we were standing in a landscape of rolling grassy hills, little blue meandering creeks, and drifting white puffy clouds. We could see farms and villages in every direction, but no cities, no cars or planes or smog. We hiked down into the nearest village and got a bit of a shock—nobody was around, no people, or animals for that matter—the place was abandoned. And we all got the strong feeling that the whole world was abandoned, too—that we were the only living creatures in it. I mean, there weren't even any bugs. It was lonesome as hell. We went home after an hour and ate our picnic back in the clearing.

The third time we went through, we ended up in this crazy city—honestly, it was too much. Guys selling stuff, people zipping around in hovercars, drunks staggering in the streets, cats and dogs and these weirdly intelligent-looking animals that were sort of like deer but striped and half as large. Everybody wore hats—the men seemed to favor these rakish modified witch-hat things with a floppy brim, and women wore a kind of collapsed cylinder, like a soufflé. Nobody seemed to notice us, they were busy, busy, busy. And the streets! None of them was straight. It was like a loud, crowded, spaghetti maze, and for about half an hour we were terrified that we'd gotten lost and would never find the portal again, which miraculously had opened into the only uninhabited dark alley in the whole town. (We'd planted our bicycle flag between two paving stones, and almost lost it to a thing that was definitely *not* a rat.) Chester demanded a witch hat, but the only place we found that sold them wouldn't take our money, and we didn't speak the language anyway, which was this whacked-out squirrel chatter. Oh, yeah, and everybody had a big jutting chin. I mean everybody. When we finally got home that night the four of us got into a laughing fit about the chins—I don't know what it was, they just struck us as wildly hilarious.

Annoying as that trip was, I have to admit now that it was the best time we ever had together, as a family I mean. Even when we were freaked out, we were all on the same page—we were a team. I suppose it's perfectly normal for this to change, I mean, the kids have to strike out on their own someday, right? They have to develop their own interests and their own way of doing things, or else they'd never leave, god forbid. But I miss that time. And just like every other asshole who fails to appreciate what he's got while he still has it, all I ever did was complain.

I'm thinking here of the fourth trip through the portal. When I stuck my head through for a peek, all I saw was fog and all I heard was clanking, and I pictured some kind of waterfront, you know, with the moored boats bumping up against each other and maybe a nice seafood place tucked in among the warehouses and such. I guess I'd gotten kind of reckless. I led the family through and after about fifteen seconds I realized that the fog was a hell of a lot thicker than I thought it was, and that it kind of stung the eyes and nose, and that the clanking was far too regular and far too deep and loud to be the result of some gentle ocean swell.

In fact, we had ended up in hell—a world of giant robots, acrid smoke, windowless buildings, and glowing toxic waste piles. We should have turned right around and gone back through the portal, but Chester ran ahead, talking to himself about superheroes or something. Gretchen went after him, Luann reached for my hand (maybe for the last time ever? But please, I don't want to go there), and before you knew it we had no idea where we were. The fog thickened, if anything, and nobody knew who had the flag, or if we'd even remembered to bring the thing. It took Luann and me half an hour just to find Gretchen and Chester, and two hours more to find the portal (and this only by random groping—it would have been easy to miss it entirely). By this time we were all trembling and crying—well, I wasn't crying, but I was sure close—and nearly paralyzed with fear from a series of close calls with these enormous, filthy, fast-moving machines that looked like elongated forklifts and, in one instance, a kind of chirping metal tree on wheels. When I felt my arm tingle I nearly crapped myself with relief. We piled through the portal and back into a summer evening in the yard, and were disturbed to discover a small robot that had inadvertently passed through along with us, a kind of four-slice toaster-type thing on spindly anodized bird legs. In the coming weeks it would rust with unnatural speed, twitching all the while, until it was nothing but a gritty orange stain on the ground.

Maybe I'm remembering this wrong—you know, piling all our misfortunes together in one place in my mind—but I believe it was in the coming days that the kids began to change, or rather to settle into what we thought (hoped) were temporary patterns of unsavory behavior. Chester's muttered monologuing, which for a long time we thought was singing, or an effort to memorize something, took on a new intensity—his face would turn red, spittle would gather at the corners of his mouth, and when we interrupted him he would gaze at us with hatred, some residual emotion from his violent fantasy world. As for Luann, the phone began ringing a lot more often, and she would disappear with the receiver into private corners of the house to whisper secrets to her friends. Eventually, of course, the friends turned into boys. Gretchen bought her some makeup, and the tight jeans and tee shirts she craved—because what are you going to do, make the kid wear hoop dresses and bonnets?

As for Gretchen, well—I don't know. She started giving me these *looks*, not exactly pitying, but regretful, maybe. Disappointed. And not even in me, particularly—more like, she had disappointed herself for setting her sights so low. I'm tempted to blame the portal for all this, the way it showed us how pathetic, how circumscribed our lives really were. But I didn't need a magic portal to tell me I was no Mr. Excitement—I like my creature comforts, and I liked it when my wife and kids didn't demand too much from me, and when you get down to it, maybe all that, not the portal, is the reason everything started going south. Not that Gretchen's parents helped matters when they bought Chester the video game for his birthday—an hour in front of that thing and adios, amigo. Whatever demons were battling in his mind all day long found expression through his thumbs—it became the only thing that gave the poor kid any comfort. And eventually we would come to realize that Luann was turning into, forgive me, something of a slut, and that Chester had lost what few social graces we'd managed to teach him. Today his face is riddled with zits, he wanders off from the school grounds two or three times a week, and he still gets skid marks in his tighty whities. And Luann—we bought her a used car in exchange for a promise to drive Chester where he wanted to go, but she gave him a ride maybe once— it was to, God knows why, the sheet metal fabricating place down behind the supermarket—and then forgot him there for four hours while she did god knows what with god knows who. ("It doesn't matter what I was doing! Stuff!")

But I'm getting ahead of myself. You'd think we would have quit the portal entirely after the robot fog incident, but then you're probably mistaking us for intelligent people. Instead we went back now and again—it was the only thing we could all agree to do together. Sometimes I went by myself, too. I suspect Gretchen was doing the same—she'd be missing for a couple of hours then would come back flushed and covered with burrs, claiming to have been down on the recreation path, jogging. I don't think the kids went alone—but then where did Chester get that weird knife?

In any event, what we saw in there became increasingly disturbing. Crowds of people with no faces, a world where the ground itself seemed to be alive, heaving and sweating. We generally wouldn't spend more than a few minutes wherever we ended up. The portal, in its decline into senility, seemed to have developed an independent streak, a mind of its own. It was . . . giving us things. Things it thought we wanted. It showed us a world that was almost all noise and confusion and flashing red light, with a soundtrack of something you could hardly call music made by something you maybe could mistake for guitars. Only Luann had a good time in that one. There was Chester's world, the one that wheeled around us in pixelated, rainbow 3-D, where every big-eyed armored creature exploded into fountains of glittering blood and coins, and the one that looked like ours, except thinner, everything thinner, the buildings and people and trucks and cars, and from the expression of horror on Gretchen's face, I could tell where that one was coming from. And there was the one place where all the creatures great and small appeared to have the red hair, thick ankles, and perky little boobs of the new administrative assistant at my office. Gretchen didn't talk to me for days after that, but it certainly did put me off the new assistant.

And so before the summer was over, we gave up. The kids were too busy indulging their new selves and quit playing make-believe out in the woods. And Gretchen and I were lost in our private worlds of self-disgust and conjugal disharmony. By Christmas we'd forgotten about the portal, and the clearing began to fill in. We did what people do: we heaved our grim corporeal selves through life.

I checked back there a couple of times over the next few years—you know, just to see if everything looked all right. Needless to say, last time I checked, it didn't—the humming was getting pretty loud, and the shimmering oval was all lopsided, with a sort of hernia in the lower left corner, which was actually drooping far enough to touch the ground. When I poked a stick through the opening, there was a pop and a spark and a cloud of smoke, and the portal seemed to emit a kind of hacking cough, followed by the scent of ozone and rot. When I returned to the house and told Gretchen what I'd seen, she didn't seem to care. And so I decided not to care, either. Like I said before, there were more important things to worry about.

Just a few weeks ago, though, I started hearing strange noises at night. "Didya hear that?" I'd say out loud, and if I was in bed with Gretchen (as opposed to on the sofa, alone), she would rise up out of half sleep to tell me no, it was just a dream. But it wasn't. It was a little like a coyote's yip, but deeper, more elongated. And sometimes there would be a screech of metal on metal, or a kind of random ticking; and if I got up and looked out the window, sometimes I thought I could see a strange glow coming from the woods.

And now, even in the daytime, there's a funny odor hanging around the yard. It's springtime, and Gretchen says it's just the smell of nature waking up. But I don't think so. Is springtime supposed to smell like motor oil and dog piss in the morning? To be perfectly honest, I'm beginning to be afraid of what our irresponsibility, our helplessness, has wrought. I mean, we bought this place. We own it, just like we own all our other problems.

I try to talk to Gretchen about it, but she doesn't want to hear it. "I'm on a different track right now," she says. "I can't be distracted from my healing." "Healing from *what?*" I want to know. "My psychic disharmony." I mean, what can you say to that? Meanwhile, I have no idea where our daughter is half the time, and I haven't gone up to Chester's room in three weeks. I can hear him up there, muttering; I can hear the bed squeak as he acts out his violent fantasies; I hear the menacing orchestral strings and explosions and tortured screams that emanate from his favorite games.

Problems don't just go away, you know? Problems get bigger and bigger and before you know it they're bigger than you are, and it's too late to fix them. Some days, when I've gotten a decent night's sleep and have had a few cups of coffee, I think sure, I'll just get on the phone, start calling people up and asking for help. A school guidance counselor, a marriage therapist, a pediatrician, a witch or shaman or wizard or physicist or whoever in the hell might know what to do about the portal, or even have the balls to walk down that path and see what's become of the clearing.

But on other days, days like today, when I'm too damned tired even to reach for the phone, the only emotion I can summon up is longing, for a time when the world was miraculous, when I couldn't wait to get up in the morning and start living.

I mean, the magic has to come from some place, right? It's out there, bestowing itself on somebody else's wife, somebody else's kids, somebody else's life. All I want is to get just a little of it back. Is that so much to ask?

ERIC PUCHNER
Beautiful Monsters

Eric Puchner is the author of the story collection *Music Through the Floor* and
the novel *Model Home*, which was a finalist for the PEN/Faulkner Award and the
Barnes & Noble Discover Award and won the California Book Award Silver Medal
for best work of fiction. His short stories and personal essays have appeared
in *GQ*, *Granta*, *Tin House*, *Zoetrope: All Story*, *Narrative*, *Glimmer Train*, *Best
American Short Stories*, *Best American Nonrequired Reading*, and *Pushcart
Prize: Best of the Small Presses*. He has received a Wallace Stegner Fellowship,
a National Endowment for the Arts grant, and the 2014 Arts and Letters Award
in Literature from the American Academy of Arts and Letters. In 2015 he was
awarded the $25,000 Jeannette Haien Ballard Writer's Prize, given annually to
writers "of proven excellence in poetry or prose." He is an assistant professor in
the Writing Seminars at Johns Hopkins University.

Like some of the best science-fiction stories, "Beautiful Monsters" begins
in strange surroundings, gradually filling in details until the plot crystallizes and
an extraordinary experience has occurred. The story was first published in the
literary magazine *Tin House* and was selected for inclusion in *The Best American
Short Stories*.

The boy is making breakfast for his sister—fried eggs and cheap frozen
sausages, furred with ice—when he sees a man eating an apple from the
tree outside the window. The boy drops his spatula. It is a gusty morning,
sun-sharp and beautiful, and the man's shirt flags out to one side of him,

rippling in the wind. The boy has never seen a grown man in real life, only in books, and the sight is both more and less frightening than he expected. The man picks another apple from high in the tree and devours it in several bites. He is bearded and tall as a shadow, but the weirdest things of all are his hands. They seem huge, grotesque, as clumsy as crabs. The veins on them bulge out, forking around his knuckles. The man plucks some more apples from the tree and sticks them in a knapsack at his feet, ducking his head so that the boy can see a saucer of scalp in the middle of his hair.

What do you think it wants? his sister whispers, joining him by the stove. She watches the hideous creature strip their tree of fruit; the boy might be out of work soon, and they need the apples themselves. The eggs have begun to scorch at the edges.

I don't know. He must have wandered away from the woods.

I thought they'd be less . . . ugly, his sister says.

The man's face is damp, streaked with ash, and it occurs to the boy that he's been crying. A twig dangles from his beard. The boy does not find the man ugly—he finds him, in fact, mesmerizing—but he does not mention this to his sister, who owns a comic book filled with pictures of handsome fathers, contraband drawings of twinkling, well-dressed men playing baseball with their daughters or throwing them high into the air. There is nothing well-dressed about this man, whose filthy pants—like his shirt—look like they've been sewn from deerskin. His bare feet are black with soot. Behind him the parched mountains seethe with smoke, charred by two-week-old wildfires. There have been rumors of encounters in the woods, of firefighters beset by giant, hairy-faced beasts stealing food or tents or sleeping bags, of girls being raped in their beds.

The man stops picking apples and stares right at the kitchen window, as if he smells the eggs. The boy's heart trips. The man wipes his mouth on his sleeve, then limps down the driveway and stoops inside the open door of the garage.

He's stealing something! the boy's sister says.

He barely fits, the boy says.

Trap him. We can padlock the door.

The boy goes and gets the .22 from the closet in the hall. He's never had cause to take it out before—their only intruders are skunks and possums, the occasional raccoon—but he knows exactly how to use it, a flash of certainty in his brain, just as he knows how to use the lawn mower and fix the plumbing and operate the worm-drive saw at work without thinking twice. He builds houses for other boys and girls to live in, it is what he's always done—he loves the smell of cut pine and sawdust in his nose, the *fzzzzdddt* of screws buzzing through Sheetrock into wood—and he can't imagine not doing it, any more than he can imagine leaving this gusty town ringed by mountains. He was born knowing these things, will always know them; they are as instinctive to him as breathing.

But he has no knowledge of men, only what he's learned from history books. And the illicit, sentimental fairy tales of his sister's comic.

He tells his sister to stay inside and then walks toward the garage, leading with the rifle. The wind swells the trees, and the few dead August leaves crunching under his feet smell like butterscotch. For some reason, perhaps because of the sadness in the man's face, he is not as scared as he would have imagined. The boy stops inside the shadow of the garage and sees the man hunched behind the lawn mower, bent down so his head doesn't scrape the rafters. One leg of the man's pants is rolled up to reveal a bloody gash on his calf. He picks a fuel jug off the shelf and splashes some gasoline on the wound, grimacing. The boy clears his throat, loudly, but the man doesn't look up.

Get out of my garage, the boy says.

The man startles, banging his head on the rafters. He grabs a shovel leaning against the wall and holds it in front of him. The shovel, in his overgrown hands, looks as small as a baseball bat. The boy lifts the .22 up to his eye, so that it's leveled at the man's stomach. He tilts the barrel at the man's face.

What will you do?

Shoot you, the boy says.

The man smiles, dimpling his filthy cheeks. His teeth are as yellow as corn. I'd like to see you try.

I'd aim right for the apricot. The medulla. You'd die instantly.

You look like you're nine, the man mutters.

The boy doesn't respond to this. He suspects the man's disease has infected his brain. Slowly, the man puts down the shovel and ducks out of the garage, plucking cobwebs from his face. In the sunlight, the wound on his leg looks even worse, shreds of skin stuck to it like grass. He reeks of gasoline and smoke and something else, a foul body smell, like the inside of a ski boot.

I was sterilizing my leg.

Where do you live? the boy asks.

In the mountains. The man looks at his gun. Don't worry, I'm by myself. We split up so we'd be harder to kill.

Why?

Things are easier to hunt in a herd.

No, the boy says. Why did you leave?

The fire. Burned up everything we were storing for winter. The man squints at the house. Can I trouble you for a spot of water?

The boy lowers his gun, taking pity on this towering creature that seems to have stepped out of one of his dreams. In the dreams, the men are like beautiful monsters, stickered all over with leaves, roaming through town in the middle of the night. The boy leads the man inside the house, where his sister is still standing at the window. The man looks at her and nods. That someone should have hair growing out of his face appalls her even more than the smell. *There's a grown man in my house*, she says to herself, but she cannot reconcile the image this arouses in her brain with the stooped creature she sees limping into the kitchen. She's often imagined what it would be like to live with a father—a dashing giant, someone who'd buy her presents and whisk her chivalrously from danger, like the brave, mortal fathers she reads about—but this man is as far from these handsome creatures as can be.

And yet the sight of his sunburned hands, big enough to snap her neck, stirs something inside her, an unreachable itch.

They have no chairs large enough for him, so the boy puts two side by side. He goes to the sink and returns with a mug of water. The man drinks the water in a single gulp, then immediately asks for another.

How old are you? the girl says suspiciously.

The man picks the twig from his beard. Forty-six.

The girl snorts.

No, really. I'm aging by the second.

The girl blinks, amazed. She's lived for thirty years and can't imagine what it would be like for her body to mark the time. The man lays the twig on the table, ogling the cantaloupe sitting on the counter. The boy unsheathes a cleaver from the knife block and slices the melon in two, spooning out the pulp before chopping off a generous piece. He puts the orange smile of cantaloupe on a plate. The man devours it without a spoon, holding it like a harmonica.

Where do you work? the man asks suddenly, gazing out the window at the pickup in the driveway. The toolbox in the bed glitters in the sun.

Out by Old Harmony, the boy says. We're building some houses.

Anything to put your brilliant skills to use, eh?

Actually, we're almost finished, the boys says. The girl looks at him: increasingly, the boy and girl are worried about the future. The town has reached its population cap, and rumor is there are no plans to raise it again.

Don't worry, the man says, sighing. They'll just repurpose you. Presto chango.

How do *you* know? the girl asks.

I know about Perennials. You think I'm an ignorant ape? The man shakes his head. Jesus. The things I could teach you in my sleep.

The girl smirks at her brother. Like what?

The man opens his mouth as if to speak but then closes it again, staring at the pans hanging over the stove. They're arranged, like the tail bones of a dinosaur, from large to small. His face seems to droop. I bet you, um, can't make the sound of a loon.

What?

With your hands and mouth? A loon call?

The boy feels nothing in his brain: an exotic blankness. The feeling frightens him. The man perks up, seeming to recover his spirits. He cups his hands together as if warming them and blows into his thumbs, fluttering one hand like a wing. The noise is perfect and uncanny: the ghostly call of a loon.

The girl grabs the cleaver from the counter. How did you do that?

Ha! Experts of the universe! The man smiles, eyes bright with disdain. Come here and I'll teach you.

The girl refuses, still brandishing the knife, but the boy swallows his fear and approaches the table. The man shows him how to cup his hands together in a box and then tells him to blow into his knuckles. The boy tries, but no sound comes out. The man laughs. The boy blows until his cheeks hurt, until he's ready to give up, angry at the whole idea of birdcalls and at loons for making them, which only makes the man laugh harder. He pinches the boy's thumbs together. The boy recoils, so rough and startling is the man's touch. Trembling, the boy presses his lips to his knuckles again and blows, producing a low airy whistle that surprises him—his chest filling with something he can't explain, a shy arrogant pleasure, like a blush.

The boy and girl let the man use their shower. While he's undressing, they creep outside and take turns at the bathroom window, their hands cupped to the glass, sneaking looks at his strange hairy body and giant shoulders tucked in like a vulture's and long terrible penis, which shocks them when he turns. The girl is especially shocked by the scrotum. It's limp and bushy and speckled with veiny bursts. She has read about the ancient way of making babies, has sometimes even tried to imagine what it would be like to grow a fetus in her belly, a tiny bean-sized thing blooming into something curled and sac-bound and miraculous. She works as an assistant in a lab where embryos are grown, and she wonders sometimes, staring at the tanks of black-eyed little beings, all the brothers and sisters farmed from frozen eggs, what it would be like to raise one of them and smoosh him to her breast, like a gorilla mother does. Sometimes she even feels a pang of loneliness when they're hatched, encoded with all the knowledge they'll ever need, sent off to the orphanage to be raised until they're old enough for treatments, the shots that keep them from getting the disease. But, of course, the same thing happened to her, and what does she have to feel lonely about?

Once in a while the girl will peek into her brother's room and see him getting dressed for work, see his little bobbing string of a penis, vestigial as his appendix, and her mouth will dry up. It lasts only for a second, this feeling, before her brain commands it to stop.

Now, staring at the man's hideous body, she feels her mouth dry up in the same way, aware of each silent bump of her heart.

The man spends the night A fugitive, the boy calls him, closing the curtains so that no one can see in. The man's clothes are torn and stiff with blood, stinking of secret man-things, so the boy gives him his bathrobe to wear as a T-shirt and fashions a pair of shorts out of some sweatpants, slitting the elastic so that they fit his waist. The man changes into his new clothes, exposing the little beards under his arms. He seems happy with his ridiculous outfit and even does a funny bow that makes the boy laugh. He tries it on the girl as well, rolling his hand through the air in front of him, but she scowls and shuts the door to her room.

As the week stretches on, the girl grows more and more unhappy. There's the smell of him every morning, a sour blend of sweat and old-person breath and nightly blood seeping into the gauze the boy uses to dress his wound. There's his ugly limp, the hockey stick he's taken to using as a cane and which you can hear clopping from every room of the house. There's the cosmic stench he leaves in the bathroom, so powerful it makes her eyes water. There are the paper airplanes littering the backyard, ones he's taught the boy to make, sleek and bird-nosed and complicated as origami. Normally, the boy and girl drink a beer together in the kitchen after work—sometimes he massages her feet while they listen to music—but all week when she gets home he's out back with the man, flying his stupid airplanes around the yard. He checks the man's face after every throw, which makes her feel like going outside with a flyswatter and batting the planes down. The yard is protected by a windbreak of pines, but the girl worries one of the neighbors might see somehow and call the police. If anyone finds out there's a man in their house, she could get fired from the lab. Perhaps they'll even put her in jail.

Sometimes the man yells at them. The outbursts are unpredictable. *Turn that awful noise down!* he'll yell if they're playing music while he's trying to watch the news. Once, when the girl answers her phone during dinner, the man grabs it from her hand and hurls it into the sink. Next time, he tells her, he'll smash it with a brick. The worst thing is that they have to do what he says to quiet him down.

If it comes to it, she will kill the man. She will grab the .22 and shoot him while he's asleep.

On Saturday, the girl comes back from the grocery store and the man is limping around the backyard with the boy on his shoulders. The lawn mower sits in a spiral of mown grass. The boy laughs, and she hisses at them that the neighbors will hear. The man plunks the boy down and then sweeps her up and heaves her onto his shoulders instead. The girl is taller than she's ever imagined, so tall that she can see into the windows of her upstairs room. The mulchy smell of grass fills her nose. She wraps her legs around the man's neck. A shiver goes through her, as if she's climbed out of a lake. The shiver doesn't end so much as work its way inside her, as elusive as a hair in her throat. The man trots around the yard and she can't help herself, she begins to laugh as the boy did, closing her legs more tightly around his neck, giggling in a way she's never giggled before—a weird, high-pitched sound, as if she can't control her own mouth—ducking under the lowest branches of the pin oak shading the back porch. The man starts to laugh, too. Then he sets her down and falls to all fours on the lawn and the boy climbs on top of him, spurring him with the heels of his feet, and the man tries in vain to buck him off, whinnying like a horse in the fresh-mown grass. The boy clutches the man's homemade shirt. The girl watches them ride around the yard for a minute, the man's face bright with joy, their long shadow bucking like a single creature, and then she comes up from behind and pushes the boy off, so hard it knocks the wind out of him.

The boy squints at the girl, whose face has turned red. She has never pushed him for any reason. The boy stares at her face, so small and smooth and freckled compared to the man's, and for the first time is filled with disgust.

The man hobbles to his feet, gritting his teeth. His leg is bleeding. The gauze is soaked, a dark splotch of blood leaking spidery trickles down his shin.

Look what you've done! the boy says before helping the man to the house.

That night, the girl startles from a dream, as if her spine has been plucked. The man is standing in the corner of her room, clutching the hockey stick. His face—hideous, weirdly agleam—floats in the moonlight coming through the window. Her heart begins to race. She wonders if he's come to rape her. The man wipes his eyes with the end of his robe, first one, then the other. Then he clops toward her and sits on the edge of the bed, so close she can smell the sourness of his breath. His eyes are still damp. I was just watching you sleep, he says. He begins to sing to her, the same sad song he croons in the shower, the one about traveling through this world of woe. *There's no sickness, toil, or danger, in that bright land to which I go.* While he sings, he strokes the girl's hair with the backs of his fingers, tucking some loose strands behind her ear. His knuckles, huge and scratchy, feel like acorns.

What's the bright land? the girl asks.

The man stops stroking her hair. Heaven, he says.

The girl has heard about these old beliefs; to think that you could live on after death is so quaint and gullible, it touches her strangely.

Did someone you know die?

The man doesn't answer her. She can smell the murk of his sweat. Trembling, the girl reaches out and touches his knee where the sweatpants end, feeling its wilderness of hair. She moves her fingers under the hem of his sweats. The man does not move, closing his eyes as she inches her fingers up his leg. His breathing coarsens. Outside the wind picks up and rattles the window screen. Very suddenly, the man recoils, limping up from the bed.

You're just a girl, he whispers.

She stares at him. His face is turned, as if he can't bear to look at her. She does not know what she is.

He calls her Sleepyhead and hobbles out of the room. She wonders at this strange name for her, so clearly an insult. Her eyes burn. Outside her window the moon looks big and stupid, a sleeping head.

The next day, when the boy comes home from work, the house is humid with the smell of cooking. The man is bent over the stove, leaning to one side to avoid putting too much weight on his injured leg. It's been over a week now and the gash doesn't look any better; in fact, the smell has started to change, an almondy stink like something left out in the rain. Yesterday, when the boy changed the bandage, the skin underneath the pus was yellowish brown, the color of an old leaf. But the boy's not worried. He's begun to see the man as some kind of god. All day long he looks forward to driving home from work and finding this huge ducking presence in his house, smelling the day's sweat of his body through his robe. He feels a helpless urge to run to him. The man always seems slightly amazed to see him, unhappy, even, but in a grateful way, shaking his head as if he's spotted something he thought he'd lost, and though the boy can't articulate his feelings to himself, it's this amazement that he's been waiting for and that fills him with such restlessness at work. Ahoy there, the man says. It's not particularly funny, even kind of stupid, but the boy likes it. Ahoy, he says back. Sometimes the man clutches the boy's shoulder while he changes his bandage, squeezing so hard the boy can feel it like a live wire up his neck, and the boy looks forward to this, too, even though it hurts them both.

Now the man lifts the frying pan from the stove and serves the boy and girl dinner. The boy looks at his plate: a scrawny-looking thing with the fur skinned off, like a miniature greyhound fried to a crisp. A squirrel.

I caught them in the backyard, the man explains.

Disgusting! the girl says, making a face.

Would you rather go to your room, young lady? the man says.

She pushes her chair back.

No, please. I'm sorry. You don't have to eat. He looks at his plate and frowns. My mother was the real cook. She could have turned this into a fricassee.

What are they like? the boy asks.

What?

Mothers.

They're wonderful, the man says after a minute. Though sometimes you hate them. You hate them for years and years.

Why?

That's a good question. The man cuts off a piece of squirrel but doesn't eat it, instead staring at the window curtain, still bright with daylight at six o'clock. I remember when I was a kid, how hard it was to go to sleep in the summer. I used to tell my mom to turn off the day. That's what I'd say, *Turn off the day*, and she'd reach up and pretend to turn it off.

The man lifts his hand and yanks at the air, as if switching off a light.

The boy eats half his squirrel even though it tastes a little bit like turpentine. He wants to make the man happy. He knows that the man is sad, and that it has to do with something that happened in the woods. The man has told him about the town where he grew up, nestled in the mountains many miles away—the last colony of its kind—and how some boys and girls moved in eventually and forced everyone out of their homes. How they spent years traveling around, searching for a spot where there was enough wilderness to hide in so they wouldn't be discovered, where the food and water were plentiful, eventually settling in the parklands near the boy and girl's house. But the boy's favorite part is hearing about the disease itself: how exciting it was for the man to watch himself change, to grow tall and hairy and dark-headed, as strong as a beast. To feel ugly sometimes and hear his voice deepen into a stranger's. To fall in love with a woman's body and watch a baby come out of her stomach, still tied to her by a rope of flesh. The boy loves this part most of all, but when he asks about it, the man grows quiet and then says he understands why Perennials want to live forever. Did you have a baby like that? the boy asked him yesterday, and the man got up and limped into the backyard and stayed there for a while, picking up some stray airplanes and crumpling them into balls.

After dinner, they go into the living room to escape the lingering smell of squirrel. Sighing, the man walks to the picture window and opens up the curtains and looks out at the empty street. Bats flicker under the street lamps. He's told them that when he was young the streets were filled with children: they played until it was dark, building things or shooting each other with sticks or playing Butts Up and Capture the Flag and Ghost in the Graveyard, games that he's never explained.

It's a beautiful evening, he says, sighing again.

The girl does not look up from her pocket computer, her eyes burning as they did last night. Just listening to him talk about how nice it is outside, like he knows what's best for them, makes her clench her teeth.

What did you do when it rained? the boy asks.

Puppet shows, the man says, brightening.

Puppet shows?

The man frowns. Performances! For our mom and dad. My brother and I would write our own scripts and memorize them. The man glances at the girl on the floor, busy on her computer. He claps in her face, loudly, but she doesn't look up. Can you get me a marker and some different colored socks?

They won't fit you, the boy says.

We'll do a puppet show. The three of us.

The boy grins. What about?

Anything. Pretend you're kids like I was.

We'll do one for *you*, the boy says, sensing how much this would please the man.

He goes to get some socks from his room and then watches as the man draws eyes and a nose on each one. The girl watches, too, avoiding the man's face. If it will make the boy happy, she will do what he wants. They disappear into the boy's room to think up a script. After a while, they come out with the puppets on their hands and crouch behind the sofa, as the man's instructed them. The puppet show begins.

Hello, red puppet.

Hello, white puppet.

I can't even drive.

Me either.

Let's play capture the graveyard.

Okay.

In seventy years I'm going to die. First, though, I will grow old and weak and disease-ridden. This is called aging. It was thought to be incurable, in the Age of Senescence.

Will you lose your hair?

I am male, so there's a four in seven chance of baldness.

If you procreate with me, my breasts will become engorged with milk.

I'm sorry.

Don't apologize. The milk will feed my baby.

But how?

It will leak from my nipples.

I do not find you disgusting, red puppet. Many animals have milk-producing mammary glands. I just wish it wasn't so expensive to grow old and die.

Everyone will have to pay more taxes, because we'll be too feeble to work and pay for our useless medicines.

Jesus Christ, the man says, interrupting them. He limps over and yanks the socks from their hands. What's wrong with you?

Nothing, the girl says.

Can't you even do a fucking puppet show?

He limps into the boy's room and shuts the door. The boy does not know what he's done to make him angry. Bizarrely, he feels like he might cry. He sits on the couch for a long time, staring out the window at the empty street. Moths eddy under the street lamps like snow. The girl is jealous of his silence; she has never made the boy look like this, as if he might throw up from unhappiness. She walks to the window and shuts the curtains without speaking and shows him something on her computer: a news article, all about the tribe of Senescents. There have been twelve sightings in three days. Most have managed to elude capture, but one, a woman, was shot by a policeboy as she tried to climb through his neighbor's window. There's a close-up of her body, older even than the man's, her face gruesome with wrinkles. A detective holds her lips apart with two fingers to reveal the scant yellow teeth, as crooked as fence posts. The girl calls up another picture: a crowd of children, a search party, many of them holding rifles. They are standing in someone's yard, next to a garden looted of vegetables. The town is offering an official reward for any Senescent captured. Five thousand dollars, dead or alive. The girl widens her eyes, hoping the boy will widen his back, but he squints at her as if he doesn't know who she is.

At work, the boy has fallen behind on the house he's drywalling. The tapers have already begun on the walls downstairs. In the summer heat, the boy hangs the last panel of Sheetrock upstairs and then sits down to rest in the haze of gypsum dust. He has always liked this chalky smell, always felt that his work meant something: he was building homes for new Perennials to move into and begin their lives. But something has changed. The boy looks through the empty window square beside him and sees the evergreens that border the lot. Before long they'll turn white with snow and then drip themselves dry and then go back to being as green and silent and lonely-looking as they are now. It will happen, the boy thinks, in the blink of an eye.

There's a utility knife sitting by his boot, and he picks it up and imagines what it would be like to slit his throat.

Did you see the news this morning? his coworker, a taper who was perennialized so long ago he's stopped counting the years, asks at lunch.

The boy shakes his head, struggling to keep his eyes open. He has not been sleeping well on the couch.

They found another Senescent, at the hospital. He wanted shots.

But it's too late, the boy says. Their cells are corrupted.

Apparently the dumbfuck didn't know that. The police promised to treat him if he told them where the new camp is.

The boy's scalp tightens. What camp?

Where most of them ended up 'cause of the fire.

Did he tell them?

Conover Pass, the taper says, laughing. I wouldn't be surprised if there's a mob on its way already.

The boy drives home after work, his eyes so heavy he can barely focus on the road. Conover Pass is not far from his house; he would have taken the man there, perhaps, if he'd known. It's been a month since the boy first saw him in the yard, devouring apples, so tall and mighty that he seemed invincible. Now the man can barely finish a piece of toast. The boy changes his bandages every night, without being asked, though secretly he's begun to dread it. The wound has stopped bleeding and is beginning to turn black and fungal. It smells horribly, like a dead possum. When the man needs a bath, the boy has to undress him, gripping his waist to help him into the tub. His arms are thinner than the boy's, angular as wings, and his penis floating in the bath looks shriveled and weedlike. The boy leaves the bathroom, embarrassed. It's amazing to think that this frail, bony creature ever filled him with awe.

Last night the man asked the boy to put his dead body under the ground. Don't let them take it away, he said.

Shhhh, the boy said, tucking a pillow under the man's head.

I don't want to end up in a museum or something.

You're not going to die, the boy said stupidly. He blushed, wondering why he felt compelled to lie. Perhaps this was what being a Senescent was like. You had to lie all the time, convincing yourself that you weren't going to disappear. He said it again, more vehemently, and saw a gleam of hope flicker in the man's eye.

Ahoy there, the man says now when he gets home.

Ahoy.

The smell is worse than usual. The man has soiled his sheets. The boy helps him from bed and lets him lean his weight on one shoulder and then walks him to the bathtub, where he cleans him off with a washcloth. The blackness has spread down to his foot; the leg looks like a rotting log. The boy has things to do—it's his turn to cook dinner, and there's a stack of bills that need to go out tomorrow—and now he has to run laundry on top of everything else. He grabs the man's wrists and tries to lift him out of the bathtub, but his arms are like dead things. The man won't flex them enough to be useful. The boy kneels and tries to get him out by his armpits, but the man slips from his hands and crashes back into the tub. He howls in pain, cursing the boy.

The boy leaves him in the tub and goes into the kitchen, where the girl is washing dishes from breakfast. The bills on the table have not been touched.

He'll be dead in a week, the girl says.

The boy doesn't respond.

I did some math this morning. We've got about three months, after you're furloughed.

The boy looks at her. The man has become a burden to him as well—she can see this in his face. She can see, too, that he loves this pathetic creature that came into their life to die, though she knows just as certainly that he'll be relieved once it happens. He might not admit it, but he will be.

I'll take care of us, the girl says tenderly.

How?

She looks down at the counter. Go distract him.

The boy does not ask why. The man will die, but he and the girl will be together forever. He goes back into the bathroom; the man has tried to get out of the tub and has fallen onto the floor. He is whimpering. The boy slides an arm around his waist and helps him back to bed. A lightning bug has gotten through the window, strobing very slowly around the room, but the man doesn't seem to notice.

What do you think about when you're old? the boy asks.

The man laughs. Home, I guess.

Do you mean the woods?

Childhood, he says, as if it were a place.

So you miss it, the boy says after a minute.

When you're a child, you can't wait to get out. Sometimes it's hell.

Through the wall, the boy hears his sister on the phone: the careful, well-dressed voice she uses with strangers. He feels sick.

At least there's heaven, he says, trying to console the man.

The man looks at him oddly, then frowns. Where I can be like you?

A tiny feather, small as a snowflake, clings to the man's eyelash. The boy does something strange. He wets his finger in the glass on the bedside table and traces a T on the man's forehead. He has no idea what this means; it's half-remembered trivia. The man tries to smile. He reaches up and yanks the air.

The man closes his eyes; it takes the boy a moment to realize he's fallen asleep. The flares of the lightning bug are brighter now. Some water trickles from the man's forehead and drips down his withered face. The boy tries to remember what it was like to see it for the first time—chewing on an apple, covered in ash—but the image has already faded to a blur, distant as a dream.

He listens for sirens. The screech of tires. Except for the chirring of crickets, the evening is silent.

The boy feels suddenly trapped, frightened, as if he can't breathe. He walks into the living room, but it doesn't help. The hallway, too, oppresses him. It's like being imprisoned in his own skin. His heart beats inside his neck, strong and steady. Beats and beats and beats. Through the skylight in the hall, he can see the first stars beginning to glimmer out of the dusk. They will go out eventually, shrinking into nothing. When he lifts the .22 from the closet, his hands—so small and tame and birdlike—feel unbearably captive.

He does not think about what he's doing, or whether there's time or not to do it—only that he will give the man what he wants: bury his body in the ground, like a treasure.

He walks back into the bedroom with the gun. The man is sleeping quietly, his breathing dry and shallow. His robe sags open to reveal a pale triangle of chest, bony as a fossil. The boy tries to imagine what it would be like to be on earth for such a short time. Forty-six years. It would be like you never even lived. He can actually see the man's skin moving with his heart, fluttering up and down. The boy aims the gun at this mysterious failing thing.

He touches the trigger, dampening it with sweat, but can't bring himself to squeeze it. He cannot kill this doomed and sickly creature. Helplessly, he imagines the policeboys carrying the man away, imagines the look on the man's face as he realizes what the boy has done. His eyes hard with blame. But no: the man wouldn't know he had anything to do with it. He won't get in trouble.

The boy and girl will go back to their old lives again. No one to grumble at them or cook them dinners they don't want or make him want to cry.

The boy's relief gives way to a ghastly feeling in his chest, as if he's done something terrible.

Voices echo from the street outside. The boy rushes to the window and pulls back the curtains. A mob of boys and girls yelling in the dusk, parading from the direction of Conover Pass, holding poles with human heads on top of them. The skewered heads bob through the air like puppets. *Off to bed without your supper!* one of the boys says in a gruff voice, something he's read in a book, and the others copy him—*Off to bed! Off to bed!*—pretending to be grown-ups. The heads gawk at each other from their poles. They look startled to the boy, still surprised by their betrayal. One turns in the boy's direction, haloed by flies, and for a moment its eyes seem to get even bigger, as though it's seen a monster. Then it spins away to face the others. Freed from their bodies, nimble as children, the heads dance down the street.

BEN LOORY

The Squid Who Fell in Love with the Sun

A converted screenwriter, **Ben Loory** has published a collection of short stories, *Stories for Nighttime and Some for the Day*, and a children's book, *The Baseball Player and the Walrus*. *Stories for Nighttime* was both a Fall selection of the Barnes & Noble Discover Great New Writers program and an August selection of the Starbucks Bookish Reading Club. He has written for the *New Yorker*, Weekly Reader's *READ Magazine*, and *Fairy Tale Review*. Although only a few of Loory's stories have appeared in genre magazines, he has been spotted not infrequently at science-fiction conventions. He has an MFA in screenwriting and teaches at UCLA Extension. He has also appeared on *This American Life*.

Most of Loory's stories are fantasy written in an unusually idiosyncratic voice, where simple words and phrases seem to pile up, almost at random, until something resembling a story for (very odd) children begins to emerge. "The Squid Who Fell in Love with the Sun" is one of his few SF stories. It was originally published in *xo Orpheus: Fifty New Myths*, edited by Kate Bernheimer.

Once there was a squid who fell in love with the sun. He'd been a strange squid ever since he was born—one of his eyes pointed off in an odd direction, and one of his tentacles was a little deformed. So, as a result, all the other squids made fun of him. They called him Gimpy and Stupid and Lame. And when he'd come around, they'd shoot jets of ink at him and laugh at him as they swam away.

So after a while, the squid gave up and started hanging out by himself. He'd swim around alone near the surface of the water, gazing upward—and that's when he saw the sun.

The sun looked to him like the greatest thing in the world.

It's just so beautiful, he'd think.

And he'd stretch out his arms and try to grab hold of it.

But the sun was always out of reach.

What are you doing? the other squids would say when they saw him grasping for it like that.

Nothing, he'd say. Just trying to touch the sun.

God, you're such an idiot, the squids would say.

Why do you say that? the squid would ask.

Because, the others would say, the sun is too high; you'll never be able to reach it.

I will, someday, the squid would say.

And the other squids laughed, but the squid kept trying. He didn't give up—he reached and stretched and reached.

And then one day, he saw a fish jump out of the water.

I should try jumping! he said.

So the squid started trying to jump to reach the sun. At first, he couldn't jump very high. He'd lurch out of the water and then fall right back in.

But he kept trying more and more every day.

And, in time, the squid could jump pretty high. He could make it eight or nine feet out of the water. He'd make a big dash in order to build up some steam, and then leap up with all his tentacles waving.

But no matter how high and how far the squid jumped, he never could quite reach the sun.

You really are a stupid squid! the squids would say. You really get dumber all the time.

The squid didn't understand how what he was doing was dumb. But it was true that he didn't seem to be getting much closer.

Then one day in mid-jump he saw a bird flying by.

Wings! I need wings! the squid said.

So the squid set out to build himself a pair of wings. He did some research into different kinds of materials. He'd found some ancient books in a sunken ship he'd discovered, and he read the ones about metallurgy and aeroscience.

And, in time, the squid built himself some wings. They were made of a super-lightweight material that also had a very high tensile strength. (He'd had to build a small smelting plant to make them.)

Looks like these wings are ready to go, the squid said.

And he leapt up out of the water. And he flapped and flapped, and he rose and rose. He rose up above the clouds and flapped on.

It's working! the squid said.

He looked up toward the sun.

I'm coming, I'm coming! he said.

But then something happened—his wings stopped working. Up that high, the air was too thin.

Uh-oh, the squid said, and he started to fall.

He fell all the way back down to the sea. Luckily, he wasn't hurt— he'd had the foresight to bring a parachute. (He even had a back-up for emergencies.)

But he splashed down in the water and as he did, his wings shattered. And of course, the other squids laughed again.

When is this squid ever going to learn? they said.

But the squid no longer took notice of them.

———————

You see, the squid had had an idea—all the way up there at the top of his climb. Just as he was perched at the outer limit of the atmosphere—

What I need is an interplanetary spaceship, he said.

Because at that very moment, the squid had finally grasped something: he'd finally understood the layout of the solar system. Before he'd been bound by his terrestrial beginnings. Now he understood the vast distances involved.

Of course, building an interplanetary spaceship was complicated—much more complicated than a simple set of wings. But the squid was not discouraged; if anything, he was excited.

It's good to have a purpose, he said.

So the squid set out designing himself a spaceship. The body was easy; it was the propulsion system that was hard. He had to cover about a hundred million miles.

I'm going to need a lot of speed, he said.

At first, the squid designed an atomic reactor. But it turned out that wouldn't provide power enough. He'd gotten pretty heavily into physics by this point.

I need to harness dark matter and energy, he said.

And so the squid did. He designed and built the world's first dark matter and energy reactor. It took a lot of time and about a thousand scientific breakthroughs.

All right, he said. That should be fast enough.

And finally, one day, the squid's interplanetary spaceship was built and ready to take off. The squid put on his helmet and climbed inside.

Well, here goes nothing, he said.

He pushed a single button and took off in a burst of light and plowed straight up out of the atmosphere. He tore free of Earth's orbit and whizzed past the moon, burned past Venus, and sped on past Mercury.

There in his command chair, the squid stared at the sun as it grew larger before him on the screen.

I'm coming, I'm coming, my beautiful Sun! he said. I'll finally hold you, after all this time!

But as he got closer, something strange started to happen—something the squid hadn't foreseen. The ship started getting hotter. And then hotter and hotter still.

Why's it so hot? the squid said.

You see, the squid really knew nothing about the sun. He didn't even know what it was. It had always just been a symbol to him—an abstraction that filled a hole in his life. He'd never even figured out that it was a great ball of fire—that is, until this very moment. But now the truth finally dawned on him.

That thing's gonna kill me! he said.

He slammed on the brakes, but the ship just kept on going. He threw the engines into reverse, and they whined, but still he kept going—getting closer and closer.

I'm stuck in the sun's gravity! he said.

He did some calculations and realized he was lost. He'd gone too far; he was over the edge. Even with his engines all strained to the limit, he had only a few hours to live.

And as he sat there in his chair, just waiting to die, something even worse started to happen. The squid started ruminating and thinking about his life.

Oh my god, he said. I really *have* been an idiot!

Suddenly it was all just painfully clear: everything he'd done, all his work, had been for nothing.

I'm a moron, he said. I wasted my whole life.

That's not true; you built me, the ship said.

And the squid thought about it, and he realized the ship was right.

But you'll be destroyed too, he said.

Yes, said the ship. But I have a transmitter. If we work fast, at least the knowledge can be saved.

So the squid started working like he'd never worked before—feverishly, as he fell into the sun. He wrote out all his knowledge, his equations and theorems, clarified the workings of everything he'd done.

And in the moments left over, the squid went even further. He pushed out into other realms of thought. He explored biology and psychology and ethics and medicine and architecture and art. He made great leaps, he overcame boundaries; he shoved back the limits of ignorance. It was like his whole mind came alive for that moment and did the work that millions had never done.

And in the very last second before his ship was destroyed, and he himself was annihilated completely, the squid sat back.

That's all I got, he said.

And the ship beamed it all into space.

And the knowledge of the squid sailed out through the dark, and it sped its way back toward Earth. But of course when it got there, the other squids didn't get it, because they were too dumb to build radios.

And the story would end there, with the squid's sad and lonely death, but luckily, those signals kept going. They moved out past Earth, past Mars and the asteroid belt, past Jupiter and all the other planets.

And then they kept going, out beyond the solar system, out into and through the darkness of space. They moved through the void, through other galaxies and clusters. They kept going for billions of years.

And finally one day—untold millenniums later—they were picked up by an alien civilization. Just a tiny backwards race on some tiny, backwards planet, all alone at the darkest end of space.

And that alien civilization decoded those transmissions, and they examined them and took them to heart. And they started to think, and they started to build, and they changed their whole way of life.

They built shining cities of towering beauty; they built hospitals and schools and parks. They obliterated disease, and stopped fighting wars.

And then they turned their eyes to space.

And they took off and spread out through the whole universe, helping everyone, no matter how different or how far.

And their spaceships were golden, and emblazoned with the image of the squid who spoke to them from beyond the stars.

JONATHAN LETHEM
Five Fucks

Jonathan Lethem began his career writing science fiction. He is one of only two writers in this anthology to have spent a significant portion of his career writing SF (the other is Karen Heuler). His first novel, *Gun, with Occasional Music*, merges science-fiction tropes with those of hardboiled detective novels. He later found his home in literary fiction, winning the National Book Critics Circle Award and a MacArthur Fellowship. He has written nine novels to date, including *Motherless Brooklyn*, *The Fortress of Solitude*, and *Dissident Gardens*. Lethem's work appears in *The Secret History of Science Fiction* and *The Secret History of Fantasy*. He was born and lives in Brooklyn, New York.

"Five Fucks" first appeared in Lethem's collection *The Wall of the Sky, the Wall of the Eye* (1996). Although the stories published in *The Wall of the Sky* date from his tenure as a science-fiction writer, it is worth noting that "Five Fucks" was written expressly for that collection and—with its title and the way it plays with familiar themes—it would have been a very uncomfortable fit for any of the SF magazines.

1.

"I feel different from other people. Really different. Yet whenever I have a conversation with a new person it turns into a discussion of things we have in common. Work, places, feelings. Whatever. It's the way people talk, I know, I share the blame, I do it too. But I want to stop and shout no, it's not like that, it's not the same for me. I feel different."

"I understand what you mean."

"That's not the right response."

"I mean what the fuck are you talking about."

"Right." Laughter.

She lit a cigarette while E. went on.

"The notion is like a linguistic virus. It makes any conversation go all pallid and reassuring. 'Oh, I know, it's like that for me too.' But the virus isn't content just to eat conversations, it wants to destroy lives. It wants you to fall in love."

"There are worse things."

"Not for me."

"Famine, war, floods."

"Those never happened to me. Love did. Love is the worst thing that ever happened to me."

"That's fatuous."

"What's the worst thing that ever happened to you?"

She was silent for a full minute.

"But there, *that's* the first fatuous thing I've said. Asking you to consider *my* situation by consulting *your* experience. You see? The virus is loose again. I don't want you to agree that our lives are the same. They aren't. I just want you to listen to what I say seriously, to believe me."

"I believe you."

"Don't say it in that tone of voice. All breathy."

"Fuck you." She laughed again.

"Do you want another drink?"

"In a minute." She slurped at what was left in her glass, then said, "You know what's funny?"

"What?"

"Other people do feel the way you do, that they're apart from everyone else. It's the same as the way every time you fall in love it feels like something new, even though you do the exact same things over again. Feeling unique is what we all have in common, it's the thing that's always the same."

"No, I'm different. And falling in love is different for me each time, different things happen. Bad things."

"But you're still the same as you were before the first time. You just feel different."

"No, I've changed. I'm much worse."

"You're not bad."

"You should have seen me before. Do you want another drink?"

The laminated place mat on the table between them showed pictures of exotic drinks. "This one," she said. "A zombie." It was purple.

"You don't want that."

"Yes I do. I love zombies."

"No you don't. You've never had one. Anyway, this place makes a terrible zombie." He ordered two more margaritas.

"You're such an expert."

"Only on zombies."

"On zombies and love is bad."

"You're making fun of me. I thought you promised to take me seriously, believe me."

"I was lying. People always lie when they flirt."

"We're not flirting."

"Then what are we doing?"

"We're just drinking, drinking and talking. And I'm trying to warn you."

"And you're staring."

"You're beautiful. Oh God."

"That reminds me of one. What's the worst thing about being an atheist?"

"I give up."

"No one to talk to when you come."

2.

Morning light seeped through the macramé curtain and freckled the rug. Motes seemed to boil from its surface. For a moment she thought the rug was somehow on the ceiling, then his cat ran across it, yowling at her. The cat looked starved. She was lying on her stomach in his loft bed, head over the side. He was gone. She lay tangled in the humid sheets, feeling her own body.

Lover—she thought.

She could barely remember.

She found her clothes, then went and rinsed her face in the kitchen sink. A film of shaved hairs lined the porcelain bowl. She swirled it out with hot water, watched as the slow drain gulped it away. The drain sighed.

The table was covered with unopened mail. On the back of an envelope was a note: *I don't want to see you again. Sorry. The door locks.* She read it twice, considering each word, working it out like another language. The cat crept into the kitchen. She dropped the envelope.

She put her hand down and the cat rubbed against it. Why was it so thin? It didn't look old. The fact of the note was still sinking in. She remembered the night only in flashes, visceral strobe. With her fingers she combed the tangles out of her hair. She stood up and the cat dashed away. She went out into the hall, undecided, but the weighted door latched behind her.

Fuck him.

The problem was of course that she wanted to.

It was raining. She treated herself to a cab on Eighth Avenue. In the backseat she closed her eyes. The potholes felt like mines, and the cab squeaked like rusty bedsprings. It was Sunday. Coffee, corn muffin, newspaper; she'd insulate herself with them, make a buffer between the night and the new day.

But there was something wrong with the doorman at her building.

"You're back!" he said.

She was led incredulous to her apartment full of dead houseplants and unopened mail, her answering machine full of calls from friends, clients, the police. There was a layer of dust on the answering machine. Her address book and laptop disks were gone; clues, the doorman explained.

"Clues to what?"

"Clues to your case. To what happened to you. Everyone was worried."

"Well, there's nothing to worry about. I'm fine."

"Everyone had theories. The whole building."

"I understand."

"The man in charge is a good man, Miss Rush. The building feels a great confidence in him."

"Good."

"I'm supposed to call him if something happens, like someone trying to get into your place, or you coming back. Do you want me to call?"

"Let me call."

The card he handed her was bent and worn from traveling in his pocket. Cornell Pupkiss, Missing Persons. And a phone number. She reached out her hand; there was dust on the telephone too. "Please go," she said.

"Is there anything you need?"

"No." She thought of E.'s cat, for some reason.

"You can't tell me at least what happened?"

"No."

She remembered E.'s hands and mouth on her—a week ago? An hour?

Cornell Pupkiss was tall and drab and stolid, like a man built on the model of a tower of suitcases. He wore a hat and a trench coat, and shoes which were filigreed with a thousand tiny scratches, as though they'd been beset by phonograph needles. He seemed to absorb and deaden light.

On the telephone he had insisted on seeing her. He'd handed her the disks and the address book at the door. Now he stood just inside the door and smiled gently at her.

"I wanted to see you in the flesh," he said. "I've come to know you from photographs and people's descriptions. When I come to know a person in that manner I like to see them in the flesh if I can. It makes me feel I've completed my job, a rare enough illusion in my line."

There was nothing bright or animated in the way he spoke. His voice was like furniture with the varnish carefully sanded off. "But I haven't really completed my job until I understand what happened," he went on.

"Whether a crime was committed. Whether you're in some sort of trouble with which I can help."

She shook her head.

"Where were you?" he said.

"I was with a man."

"I see. For almost two weeks?"

"Yes."

She was still holding the address book. He raised his large hand in its direction, without uncurling a finger to point. "We called every man you know."

"This—this was someone I just met. Are these questions necessary, Mr. Pupkiss?"

"If the time was spent voluntarily, no." His lips tensed, his whole expression deepened, like gravy jelling. "I'm sorry, Miss Rush."

Pupkiss in his solidity touched her somehow. Reassured her. If he went away, she saw now, she'd be alone with the questions. She wanted him to stay a little longer and voice the questions for her.

But now he was gently sarcastic. "You're answerable to no one, of course. I only suggest that in the future you might spare the concern of your neighbors, and the effort of my department—a single phone call would be sufficient."

"I didn't realize how much time had passed," she said. He couldn't know how truthful that was.

"I've heard it can be like that," he said, surprisingly bitter. "But it's not criminal to neglect the feelings of others; just adolescent."

You don't understand, she nearly cried out. But she saw that he would view it as one or the other, a menace or self-indulgence. If she convinced him of her distress, he'd want to protect her.

She couldn't let harm come to E. She wanted to comprehend what had happened, but Pupkiss was too blunt to be her investigatory tool.

Reflecting in this way, she said, "The things that happen to people don't always fit into such easy categories as that."

"I agree," he said, surprising her again. "But in my job it's best to keep from bogging down in ontology. Missing Persons is an extremely large and various category. Many people are lost in relatively simple ways, and those are generally the ones I can help. Good day, Miss Rush."

"Good day." She didn't object as he moved to the door. Suddenly she was eager to be free of this ponderous man, his leaden integrity. She wanted to be left alone to remember the night before, to think of the one who'd devoured her and left her reeling. That was what mattered.

E. had somehow caused two weeks to pass in one feverish night, but Pupkiss threatened to make the following morning feel like two weeks.

He shut the door behind him so carefully that there was only a little huff of displaced air and a tiny click as the bolt engaged.

"It's me," she said into the intercom.

There was only static. She pressed the button again. "Let me come up."

He didn't answer, but the buzzer at the door sounded. She went into the hall and upstairs to his door.

"It's open," he said.

E. was seated at the table, holding a drink. The cat was curled up on the pile of envelopes. The apartment was dark. Still, she saw what she hadn't before: he lived terribly, in rooms that were wrecked and provisional. The plaster was cracked everywhere. Cigarette stubs were bunched in the baseboard corners where, having still smoldered, they'd tanned the linoleum. The place smelled sour, in a way that made her think of the sourness she'd washed from her body in her own bath an hour before.

He tilted his head up, but didn't meet her gaze. "Why are you here?"

"I wanted to see you."

"You shouldn't."

His voice was ragged, his expression had a crushed quality. His hand on the glass was tensed like a claw. But even diminished and bitter he seemed to her effervescent, made of light.

"We—something happened when we made love," she said. The words came tenderly. "We lost time."

"I warned you. Now leave."

"My life," she said, uncertain what she meant.

"Yes, it's yours," he shot back. "Take it and go."

"If I gave you two weeks, it seems the least you can do is look me in the eye," she said.

He did it, but his mouth trembled as though he were guilty or afraid. His face was beautiful to her.

"I want to know you," she said.

"I can't let that happen," he said. "You see why." He tipped his glass back and emptied it, grimacing.

"This is what always happens to you?"

"I can't answer your questions."

"If that happens, I don't care." She moved to him and put her hands in his hair.

He reached up and held them there.

3.

A woman has come into my life. I hardly know how to speak of it.

I was in the station, enduring the hectoring of Dell Armickle, the commander of the Vice Squad. He is insufferable, a toad from Hell. He follows the donut cart through the offices each afternoon, pinching the buttocks of the Jamaican woman who peddles the donuts and that concentrated urine others call coffee. This day he stopped at my desk to gibe at the headlines in my morning paper. "'Union Boss Stung In Fat Farm Sex Ring'—ha! Made you look, didn't I?"

"What?"

"Pupkiss, you're only pretending to be thick. How much you got hidden away in that Swedish bank account by now?"

"Sorry?" His gambits were incomprehensible.

"Whatsis?" he said, poking at my donut, ignoring his own blather better than I could ever hope to. "Cinnamon?"

"Whole wheat," I said.

Then she appeared. She somehow floated in without causing any fuss, and stood at the head of my desk. She was pale and hollow-eyed and beautiful, like Renée Falconetti in Dreyer's *Jeanne d'Arc*.

"Officer Pupkiss," she said. Is it only in the light of what followed that I recall her speaking my name as though she knew me? At least she spoke it with certainty, not questioning whether she'd found her goal.

I'd never seen her before, though I can only prove it by tautology: I knew at that moment I was seeing a face I would never forget.

Armickle bugged his eyes and nostrils at me, imitating both clown and beast. "Speak to the lady, Cornell," he said, managing to impart to the syllables of my given name a childish ribaldry.

"I'm Pupkiss," I said awkwardly.

"I'd like to talk to you," she said. She looked only at me, as though Armickle didn't exist.

"I can take a hint," said Armickle. "Have fun, you two." He hurried after the donut cart.

"You work in Missing Persons," she said.

"No," I said. "Petty Violations."

"Before, you used to work in Missing Persons—"

"Never. They're a floor above us. I'll walk you to the elevator if you'd like."

"No." She shook her head curtly, impatiently. "Forget it. I want to talk to you. What are Petty Violations?"

"It's an umbrella term. But I'd sooner address your concerns than try your patience with my job description."

"Yes. Could we go somewhere?"

I led her to a booth in the coffee shop downstairs. I ordered a donut, to replace the one I'd left behind on my desk. She drank coffee, holding the cup with both hands to warm them. I found myself wanting to feed her, build her a nest.

"Cops really do like donuts," she said, smiling weakly.

"Or toruses," I said.

"Sorry? You mean the astrological symbol?"

"No, the geometric shape. A torus. A donut is in the shape of one. Like a life preserver, or a tire, or certain space stations. It's a little joke of mine: cops don't like donuts, they like toruses."

She looked at me oddly. I cursed myself for bringing it up. "Shouldn't the plural be *tori*?" she said.

I winced. "I'm sure you're right. Never mind. I don't mean to take up your time with my little japes."

"I've got plenty of time," she said, poignant again.

"Nevertheless. You wished to speak to me."

"You knew me once," she said.

I did my best to appear sympathetic, but I was baffled.

"Something happened to the world. Everything changed. Everyone that I know has disappeared."

"As an evocation of subjective truth—" I began.

"No. I'm talking about something real. I used to have friends."

"I've had few, myself."

"Listen to me. All the people I know have disappeared. My family, my friends, everyone I used to work with. They've all been replaced by strangers who don't know me. I have nowhere to go. I've been awake for two days looking for my life. I'm exhausted. You're the only person that looks the same as before, and has the same name. The Missing Persons man, ironically."

"I'm not the Missing Persons man," I said.

"Cornell Pupkiss. I could never forget a name like that."

"It's been a burden."

"You don't remember coming to my apartment? You said you'd been looking for me. I was gone for two weeks."

I struggled against temptation. I could extend my time in her company by playing along, indulging the misunderstanding. In other words, by betraying what I knew to be the truth: that I had nothing at all to do with her unusual situation.

"No," I said. "I don't remember."

Her expression hardened. "Why should you?" she said bitterly.

"Your question's rhetorical," I said. "Permit me a rhetorical reply. That I don't know you from some earlier encounter we can both regret. However, I know you now. And I'd be pleased to have you consider me an ally."

"Thank you."

"How did you find me?"

"I called the station and asked if you still worked there."

"And there's no one else from your previous life?"

"No one—except him."

Ah.

"Tell me," I said.

She'd met the man she called E. in a bar, how long ago she couldn't explain. She described him as irresistible. I formed an impression of a skunk, a rat. She said he worked no deliberate charm on her, on the contrary seemed panicked when the mood between them grew intimate and full of promise. I envisioned a scoundrel with an act, a crafted diffidence that allured, a backpedaling attack.

He'd taken her home, of course.

"And?" I said.

"We fucked," she said. "It was good, I think. But I have trouble remembering."

The words stung. The one in particular. I tried not to be a child, swallowed my discomfort away. "You were drunk," I suggested.

"No. I mean, *yes*, but it was more than that. We weren't clumsy like drunks. We went into some kind of trance."

"He drugged you."

"No."

"How do you know?"

"What happened—it wasn't something he wanted."

"And what did happen?"

"Two weeks disappeared from my life overnight. When I got home I found I'd been considered missing. My friends and family had been searching for me. You'd been called in."

"I thought your friends and family had vanished themselves. That no one knew you."

"No. That was the *second* time."

"Second time?"

"The second time we fucked." Then she seemed to remember something, and dug in her pocket. "Here." She handed me a scuffed business card: Cornell Pupkiss, Missing Persons.

"I can't believe you live this way. It's like a prison." She referred to the seamless rows of book spines that faced her in each of my few rooms, including the bedroom where we now stood. "Is it all criminology?"

"I'm not a policeman in some cellular sense," I said, and then realized the pun. "I mean, not intrinsically. They're novels, first editions."

"Let me guess; mysteries."

"I detest mysteries. I would never bring one into my home."

"Well, you have, in me."

I blushed, I think, from head to toe. "That's different," I stammered. "Human lives exist to be experienced, or possibly endured, but not solved. They resemble any other novel more than they do mysteries. Westerns, even. It's that lie the mystery tells that I detest."

"Your reading is an antidote to the simplifications of your profession, then."

"I suppose. Let me show you where the clean towels are kept."

I handed her fresh towels and linen, and took for myself a set of sheets to cover the living room sofa.

She saw that I was preparing the sofa and said, "The bed's big enough."

I didn't turn, but I felt the blood rush to the back of my neck as though specifically to meet her gaze. "It's four in the afternoon," I said. "I won't be going to bed for hours. Besides, I snore."

"Whatever," she said. "Looks uncomfortable, though. What's Barbara Pym? She sounds like a mystery writer, one of those stuffy English ones."

The moment passed, the blush faded from my scalp. I wondered later, though, whether this had been some crucial missed opportunity. A chance at the deeper intervention that was called for.

"Read it," I said, relieved at the change of subject. "Just be careful of the dust jacket."

"I may learn something, huh?" She took the book and climbed in between the covers.

"I hope you'll be entertained."

"And she doesn't snore, I guess. That was a joke, Mr. Pupkiss."

"So recorded. Sleep well. I have to return to the station. I'll lock the door."

"Back to Little Offenses?"

"Petty Violations."

"Oh, right." I could hear her voice fading. As I stood and watched, she fell soundly asleep. I took the Pym from her hands and replaced it on the shelf.

I wasn't going to the station. Using the information she'd given me, I went to find the tavern E. supposedly frequented.

I found him there, asleep in a booth, head resting on his folded arms. He looked terrible, his hair a thatch, drool leaking into his sweater arm, his eyes swollen like a fevered child's, just the picture of raffish haplessness a woman would find magnetic. Unmistakably the seedy vermin I'd projected and the idol of Miss Rush's nightmare.

I went to the bar and ordered an Irish coffee, and considered. Briefly indulging a fantasy of personal power, I rebuked myself for coming here and making him real, when he had only before been an absurd story, a neurotic symptom. Then I took out the card she'd given me and laid it on the bar top. CORNELL PUPKISS, MISSING PERSONS. No, I myself was the symptom. It is seldom as easy in practice as in principle to acknowledge one's own bystander status in incomprehensible matters.

I took my coffee to his booth and sat across from him. He roused and looked up at me.

"Rise and shine, buddy boy," I said, a little stiffly. I've never thrilled to the role of Bad Cop.

"What's the matter?"

"Your unshaven chin is scratching the table surface."

"Sorry." He rubbed his eyes.

"Got nowhere to go?"

"What are you, the house dick?"

"I'm in the employ of any taxpayer," I said. "The bartender happens to be one."

"He's never complained to me."

"Things change."

"You can say that again."

We stared at each other. I supposed he was nearly my age, though he was more boyishly pretty than I'd been even as an actual boy. I hated him for that, but I pitied him for the part I saw that was precociously old and bitter.

I thought of Miss Rush asleep in my bed. She'd been worn and disarrayed by their two encounters, but she didn't yet look this way. I wanted to keep her from it.

"Let me give you some advice," I said, as gruffly as I could manage. "Solve your problems."

"I hadn't thought of that."

"Don't get stuck in a rut." I was aware of the lameness of my words only as they emerged, too late to stop.

"Don't worry, I never do."

"Very well then," I said, somehow unnerved. "This interview is concluded." If he'd shown any sign of budging I might have leaned back in the booth, crossed my arms authoritatively, and stared him out the door. Since he remained planted in his seat, I stood up, feeling that my last spoken words needed reinforcement.

He laid his head back into the cradle of his arms, first sliding the laminated place mat underneath. "This will protect the table surface," he said.

"That's good, practical thinking," I heard myself say as I left the booth.

It wasn't the confrontation I'd been seeking.

On the way home I shopped for breakfast, bought orange juice, milk, bagels, fresh coffee beans. I took it upstairs and unpacked it as quietly as I could in the kitchen, then removed my shoes and crept in to have a look at Miss Rush. She was peaceably asleep. I closed the door and prepared my bed on the sofa. I read a few pages of the Penguin softcover edition of Muriel Spark's *The Bachelors* before dropping off.

Before dawn, the sky like blued steel, the city silent, I was woken by a sound in the apartment, at the front door. I put on my robe and went into the kitchen. The front door was unlocked, my key in the deadbolt. I went back through the apartment; Miss Rush was gone.

I write this at dawn. I am very frightened.

4.

In an alley which ran behind a lively commercial street there sat a pair of the large trash receptacles commonly known as Dumpsters. In them accumulated the waste produced by the shops whose rear entrances shared the alley—a framer's, a soup kitchen, an antique clothing store, a donut bakery, and a photocopyist's establishment, and by the offices above those storefronts. On this street and in this alley, each day had its seasons: Spring, when complaining morning shifts opened the shops, students and workers rushed to destinations, coffee sloshing in paper cups, and in the alley, the sanitation contractors emptied containers, sorted recyclables and waste like bees pollinating garbage truck flowers; Summer, the ripened afternoons, when the workday slackened, shoppers stole long lunches from their employers, the cafes filled with students with highlighter pens, and the indigent beckoned for the change that jingled in incautious pockets, while in the alley new riches piled up; Autumn, the cooling evening, when half the shops closed, and the street was given over to prowlers and pacers, those who lingered in bookstores and dined alone in Chinese restaurants, and the indigent plundered the fatted Dumpsters for half-eaten paper bag lunches, batches of botched donuts, wearable cardboard matting and unmatched socks, and burnable wood scraps; Winter, the selfish night, when even the cafes battened down iron gates through which night-watchmen fluorescents palely flickered, the indigent built their overnight camps in doorways and under side-street hedges, or in wrecked cars, and the street itself was an abandoned stage.

On the morning in question the sun shone brightly, yet the air was bitingly cold. Birds twittered resentfully. When the sanitation crew arrived to wheel the two Dumpsters out to be hydraulically lifted into their screeching, whining truck, they were met with cries of protest from within.

The men lifted the metal tops of the Dumpsters and discovered that an indigent person had lodged in each of them, a lady in one, a gentleman in the other.

"Geddoudadare," snarled the eldest sanitation engineer, a man with features like a spilled plate of stew.

The indigent lady rose from within the heap of refuse and stood blinking in the bright morning sun. She was an astonishing sight, a ruin. The colors of her skin and hair and clothes had all surrendered to gray; an archaeologist might have ventured an opinion as to their previous hue. She could have been anywhere between thirty and fifty years old, but speculation was absurd; her age had been taken from her and replaced with a timeless condition, a state. Her eyes were pitiable; horrified and horrifying; witnesses, victims, accusers.

"Where am I?" she said softly.

"Isedgeddoudadare," barked the garbage operative.

The indigent gentleman then raised himself from the other Dumpster. He was in every sense her match; to describe him would be to tax the reader's patience for things worn, drab, desolate, crestfallen, unfortunate, etc. He turned his head at the trashman's exhortation and saw his mate.

"What's the—" he began, then stopped.

"You," said the indigent lady, lifting an accusing finger at him from amidst her rags. "You did this to me."

"No," he said. "No."

"Yes!" she screamed.

"C'mon," said the burly sanitateur. He and his second began pushing the nearer container, which bore the lady, towards his truck.

She cursed at them and climbed out, with some difficulty. They only laughed at her and pushed the cart out to the street. The indigent man scrambled out of his Dumpster and brushed at his clothes, as though they could thereby be distinguished from the material in which he'd lain.

The lady flew at him, furious. "Look at us! Look what you did to me!" She whirled her limbs at him, trailing banners of rag.

He backed from her, and bumped into one of the garbagemen, who said, "Hey!"

"It's not my fault," said the indigent man.

"Yugoddagedoudahere!" said the stew-faced worker.

"What do you mean it's not your fault?" she shrieked.

Windows were sliding open in the offices above them. "Quiet down there," came a voice.

"It wouldn't happen without you," he said.

At that moment a policeman rounded the corner. He was a large man named Officer McPupkiss who even in the morning sun conveyed an aspect of night. His policeman's uniform was impeccably fitted, his brass polished, but his shoetops were exceptionally scuffed and dull. His presence stilled the combatants.

"What's the trouble?" he said.

They began talking all at once; the pair of indigents, the refuse handlers, and the disgruntled office worker leaning out of his window.

"Please," said McPupkiss, in a quiet voice which was nonetheless heard by all.

"He ruined my life!" said the indigent lady raggedly.

"Ah, yes. Shall we discuss it elsewhere?" He'd already grasped the situation. He held out his arms, almost as if he wanted to embrace the two tatterdemalions, and nodded at the disposal experts, who silently resumed their labors. The indigents followed McPupkiss out of the alley.

"He ruined my life," she said again when they were on the sidewalk.

"She ruined mine," answered the gentleman.

"I wish I could believe it was all so neat," said McPupkiss. "A life is simply *ruined*; credit for the destruction goes *here* or *here*. In my own experience things are more ambiguous."

"This is one of the exceptions," said the lady. "It's strange but not ambiguous. He fucked me over."

"She was warned," he said. "She made it happen."

"The two of you form a pretty picture," said McPupkiss. "You ought to be working together to improve your situation; instead you're obsessed with blame."

"We can't work together," she said. "Anytime we come together we create a disaster."

"Fine, go your separate ways," said the officer. "I've always thought 'We got ourselves into this mess and we can get ourselves out of it' was a laughable attitude. Many things are irreversible, and what matters is moving on. For example, a car can't reverse its progress over a cliff; it has to be abandoned by those who survive the fall, if any do."

But by the end of this speech the gray figures had fallen to blows and were no longer listening. They clutched one another like exhausted boxers, hissing and slapping, each trying to topple the other. McPupkiss chided himself for wasting his breath, grabbed them both by the back of their scruffy collars, and began smiting their hindquarters with his dingy shoes until they ran down the block and out of sight together, united again, McPupkiss thought, as they were so clearly meant to be.

5.

The village of Pupkinstein was nestled in a valley surrounded by steep woods. The villagers were a contented people except for the fear of the two monsters that lived in the woods and came into the village to fight their battles. Everyone knew that the village had been rebuilt many times after being half destroyed by the fighting of the monsters. No one living could remember the last of these battles, but that only intensified the suspicion that the next time would surely be soon.

Finally the citizens of Pupkinstein gathered in the town square to discuss the threat of the two monsters, and debate proposals for the prevention of their battles. A group of builders said, "Let us build a wall around the perimeter of the village, with a single gate which could be fortified by volunteer soldiers."

A group of priests began laughing, and one of them said, "Don't you know that the monsters have wings? They'll flap twice and be over your wall in no time."

Since none of the builders had ever seen the monsters, they had no reply.

Then the priests spoke up and said, "We should set up temples which can be filled with offerings: food, wine, burning candles, knitted scarves, and the like. The monsters will be appeased."

Now the builders laughed, saying, "These are monsters, not jealous gods. They don't care for our appeasements. They only want to crush each other, and we're in the way."

The priests had no answer, since their holy scriptures contained no accounts of the monsters' habits.

Then the Mayor of Pupkinstein, a large, somber man, said, "We should build our own monster here in the middle of the square, a scarecrow so huge and threatening that the monsters will see it and at once be frightened back into hiding."

This plan satisfied the builders, with their love of construction, and the priests, with their fondness for symbols. So the very next morning the citizens of Pupkinstein set about constructing a gigantic figure in the square. They began by demolishing their fountain. In its place they marked out the soles of two gigantic shoes, and the builders sank foundations for the towering legs that would extend from them. Then the carpenters built frames, and the seamstresses sewed canvases, and in less than a week the two shoes were complete, and the beginnings of ankles besides. Without being aware of it, the citizens had begun to model their monster on the

Mayor, who was always present as a model, whereas no one had ever seen the two monsters.

The following night it rained. Tarpaulins were thrown over the half-constructed ankles that rose from the shoes. The Mayor and the villagers retired to an alehouse to toast their labors and be sheltered from the rain. But just as the proprietor was pouring their ale, someone said, "Listen!"

Between the crash of thunder and the crackle of lightning there came a hideous bellowing from the woods at either end of the valley.

"They're coming!" the citizens said. "Too soon—our monster's not finished!"

"How bitter," said one man. "We've had a generation of peace in which to build, and yet we only started a few days ago."

"We'll always know that we tried," said the Mayor philosophically.

"Perhaps the shoes will be enough to frighten them," said the proprietor, who had always been regarded as a fool.

No one answered him. Fearing for their lives, the villagers ran to their homes and barricaded themselves behind shutters and doors, hid their children in attics and potato cellars, and snuffed out candles and lanterns that might lead an attacker to their doors. No one dared even look at the naked, miserable things that came out of the woods and into the square; no one, that is, except the Mayor. He stood in the shadow of one of the enormous shoes, rain beating on his umbrella, only dimly sensing that he was watching another world being fucked away.

6.

I live in a shadowless pale blue sea.

I am a bright pink crablike thing, some child artist's idea of an invertebrate, so badly drawn as to be laughable.

Nevertheless, I have feelings.

More than feelings. I have a mission, an obsession.

I am building a wall.

Every day I move a grain of sand. The watercolor sea washes over my back, but I protect my accumulation. I fasten each grain to the wall with my comic-book feces. (Stink lines hover above my shit, also flies which look like bow ties, though I am supposed to be underwater.)

He is on the other side. My nemesis. Someday my wall will divide the ocean, someday it will reach the surface, or the top of the page, and be called a reef. He will be on the other side. He will not be able to get to me.

My ridiculous body moves only sideways, but it is enough.

I will divide the watercolor ocean, I will make it two. We must have a world for each of us.

I move a grain. When I come to my wall, paradoxically, I am nearest him. His little pink body, practically glowing. He is watching me, watching me build.

There was a time when he tried to help, when every day for a week he added a grain to my wall. I spent every day that week removing his grain, expelling it from the wall, and no progress was made until he stopped. He understands now. My wall must be my own. We can be together in nothing. Let him build his own wall. So he watches.

My wall will take me ten thousand years to complete. I live only for the day that it is complete.

The Pupfish floats by.

The Pupfish is a fish with the features of a mournful hound dog and a policeman's cap. The Pupfish is the only creature in the sea apart from me and my pink enemy.

The Pupfish, I know, would like to scoop me up in its oversized jaws and take me away. The Pupfish thinks it can solve my problem.

But no matter how far the Pupfish took me, I would still be in the same ocean with *him*. That cannot be. There must be two oceans. So I am building a wall.

I move a grain.

I rest.

I will be free.

JULIA ELLIOTT

LIMBs

Julia Elliott is the author of a recently published novel, *The New and Improved Romie Futch* (2015). Billed as "part surreal satire, part Southern Gothic tall tale," *Romie Futch* features Cybernetic Neuroscience, biotech operatives, and a thousand-pound feral hog. Elliott's writing has appeared in *Tin House*, the *Georgia Review, Conjunctions*, the *New York Times*, and other publications. She has won the Rona Jaffe Writer's Award, and her stories have been anthologized in *Pushcart Prize: Best of the Small Presses* and *Best American Short Stories*. She teaches at the University of South Carolina.

"LIMBs" was first published in *Tin House* in 2012, which also published her first collection *The Wilds*, which was chosen by *Kirkus, BuzzFeed, Book Riot*, and *Electric Literature* as one of the Best Books of 2014 and was a *New York Times Book Review* Editors' Choice. "LIMBs" is one of the few SF stories to attempt to envision what it might be like to grow old in the future.

On a gauzy day in early autumn, senior citizens stroll around the pear orchard on robot legs. Developed by the Japanese, manufactured by Boeing, one of the latest installments in the mechanization of geriatric care, Leg Intuitive Motion Bionics (LIMBs) have made it all the way to Gable, South Carolina, to this little patch of green behind Eden Village Nursing Home. And Elise Mood is getting the hang of them. Every time her brain sends a signal to her actual legs, the exoskeletal LIMBs respond, marching her along in the gold light. A beautiful day—even though Elise can smell chickens from the poultry complex down the road and exhaust from the interstate, even though the pear trees in this so-called orchard bear no fruit. The mums are in bloom. Bees glitter above the beds. And a skinny man comes toward her, showing off his mastery of the strap-on LIMBs.

"Elise." He squints at her. "You still got it. Prettiest girl at Eden Village."

She flashes her dentures but says nothing.

"You remember me. Ulysses Stukes, aka Pip. We went to the BBQ place that time."

Elise nods, but she doesn't remember. And she's relieved to see a tech nurse headed her way, the one with the platinum hair.

"Come on, Miss Elise," the nurse says. "You got Memories at three."

Elise points at the plastic Power Units strapped to her lower limbs.

"You're gonna walk it today," says the nurse. "I think you got it down."

Elise grins. Three people from the Dementia Ward were chosen for the test group, and so far, she's the only one with nerve signals strong enough to stimulate the sensors. As she strides along among flowers and bees, she rolls the name around on her tongue—Pip Stukes—recalling something familiar in the wry twist of his mouth.

For the past few months, nanobots have been rebuilding Elise's degenerated neural structures, refortifying the cell production of her microglia in an experimental medical procedure. Now she sits in the Memory Lane Neurotherapy Lounge, strapped into a magnetoencephalographic (MEG) scanner that looks like a 1950s beauty parlor hair-drying unit. As a young female therapist monitors a glowing map of Elise's brain, a male spits streams of nonsense at her.

"Corn bread," he says. "Corn-fed coot. Corny old colonel with corns on his feet."

Elise snorts. Who was that colonel she knew? Not a colonel, but a corporal. She once kissed him during a thunderstorm. But she was all of sixteen and he was fresh from Korea, drenched in mystique and skinny from starving in a bamboo cage. Elise vaguely recollects his inflation into a three-hundred-pounder who worked the register at Stukes Feed and Seed. Pip Stukes.

In a flash, she remembers the night they ate barbecue together, back when the world was still green, back when Hog Heaven hung paper lanterns over the picnic tables and Black River Road was dirt. After wiping his lips with a paper napkin, he'd said, *You ought to be my wife* in his half-joking way—and she'd dropped her fork.

"Look," says the female therapist. "We've got action between the inferior temporal and the frontal."

"Let's try another round," says the male, the one with the ponytail so little and scraggly that Elise wants to snip it off with a pair of scissors.

"One unit of BDNF," says the female. "And self-integration image therapy with random auditory sequencing and a jolt of EphB2."

The boy clamps Elise's head into a padded dome, and the room gets darker. She hears birdsong and distant traffic as a screen lights up to display a photo of a couple, the girl decked out in a wiggle dress and heels, the man slouching beside her in baggy tweed, his face obscured by a straw hat. At first Elise thinks they're walking on water, but then she realizes they're standing at the edge of a pier, a lake glinting all around them.

Something about the lake makes her gasp, and Elise wonders if the young woman in the photograph is her daughter—though she's pretty sure she never had a daughter, so maybe it's her mother's daughter, which means she and the girl are the same person.

"We've got action all over," says the female therapist, "mostly in the temporal and right parietal lobes."

"Emotional memory and spatial identity," says the male, tapping a rhythm on the desk with his fingertips.

Elise glares at him for breaking her stream of thought, then looks back up at the image, noting a streak of silver in the upper-right corner.

"Boat," she whispers.

And then she sees him clear as day: Pip Stukes at the wheel of the boat, his hair swept into a ducktail by the wind.

In the pear orchard, Elise takes long strides, easy as thought, around the bed of mums. Scanning the lawn for Pip Stukes, she notes a cluster of wheelchair-bound patients idling at the edge of the flower bed, two women and a sleeping man, his shoulders slumped forward, his chin resting on his chest.

"Hey, good-lookin', what you got cookin'?" Pip Stukes struts toward her on cyborg legs. The skin around his eye sockets looks delicate, parchment shrunk down to the bone. While one of his eyes shines as blue as a tropical sea, the other is frosted with glaucoma. But Pip still flirts like a demon, sadness nestled under the happy talk.

Elise blushes and Pip laughs, stands with his hip cocked.

"Pretty day for a walk." He holds out his arm and she takes it.

He leads her into a stand of planted pine. Interstate 95 drones, but Elise thinks she hears a river. Looking for a thread of blue, she gazes through the trees, but all she sees is the blurry outline of a brick building. A crow flutters down in a shaft of green light. And Pip turns to her with an aching look from long ago.

"Elise."

She studies him, mentally peeling back layers of wrinkled skin to glimpse the shining young man inside. She thinks he may have been *the one*, the dark shape in the bed beside her when she came up gasping from the depths of a bad dream.

She practices the phrase in her head first—*Are you my husband?*—but her lips twitch when she tries to say it.

"What?" says Pip.

And then a male tech nurse, alerted by their RFID alarms, rushes into the patch of woods to retrieve them.

Elise sits by the lake on a towel in early spring, delighted to see that she's young again. As the sun sinks behind the tree line, she shivers, waiting for someone. She spots a wet glimmer of motion out past the end of the pier, a lithe young man doing tricks in the water. He crawls dripping from the lake, a merman with seal-black hair and familiar green eyes. As he inches toward her, his tail, a long fishy appendage glistening with aqua scales, swishes behind him in the sand.

Elise wakes, panting, in her semi-electric bed. She reaches into the dark, claws at the aluminum railing. She's cold, her blanket wadded beneath her feet. And her roommate moans, a steady animal keening. The night nurse drifts in with pills in tiny cups. Though Elise can't see her, she knows her voice, low and soothing like a sheep's. The night nurse fixes her blanket, checks her diaper, gives her a drink of water, and then slips out of the room. Now her roommate's snoring. The air conditioner hums. And Elise lies awake, thinking about the beautiful swimmer from her dream.

Elise can smell the stuffiness of Eden Village Nursing Home only when she returns from being outside for a while. It's as if they've shellacked the floors with urine and Lysol. And in the cafeteria, some gravy is always boiling, spiked with the sweat and waste and blood of the dying, all the juices that leak from withering people—huge cauldrons of gravy that emit a meaty, medicinal steam.

Now that Elise can walk, now that she's thinking a little faster, she feels up to exploring. She wants to find the room where Pip Stukes lives, ask him point-blank if he's the man she married.

Someone's approaching down the endless hallway, a speck swelling bigger and bigger until it transforms into a nurse, a boy with a golden dab of beard.

"Looking for the Dogwood Library?" he says. "Elvis and the Chipmunks?" He points toward a small corridor, then shuffles off into nonexistence.

Peering down the passageway, Elise sees a parlor: wingback chairs, sofas, a crowd of patients in wheelchairs. She wills her strap-on LIMBs to move and, after a heartbeat pause, lurches down the hall. Over by a makeshift stage, the wheelchair-bound patients watch some middle-aged men set up equipment. A few people with LIMBs weave among the furnishings. Elise recognizes a tall woman with bald spots and a stubby old man with big ears. She creeps behind a potted palm to watch Elvis and the Chipmunks take the stage. Three large plush rodents sporting high pompadours, they jump into a brisk, twittering version of "Jailhouse Rock." Elise is about to leave in disgust when she spots a man slumped in a wheelchair, dozing, his face so familiar that the shock of it interrupts the signals pulsing from her brain to her legs and into the sensors of her Power Units. She collapses onto a brocade couch. Sits there wheezing in the blotchy light. Then she calms herself and looks the man over. She remembers the hawk nose, the big, creased forehead.

The Chipmunks croon "Love Me Tender" in their earsplitting rodent way, and Elise snorts. The man in the wheelchair had a great voice, could play guitar by ear. All those summer evenings they spent on the porch have been streamlined into archetypes and filed away in different sections of her cerebral cortex. And now the memories come trickling out. She remembers the sound of the porch fan and the smell of the lake and the feel of his hand on the back of her neck. She recalls swimming under stars and singing folk songs and drinking wine until their heads floated off their necks.

Elise steps around a coffee table heaped with *Reader's Digest*s. She studies the pink bulges of the man's closed eyes, the blanket draped over his legs, the big, fleshy head, humming with mysterious thoughts. The mouth is what strikes her hardest, the lips full, just a quirk feminine. When he opens his eyes and she sees the strange green, she knows it's him, the man who once kissed her in a birch canoe, moonlight twitching on the water.

"Who are you?" she says, the words pouring miraculously from her tongue.

He studies her, and she fears he's been drained dry, all of his memories siphoned by therapists into that electric box, where they bump around like trapped moths.

He makes a gurgling sound, small and goatish. His left eye is blighted with red veins. His hands rest on his knees, and she wonders if he can move them at all.

"Are you my husband?" she says.

The man's tongue pokes out and then retreats back into the cave of his mouth. He grunts. His left hand closes into a fist.

"I thought you were dead," she says.

"Bwa," he says, but then a nurse seizes his wheelchair, jerks him around, and trundles him off toward the corridor. Elise staggers in a panic and her LIMBs malfunction, leaving her crumpled on the carpet as the chipmunks mock her with "Heartbreak Hotel."

She pulls herself up, squats, then stands, wills her legs to move fast, and they do, speeding her along like a power walker, but then a CNA with dyed black hair stops her. Scans her tag, beeps the Dementia Ward, and shuffles her back to the place she's supposed to be.

Hands folded in her lap, Elise slumps in the MEG scanner. Groggy from an antipsychotic called Vivaquel, she's having a hard time concentrating on what the therapists are saying.

"Barbecue bubba," says the boy. "Magnolia, moonshine, Maw and Paw."

"Very original," says the girl. "How about some limbic work? Aural olfactory?"

"Whatever," says the boy.

"Doo-wop and gardenias." The girl giggles. "Who the hell makes this shit up?"

Elise wishes they'd quit flirting and get on with it. She has half a mind to tell the boy that he'd be attractive with a decent haircut, but she doesn't. She sits with her arms crossed until the boy slips in her ear buds and clamps a plastic cup over her nose. In minutes Elise smells sickly sweet aerosol air freshener. She coughs, and they lower her olfactory levels. As the Everly Brothers croon "All I Have to Do Is Dream" in their wistful Appalachian twang, she can't help but sway to the music, breathing in a whiff of synthetic cherry, the exact scent of a Lysol spray that was marketed in the 1980s.

"She doesn't like it," says the boy.

"She's responding," says the girl. "Look at her amygdala. It's glowing."

Elise recalls a cramped hospital room that smelled of cherry Lysol, the green-eyed man hunched in a bed, looking at the wall. He dove into the lake one summer night and bashed his head against a rock. Now his legs wouldn't work right and he refused to look her in the eye. She held his balled fist in both hands and squeezed. The doctor said his motor neurons were damaged, compromising his leg muscles. The doctor went on and on about *partial recovery* and *physical therapy*, but the man didn't seem to be listening.

Elise remembers the smell of the man and the way he cleared his throat when he got nervous. She remembers how his silence filled the room every time he heard a motorboat fly by on the water. Stiffly, they'd wait for the sound to fade, and then pretend they hadn't heard it.

She wakes up with his name on her tongue: Robert Graham Mood, otherwise known as Bob. In the depths of her Vivaquel nap, she saw him, swimming in the lake's brown murk, down near the silty bottom. Enormous primordial catfish flickered through the hydrilla, and Bob fed them night crawlers with his hands. Right where his sick legs used to be, Bob was growing flippers, two stunted incipient fins sprouting from his knees.

This merman *was* her husband, Elise realized, and he was swimming away from her, toward the deepest part of the lake, where the Morrisons' pontoon had sunk during a severe thunderstorm. The whole family had drowned: mother, father, three sons. And scuba divers swore they'd seen ghosts slithering near the wreck, glowing like electric eels.

Elise rolls onto her side. Her room has a window, but an air-conditioning unit blocks the view. And now a tech nurse is here to attach her LIMBs to her scrawny legs. As he hooks up her sensors, he doesn't say one word, doesn't make eye contact: he might as well be tinkering with an old lawn mower.

Out in the pear orchard, Pip Stukes comes strutting, does a little turn around a park bench, and stoops to pluck a fistful of chrysanthemums, which he presents with a debonair smirk.

"Thank you," says Elise, shocked when the words pop out of her mouth.

"So you *can* talk!" says Pip. "I knew it. I could tell by the look in your eyes. I knew Elise Boykin was in there somewhere."

Elise Mood she wants to say, but keeps her lips zipped. Elise Boykin married Bob Mood, but Pip Stukes had refused to honor her changed name.

"Have you seen the goldfish pond?" Pip extends his arm, and she takes it in spite of herself. Curls her fingers around his bicep and gives it a squeeze, surprised by the wobble of muscle encased in the sagging skin. They amble over to the pond, which is tucked behind a stand of canna lilies.

"Watch this," says Pip. He pulls a plastic bag from his pocket, shakes bread crumbs into his hand, and flings them into the water.

Elise concentrates on the oblong circle of liquid, eyeing it like an old queen gazing into a magic mirror. She sees a glimmer of orange, and then another, and another: six fish flitting up from the black depths. Lovely, greedy, they pucker their lips to suck up bits of bread.

Pip laughs and slips his arm around her, a gesture so familiar that she mechanically follows suit, twining her arm around his waist. She ought to pull away, but she doesn't.

She studies his profile and sees him as a younger man, after his grandfather died and left him the money, after the Feed and Seed shut down and he took up jogging. He'd run by her house at dawn, handsomeness emerging from his body in the form of cheekbones and muscle tone. Meanwhile, Bob slumped, staring at the TV—a man who used to hate the tube. Called it *the idiot box, the shit pump, opiate of the masses.* But now he said nothing, just eyeballed the screen, silence filling the house like swamp gas.

She took up smoking again, would slip down to the dock and sit with her feet in the water. She's the one who checked the catfish traps. She's the one who picked the vegetables that summer and trucked them to the market. She still sold her chowchow and blueberry jam and eggs from the chickens, whose house needed a new roof. She sold azalea seedlings to the Yankees who were buying up every last waterfront lot on the lake. After Bob's accident, they'd sold fifty acres of their land, the woods shrinking around them, big houses popping up in every bay.

One day in July she took a break to go swimming. Just before Bob's accident, she'd bought a French-cut one-piece that now seemed shameless—too young for forty-three—but she was alone in the cove. She dove into the water and swam out to the floating dock. Let the sun dry her hair, which had darkened to auburn over the years. And then Pip Stukes whisked by in his new motorboat, a dolphin-blue Savage Electra. He looked sharp in aviator sunglasses, slender and tan, a cigarette clenched in his teeth.

Elise eats every bit of her supper, fast, even the creamed corn. Remembering the ears of sweet corn Bob used to roast on the grill, she swallows the filthy goop. Smiles at the CNA when he sweeps up her tray. Sits waiting in bed, listening to her roommate smack up her gruel. Then she stands and teeters toward her LIMBs, which rest against a La-Z-Boy. Panting, she sits in the chair and grapples for one of the units, grabs it by the upper thigh and drags it to her, shocked by how light it is. She's been watching the tech nurse, knows exactly how to strap the contraptions onto her legs, fastens the Velcro and then a hundred little metal snaps. She stands up. Takes a test run around the room. Pokes her head out into the hall, looks both ways, and then lurches into the white light.

Since most of the Dementia Ward nurses are in the dining room with patients, Elise has a clear shot down the hall. She makes it all the way to the main desk without incident, then stops, baffled, trying to remember which passage she took the time she came upon Robert Graham Mood. She recalls a different kind of fluorescent light, bluer than usual, a lower ceiling. *That's the one*, she thinks, the one with the green wall. Elise ambles down the hall, finds the library. Over by the front desk, a solitary CNA reads a magazine.

Elise recognizes the corridor down which that bitch of a nurse took her husband, a man she thought was dead. She ambles down the hallway, peeks into dim rooms, sees lumps curled on beds, aged figures zoned out before televisions. When a wheelchair emerges from one of the doorways, her heart catches, but it's not Robert Graham Mood. She keeps walking as though she knows where she's going, nods whenever she passes a nurse. The hallway narrows. At the end of the hall, she spots a nurses station around the corner, the CNA at the desk bent over a gadget.

Elise squats, scampers like a crab around the desk, almost laughing at the ease of it, and enters the little hall where the severely disabled are stashed away. She sniffs, the burn of disinfectant stronger here. And then she peers into each room until she finds him, three doors down on the left, her husband, Bob, drooping in his wheelchair before a muted TV.

She remembers that summer—when the stubble on his face grew into a dirty beard and his sideburns fanned into wild whiskers. Jimmy Carter was floundering, the oil running out, those hostages still rotting in Iran. And Bob, TV-obsessed, sat wordless as a bear. Soviets in Afghanistan and J.R. Ewing shot and Bob's legs as weak as they were the day before. She couldn't keep up with the okra picking. Blight had taken the tomatoes. One of their hens had an abscess that needed to be lanced. It wasn't Bob's sick legs that had pushed her over the edge, but his refusal to talk about the details of their shared life.

Elise steps between Bob and the TV, just like she did that day in July when she'd had enough of his silence.

His eyes stray from the screen—still the strange green, steeped in obscure feelings.

"Robert Graham Mood," she says. And he blinks.

"Elise." His voice rattles like a rusty cotton gin, but to her the word sounds exquisitely feminine, the name of some flower that blooms for just half a day, almost too small to see but insanely perfumed in the noon heat.

"How long have you been here?" she asks.

He looks her up and down.

"You're my husband?" she says.

"Yes," Bob rasps. The air conditioner drones and they stare at each other.

Elise is about to touch his arm when a CNA rushes in, smiles, speaks softly, as to a cornered kitten, and takes her firmly by the arm.

———————

When Elise wakes up from her Vivaquel nap, a boy looms over her—Robert Graham Mood, a sleek young stunner with red hair. She frowns, for Bob's hair had been black, his lips plump and just a tad crooked. She thinks she may be dead at last, Bob's golden spirit hovering to welcome her to the next phase.

"Mom," says the boy.

When her eyes adjust, she notes lines around his eyes, the bulge of a budding gut. Not the father but the son.

"Just give her a few minutes," says the nurse. "According to the neuro-therapists, she's made enormous strides. Her roaming incident shows some planning, thinking ahead, which indicates enhanced semantic memory."

"And you think she knows he's my father?"

"She knows he's somebody. Found him halfway across the complex. I had no idea they'd even been married."

"They still are, technically, you know."

Elise snorts at this, but nobody pays one bit of attention.

"Of course. Very odd, though it happens from time to time. Married people in different wings. We don't do couples at Eden Village."

"It really didn't matter until now," says the boy, sinking into the chair by the bed. "I didn't think the therapies would lead to anything, with her so far gone. But still, I figured *why not?*"

Elise claws at her throat, her tongue as dead as a slab of pickled beef. She knows the boy is her son, but she can't remember when he was born or how he got to be grown so fast.

"Mom," says the boy, that familiar tinge of whininess in his voice, and it comes to her: her son home from college for a few days, pacing from window to window, restless as a cooped rooster. He said the house felt smaller than he remembered. Stayed out on the boat all day with the spoiled-rotten Morrison boys. Acted skittish when he came in from the water, pained eyes hiding behind the soft flounce of his bangs. He'd gone vegetarian, looked as skinny as Gandhi, and she fed him fried okra and butterbeans.

As the two of them sat at the kitchen table making conversation, Bob's silence leaked from the boy's old bedroom like nuclear radiation from a triple-sealed vault—the kind of poison you can't smell but that sinks into your cells, making you mutant from the inside out.

"Bye, Mom." The boy pats her crimped hand. "I'll be back soon." And they leave her in the semidarkness, window shades down, unable to tell if it's night or day.

The therapists have strapped her into the MEG scanner and popped in a retro-TV sense-enhanced module. While they play footsy under the desk, Elise turns her attention to a montage of *The Incredible Hulk* episodes, breathing in smells of Hamburger Helper and Bounce fabric-softening sheets. She never cooked Hamburger Helper; she never wasted money on fabric softeners. She never sat through a complete episode of *The Hulk*, but the seething mute giant reminds her of Bob, who watched it religiously after his accident. She remembers peering into his room, standing there in the hallway for just one minute to watch the green monster rage. Then she'd close the door, drift out into the night with her pack of cigarettes.

Now the screen goes dim and Elise hears crickets, smells cigarette smoke and a hint of gas. Pip's boat had a leak that summer, and everything they did was enveloped in the haze of gasoline. What did they do? Zigzagged over the lake. Dropped the anchor and sat rocking in the waves, drinking wine coolers and watching for herons. Then they'd drift up to this island he knew. The first time Pip took her to his secret island—the one with the feral goats and rotting shed—she drank until her head thrummed. Bob had not said one word for sixty-two days. Each night before bed she'd stick her head into the toxic glow of his room to say good night, and he'd grunt. She kept track of the days. Ticked them off with a pencil on a yellow legal pad.

He sat there glued to the TV, waiting for news on the hostages, wondering if Afghanistan had turned Communist yet, trying to figure out who shot J.R. She even caught him watching soaps in the middle of the day—*like sands through the hourglass, so are the days of our lives*—foolishness he used to laugh at. Now he sat grimly as Marlena mourned the death of her premature son and her marriage to a two-timing lawyer fell apart. The dismal music, the tedious melodrama, and the flimsy opulent interiors sank Elise into a malaise. And she'd leave Bob in the eternal twilight of the TV.

Out in the humming afternoon heat, Elise had started talking to herself. *Goddamn grass*, she'd hiss. *Bastard ants.* One day, in the itchy okra patch, where unpicked pods had swollen into eight-inch monsters, where fire ants marched up and down the sticky stalks, crawling onto her hands and stinging her in the tender places between her fingers, Elise ripped off her sun hat and shrieked. Then she stormed inside and changed into her swimsuit. Without looking in on Bob, she grabbed her smokes and jogged out to the cove, walked waist-deep into the water while taking deep drags. *Fuck*, she hissed—a trashy cuss she never indulged in. And then she felt drained of wrath.

She tossed her cigarette butt and swam out to the floating dock, where the water was cooler. Pip Stukes came knifing through the waves, skinny again, his sunglasses two mirrors that hid his sad eyes, and Elise crawled up into his glittery boat. She swigged wine coolers like they were Cokes and laughed a high, dry laugh that was half cough. She lost track of herself: let another man kiss her on an island where shadowy goats watched from the woods. She stayed out past dusk and got a sunburn, a bright red affliction that she didn't feel until the next day.

When she came in that night, Bob didn't ask where she'd been. Didn't say one word. Just kept clearing his throat over and over, as though he had something stuck in it—a bit of gristle in his windpipe, a dry spot on his glottis, acid gushing up from his bad stomach. He cleared his throat when she served him supper (one hour later than usual). Cleared his throat when she changed his sheets and punched his pillow with her small fist. Cleared his throat when she quietly shut his door, and kept on clearing his throat as she brushed her teeth and crawled into the bed they'd shared for twenty years.

Elise's skin blistered and peeled. For several nights she lay in bed rolling it into little balls that she'd flick into the darkness. And then, one week later, her skin tender, the pale pink of a seashell's interior, she went off with Pip Stukes again.

——————

"I figured out how they catch us," whispers Pip.

Elise widens her eyes. As they take a little turn around the birdbath, she scans the crowd for wheelchairs. They sit down on a concrete bench.

"Feel that bump on your arm?" Pip slides the tip of his index finger over her forearm, stops when he reaches that hard little pimple that won't go away. Maybe it's a wart. Maybe it's a mole. Elise doesn't know what it is, but she blushes when he touches the spot.

"Microchip," he says. "My son put one in his dog's ear. A good idea. Except we're not dogs."

Pip laughs, the old, dark laugh that lingers in the air. Elise can't remember Pip's children. And what about his wife? He must have had one. But now she's unsettled by his eyes, the clear one at least, which drills her with a secret force while the other stares at nothing.

Something about his laugh and fading smile, something about the slant of light and the wash of distant traffic remind her— of what, she's not sure, not until the blush spreads from her hairline to her chest, not until she sees Pip walking naked from the lake, sees the scar on his chest, the sad apron of belly skin, relic of his previous life as a fat man. And then she remembers. He did have a wife, a girl named Emmy from Silver. They'd had two boys and divorced. Emmy had kept the house in Manning, and Pip moved out to the lake house, free to whip around on the empty water.

For two months they boated out to the little island almost every afternoon. Got sucked into the oblivion of the dog days: shrieking cicadas and heat like a blanket of wet velvet that made you feel half asleep. It was easy to sip wine coolers until you couldn't think. Easy to swim naked in water warm as spit. In September they finally went to his lake house, a fancy place with lots of gleaming brass, the TV built into a clever cabinet, a stash of top-notch liquor behind the wet bar. Showing her around, Pip pointed out every last effect, all bought with his grandfather's money. Something bothered her: the way he slapped her rear like a rake on *Dallas*, the way he smoked afterward in the air-conditioned bedroom. Hiding his saggy gut under the sheet, he kept checking himself out in the mirror. He ran his fingers through his gelled hair.

As Pip went on about the Corvette he wanted to buy, she thought about Bob, how, in the past, he was always quietly tinkering with something. And then poor Pip started up on Korea, told her about coming back home after starving in that bamboo cage, eating for a solid year in a trance, waking up one day to the shock of three hundred pounds. He'd lost the weight and gotten married. But then he gained it back, got divorced, lost it again—his whole life staked to that tedious fluctuation.

That night when she got home, Bob turned from the television and spoke to her.

"Look at this joker," he said, pointing at Ronald Reagan, the movie star who was running for president, the one who looked like a handsome lizard.

The next day Bob bathed himself and rolled out onto the screened porch. Watching the lake, they shelled field peas all morning. She knew that Pip would come flying out of the blue in his boat, and when he did, Bob cleared his throat and said nothing.

Pip's boat appeared every afternoon for the next week. They'd hold their breath and wait for the high whine of his motor to fade.

Bob started doing his leg exercises, made an appointment with the hot-shot therapist in Columbia. In two years he could get around the house with a walker. By Reagan's second term he was ambling with a cane. He took care of the chickens, started dabbling with quail. And every year they sold more land, acre by acre, until all they had was their cottage—mansions towering on every side, the lake a circus of Jet Skis, houseboats so big they blotted out the sun.

Bob and Elise got old on the lake, their son breezing in twice a year to say hello. And they planned to die there, right on the water, even though the place was turning to shit.

Elise fingers the scab on her arm. It's been a week since she gouged the microchip out with the sharp scissors she nabbed from the Dementia Ward desk. All this time she's kept the fleck of metal in her locket and nobody's said one word. The nurses know better than to touch her locket, a thirtieth-anniversary gift from Bob—not a heart, like you'd expect, just a circle of gold that opens via a hinge, a clip of Bob's gray hair stuffed inside as a sweet joke. *To thirty more years of glorious monotony*, Bob had said, and they'd laughed, opened another jar of mulberry wine.

A tech nurse escorts Elise out to the pear orchard. Just as soon as she's released into the flock of seniors, Pip Stukes comes swaggering across the grass.

"Hey, good lookin', what you got cookin?"

Elise takes his arm as usual and they promenade across stepping-stones, over to their favorite bench. Pip talks about his son, who dropped by this morning with Pip's grandbaby, now a grown girl. He talks about the artificial bacon he had for breakfast and the blue jay that perched on his windowsill. Then he goes quiet and just stares at her, filling the space between them with sighs. It's warm for November. The mums have dried up and the pear trees drop their last red leaves. When Pip leans in to kiss her, Elise embraces him, keeping her lips off limits while hugging him close enough to slip the microchip into his shirt pocket.

She sits back and smiles. It feels good to be invisible.

"You remember that island?" says Pip.

Elise nods, touches his cheek, stands up on her robot legs, and then walks off into the canna lilies. Behind the dead flowers are two big Dumpsters and, if she's calculated correctly, a door leading into the Dogwood Library.

When Bob wakes up, she's standing there in a shaft of late-morning light, a small-boned woman wearing strap-on plastic Power Units like something from the Sci-Fi Channel, her gray hair cropped into an elfin cap.

"Elise," he rasps.

"Bob," she says.

His thick lids slide down over watery eyes.

"Bob?" she says. He shifts in his chair but won't wake up.

She checks his pulse, grabs his blanket from the bed, and tucks it around him. Makes sure he's got on proper socks under his corduroy slippers. And then she rolls him toward the door.

Though Elise has spent many an afternoon wrinkling her nose at the smell of chickens, she isn't prepared for the endless stream of barracks southwest on Highway 301: three giant buildings as long as trains and leaking a stench so shocking she can't believe it doesn't jolt Bob from his nap. Mouth-breathing, she hustles to get past the nastiness, fingering the button that operates his chair, kicking it into high gear, the one the nurses use when they're in a tizzy.

She's been walking for an hour, on a strip of highway shoulder that comes and goes, smooth sailing for a mile and then she'll hit a patch of bumpy asphalt and veer onto the road. A number of motorists have passed—mostly big trucks, pickups, the occasional SUV—and she worries that some upstanding citizen has already called Eden Village. She expects a cop car to roll up any minute. Expects to see the officer put on his gentle smile, the one he uses with feeble-minded people and lunatics, geezers and little children. She would prefer a back road, some decent air and greenery, but she knows she wouldn't remember the way.

If she recalls correctly, 301 is almost a straight shot to the water. Though her legs don't hurt, her shoulders do, an ache that dips into her bones. Her fingers cramp as they grip the handles of Bob's chair. And she's too thirsty to spit. She imagines sweating glasses of sweet tea, cold Coca-Cola in little bottles, lemonade with hunks of fruit floating in the pitcher. She remembers the time she took Bob to meet her grandmother. They drank from a pump on the old wraparound porch, drawing cool spring water up from the earth. She recalls sipping from the garden hose and tasting rubber. Remembers the special flavor of Bob's musty canteen, the one they always took camping. She and Bob once hiked up Looking Glass Rock, crouched under a waterfall with their mouths open, taking giant gulps, the whole mountain wet with dew. Hosts of tiny frogs had clung to the stone, suckers on their toes.

When they get to the lake Elise will roll Bob to the end of their old pier. It'll be dusk by then, she thinks, catfish crowding in the shallows. She wants him to see water on every side when he wakes up, vast and black, with the sky in pink turmoil, as though it's just the two of them, out there floating in a little boat.

DEJI BRYCE OLUKOTUN
We Are the Olfanauts

After **Deji Bryce Olukotun** came to the United States and obtained degrees from Yale and Stanford, he studied at the University of Cape Town with South African writers André Brink, Mike Nicol, Andre Wiesner, and Henrietta Rose-Innes. His novel, *Nigerians in Space*, was published by Unnamed Press in Los Angeles. Olukotun's fiction and nonfiction has been published by *Vice*, *Slate*, the *New York Times*, the *Los Angeles Times*, the *Los Angeles Review of Books*, the *Atlantic*, *Guernica*, *Global Voices*, the *Huffington Post*, *PEN America*, the *London Magazine*, *Men's Health*, and *Electric Literature*. He has been a juror for the Neustadt Festival of International Literature.

Olukotun's story "We Are the Olfanauts" was first published in *Watchlist: 32 Short Stories by Persons of Interest* and deals with new Internet technologies and the social divide between those who work in tech and those who work in the surrounding areas.

U have to whyff this.

Cant.

Y not? ☹

Just cant.

Shes bak.

Dont care. Send it up.

I pasted in the link anyway, ignoring Aubrey's decision.
www.olfanautics.com/13503093!hsfi9hhhh

I knew she would whyff it eventually. One click and you were there. You may as well download it directly into your brain, and with a whyff the effect was nearly as instantaneous. I played the video again to confirm that it was as special as I remembered.

Close-up of a desk. Glass top on a chrome frame. On the desk, a knife, a leather strap, a small glass bowl, and the girl's wrist. Light tan skin. The whyff: hints of lilac, clearly the girl's perfume.

She holds the knife in her palm and waves her second hand over it, like a game show hostess displaying a valuable prize. Then she stabs the tip of her finger with the knife and lets her blood trickle into the bowl. The whyff is not of pain, nor the metallic scent of blood. It smells like the richest, freshest strawberries, collected right there in the bowl. And you can hear her laughing.

I should say that the girl *appeared* to stab the tip of her finger with the knife. You see, there was no proof that she had actually done it. When I slowed the video down, and advanced it frame by frame, her index finger and thumb obscured my view at the exact moment of puncture. She may have stabbed her own finger, or she may have somehow burst a capsule of fake blood with her fingers. Or, more likely, based on the whyff, a capsule of concentrated strawberry essence. It was either the work of a skillful illusionist or a deranged sadomasochist. With my Trunk on, it smelled hilarious.

Aubrey eventually messaged back: **Told u to send it up.**

What abt the whyff??

Send it up.

Shld Private Review.

Send it up.

Cmon, grrl. Strawberries!

This was the second video this user had posted, and each had ended with a whyff that completely subverted the image of the video with humor. It felt like she was playing with us, questioning whether we would believe our eyes or other senses. Wasn't that reason enough to Private Review? To talk it through? Last week, Aubrey and I had met in the Private Review rooms twice. I wasn't going to let her ruin my discovery, though. Instead of sending it up, as she had ordered, I posted the link to ALL-TEAM. Immediately I heard gasps in the cubicles around me.

"Oh, shit, Renton!"

"She's back!"

"Aw, man, I bet she's hot!"

Then they went back to their keypads and we began a group chat.

You gonna send it up?

What do you think?

Think we shld.

You smell the strawberries?

I thought it was raspberries.

You cant see the wound.

She a kid?

No, shes 18+.

You hear her laughing?

Crazy grl.

I let the discussion go on for some time as the team chatted amongst themselves, enjoying the fact that with every passing moment the post was staying online, and some new stranger could appreciate its artistry. There was something beautiful about the glass and the steel and the blood. Only the essentials, the sterility of the table against the violence engendered in the blade. The whorls in the redness as the blood filled the bowl, the burst of strawberries and the laughter, ethereal, hovering above it all.

In the end someone sent it up. I wasn't surprised. We were paid to be cautious, to keep the slipstream of information flowing at all costs, even if it meant removing some of it from the world.

Our team was based in a multibillion-dollar technology park fifteen kilometers outside Nairobi, and our data servers, which would have made us liable under Kenyan law, floated above national airspace in tethered balloons. The Danish architect had modeled the Olfanautics complex after a scene from Karen Blixen's novel, as if that was what we secretly aspired to, a coffee ranch nestled against the foothills of some dew-soaked savannah. The cafeteria was intended to replicate the feel of a safari tent. Catenary steel cables held up an undulating layer of fabric, which gleamed white in the midday sun. In reality, the tent was the closest I had ever been to a safari. I only left Nairobi to go rock climbing.

Aubrey found me as I was ordering a double veggie burger with half a bun and six spears of broccolini. I could tell from the few frayed braids poking out of her headwrap that she had not slept well last night, nor had she gone to the campus hairdresser to clean herself up. I reached for her thigh as soon as she sat down but she swatted it away.

"I told you to send it up."

"Nice to see you, too, Aubrey," I said.

"I'm your boss, Renton. If I say send the video up, then send it up. You're making me look bad."

That was the problem with dating your supervisor. She thought any discussion could be resolved by pulling rank.

"Didn't you whyff the strawberries? They were hilarious, hey. That girl's an actress or something."

"We don't know that, Renton. She could have really been cutting herself. Or someone could have been forcing her off camera and layered in that whyff afterward. We don't even know if she's a she. It could be a man."

Aubrey always pulled her liberal philosophy on me, as if I couldn't trust my own nose.

"The metadata said she was a twenty-four-year-old woman," I said. "I looked at the time signatures. The whyff was recorded simultaneously."

"The signatures could have been spoofed."

"That's only happened once."

I wasn't concerned about speaking to Aubrey so intimately in the cafeteria. No one would have believed that we were together, because for all appearances, I was a handsome young Kenyan man with his pick of eligible women, and Aubrey was a frumpy foreigner from Somewhere Else. But they were using the wrong sense when they judged her.

"Aubs, maybe you should eat something."

"We can't Private Review anymore, Renton."

"Here, have one," I offered. I liked to eat broccolini from the spear to the tip, leaving the head for last.

"Those rooms are set aside for us to do our jobs."

"It's high in folate. And iron."

She glanced around. "Would you stop bloody ignoring me!"

"I think you need to eat something."

"I don't want any of those bloody things. They're not natural. They were invented by some scientist."

"At least it's food." I showed her the screen of my Quantiband on my wrist. "Says I need five hundred milligrams of iron today, and these will give me a thousand. Don't shoot the messenger, hey. I do what I'm told."

"Just not when your boss is the one telling you," she said, and walked away. Only after I had finished my broccolini spears did I realize that she hadn't been wearing her Quantiband.

That evening I tried to forget my conversation with Aubrey because I wanted to be totally focused on my Passion. In three years, I planned to free-climb the sheer granite face of the Orabeskopf Wall in Namibia, one of the most difficult routes in southern Africa, and I had meticulously plotted out my conditioning, fitness, and routes with my personal fitness instructor, whose name was Rocky. You see, because of my work on Trust & Safety, we were afforded certain additional privileges: a trainer (mine was Rocky), a psychologist, a full subscription Quantiband, an additional five floating holidays, a stipend of OlfaBucks that we could use at the gift shop, and access to a sleep specialist. The company would support one Passion for each of us. It could be running a marathon, completing a competitive Scrabble tournament, or knitting a quilt. What mattered is that you chose a Passion with a measurable goal. That's why I loved my Quantiband: it calculated my heart rate, blood pressure, distance walked, calories, alertness, mood, sleep quality, and even the frequency with which I had sex. When I was treating my body well, my Quantiband felt as light as air, but it could constrict itself around my wrist like a snake when I veered off my programmed routine.

My role at T&S was fairly simple: to respond to content flagged by our users that violated our Terms of Service. Olfanautics was the global pioneer in scented social media. Our Whyff product allowed users to send scents to people around the world. It was originally a stand-alone device that utilized four fundamental scents—woody, pungent, sweet, and decayed— and combined them proportionately in a spray to mimic real scents, but few people could afford to buy it. As the technology grew better, and tinier, Olfanautics became a standard feature of smartphones that could also record video and audio. Many users would whyff frequently at first and then save it for special occasions, like showing off a fresh baked pie during the holidays, or sharing a vacation by the beach. Some users would turn off the feature when they wanted more privacy but most preferred to have the ability to whyff, if they might need it, than not to have it. Then there were people like me who whyffed incessantly, who became so enthralled by the unlimited palate of experience that we sought out its very source.

My main job was to monitor the whyffs that users considered suspicious or objectionable. I did so through my Trunk, a tube that looked like the oxygen mask of a fighter jet pilot. Between each whyff, the Trunk would inject a neutral scent to cleanse my palate. You see, scent is determined more by your tongue than your nose—think of how hard it is to taste anything when you have a bad cold—and everyone on my team had a significantly higher number of papillae on our tongues than your average user. In another era, we might have been perfumers selling bottles of lavender along the cobblestones of Grasse. Today we were the Olfanauts. We transported our users safely and peacefully to exciting realms of discovery. So went our tagline.

I loved our tagline.

The video safety team would pull down the usual garbage: sexual content, violence, self-mutilation, and child pornography. But sometimes people would inject a whyff into an otherwise normal video. A video of a birthday cake might stink like feces, or a trickling stream might reek of decomposition. Usually these were hatchet jobs that were crudely added to the video, and our software would automatically flag the whyffs because of their metadata. Occasionally we'd come across a whyff of skilled artistry, when the scent would waft through the Trunk like a sublime wind. Like the girl with the knife.

When I couldn't decide on a case by myself, I could present it to my supervisor, Aubrey, and then she had the option of sending it up to the Deciders—members of the legal and marketing teams back in Denmark. Only Aubrey had ever met them, although we had all been flown to Copenhagen for orientation when we were hired. (That was a legendary trip, hey.)

Rocky was waiting for me at the gym when I arrived. He was a grizzly, colored South African with a bursting Afro and wind-seared skin. He claimed to have broken thirty-two bones, fifteen of which he had shattered on the same fall in the Dolomites back when he was a competitive climber. He wore glasses with thick black plastic rims that he had owned for so long that they had twice gone in, and out, of fashion while they were still on his nose. He'd switched from rock climbing to bouldering after he had gnarled his right leg, and I had seen videos of him skittering under impossible slabs of granite like a dassie.

I began strapping on my harness.

"Wait, wait, bru," Rocky said. "Let's hit the fingerboard first."

"Quantiband says I don't need to get on the fingerboard until next week. I'm supposed to climb."

"That thing doesn't know how to climb."

"It knows how to measure my progress. That's what it's supposed to do."

Rocky sighed. "All right, big man. Think you know what you're doing? Give this route a try, then." He hooked me in to his carabiner and illuminated a green climbing path for me to follow on the wall.

I gleefully dipped my hands in my powder bag. I love the smell of the powder as you grab the first holds. It smells like freedom, hey, as if I am climbing towards my dreams. Before long I had pulled myself about ten meters off the ground. Then I got to a problem that I couldn't navigate. There was a nasty slither of a hold that I thought I could crimp, and as I dug my fingers in, my hand stiffened from fatigue and my feet slid out from under me. I tried to dyno my hip onto the hold but it was too late. And I was falling rapidly towards the mats below.

My head snapped forward so hard that my nose bashed into my kneecap.

"Got ya!" Rocky said. He gradually lowered me to the ground.

I clutched at my nose as he unclipped my harness. I could feel numbness spreading along my eye socket.

"You all right there, bru?"

"No, I'm not all right! Why the fuck didn't you catch me earlier, Rocky?"

Rocky recoiled: "Why the fuck did you fall?"

"I couldn't crimp it. The route was too hard."

"Here, let me look at your nose. Come on, move your hand out of the way." I let go, and the blood rushed in painfully. "It's all right, bru. You're not bleeding. It was a light knock."

"Bloody hell." I was relieved but I could feel my nostrils filling with something. Mucus? Blood? The air was already starting to feel stale. It was as if the smells were slipping past me, as if the room was coated in a skein of mud.

"You weren't prepared for it, bru," he went on, tapping his temple with his finger. "It was a simple problem. It wasn't your finger strength but your mind that failed you."

I didn't like Rocky's tone. I paid him to help me fulfill my Passion, not to cause me more problems. I was in line for a promotion soon. "How am I supposed to go to work tomorrow if I can't even smell your stinking breath? You made a mistake, Rocky. Just admit it."

"That's kak. I'm not the one who fell."

I began tapping away on my Quantiband. "Says here that I shouldn't have been doing this route for three weeks. This wasn't part of the program. I could report you for this."

Now I had his attention. "Calm down there, bru. There's no need to report it."

At Olfanautics, the numbers didn't lie. The Quantiband would have measured the speed of my fall in meters per second as well as my rise in pulse. If I could show, objectively, that someone had put my work at risk then he would be dismissed immediately. The same went for all of us.

"Why shouldn't I report you?"

"Because then you wouldn't get any better at climbing. I wanted to challenge you, bru. You can't control everything when you're out there. That's part of climbing."

"But it's not part of the program. The program says I get better in three weeks. That's the whole point. If you want to challenge me then put it in the program."

"Come on, let's forget it, Renton. You're right. My mistake, bru. I put in the wrong route." He tapped on the wall and illuminated a yellow route, one that I had already successfully completed twice before. "This is what the program wanted, right?"

He grabbed for the carabiner on my harness, but I pushed his hand away. "No, I need to get some ice for my nose."

"Come on, bru. Your nose is fine. You took a small knock, is all. Let's hook you in. Yellow's still a bastard of a route. You haven't even free-climbed it yet."

It was so easy to screenshot my Quantiband, and even easier to send it to security. I looked at him blankly as if I didn't understand, buying time. He began pleading with me to hook me in, insistently, pathetically even.

"What are you waiting for, Renton? It was a simple mistake. Let me hook you in!"

"No, it's too late."

Olfanautics only allowed the perimeter security to carry guns. So the ones who arrived wielded batons, but the effect was still intimidating enough to prevent Rocky from putting up any sort of struggle.

"You think the Orabeskopf Wall gives a shit about that thing on your wrist, bru?" he shouted back. "You think that thing is going to save you when you're on the wall and a vulture starts pecking at your fingers? That's what happened to me! I was like Prometheus, getting my liver pecked out by an eagle, bru. I didn't have one of those kak wristbands. I let it eat my own hand and then I climbed up that wall! The Orabeskopf says fuck-all to your wrist! That wind will tear you off that route and splatter your brains in the sand!"

But I'd heard that story about the vulture many times before, and it didn't scare me anymore. My Quantiband told me that there was a one in ten million chance of it ever happening to me. I had whyffed some terrible things during my time at Olfanautics—ritual dismemberment by a militia in Bukavu with a volcano looming in the background, a woman being raped on a frozen canal in Ottawa, and once, a manhole cover in Nagoya crushing an old nun on the sidewalk after it was ejected by a blast of gas. If Rocky had whyffed these things, too, he might have left with a little more dignity. The world was not a fair place, and I was the one who helped people forget that fact. As soon as he had left, I put in an order for a new fitness instructor.

Except for the death of the nun in Nagoya, which crept into my dreams and made me sad in a way that I don't think I'll ever understand (the ferocious spin of the manhole cover, the febrile skull), I had learned to forget the horrific smells that permeated my Trunk. I had trained for months at Olfanautics to expunge them from my mind, and the regimen had worked for the most part. You have to let things go, you see.

But I hadn't finished my climbing routine, so I felt edgy when I took the shuttle back to the Olfanautics housing complex, and my nose hurt like hell. The pain from my fall had spread from the base of my skull to my shoulders, and seemed to be wrapping itself around my chest.

My apartment had two bedrooms, a small balcony, and one-and-a-half bathrooms. Behind it, I had a tolerable view of a tennis court surrounded by electrified razor wire. My unit was subsidized so it was still cheaper than living in the city, and I was permitted to invite guests, usually my parents, to stay with me for six days per month.

Aubrey was sipping on a beer at the living room table when I opened the door.

"What happened to your face?"

"Took a fall at the gym."

"What about those bandages?"

"It's to keep my nostrils open. Doctor said there might be some temporary blockage." When she didn't say anything, I added: "I should still be able to put in my shift tomorrow."

"I'm not worried about that anymore."

Her face was as distraught as when we'd met in the cafeteria. If she'd been wearing her Quantiband, it would have been twisted tight around her wrist like a tourniquet. But she still didn't have it on. Maybe it was that sense of freedom that made her come over to me. Because the next thing I knew, she began opening the buttons of my shirt. I didn't stop her. Aubrey was the most beautiful woman I had ever met. Her natural odor was enough to turn my head, and she layered on essential oils so that she was a fragrant mosaic, a true artiste who could compose entire olfascapes of inspired brilliance. I had never been able to resist her. On our first secret date, she had guessed what cologne I would wear and applied an extract of argan nuts on her skin, so that when we touched we smelled like buttered popcorn. I found other women repulsive by comparison, as if they had showered themselves in crude perfume.

But as she slowly peeled off my shirt, my bashed-in nose seemed to be obscuring everything. "I can't smell you."

"Then feel me."

In the Private Review rooms, Aubrey and I would sniff each other more than we licked or kissed, and this took time. When we were really horny, we'd inhale each other's most private scents—our groins, armpits, and anuses—like animals in the throes of estrus. But with my swollen nose I felt clumsy, as if I was watching myself make love from a distance, and my fingertips couldn't make up for the lack of sensation. Aubrey, on the other hand, enjoyed every second of it. She lingered over my bandages and wrapped herself around me. Then she dug her hips into mine until she came. Even with her breasts flopping against my face and her full buttocks in my hands, I couldn't stay aroused without my sense of smell, and we both gave up trying.

As we lay on my bed, Aubrey announced: "This isn't working." She always said depressing things after sex.

"It's my fault. I couldn't get into it."

"No, Renton. I mean us. I'm your boss. We can't do this anymore."

I turned to face her, suddenly concerned. "What do you mean?"

"The Deciders know."

"You told them?"

"No, the Private Review rooms are all monitored. They've known for some time and they confronted me about it."

I tried to remember everything we might have done or said to each other. She normally made me take off my Quantiband in the Private Review rooms.

"Did they whyff it, too?"

"I don't think so—at least, I wouldn't see the point of that. They tracked our bands to see how often we were meeting. I clearly violated my Terms of Reference. I'm your boss and it should never have happened. I've got to go see them tomorrow."

"They're flying you to Copenhagen?"

"Yeah."

"That's a good sign, right? They wouldn't fly you up there if they wanted to fire you."

She considered this. "I suppose so."

"Why did you come here tonight, Aubs?"

"I wanted to do it one last time."

I raised from the bed to look out the window. Beyond the tennis court were rows upon rows of sagging acacia trees that the Danish architect had planted all around the campus, but the soil was too damp for the trees and their roots were slowly drowning. I had never liked them. Their pollen gave me sneezing fits. If I had my way, I'd have them all cut down. "How can you say it's the last time? How is that fair? Shouldn't I also know when it's the last time? You can't break it off and say it's the last time without telling me!"

"I'm sorry, Renton. It's not just the Deciders. It's—it's the unreality of it."

"Was it the video of the girl? The strawberries?"

"No, that's not it."

"I meant it as a joke. There's no need to break up over a thing like that."

"You know what I spent this morning doing? Watching a woman eat a goat alive. She had filed her teeth into points, Renton. Like a vampire. Even had the makeup on. Her girlfriend—I think that's who it was—was screaming at her to eat more. Shrieking at her to eat more. The poor beast was pinned down by stakes and the girl was tearing into its belly. The stench! Of piss and shit, the goat was in so much pain it was expelling what little bit of life it had left in it. Trying to die."

I had never seen Aubrey cry before, and I feared what it might mean.

"Who would do such a thing, Renton? To a harmless animal? I vomited into my Trunk it was so disgusting."

I could see that she wanted me to feel what she had felt, smell what she had smelled, but I couldn't let her get to me. Every Olfanaut who burned out tried to drag everyone else down with them. The psychologists had taught us it was called transference. I began searching desperately for my Quantiband, which she must have torn off during sex.

"Why don't you go see the psychologists, Aubs? That's what they're there for."

"They wouldn't understand."

"Of course they would! Mimi helped me with the nun thing. I'm sure she can help you with whatever is bothering you."

I found my Quantiband beneath my sock at the foot of the bed. I didn't remember taking the sock off, because I was still wearing the other one.

"Mimi can't help me, Renton. She can't help a thing like that. Tell me, when was the last time you left the campus?"

"I go to the Rain Drop all the time."

"That's still on the campus!"

"So what? It's a bar. I like the people there. We have a lot in common."

"I mean, when was the last time you went downtown? Or anywhere people don't have to whyff a conversation?"

"My family doesn't live downtown. They're out in Kibera."

"That's not my point. What we see all day—it's not right. We made love over a Nazi bookburning last week. A bloody bookburning."

"We took that video down, Aubrey. We prevented the rest of the world from smelling that filth. That's something to be proud of. Sure, we had sex in there but we did our job in the end. That's what matters. We have one job here, and we do it right. I'm sure that's all the Deciders care about too. That's why I fired Rocky."

"What are you talking about?"

I hadn't meant to tell her, because I knew she'd try to make me feel bad, but now it was too late. "He put me on a dangerous route. That's how I hurt my nose."

"So you fired him?"

"Of course! Rocky had it coming to him, Aubs. I'd told him a thousand times that we had to follow the program. It's not my fault he can't listen to directions."

"That's what I mean by unreality. So what if you hurt your nose—he has a family! How will he survive without this job?"

"What about my family?" I grabbed a glass from the kitchen, and filled it in the sink. "Do you realize this is the only neighborhood within twenty kilometers where you can do this? Drink water straight from the tap? My parents drive here for their drinking water. I'm putting my sister through school. I pay for every funeral in my family. That's as real as it gets." I pointed to my Quantiband. "This says right here that I was climbing the wrong route when I fell. Rocky hurt my nose, the tool of my trade. I'm in line for a promotion now and I can't take the risk. I need someone reliable. Trustworthy. I don't need his bloody war stories. I need someone safe. Who can commit to the program."

Aubrey stared at me blankly for a few moments. "You don't see what this does to us, do you? Today was my big test to determine if I could join the Deciders. And I failed it, Renton. I failed it horribly. Because I told them that if I had my way I'd exterminate those girls from the face of the Earth. I wasn't thinking about justice. I was thinking about revenge. Revenge on behalf of a mangy fucking goat."

I drank my glass slowly, trying to taste the filtered water. They ran it through reverse osmosis and then a layer of sand, which normally gave it a delightful mineral quality. But I couldn't taste a thing.

"You're not going to get a promotion, Renton. Look at yourself in the mirror and then take a look at management. I recommended you twice but they said you don't have the pedigree. When was the last time a local was promoted?"

Now I knew Aubrey was planning to move away all along. And she wanted to hurt me while doing it, whatever for I had no idea. That was what happened in the videos. That was what those people did to each other. Even after all we'd been through, I refused to let her do this to me. It was the slippery hold on the wall. The tumble from the granite, the brains in the sand.

"I'm going to be the first one, then."

You can't let it all weigh on your shoulders. That's what Mimi had told me about the nun. You've got to let things go.

I snapped my finger. "I know what's changed—it's you, Aubrey."

"Me?"

"Yes, you need a new Passion."

"You weren't listening."

"You made that short film last year, right? That was too close to home. We whyff videos all day, hey. You've got to choose something else. Something that really gets you chuffed! Like writing a book. Or dancing. You've got to focus on the positive, Aubs! Think of all the value we're creating for our users. Think about how we protected them from that Nazi video. We saved a little bit of joy for two billion users around the world. We have to celebrate that! You can't dwell on these things. We're watching so no one else has to!"

As I went on like this, Aubrey's face brightened, and before long she seemed to be coming around to the idea. So I was surprised, when I pulled her in for a kiss, and she said: "If evil is humanity turned against itself, Renton, then who are we?"

"We're the Olfanauts," I said proudly.

Aubrey left Olfanautics two weeks later, and she was kind enough to say goodbye to me. She also transferred me all of her OlfaBucks, which would allow me to order something from the gift shop, and I think she knew, in her heart, that I would spend it on a Hyperlite Bivouack that I had told her about a few months ago, which I planned to use when I free-climb the Orabeskopf Wall in Namibia. I won't lie—I started dreaming about the nun again as soon as Aubrey left, and I had to work extra hard at my Passion to get that old woman to leave me alone in my sleep. It's funny how sometimes you only understand what people mean well after they say it. Because I realized that Rocky had been right all along, that I had to be like Prometheus giving the fire to humanity, and that I couldn't worry about some bird pecking at my fingers as I made my grand ascent.

RIVKA GALCHEN
The Region of Unlikeness

Rivka Galchen is a Canadian American writer who received her MD from Mount Sinai and an MFA from Columbia University. Her first novel, *Atmospheric Disturbances*, won the Danuta Gleed Literary Award and the William Saroyan International Prize. Her short stories have been collected in *American Innovations*. Galchen's work has been published in the *New Yorker*, *Harper's*, the *New York Times Magazine*, the *Believer*, *Open City*, and the *Walrus*. She is a recipient of the Rona Jaffe Foundation Writer's Award and was the Mary Ellen von der Heyden Fiction Fellow at the American Academy in Berlin. Galchen was chosen in 2010 by the *New Yorker* as one of its "20 Under 40."

"The Region of Unlikeness" follows the fleeting relationship between a young woman and two strange men, Ilan and Jacob, who may be academics, eccentric dilettantes, or something entirely different. The story was first published in the *New Yorker*.

Some people would consider Jacob a physicist, some would consider him a philosopher or simply a "time expert," though I tend to think of him in less reverent terms. But not terms of hatred. Ilan used to call Jacob "my cousin from Outer Swabia." That obscure little joke, which I heard Ilan make a number of times, probably without realizing how many times he'd made it before, always seemed to me to imply a distant blood relation between the two of them. I guess I had the sense (back then) that Jacob and Ilan were shirttail cousins of some kind. But later I came to believe, at least intermittently, that actually Ilan's little phrase was both a misdirection and a sort of clue, one that hinted at an enormous secret that they'd never let me in on. Not a dully personal secret, like an affair or a small crime or, say, a missing testicle—but a scientific secret, that rare kind of secret that, in our current age, still manages to bend our knee.

I met Ilan and Jacob by chance. Sitting at the table next to mine in a small Moroccan coffee shop on the Upper West Side, they were discussing *Wuthering Heights*, too loudly, having the kind of reference-laden conversation that unfortunately never fails to attract me. Jacob looked about forty-five; he was overweight, he was munching obsessively on these unappetizing green leaf-shaped cookies, and he kept saying "obviously." Ilan was good-looking, and he said that the tragedy of Heathcliff was that he was essentially, on account of his lack of property rights, a woman. Jacob then extolled Catherine's proclaiming, "I *am* Heathcliff." Something about passion was said. And about digging up graves. And a bearded young man next to them moved to a more distant table. Jacob and Ilan talked on, unoffended, praising Brontë, and at some point Ilan added, "But since Jane Austen's usually the token woman on university syllabi, it's understandable if your average undergraduate has a hard time shaking the idea that women are half-wits, moved only by the terror that a man might not be as rich as he seems."

Not necessarily warmly, I chimed in with something. Ilan laughed. Jacob refined Ilan's statement to "straight women." Then to straight women "in the Western tradition." Then the three of us spoke for a long time. That hadn't been my intention. But there was something about Ilan—manic, fragile, fidgety, womanizing (I imagined) Ilan—that was all at once like fancy coffee and bright-colored smutty flyers. He had a great deal to say, with a steady gaze into my eyes, about my reading the *New York Post*, which he interpreted as a sign of a highly satiric yet demotically moral intelligence. Jacob nodded. I let the flattery go straight to my heart, despite the fact that I didn't read the *Post*—it had simply been left on my table by a previous customer. Ilan called *Post* writers naïve Nabokovs. Yes, I said. The headline, I remember, read AXIS OF WEASEL. Somehow this led to Jacob's saying something vague about Proust, and violence, and perception.

"Jacob's a boor, isn't he?" Ilan said. Or maybe he said "bore" and I heard "boor" because Ilan's way of talking seemed so antiquated to me. I had so few operating sources of pride at that time. I was tutoring and making my lonely way through graduate school in civil engineering, where my main sense of joy came from trying to silently outdo the boys—they still played video games—in my courses. I started going to that coffee shop every day.

Everyone I knew seemed to find my new companions arrogant and pathetic, but whenever they called me I ran to join them. Ilan and Jacob were both at least twenty years older than me, and they called themselves philosophers, although only Jacob seemed to have an actual academic position, and maybe a tenuous one, I couldn't quite tell. I was happy not to care about those things. Jacob had a wife and daughter, too, though I never met them. It was always just the three of us. We would get together and Ilan would go on about Heidegger and "thrownness," or about Will Ferrell, and Jacob would come up with some way to disagree, and I would mostly just listen, and eat baklava and drink lots of coffee. Then we'd go for a long walk, and Ilan might have some argument in defense of, say, Fascist architecture, and Jacob would say something about the striated and the smooth, and then a pretty girl would walk by and they would talk about her outfit for a long time. Jacob and Ilan always had something to say, which gave me the mistaken impression that I did, too.

Evenings, we'd go to the movies, or eat at an overpriced restaurant, or lie around Ilan's spacious and oddly neglected apartment. He had no bed frame, nothing hung on the walls, and in his bathroom there was just a single white towel and a T.W.A. mini-toothbrush. But he had a two-hundred-dollar pair of leather gloves. One day, when I went shopping with the two of them, I found myself buying a simple striped sweater so expensive that I couldn't get to sleep that night.

None of this behavior—the laziness, the happiness, the subservience, even the pretentiousness—was "like me." I was accustomed to using a day planner and eating my lunch alone, in fifteen minutes; I bought my socks at street fairs. But when I was with them I felt like, well, a girl. Or "the girl." I would see us from the outside and recognize that I was, in an old-fashioned and maybe even demeaning way, the sidekick, the mascot, the decoration; it was thrilling. And it didn't hurt that Ilan was so generous with his praise. I fixed his leaking shower and he declared me a genius. Same when I roasted a chicken with lemons. When I wore orange socks with jeans, he kissed my feet. Jacob told Ilan to behave with more dignity; he was just jealous of Ilan's easy pleasures.

It's not as if Jacob wasn't lovable in his own abstruse and awkward way. I admired how much he read—probably more than Ilan, certainly more than me (he made this as clear as he could)—but Jacob struck me as pedantic, and I thought he would do well to button his shirts a couple buttons higher. Once, we were all at the movies—I had bought a soda for four dollars—and Jacob and I were waiting wordlessly for Ilan to return from the men's room. It felt like a very long wait. Several times I had to switch the hand I was holding the soda in because the waxy cup was so cold. "He's taking such a long time," I said, and shrugged my shoulders, just to throw a ripple into the strange quiet between us.

"You know what they say about time," Jacob said idly. "It's what happens even when nothing else does."

"O.K.," I said. The only thing that came to my mind was the old joke that time flies like an arrow and fruit flies like a banana. I couldn't bear to say it, so I remained silent. It was as if, without Ilan, we couldn't even pretend to have a conversation.

There were, I should admit, things about Ilan (in particular) that didn't make me feel so good about myself. For example, once I thought he was pointing a gun at me, but it turned out to be a remarkably good fake. Occasionally when he poured me a drink he would claim he was trying to poison me. One night I even became very sick, and wondered. Another evening—maybe the only time Jacob wasn't with us; he said his daughter had appendicitis—Ilan and I lay on his mattress watching TV. For years, watching TV had made me sick with a sense of dissoluteness, but now suddenly it seemed great. That night, Ilan took hold of one of my hands and started idly to kiss my fingers, and I felt—well, I felt I'd give up the rest of my life just for that. Then Ilan got up and turned off the television. Then he fell asleep, and the hand-kissing never came up again.

Ilan frequently called me his "dusty librarian." And once he called me his "Inner Swabian," and this struck him as very funny, and even Jacob didn't seem to understand why. Ilan made a lot of jokes that I didn't understand— he was a big fan of Poe, so I chalked his occasionally morbid humor up to that. But he had that handsome face, and his pants fit him just so, and he liked to lecture Jacob about how smart I was after I'd, say, nervously folded up my napkin in a way he found charming. I got absolutely no work done while I was friends with them. And hardly any reading, either. What I mean to say is that those were the happiest days of my entire life.

Then we fell apart. I just stopped hearing from them. Ilan didn't return my calls. I waited and waited, but I was remarkably poised about the whole thing. I assumed that Ilan had simply found a replacement mascot. And I imagined that Jacob—in love with Ilan, in his way—hardly registered the swapping out of one girl for another. Suddenly it seemed a mystery to me that I had ever wanted to be with them. Ilan was just a charming parrot. And Jacob the parrot's parrot. And if Jacob was married and had a child wasn't it time for him to grow up and spend his days like a responsible adult? That, anyway, was the disorganized crowd of my thoughts. Several months passed, and I almost convinced myself that I was glad to be alone again. I took on more tutoring work.

Then one day I ran randomly (O.K., not so randomly—I was haunting our old spots like the most unredeemed of ghosts) into Jacob.

For the duration of two iced teas, Jacob sat with me, repeatedly noting that, sadly, he really had no time at all, he really would have to be going. We chatted about this and that and about the tasteless yet uncanny ad campaign for a B movie called *Silent Hill* (the poster image was of a child normal in all respects except for the absence of a mouth), and Jacob went on and on about how much some prominent philosopher adored him, and about how deeply unmutual the feeling was, and about the burden of unsolicited love, until finally, my heart a hummingbird, I asked, "And how is Ilan?"

Jacob's face went the proverbial white. I don't think I'd ever actually seen that happen to anyone. "I'm not supposed to tell you," he said.

Not saying anything seemed my best hope for remaining composed; I sipped at my tea.

"I don't want your feelings to be hurt," Jacob went on. "I'm sure Ilan wouldn't have wanted them hurt, either."

After a long pause, I said, "Jacob, I really am just a dusty librarian, not some disastrous heroine." It was a bad imitation of something Ilan might have said with grace. "Just tell me."

"Well, let's see. He died."

"What?"

"He had, well, so it is, well, he had stomach cancer. Inoperable, obviously. He kept it a secret. Told only family."

I recalled the cousin from Outer Swabia line. Also, I felt certain—somehow really certain—that I was being lied to. That Ilan was actually still alive. Just tired of me. Or something. "He isn't dead," I said, trying to deny the creeping sense of humiliation gathering at my liver's portal vein.

"Well, this is very awkward," Jacob said flatly. "I feel suddenly that my whole purpose on earth is to tell you the news of Ilan—that this is my most singular and fervent mission. Here I am, failing, and yet still I feel as though this job were, somehow, my deepest essence, who I really—"

"Why do you talk like that?" I interrupted. I had never, in all our time together, asked Jacob (or Ilan) such a thing.

"You're in shock—"

"What does Ilan even do?" I asked, ashamed of this kind of ignorance above all. "Does he come from money? What was he working on? I never understood. He always seemed to me like some kind of stranded time traveller, from an era when you really could get away with just being good at conversation—"

"Time traveller. Funny that you say that." Jacob shook extra sugar onto the dregs of his iced tea and then slurped at it. "Ilan may have been right about you. Though honestly I could never see it myself. Well, I need to get going."

"Why do you have to be so obscure?" I asked. "Why can't you just be sincere?"

"Oh, let's not take such a genial view of social circumstances so as to uphold sincerity as a primary value," Jacob said, with affected distraction, stirring his remaining ice with his straw. "Who you really are—very bourgeois myth, that, obviously an anxiety about social mobility."

I could have cried, trying to control that conversation. Maybe Jacob could see that. Finally, looking at me directly, and with his tone of voice softened, he said, "I really am very sorry for you to have heard like this." He patted my hand in what seemed like a genuine attempt at tenderness. "I imagine I'll make this up to you, in time. But listen, sweetheart, I really do have to head off. I have to pick my wife up from the dentist and my kid from school, and there you go, that's what life is like. I would advise you to seriously consider avoiding it—life, I mean—altogether. I'll call you. Later this week. I promise."

He left without paying.

He had never called me "sweetheart" before. And he'd never so openly expressed the opinion that I had no life. He didn't phone me that week, or the next, or the one after that. Which was O.K. Maybe, in truth, Jacob and I had always disliked each other.

I found no obituary for Ilan. If I'd been able to find any official trace of him at all, I think I might have been comforted. But he had vanished so completely that it seemed like a trick. As if for clues, I took to reading the *New York Post*. I learned that pro wrestlers were dying mysteriously young, that baseball players and politicians tend to have mistresses, and that a local archbishop who'd suffered a ski injury was now doing, all told, basically fine. I was fine, too, in the sense that every day I would get out of bed in the morning, walk for an hour, go to the library and work on problem sets, drink tea, eat yogurt and bananas and falafel, avoid seeing people, rent a movie, and then fall asleep watching it. But I couldn't recover the private joy I'd once taken in the march of such orderly, productive days.

One afternoon—it was February—a letter showed up in my mailbox, addressed to Ilan. It wasn't the first time this had happened; Ilan had often, with no explanation, directed mail to my apartment, a habit I'd always assumed had something to do with evading collection agencies. But this envelope had been addressed by hand.

Inside, I found a single sheet of paper with an elaborate diagram in Ilan's handwriting: billiard balls and tunnels and equations heavy with Greek. At the bottom it said, straightforwardly enough, "Jacob will know."

This struck me as a silly, false clue—one that I figured Jacob himself had sent. I believed it signified nothing. But. My face flushed, and my heart fluttered, and I felt as if a morning-glory vine were snaking through all my body's cavities.

I set aside my dignity and called Jacob.

Without telling him why, assuming that he knew, I asked him to meet me for lunch. He excused himself with my-wife-this, my-daughter-that; I insisted that I wanted to thank him for how kind he'd always been to me, and I suggested an expensive and tastelessly fashionable restaurant downtown and said it would be my treat. Still he turned me down.

I hadn't thought this would be the game he'd play.

"I have something of Ilan's," I finally admitted.

"Good for you," he said, his voice betraying nothing but a cold.

"I mean work. Equations. And what look like billiard-ball diagrams. I really don't know what it is. But, well, I had a feeling that you might." I didn't know what I should conceal, but it seemed like I should conceal something. "Maybe it will be important."

"Does it smell like Ilan?"

"It's just a piece of paper," I answered, not in the mood for a subtext I couldn't quite make out. "But I think you should see it."

"Listen, I'll have lunch with you, if that's going to make you happy, but don't be so pathetic as to start thinking you've found some scrap of genius. You should know that Ilan found your interest in him laughable, and that his real talent was for convincing people that he was smarter than he was. Which is quite a talent, I won't deny it, but other than that the only smart ideas that came out of his mouth he stole from other people, usually from me, which is why most everyone, although obviously not you, preferred me—"

Having a "real" life seemed to have worn on Jacob.

At the appointed time and place, Ilan's scrawl in hand, I waited and waited for Jacob. I ordered several courses and ate almost nothing, except for a little side of salty cucumbers. Jacob never showed. Maybe he hadn't been the source of the letter. Or maybe he'd lost the spirit to follow through on his joke, whatever it was.

A little detective work on my part revealed that Ilan's diagrams had something to do with an idea often played with in science fiction, a problem of causality and time travel known as the grandfather paradox. Simply stated, the paradox is this: if travel to the past is possible—and much in physics suggests that it is—then what happens if you travel back in time and set out to murder your grandfather? If you succeed, then you will never be born, and therefore your grandfather won't be murdered by you, and therefore you will be born, and will be able to murder him, et cetera, ad paradox. Ilan's billiard-ball diagrams were part of a tradition (the seminal work is Feynman and Wheeler's 1949 Advanced Absorber Theory) of mathematically analyzing a simplified version of the paradox: imagine a billiard ball enters a wormhole, and then emerges five minutes in the past, on track to hit its past self out of the path that sent it into the wormhole in the first place. The surprise is that, just as real circles can't be squared, and real moving matter doesn't cross the barrier of the speed of light, the mathematical solutions to the billiard-ball wormhole scenario seem to bear out the notion that real solutions don't generate grandfather paradoxes. The rub is that some of the real solutions are very strange, and involve the balls behaving in extraordinarily unlikely, but not impossible, ways. The ball may disintegrate into a powder, or break in half, or hit up against its earlier self at just such an angle so as to enter the wormhole in just such a way that even more peculiar events occur. But the ball won't, and can't, hit up against its past self in any way that would conflict with its present self's trajectory. The mathematics simply don't allow it. Thus no paradox. Science-fiction writers have arrived at analogous solutions to the grandfather paradox: murderous grandchildren are inevitably stopped by something—faulty pistols, slippery banana peels, flying squirrels, consciences—before the impossible deed can be carried out.

Frankly, I was surprised that Ilan—if it was Ilan—was any good at math. He hadn't seemed the type.

Maybe I was also surprised that I spent so many days trying to understand that note. I had other things to do. Laundry. Work. I was auditing an extra course in Materials. But I can't pretend I didn't harbor the hope that eventually—on my own—I'd prove that page some sort of important discovery. I don't know how literally I thought this would bring Ilan back to me. But the oversimplified image that came to me was, yes, that of digging up a grave.

I kind of wanted to call Jacob just to say that he hadn't hurt my feelings by standing me up, that I didn't need his help, or his company, or anything.

Time passed. I made no further progress. Then, one Thursday—it was August—I came across two (searingly dismissive) reviews of a book Jacob had written called *Times and Misdemeanors*. I was amazed that he had completed anything at all. And frustrated that "grandfather paradox" didn't appear in the index. It seemed to me implied by the title, even though that meant reading the title wrongly, as literature. Though obviously the title invited that kind of "wrongness." Which I thought was annoying and ambiguous in precisely a Jacob kind of way. I bought the book, but, in some small attempt at dignity, I didn't read it.

The following Monday, for the first time in his life, Jacob called me up. He said he was hoping to discuss something rather delicate with me, something he'd rather not mention over the phone. "What is it?" I asked.

"Can you meet me?" he asked.

"But what is it?"

"What time should we meet?"

I refused the first three meeting times he proposed, because I could. Eventually, Jacob suggested we meet at the Moroccan place at whatever time I wanted, that day or the next, but urgently, not farther in the future, please.

"You mean the place where I first met Ilan?" This just slipped out.

"And me. Yes. There."

In preparation for our meeting, I reread the negative reviews of Jacob's book.

And I felt so happy; the why of it was opaque to me.

Predictably, the coffee shop was the same but somehow not quite the same. Someone, not me, was reading the *New York Post*. Someone, not Ilan, was reading Deleuze. The fashion had made for shorter shorts on many of the women, and my lemonade came with slushy, rather than cubed, ice. But the chairs were still trimmed with chipping red paint, and the floor tile seemed, as ever, to fall just short of exhibiting a regular pattern.

Jacob walked in only a few minutes late, his gaze beckoned in every direction by all manner of bare legs. With an expression like someone sucking on an unpleasant cough drop, he made his way over to me.

I offered my sincerest consolations on the poor reviews of his work.

"Oh, time will tell," he said. He looked uncomfortable; he didn't even touch the green leaf cookies I'd ordered for him. Sighing, wrapping his hand tightly around the edge of the table and looking away, he said, "You know what Augustine says about time? Augustine describes time as a symptom of the world's flaw, a symptom of things in the world not being themselves, having to make their way back to themselves, by moving through time—"

Somehow I had already ceded control of the conversation. No billiard-ball diagrams. No Ilan. No reviews. Almost as if I weren't there, Jacob went on with his unencouraged ruminations: "There's a paradox there, of course, since what can things be but themselves? In Augustine's view, we live in what he calls the region of unlikeness, and what we're unlike is

God. We are apart from God, who is pure being, who is himself, who is outside of time. And time is our tragedy, the substance we have to wade through as we try to move closer to God. Rivers flowing to the sea, a flame reaching upward, a bird homing: these movements all represent objects yearning to be their true selves, to achieve their true state. For humans, the motion reflects the yearning for God, and everything we do through time comes from moving—or at least trying to move—toward God. So that we can be"—someone at a nearby table cleared his throat judgmentally, which made me think of Ilan also being there—"our true selves. So there's a paradox there again, that we must submit to God—which feels deceptively like *not* being ourselves   in order to become ourselves. We might call this yearning love, and it's just that we often mistake *what* we love. We think we love sensuality. Or admiration. Or, say, another person. But loving another person is just a confusion, an error. Even if it is the kind of error that a nice, reasonable person might make—"

It struck me that Jacob might be manically depressed and that, in addition to his career, his marriage might not be going so well, either.

"I mean," Jacob amended, "it's all bullshit, of course, but aren't I a great guy? Isn't talking to me great? I can tell you about time and you learn all about Western civilization. And Augustine's ideas are beautiful, no? I love this thought that motion is *about* something, that things have a place to get to, and a person has something to become, and that thing she must become is herself. Isn't that nice?"

Jacob had never sounded more like Ilan. It was getting on my nerves. Maybe Jacob could read my very heart, and was trying to insult—or cure—me. "You've never called me before," I said. "I have a lot of work to do, you know."

"Nonsense," he said, without making it clear which statement of mine he was dismissing.

"You said," I reminded him, "that you wanted to discuss something 'delicate.'"

Jacob returned to the topic of Augustine; I returned to the question of why the two of us had come to sit together right then, right there. We ping-ponged in this way, until eventually Jacob said, "Well, it's about Ilan, so you'll like that."

"About the grandfather paradox?" I said, too quickly.

"Or it could be called the father paradox. Or even the mother paradox."

"I guess I've never thought of it that way, but sure." My happiness had dissipated; I felt angry, and manipulated.

"Not only about Ilan but about my work as well." Jacob actually began to whisper. "The thing is, I'm going to ask you to try to kill me. Don't worry, I can assure you that you won't succeed. But in attempting you'll prove a glorious, shunned truth that touches on the nature of time, free will, causal loops, and quantum theory. You'll also probably work out some aggression you feel toward me."

Truth be told, through the thin haze of my disdain, I had always been envious of Jacob's intellect; I had privately believed—despite what those reviews said, or maybe partly because of what those reviews said—that Jacob was a rare genius. Now I realized that he was just crazy.

"I know what you're thinking," Jacob said. "Unfortunately, I can't explain everything to you right here, right now. It's too psychologically trying. For you, I mean. Listen, come over to my apartment on Saturday. My family will be away for the weekend, and I'll explain everything to you then. Don't be alarmed. You probably know that I've lost my job"—I hadn't known that, but I should have been able to guess it—"but those morons, trust me, their falseness will become obvious. They'll be flies at the horse's ass. My ideas will bestride the world like a colossus. And you, too—you'll be essential."

I promised to attend, fully intending not to.

"Please," he said.

"Of course," I said, without meaning it.

All the rest of that week I tried to think through my decision carefully, but the more I tried to organize my thoughts the more ludicrous I felt for thinking them at all. I thought: As a friend, isn't it my responsibility to find out if Jacob has gone crazy? But really we're not friends. And if I come to know too much about his madness he may destroy me in order to preserve his psychotic worldview. But maybe I should take that risk, because, in drawing closer to Jacob—mad or no—I'll learn something more of Ilan. But why do I need to know anything? And do my propositions really follow one from the other? Maybe my *not going* will entail Jacob's having to destroy me in order to preserve his psychotic worldview. Or maybe Jacob is utterly levelheaded, and just bored enough to play an elaborate joke on me. Or maybe, despite there never having been the least spark of sexual attraction between us, despite the fact that we could have been locked in a closet for seven hours and nothing would have happened, maybe, for some reason, Jacob is trying to seduce me. Out of nostalgia for Ilan. Or as consolation for the turn in his career. Was I really up for dealing with a desperate man?

Or: Was I, in my dusty way, passing up the opportunity to be part of an idea that would, as Jacob had said, "bestride the world like a colossus"?

Early Saturday morning, I found myself knocking on Jacob's half-open door; this was when my world began to grow strange to me—strange, and yet also familiar, as if my destiny had once been known to me and I had forgotten it incompletely. Jacob's voice invited me in.

I'd never been to his apartment before. It was tiny, and smelled of orange rinds, and had—incongruously, behind a futon—a chalkboard; also so many piles of papers and books that the apartment seemed more like the movie set for an intellectual's rooms than like the real McCoy. I had once visited a ninety-one-year old great-uncle who was still conducting research on fruit flies, and his apartment was cluttered with countless hand-stoppered jars of cloned fruit flies and a few hot plates for preparing some sort of agar; that apartment is what Jacob's brought to mind.

I found myself doubting that Jacob truly had a wife and child, as he had so often claimed.

"Thank God you've come," Jacob said, emerging from what appeared to be a galley kitchen but may have been simply a closet. "I knew you'd be reliable, that at least." And then, as if reading my mind, "Natasha sleeps in the loft we built. My wife and I sleep on the futon. Although, yes, it's not much for entertaining. But can I get you something? I have this tea that one of my students gave me, exceptional stuff from Japan, harvested at high altitude—"

"Tea, great, yes," I said. To my surprise, I was relieved that Jacob's ego seemed to weather his miserable surroundings just fine. Also to my surprise I felt tenderly toward him. And toward the scent of old citrus.

On the main table I noticed what looked like the ragtag remains of some Physics 101 lab experiments: rusted silver balls on different inclines, distressed balloons, a stained funnel, a markered flask, a calcium-speckled Bunsen burner, iron filings and sandpaper, large magnets, and batteries that could have been bought from a Chinese immigrant on the subway. Did I have the vague feeling that "a strange traveller" might show up and tell "extravagant stories" over a meal of fresh rabbit? I did.

I also considered that Jacob's asking me to murder him had just been an old-fashioned suicidal plea for help.

"Here, here." Jacob brought me tea (in a cracked porcelain cup), and I thought—somewhat fondly—of Ilan's old inscrutable poisoning jokes.

"Thanks so much." I moved away from that table of hodgepodge and sat on Jacob's futon.

"Well," Jacob said gently, also sitting down.

"Yes, well."

"Well, well," he said.

"Yes," I said.

"I'm not going to hit on you," Jacob said.

"Of course not," I said. "You're not going to kiss my hand."

"Of course not."

The tea tasted like damp cotton.

Jacob rose and walked over to the table, spoke to me from across the compressed distance. "I presume that you learned what you could. From those scribblings of Ilan. Yes?"

I conceded—both that I had learned something and that I had not learned everything, that much was still a mystery to me.

"But you understand, at least, that in situations approaching grandfather paradoxes very strange things can become the norm. Just as, if someone running begins to approach the speed of light, he grows unfathomably heavy." He paused. "Didn't you find it odd that you found yourself lounging so much with me and Ilan? Didn't it seem to beg explanation, how happy the three of us—"

"It wasn't strange," I insisted, and surely I was right almost by definition. It wasn't strange because it had already happened and so it was conceivable. Or maybe that was wrong. "I think he loved us both," I said, confused for no reason. "And we both loved him."

Jacob sighed. "Yes, O.K, I hope you'll appreciate the elaborate calculations I've done in order to set up these demonstrations of extraordinarily unlikely events. Come over here. Please. You'll see that we're in a region of, well, not exactly a region of unlikeness, that would be a cheap association—very Ilan-like, though, a fitting tribute—but we'll enter a region where things seem not to behave as themselves. In other words, a zone where events, teetering toward interfering"—I briefly felt that I was a child again, falling asleep on our scratchy blue sofa while my coughing father watched reruns of *Twilight Zone*—"with a fixed future, are pressured into revealing their hidden essences."

I felt years or miles away.

Then this happened, which is not the crux of the story, or even the center of what was strange to me:

Jacob tapped one of the silver balls and it rolled up the inclined plane; he set a flask of water on the Bunsen burner and marked the rising level of the fluid; a balloon distended unevenly; a magnet under sandpaper moved iron filings so as to spell the word "egregious."

Jacob turned to me, raised his eyebrows. "Astonishing, no?'

I felt like I'd seen him wearing a dress or going to the bathroom.

"I remember those science-magic shows from childhood," I said gently, tentatively. "I always loved those spooky caves they advertised on highway billboards." I wasn't *not* afraid. Cousin or no cousin, Ilan had clearly run away from Jacob, not from me.

"I can see you're resistant," Jacob said. "Which I understand, and even respect. Maybe I scared you, with that killing-me talk, which you weren't ready for. We'll return to it. I'll order us in some food. We'll eat, we'll drink, we'll talk, and I'll let you absorb the news slowly. You're an engineer, for God's sake. You'll put the pieces together. Sometimes sleep helps, sometimes spearmint—just little ways of sharpening a mind's ability to synthesize. You take your time."

Jacob transferred greasy Chinese food into marginally clean bowls, "for a more homey feel." There at the table, that shabby impromptu lab, I found myself eating slowly. Jacob seemed to need something from me, something more, even, than just a modicum of belief. And he had paid for the takeout. Halfway through a bowl of wide beef-flavored noodles—we had actually been comfortable in the quiet, at ease—Jacob said, "Didn't you find Ilan's ideas uncannily fashionable? Always a nose ahead? Even how he started wearing pink before everyone else?"

"He was fashionable in all sorts of ways," I agreed, surprised by my appetite for the slippery and unpleasant food. "Not that it ever got him very far, always running after the next new thing like that. Sometimes I'd copy what he said, and it would sound dumb coming out of my mouth, so maybe it was dumb in the first place. Just said with charm." I shrugged. Never before had I spoken aloud anything unkind about Ilan.

"You don't understand. I guess I should tell you that Ilan is my as yet unborn son, who visited me—us—from the future." He took a metal ball between two greasy fingers, dropped it twice, and then once again demonstrated it rolling up the inclined plane. "The two of us, Ilan and I, we collaborate." Jacob explained that part of what Ilan had established in his travels—which were repeated, and varied—was that, contrary to popular movies, travel into the past didn't alter the future, or, rather, that the future was already altered, or, rather, that it was all far more complicated than that. "I, too, was reluctant to believe," Jacob insisted. "Extremely reluctant. And he's my son. A pain in the ass, but also a dear." Jacob ate a dumpling in one bite. "A bit too much of a moralist, though. Not a good business partner, in that sense."

Although I felt the dizziness of old heartbreak—had I really loved Ilan so much?—the fact that, in my first reaction to Jacob's apartment, I had kind of foreseen this turn of events obscurely satisfied me. I played along: "If Ilan was from the future, that means he could tell you about your future." I no longer felt intimidated by Jacob. How could I?

"Sure, yes. A little." Jacob blushed like a schoolgirl. "It's not important. But certain things he did know. Being my son and all."

"Ah so." I, too, ate a dumpling whole. Which isn't the kind of thing I normally do. "What about my future? Did he know anything about my future?"

Jacob shook his head. I couldn't tell if he was responding to my question or just disapproving of it. He again nudged a ball up its inclined plane. "Right now we have my career to save," he said. I saw that he was sweating, even along his exposed collarbone. "Can I tell you what I'm thinking? What I'm thinking is that we *perform* the impossibility of my dying before fathering Ilan. A little stunt show of sorts, but for real, with real guns and rope and poison and maybe some blindfolded throwing of knives. Real life. And this can drum up a bit of publicity for my work." I felt myself getting sleepy during this speech of his, getting sleepy and thinking of circuses and of dumb pornography and of Ilan's mattress and of the time a small binder clip landed on my head when I was walking outside. "I mean, it's a bit lowbrow, but lowbrow is the new highbrow, of course, or maybe the old highbrow, but, regardless, it will be fantastic. Maybe we'll be on Letterman. And we'll probably make a good deal of money in addition to getting me my job back. We have to be careful, though. Just because I can't die doesn't mean I can't be pretty seriously injured. But I've been doing some calculations and we've got some real showstoppers."

Jacob's hazel eyes stared into mine. "I'm not much of a showgirl," I said, suppressing a yawn. "You can find someone better than me for the job."

"We're meant to have this future together. My wife—she really will want to kill me when she finds out the situation I'm in. She won't cooperate."

"I know people who can help you, Jacob," I said, in the monotone of the half-asleep. "But I can't help you. I like you, though. I really, really do."

"What's wrong with you? Have you ever seen a marble roll up like that? I mean, these are just little anomalies, I didn't want to frighten you, but there are many others. Right here in this room, even. We have the symptoms of leaning up against time here."

I thought of Jacob's blathering on about Augustine and meaningful motion and yearning. I also felt convinced I'd been drugged. Not just because of my fatigue but because I was beginning to find Jacob vaguely attractive. His sweaty collarbone was pretty. The room around me—the futon, the Chinese food, the porcelain teacup, the rusty laboratory, the piles of papers, Ilan's note in my back pocket, Jacob's cheap dress socks, the dust, Jacob's ringed hand on his knee—these all seemed like players in a life of mine that had not yet become real, a life I was coursing toward, one for which I would be happy to waste every bit of myself. "Do you think," I found myself asking, maybe because I'd had this feeling just once before in my life, "that Ilan was a rare and tragic genius?"

Jacob laughed.

I shrugged. I leaned my sleepy head against his shoulder. I put my hand to his collarbone.

"I can tell you this about your future," Jacob said quietly. "I didn't not hear that question. So let me soothsay this. You'll never get over Ilan. And that will one day horrify you. But soon enough you'll settle on a replacement object for all that love of yours, which does you about as much good as a proverbial stick up the ass. Your present, if you'll excuse my saying so, is a pretty sorry one. But your future looks pretty damn great. Your work will amount to nothing. But you'll have a brilliant child. And a brilliant husband. And great love."

He was saying we would be together. He was saying we would be in love. I understood. I had solved the puzzle. I knew who I, who we, were meant to be. I fell asleep relieved.

———

I woke up alone on Jacob's futon. At first I couldn't locate Jacob, but then I saw he was sleeping in his daughter's loft. His mouth was open; he looked awful. The room smelled of MSG. I felt at once furious and small. I left the apartment, vowing never to go to the coffee shop—or anywhere else I might see Jacob—again. I spent my day grading student exams. That evening, I went to the video store and almost rented *Wuthering Heights*, then switched to *The Man Who Wasn't There*, then, feeling haunted in a dumb way, ended up renting nothing at all.

Did I, in the following weeks and months, think of Jacob often? Did I worry for or care about him? I couldn't tell if I did or didn't, as if my own feelings had become the biggest mystery to me of all. I can't even say I'm absolutely sure that Jacob was delusional. When King Laius abandons baby Oedipus in the mountains on account of the prophecy that his son will murder him, Laius's attempt to evade his fate simply serves as its unexpected engine. This is called a predestination paradox. It's a variant of the grandfather paradox. At the heart of it is your inescapable fate.

We know that the general theory of relativity is compatible with the existence of space-times in which travel to the past or remote future is possible. The logician Kurt Gödel proved this back in the late nineteen-forties, and it remains essentially undisputed. Whether or not humans (in our very particular space-time) can in fact travel to the past—we still don't know. Maybe. Surely our world obeys rules still alien to our imaginations. Maybe Jacob is my destiny. Regardless, I continue to avoid him.

STEVEN MILLHAUSER

A Precursor of the Cinema

Steven Millhauser won the Pulitzer Prize for fiction for his novel *Martin Dressler* and the Story Prize for *We Others*. He has written thirteen books of fiction, including *Voices in the Night*, *Edwin Mulhouse*, *The Barnum Museum*, and *Dangerous Laughter*. His short story "Eisenheim the Illusionist" became the basis for the popular movie *The Illusionist* in 2006. Millhauser has stories in *The Secret History of Science Fiction* and *The Secret History of Fantasy*. He lives in Saratoga Springs and teaches at Skidmore College.

"A Precursor of the Cinema" is a piece of historical trickery reminiscent of the work of Jorge Luis Borges, the story of a totally forgotten nineteenth-century painter who may be the missing link between painting and motion pictures.

E very great invention is preceded by a rich history of error. Those false paths, wrong turns, and dead ends, those branchings and veerings, those wild swerves and delirious wanderings—how can they fail to entice the attention of the historian, who sees in error itself a promise of revelation? We need a taxonomy of the precursor, an esthetics of the not-quite-yet. Before the cinema, that inevitable invention of the mid-1890s, the nineteenth century gave birth to a host of brilliant toys, spectacles, and entertainments, all of which produced vivid and startling illusions of motion. It's a seductive pre-history, which divides into two lines of descent. The true line is said to be the series of rapidly presented sequential drawings that create an illusion of motion based on the optical phenomenon known as persistence of vision

(Plateau's Phenakistoscope, Horner's Zoetrope, Reynaud's Praxinoscope); the false line produces effects of motion based on visual illusions of another kind (Daguerre's Diorama, with its semi-transparent painted screens and shifting lights; sophisticated magic-lantern shows with double projectors and overlapping views). But here and there we find experiments in motion that are less readily explained, ambiguous experiments that invite the historian to follow obscure, questionable, and at times heretical paths. It is in this twilit realm that the work of Harlan Crane (1844–1888?) leads its enigmatic life, before sinking into a neglect from which it has never recovered.

Harlan Crane has been called a minor illustrator, an inventor, a genius, a charlatan. He is perhaps all and none of these things. So little is known of his first twenty-nine years that he seems almost to have been born at the age of thirty, a tall, reserved man in a porkpie hat, sucking on a pipe with a meerschaum bowl. We know that he was born in Brooklyn, in the commercial district near the Fulton Ferry; many years later he told W. C. Curtis that as a child he had a distant view from his bedroom window of the church steeples and waterfront buildings of Manhattan, which seemed to him a picture that he might step into one day. His father was a haberdasher who liked to spend Sundays in the country with oil paints and an easel. When Harlan was thirteen or fourteen, the Cranes moved across the river to Manhattan. Nothing more is known of his adolescence.

We do know, from records discovered in 1954, that Crane studied drawing in his early twenties at Cooper Union and the National Academy of Design (1866–68). His first illustrations for *Harper's Weekly*—"Selling Hot Corn," "The Street Sweeper," "Fire Engine at the Bowery Theater," "Unloading Flour at Coenties Slip"—date from 1869; the engravings are entirely conventional, without any hint of what was to come. It is of course possible that the original drawings (since lost) contained subtleties of line and tone not captured by the crude wood engravings of the day, but unfortunately nothing remains except the hastily executed and poorly printed woodcuts themselves. There is evidence, in the correspondence of friends, to suggest that Crane became interested in photography at this time. In the summer of 1870 or 1871 he set up against one wall of his walk-up studio a long table that became a kind of laboratory, where he is known to have conducted experiments on the properties of paint. During this period he also worked on a number of small inventions: a doll with a mechanical beating heart; an adaptation of the kaleidoscope that he called the Phantasmatrope, in which the turning cylinder contained a strip of colored sequential drawings that gave the illusion of a ceaselessly repeated motion (a boy tossing up and catching a blue ball, a girl in a red dress skipping rope); and a machine that he called the Vivograph, intended to help amateurs draw perfect still lifes every time by the simple manipulation of fourteen knobs and levers. As it turned out, the Vivograph produced drawings that resembled the scrawls of an angry child, the Phantasmatrope, though patented, was never put on the market because of a defect in the shutter mechanism that was essential for masking each phase of motion, and the beating hearts of his dolls kept suddenly dying. At about this time he began to paint in oils and to take up with several artists who later became part of the Verisimilist movement. In 1873 he is known to have worked on a group of paintings clearly influenced by his photographic studies: the Photographic Print series, which consisted of several blank canvases that were said to fill gradually with painted scenes. By the age of thirty, Harlan Crane seems to have settled into the career of a diligent and negligible magazine illustrator, while in his spare time he painted in oils, printed photographs on albumen paper, and performed chemical experiments on his laboratory table, but the overwhelming impression he gives is one of restlessness, of not knowing what it is, exactly, that he wants to do with his life.

Crane first drew attention in 1874, when he showed four paintings at the Verisimilist Exhibition held in an abandoned warehouse on the East River. The Verisimilists (Linton Burgis, Thomas E. Avery, Walter Henry Hart, W. C. Curtis, Octavius Ward, and Arthur Romney Ropes) were a group of young painters who celebrated the precision of photography and rejected all effects of a dreamy, suggestive, or symbolic kind. In this there was nothing new; what set them apart from other realist schools was their fanatically meticulous concern for minuscule detail. In a Verisimilist canvas it was possible to distinguish every chain stitch on an embroidered satin fan, every curling grain in an open package of Caporal tobacco, every colored kernel and strand of silk on an ear of Indian corn hanging from a slanted nail on the cracked and weather-worn door of a barn. But their special delight was in details so marvelously minute that they could be seen only with the aid of a magnifying glass. Through the lens the viewer would discover hidden minutiae—the legs of a tiny white spider half hidden in the velvet folds of a curtain, a few breadcrumbs lying in the shadow cast by a china plate's rim. Arthur Romney Ropes claimed that his work could not be appreciated without such a glass, which he distributed free of charge to visitors at his studio. Although the Verisimilists tended to favor the still life (a briarwood pipe lying on its side next to three burnt matches, one of which was broken, and a folded newspaper with readable print; a slightly uneven stack of lovingly rendered silver coins rising up beside a wad of folded five-dollar bills and a pair of reading glasses lying on three loose playing cards), they ventured occasionally into the realm of the portrait and the landscape, where they painstakingly painted every individual hair on a gentleman's beard or a lady's muff, every lobe and branching vein on every leaf of every sycamore and oak. The newspaper reviews of the exhibition commended the paintings for illusionistic effects of a remarkable kind, while agreeing that as works of art they had been harmed by the baleful influence of photography, but the four works (no longer extant) of Harlan Crane seemed to interest or irritate them in a new way.

From half a dozen newspaper reports, from a letter by Linton Burgis to his sister, and from a handful of scattered entries in journals and diaries, we can reconstruct the paintings sufficiently to understand the perplexing impressions they caused, though many details remain unrecoverable.

Still Life with Fly appears to have been a conventional painting of a dish of fruit on a table: three apples, a yellow pear, and a bunch of red grapes in a bronze dish with repoussé rim, beside which lay a woman's slender tan-colored kid glove with one slightly curling fingertip and a scattering of envelopes with sharply rendered stamps and postmarks. On the side of one of the red-and-green apples rested a beautifully precise fly. Again and again we hear of the shimmering greenish wings, the six legs with distinct femurs, tibias, and tarsi, each with its prickly hairs, the brick-red compound eyes. Viewers agreed that the lifelike fly, with its licorice-colored abdomen showing through the silken transparence of the wings, was the triumph of the composition; what bewildered several observers was the moment when the fly darted suddenly through the paint and landed on an apple two inches away. The entire flight was said to last no more than half a second. Two newspapers deny any movement whatever, and it remains uncertain whether the fly returned to its original apple during visiting hours, but the movement of the painted fly from apple to apple was witnessed by more than one viewer over the course of the next three weeks and is described tantalizingly in a letter of Linton Burgis to his sister Emily as "a very pretty simulacrum of flight."

Waves appears to have been a conventional seascape, probably sketched during a brief trip to the southern shore of Long Island in the autumn of 1873. It showed a long line of waves breaking unevenly on a sandy shore beneath a melancholy sky. What drew the attention of viewers was an unusual effect: the waves could be clearly seen to fall, move up along the shore, and withdraw—an eerily silent, living image of relentlessly falling waves, under a cheerless evening sky.

The third painting, *Pygmalion*, showed the sculptor in Greek costume standing back with an expression of wonderment as he clutched his chisel and stared at the beautiful marble statue. Observers reported that, as they looked at the painting, the statue turned her head slowly to one side, moved her wrists, and breathed in a way that caused her naked breasts to rise and fall, before she returned to the immobility of paint.

The Séance showed eight people and a medium seated in a circle of wooden chairs, in a darkened room illuminated only by candles. The medium was a stern woman with heavy-lidded eyes, a fringed shawl covering her upper arms, and tendrils of dark hair on her forehead. Rings glittered on her plump fingers. As the viewer observed the painting, the eight faces gradually turned upward, and a dim form could be seen hovering in the darkness of the room, above or behind the head of the medium.

What are we to make of these striking effects, which seem to anticipate, in a limited way, the illusions of motion perfected by Edison and the Lumière brothers in the mid-1890s? Such motions were observed in no other of the more than three hundred Verisimilist paintings, and they inspired a number of curious explanations. The "trick" paintings, as they came to be called, were said to depend on carefully planned lighting arrangements, as in the old Diorama invented by Daguerre and in more recent magic-lantern shows, where a wagon might seem to move across a landscape (though its wheels did not turn). What this explanation failed to explain was where the lights were concealed, why no one mentioned any change in light, and how, precisely, the complex motions were produced. Another theory claimed that behind the paintings lay concealed systems of springs and gears, which caused parts of the picture to move. Such reasoning might explain how a mechanical fly, attached to the surface of a painting, could be made to move from one location to another, but we have the testimony of several viewers that the fly in Crane's still life was smooth to the touch, and in any case the clockwork theory cannot explain phenomena such as the falling and retreating waves or the suddenly appearing ghostly form. It is true that Daguerre, in a late version of his Diorama, created an illusion of moving water by the turning of a piece of silver lace on a wheel, but Daguerre's effects were created in a darkened theater, with a long distance between seated viewers and a painted semi-transparent screen measuring some seventy by fifty feet, and cannot be compared with a small canvas hanging six inches from a viewer's eyes in a well-lit room.

A more compelling theory for the historian of the cinema is that Harlan Crane might have been making use of a concealed magic lantern (or a projector of his own invention) adapted to display a swift series of sequential drawings, each one illuminated for an instant and then abolished before being replaced by the next. Unfortunately there is no evidence whatever of beams of light, no one saw a tell-tale flicker, and we have no way of knowing whether the motions repeated themselves in exactly the same way each time.

The entire issue is further obscured by Crane's own bizarre claim to a reporter, at the time of the exhibition, that he had invented what he called "animate paint"—a paint chemically treated in such a way that individual particles were capable of small motions. This claim—the first sign of the future showman—led to a number of experiments performed by chemists hired by the Society for the Advancement of the Arts, where at the end of the year an exhibition of third-rate paintings took place. As visitors passed from picture to picture, the oils suddenly began to drip down onto the frames, leaving behind melting avenues, wobbly violinists, and dissolving plums. The grotesque story does not end here. In 1875 a manufacturer of children's toys placed on the market a product called Animate Paint, which consisted of a flat wooden box containing a set of brightly colored metal tubes, half a dozen slender brushes, a manual of instruction, and twenty-five sheets of specially prepared paper. On the advice of a friend, Crane filed suit; the case was decided against him, but the product was withdrawn after the parents of children with Animate Paint sets discovered that a simple stroke of chrome yellow or crimson lake suddenly took on a life of its own, streaking across the page and dripping brightly onto eiderdown comforters, English-weave rugs, and polished mahogany tables.

An immediate result of the controversy surrounding Crane's four paintings was his expulsion from the Verisimilist group, who claimed that his optical experiments detracted from the aim of the movement: to reveal the world with ultra-photographic precision. We may be forgiven for wondering whether the expulsion served a more practical purpose, namely, to remove from the group a member who was receiving far too much attention. In any case, it may be argued that Crane's four paintings, far from betraying the aim of the Verisimilists, carried that aim to its logical conclusion. For if the intention of verisimilism was to go beyond the photograph in its attempt to "reveal" the world, isn't the leap into motion a further step in the same direction? The conventional Verisimilist wave distorts the real wave by its lack of motion; Crane's breaking wave is the true Verisimilist wave, released from the falsifying rigidity of paint.

Little is known of Crane's life during the three years following the Exhibition of 1874. We know from W. C. Curtis, the one Verisimilist who remained a friend, that Crane shut himself up all day in his studio, with its glimpse of the distant roof of the Fulton Fish Market and a thicket of masts on the East River, and refused to show his work to anyone. Once, stopping by in the evening, Curtis noticed an empty easel and several large canvases turned against the wall. "It struck me forcibly," Curtis recorded in his diary, "that I was not permitted to witness his struggles." Exactly what those struggles were, we have no way of knowing. We do know that a diminishing number of his undistinguished woodcut engravings continued to appear in *Harper's Weekly*, as well as in *Appleton's Journal* and several other publications, and that for a time he earned a small income by tinting portrait photographs. "On a long table at one side of the studio," Curtis noted on one occasion, "I observed a wet cell, a number of beakers, several tubes of paint, and two vessels filled with powders." It remains unclear what kinds of experiment Crane was conducting, although the theme of chemical experimentation raises the old question of paint with unusual properties.

In 1875 or 1876 he began to frequent the studio of Robert Allen Lowe, a leading member of a loose-knit group of painters who called themselves Transgressives and welcomed Crane as an offender of Verisimilist pieties. Crane began taking his evening meals at the Black Rose, an ale house patronized by members of the group. According to Lowe, in a letter to Samuel Hope (a painter of still lifes who later joined the Transgressives), Crane ate quickly, without seeming to notice what was on his plate, spoke very little, and smoked a big-bowled meerschaum pipe with a richly stained rim, a cherrywood stem, and a black rubber bit as he tilted back precariously in his chair and hooked one foot around a table leg. He wore a soft porkpie hat far back on his head and followed the conversation intently behind thick clouds of smoke.

The Transgressive movement began with a handful of disaffected Verisimilists who felt that the realist program of verisimilism did not go far enough. Led by Robert Allen Lowe, a painter known for his spectacularly detailed paintings of dead pheasants, bunches of asparagus, and gleaming magnifying glasses lying on top of newspapers with suddenly magnified print, the Transgressives argued that Verisimilist painting was hampered by its craven obedience to the picture frame, which did nothing but draw attention to the artifice of the painted world it enclosed. Instead of calling for the abolishment of the frame, in the manner of trompe l'oeil art, Lowe insisted that the frame be treated as a transition or "threshold" between the painting proper and the world outside the painting. Thus in a work of 1875, *Three Pears*, a meticulous still life showing three green pears on a wooden table sharply lit by sunlight streaming through a window, the long shadows of the pears stretch across the tabletop and onto the vine-carved picture frame itself. This modest painting led to an outburst of violations and disruptions by Lowe and other members of the group, and their work made its way into the Brewery Show of 1877.

The Transgressive Exhibition—better known as the Brewery Show, since the paintings were housed in an abandoned brewery on Twelfth Avenue near the meat-packing district—received a good deal of unfavorable critical attention, although it proved quite popular with the general public, who were attracted by the novelty and playfulness of the paintings. One well-known work, *The Window*, showed a life-sized casement window in a country house. Real ivy grew on the picture frame. *The Writing Desk*, by Robert Allen Lowe, showed part of a roll-top desk in close-up detail: two rows of pigeon holes and a small, partly open door with a wooden knob. In the pigeon holes one saw carefully painted envelopes, a large brass key, folded letters, a pince-nez, and a coil of string, part of which hung carelessly down over the frame. Viewers discovered that one of the pigeon holes was a real space containing a real envelope addressed to Robert Allen Lowe, while the small door, composed of actual wood, protruded from the picture surface and opened to reveal a stoneware inkbottle from which a quill pen emerged at a slant. Several people reached for the string, which proved to be a painted image. *Grapes*, a large canvas by Samuel Hope, showed an exquisitely painted bunch of purple grapes from which real grapes emerged to rest in a silver bowl on a table beneath the painting. After the first day, a number of paintings had to be roped off, to prevent the public from pawing them to pieces.

In this atmosphere of playfulness, extravagance, and illusionist wit, the paintings of Harlan Crane attracted no unusual attention, although we sometimes hear of a "disturbing" or "uncanny" effect. He displayed three paintings. *Still Life with Fly #2* showed an orange from which the rind had been partially peeled away in a long spiral, half a sliced peach with the gleaming pit rising above the flat plane of its sliced flesh, the hollow, jaggedly broken shell of an almond beside half an almond and some crumbs, and an ivory-handled fruit knife. To the side of the peach clung a vertical fly, its wings depicted against the peach-skin, its head and front legs rising above the exposed flesh of the peach. An iridescent drop of water, which seemed about to fall, clung to the peach-skin beside the fly. A number of viewers claimed that the fly suddenly left the canvas, circled above their heads, and landed on the upper right-hand corner of the frame before returning to the peach beside the glistening, motionless drop. Several viewers apparently swatted at the fly as it flew beside them, but felt nothing.

A second painting, *Young Woman,* is the only known instance of a portrait in the oeuvre of Harlan Crane. The painting showed a girl of eighteen or nineteen, wearing a white dress and a straw bonnet with a cream-colored ostrich plume, standing in a bower of white and red roses with sun and leaf-shadow stippling her face. In one hand she held a partly open letter; a torn envelope lay at her feet. She stood facing the viewer, with an expression of troubled yearning. Her free hand reached forward as if to grasp at something or someone. Despite its Verisimilist attention to detail—the intricate straw weave of the bonnet, the individual thorns on the trellis of roses—the painting looked back to the dreary conventions of narrative art deplored by Verisimilists and Transgressives alike; but what struck more than one viewer was the experience of stepping up close to the painting, in order to study the lifelike details, and feeling the unmistakable sensation of a hand touching a cheek.

The third painting, *The Escape,* hung alone in a small dusky niche or alcove. It depicted a gaunt man slumped in the shadows of a stone cell. From an unseen window a ray of dusty light fell slantwise through the gloom. Viewers reported that, as they examined the dark painting, in the twilit niche, the prisoner stirred and looked about. After a while he began to crawl forward, moving slowly over the hard floor, staring with haunted eyes. Several viewers spoke of a sudden tension in the air; they saw or felt something before or beside them, like a ghost or a wind. In the painting, the man had vanished. One journalist, who returned to observe the painting three days in succession, reported that the "escape" took place three or four times a day, at different hours, and that, if you watched the empty painting closely, you could see the figure gradually reappearing in the paint, in the manner of a photographic image appearing on albumen paper coated with silver nitrate and exposed to sunlight beneath a glass negative.

Although a number of newspapers do not even mention the Crane paintings, others offer familiar and bogus explanations for the motions, while still others take issue with descriptions published in rival papers. Whatever one may think of the matter, it is clear that we are no longer dealing with paintings as works of art, but rather with paintings as *performances*. In this sense the Brewery Show represents the first clear step in Harlan Crane's career as an inventor-showman, situated in a questionable realm between the old world of painting and the new world of moving images.

It is also worth noting that, with the exception of Lowe's *Writing Desk*, Transgressive paintings are not trompe l'oeil. The trompe l'oeil painting means to deceive, and only then to undeceive; but the real ivy and the real grapes immediately present themselves as actual objects disruptively continuing the painted representation. Harlan Crane's animate paintings are more unsettling still, for they move back and forth deliberately between representation and deception, and have the general effect of radically destabilizing the painting—for if a painted fly may at any moment suddenly enter the room, might not the painted knife slip from the painted table and cut the viewer's hand?

After their brief moment of notoriety in 1877, the Transgressives went their separate ways. Samuel Hope, Winthrop White, and C. W. E. Palmer returned to the painting of conventional still lifes, Robert Allen Lowe ventured with great success into the world of children's book illustration, and John Frederick Hill devoted his remaining years to large, profitable paintings of very white nudes on very red sofas, destined to be hung above rows of darkly glistening bottles in smoky saloons.

Crane now entered a long period of reclusion, which only in retrospect appears the inevitable preparation for his transformation into the showman of 1883. It is more reasonable to imagine these years as ones of restlessness, of dissatisfaction, of doubt and questioning and a sense of impediment. Such a view is supported by the few glimpses we have of him, in the correspondence of acquaintances and in the diary of W. C. Curtis. We know that in the summer of 1878 he took a series of photographs of picnickers on the Hudson River, from which he made half a dozen charcoal sketches that he later destroyed. Not long afterward he attempted and abandoned several small inventions, including a self-cleaning brush: through its hollow core ran a thin rubber tube filled with a turpentine-based solvent released by pressing a button. For a brief time he took up with Eliphalet Hale and the Sons of Truth, a band of painters who were opposed to the sentimental and falsely noble in art and insisted on portraying subjects of a deliberately vile or repellent kind, such as steaming horse droppings, dead rats torn open by crows, blood-soaked sheets, scrupulously detailed pools of vomit, rotting vegetables, and suppurating sores. Crane was indifferent to the paintings, but he liked Hale, a soft-spoken God-fearing man who believed fervently in the beauty of all created things.

Meanwhile Crane continued to take photographs, switching in the early 1880s from wet-collodion plates to the new dry-gelatin process in order to achieve sharper definition of detail. He also began trying his hand at serial photography. At one period he took scores of photographs of an unknown woman in a chemise with a fallen shoulder strap as she turned her face and body very slightly each time. He tested many kinds of printing paper, which he coated with varying proportions of egg white, potassium iodide, and potassium bromide, before sensitizing the prepared paper in a solution of silver nitrate. He told W. C. Curtis that he hated the "horrible fixity" of the photographic image and wished to disrupt it from within. In 1881 or 1882 we find him experimenting with a crude form of projector: to an old magic lantern he attached a large, revolving glass disk of his own invention on which transparent positives were arranged in phase. One evening, to the astonishment of Curtis, he displayed for several seconds on a wall of his studio the Third Avenue El with a train moving jerkily across.

But Crane did not pursue this method of bringing photographs to life, which others would carry to completion. Despite his interest in photography, he considered it inferior to painting. After attending a photographic exhibition with W. C. Curtis, he declared: "Painting is dead," but a week later at an oyster bar he remarked that photography was a "disappointment" and couldn't compare with paint when it came to capturing the textures of things. What is striking in the career of Harlan Crane is that more than once he seemed to be in the direct line of invention and experimentation that led to the cinema of Edison and the Lumières, and that each time he turned deliberately away. It was as if he were following a parallel line of discovery, searching for an illusion of motion based not on serial photographs and perforated strips of celluloid, but on different principles altogether.

The Phantoptic Theater opened on October 4, 1883. People purchased tickets at the door, passed through a foyer illuminated by brass gas-lamps on the walls, and made their way toward an arched opening half-concealed by a thick crimson curtain hung on gold rings. The curtain, the arch, and the rings turned out to be images painted on the wall; the actual entrance was through a second, less convincing curtain that opened into a small theater with a high ceiling, worn red-plush seats for some three hundred people, a cut-glass chandelier, and a raised stage with a black velvet curtain. Between the audience and the stage stood a piano. Newspaper reports differ in certain details, but the performance appears to have begun by the emergence from a side door of a man in evening dress and gleaming black shoes who strode to the piano bench, flung out his tails, sat grandly down, threw back his head, and began to play a waltz described variously as "lively" and "melancholy." The hissing gas-jets in the chandelier grew quiet and faint as the footlights were turned up. Slowly the black curtain rose. It revealed an immense oil painting that took up the entire rear wall of the stage and was framed on three sides by a polished dark wood carved with vine leaves and bunches of grapes.

The painting showed a ballroom filled with dancers: women with roses and ropes of pearls in their high-piled hair, heavily flounced ball-gowns that swept along the floor, and tight-corseted bosoms pressing against low-cut necklines trimmed with lace; men with beards and monocles, tight-waisted tailcoats, and very straight backs. A hearth with a fire was visible in one wall, high windows hung with dark-blue velvet curtains in another. As the audience watched and the pianist played his lively, melancholy waltz, the figures in the painting began to dance. Here the newspaper accounts differ. Some say the figures began to waltz suddenly, others report that first one pair of dancers began to move and then another—but it is clear to everyone that the figures are moving in a lifelike manner, made all the more convincing by the waltz music welling up from the piano. Other movements were also observed: the flames in the fireplace leaped and fell, a man leaning his elbow on the mantelpiece removed his monocle and replaced it in his eye, and a woman with yellow and pink roses in her hair fanned herself with a black silk fan.

The audience, exhilarated by the spectacle of the waltzing figures, soon began to notice a second phenomenon. Some of the dancers appeared to emerge from the ballroom onto the stage, where they continued waltzing. The stage, separated from the first row of seats by the piano and a narrow passageway, gradually seemed to become an extension of the ballroom. But the optical effect was unsettling because the dancers on the stage were seen against a ballroom that was itself perceived as a flat perspective painting— a painted surface with laws of its own. After no more than a minute or two the dancers returned to the painting, where for several minutes they continued to turn in the picture until the last notes of the waltz died away. Gradually—or suddenly, according to one journalist—the figures became immobile. In the auditorium, the gaslights in the chandelier were turned up.

From a door at stage-left emerged Harlan Crane, dressed in black evening clothes and a silk top hat that glistened as if wet in the glare of the gas-jets. He stepped to the front of the stage and bowed once to enthusiastic applause, sweeping his hat across his body. He rose to wait out the shouts and cheers. Holding up a hand, he invited the audience onto the stage to examine his painting, asking only that they refrain from touching it. He then turned on his heel and strode out of sight.

An assistant came onto the stage, carrying a long red-velvet rope. He suspended the rope between two wooden posts at both ends of the painting, some three feet from its surface.

Members of the audience climbed both sets of side steps onto the stage, where they gathered behind the velvet rope and examined the vast canvas. Sometimes they bent forward over the rope to study the painting more closely through a lorgnette or monocle. In this second phase of the show, the theater may be said to have withdrawn certain of its features and transformed itself into an art museum—one that contained a single painting. The evidence we have suggests that it was in fact an oil painting, with visible brushstrokes, rather than a screen or other surface onto which an image had been cast.

There were three showings daily: at two o'clock, four o'clock, and eight o'clock. Crane, who was present at every performance, never varied his routine, so that one wit said it wasn't Harlan Crane at all, but a mechanical figure, like Kempelen's Chess Player, fitted out with one of Edison's talking machines.

Contemporary accounts speculate lavishly about the secret of the motions, some seeing the Phantoptic Theater as a development of the old Diorama, others arguing that it was done with a specially adapted magic lantern that projected serial images of dancers onto a motionless background. But the motions of the Diorama were nothing like those of the Phantoptic Theater, for Daguerre's effects, produced by artful manipulation of light, were limited to extremely simple illusions, such as lava or masses of snow rushing down the side of a mountain; and the theory of serial projection, while anticipating later advances in the development of the cinema, cannot explain the emergence of the dancers onto the stage. For their part, the dancers on stage were variously explained as real actors appearing from behind a curtain, as images projected onto "invisible" screens, and as optical illusions produced by "hidden lenses" that the writer does not bother to describe. In truth, the riddle of Crane's *Ballroom* illusions has never been solved. What strikes the student of cinema is the peculiar position assumed by Crane and his theater with respect to the history of the illusion of motion. For if in one respect the Phantoptic Theater shares the late-nineteenth-century fascination with the science of moving images, in another it looks back, far back, to a dim, primitive world in which painted images are magical visions infused with the breath of life. Crane's refusal to abandon painting and embrace the new technology of serial photographs, his insistence on creating illusions of motion that cannot be accounted for in the new way, make him a minor, quirky, exasperating, and finally puzzling figure in the pre-history of the cinema, who seizes our attention precisely because he created a riddling world of motion entirely his own.

For a while the daily shows of the Phantoptic Theater continued to draw enthusiastic audiences, even as the press turned its gaze in other directions. By the end of the year, attendance had begun to decline; and by the middle of January the theater rarely held more than a few dozen people, crowded expectantly into the front rows.

We have several glimpses of Crane during this period. In the diary of W. C. Curtis we hear that Crane is hard at work on a new painting for his theater, though he refuses to reveal anything about it; sometimes he complains of "difficulties." One evening in December, Curtis notes with surprise the presence of a youngish woman at the studio, with auburn hair and a "plain, intelligent" face, whom he recognizes as the woman in the chemise. Crane introduced her first as Annie, then as Miss Merrow; she lowered her eyes and quickly disappeared behind a folding screen that stood in one corner of the studio. After this, Curtis saw her now and then on evening visits, when she invariably retreated behind the screen. Crane never spoke of her. Curtis remarks on his friend's "secretive" nature, speculates that she is his mistress, and drops the subject.

One evening at an ale house, Crane suddenly began to speak of his admiration for Thomas Edison. Unfolding a newspaper, he pointed to an interview in which the inventor insisted on the importance of "chance" in his discoveries. Crane read several passages aloud, then folded the paper and looked up at Curtis. "A methodical man who believes in chance. Now what does that sound like to you, Curtis?" Curtis thought for a moment before replying: "A gambler." Crane, looking startled and then pleased, gave a laugh and a shake of the head. "I hadn't thought of that. Yes, a gambler." "And you were thinking—" "Oh, nothing, nothing—do you have any matches, Curtis, I never seem to—but a methodical man, who believes in chance— tell me, Curtis, have you ever heard a better definition of an artist?"

Not until March of 1884 was a new piece announced. The opening took place at eight o'clock in the evening. The black velvet curtain rose to reveal *Picnic on the Hudson*, a monumental painting that showed groups of picnickers sitting in sun-checked green shade between high trees. Sunlight glowed in sudden bursts: on the corner of a white cloth spread on the grass, on a bunch of red grapes in a silver dish, on the lace sleeve of a lavender dress, on the blue-green river in the background, where sunlit portions of a two-stacked steamer were visible through the trees. As the pianist played a medley of American melodies ("Aura Lee," "Sweet Genevieve," "Carry Me Back to Old Virginny," "I'll Take You Home Again, Kathleen"), *Picnic on the Hudson* began to show signs of life: the second of the steamer's smokestacks emerged fully from behind the trunk of an oak, a squirrel moved along a branch, the hand of a picnicker held out a glistening crystal glass, into which, from the mouth of a wine bottle, poured a ruby-colored liquid. A small boy in boots and breeches and a feathered hat strolled into view, holding in one hand a red rubber ball. A young woman, wearing a straw poke bonnet trimmed with purple and gold pansies, slowly smiled. The several groups of men and women seated on the grass seemed to feel a great sense of peacefulness, in the warm shade, under the trees, on a summer afternoon beside the Hudson. A number of viewers later said that the painting created in them a feeling of deep repose.

As the picnickers relaxed on the riverbank, one of them, a mustached young man in a bowler hat who had been gazing toward the river, turned his head lazily in the direction of the audience and abruptly stopped. The woman in the straw bonnet, following his gaze, turned and stared. And now all the faces of the people in the painting turned to look toward the viewers, many of whom later spoke of feeling, at that moment, a sensation of desire or yearning. Someone in the audience rose and slowly climbed the steps to the stage; others soon followed. Once on the stage, they walked up and down along the painting, admiring its Verisimilist accuracy of detail—the brown silk stitching on the back of a woman's white kid glove, the webbed feet and overlapping feather-tips of a tiny seagull sitting on the railing of the steamer, the minuscule fibers visible in the torn corner of a folded newspaper on the grass. Contemporary reports are unclear about what happened next, but it appears that a man, reaching out to feel the canvas, experienced in his fingertips a sensation of melting or dissolving, before he stepped into the painting. Those who entered the painting later reported a "dreamlike feeling" or "a sense of great happiness," but were less clear about the physical act of entry. Most spoke of some kind of barrier that immediately gave way; several felt hard canvas and paint. One woman, a Mrs. Amelia Hartman, said that it reminded her of immersing herself in the ocean, but an ocean whose water was dry. Inside the painting, the figures watched them but did not speak. The mingling seems to have lasted from about ten minutes to half an hour, before the visitors experienced what one described as a "darkening" and another as "stepping into deep shade." The deep shade soon revealed itself to be a corridor lit by dimmed gas-jets, which led to a door that opened into the side of the auditorium.

When all the members of the audience had returned to their seats, the pianist drove his music to a crescendo, threw back his head with a great agitation of hair, struck three ringing chords, and stopped. The figures in the painting resumed their original poses. Slowly the curtain came down. Harlan Crane walked briskly out onto the apron, bowed once, and strode off. The showing was over.

Newspaper reviews outdid themselves in their attempts to explain the new range of effects produced by Crane in *Picnic on the Hudson*. The *New York News* proposed a hollow space behind the painting, with actors and a stage set; the picture, an ingenious deception, was nothing but a diaphanous screen that separated the actors from the stage. The proposed solution fails to mention the hardness of the canvas, as reported by many members of the audience, and in any case it cannot explain why no one ever detected anything resembling a "diaphanous screen," or how the mysterious screen vanished to permit entry. Other explanations are equally unsatisfactory: one columnist described the barrier as an artificially produced "mist" or "vapor" onto which magic lantern slides were projected, and another suggested that the audience, once it reached the stage, had inhaled an opiate sprayed into the atmosphere and had experienced a shared hallucination.

These explanations, far from revealing the secret of Crane's art, obscured it behind translucent, fluttering veils of language, which themselves were seductive and served only to sharpen the public's curiosity and desire.

Picnic on the Hudson was shown to a packed house every evening at eight o'clock, while *The Ballroom* continued to be displayed daily to diminishing audiences. By early summer, when evening attendance at the Phantoptic Theater showed signs of falling off, a rumor began to circulate that Crane had already started a new work, which would usher in an age of wonder; and it was said that if you listened closely, in the theater, you could hear the artist-showman moving about in the basement, pushing things out of the way, hammering, preparing.

A single anecdote survives from this period. In a dockside restaurant with a view of the Brooklyn ferry across the river, Crane told W. C. Curtis that as a child he had thought he would grow up to be a ferryboat captain. "I like rivers," he said. "I thought I'd travel a lot." Curtis, a well-traveled man who had spent three years in Europe in his twenties, urged Crane to go abroad with him, to Paris and Munich and Venice. Crane appeared to consider it. "Not far enough," he then said. Curtis had also spent six months in China; he immediately began to sing the praises of the Orient. Crane gave "an odd little laugh" and, with a shrug of one shoulder, remarked, "Still not far enough." Then he lit up his pipe and ordered another dish of Blue Point oysters.

We know very little about *Terra Incognita*, which was shown only a single time (February 6, 1885). From the foyer of the Phantoptic Theater, visitors were led down a flight of steps into a dark room illuminated by a few low-burning gas-jets in glass lanterns suspended from the ceiling. Gradually the viewers became aware of a painting rising up on all sides—a continuous twelve-foot-high canvas that stretched flat along all four walls and curved at the wall junctures.

The vast, enclosing composition seemed at first to be painted entirely black, but slowly other colors became visible, deep browns and blackish reds, while vague shapes began to emerge. Here the evidence becomes confused. Some claimed that the painting represented a dark cavern with rocks and ledges. Others spoke of a dark sea. All witnesses agreed that they gradually became aware of shadowy figures, who seemed to float up from the depths of the painting and to move closer to the surface. A woman screamed—it isn't clear when—and was harshly hushed. At some point several figures appeared to pass from the surface into the dark and crowded room. Precisely what took place from then on remains uncertain. One woman later spoke of a sensation of cold on the back of her neck; another described a soft pressure on her upper arm. Others, men and women, reported "a sensation of being rubbed up against, as by a cat," or of being touched on the face or bosom or leg. Not all impressions were gentle. Here and there, hats were knocked off, shawls pulled away, hands and elbows seized. One witness said: "I felt as though a great wind had blown through me, and I was possessed by a feeling of sweetness and despair." Someone screamed again. After a third scream, things happened very quickly: a woman burst into tears, people began pushing their way to the stairs, there were cries and shouts and violent shoving. A bearded man fell against the canvas. A young woman in a blue felt hat trimmed with dark red roses sank slowly to the floor.

The commotion was heard by a janitor sweeping the aisles of the upper theater. He came down to check and immediately ran outside for a police-man, who hurried over and appeared at the top of the stairs with a lantern and a nightstick to witness a scene of dangerous panic. People were sobbing and pushing forward, tearing at one another's bodies, trampling the fallen woman. The policeman was unable to fight his way down. Shrill blows of his whistle brought three more policemen with lanterns, who helped the terrified crowd up the narrow stairway. When it was all over, seven people were hospitalized; the young woman on the floor later died of injuries to the face and head. The painting had been damaged in many places; one portion of canvas showed a ragged hole the size of a fist. On the floor lay broken fans and crushed top hats, torn ostrich plumes, a scattering of dark red rose petals, a mauve glove, an uncoiled chignon with one unraveled ribbon, a cracked monocle at the end of a black silk cord.

Regrettably, newspaper accounts concentrated more on the panic than on the painting. There were the usual attempts at tracing the motions of the figures to hidden magic lanterns, even though not a single visitor reported a beam of light in the darkened, gas-lit room. The penetration of the figures into the room was explained either as a theatrical stunt performed by concealed actors or a delusion stimulated by the heightened anxiety of a crowd in the dark. In truth, we simply cannot explain the reported effects by means of the scant evidence that has come down to us. It is worth noting that no one has ever duplicated the motions produced in the Phantoptic Theater. On strictly objective grounds, we cannot rule out the possibility that Crane's figures in *Terra Incognita* really did what they appeared to do, that is, emerge from the paint and enter the room, perhaps as a result of some chemical discovery no longer recoverable.

By order of the mayor, Crane's theater was closed. Three weeks later, when he attempted to open a second theater, city authorities intervened. Meanwhile the parents of the trampled woman sued Crane for inciting a riot. Although he was exonerated, the judge issued a stern warning. Crane never returned to public life.

In his cramped studio and in neighborhood chophouses we catch glimpses of him over the next few years: a thin-lipped, quiet man, with a clean-shaven face and brooding eyes. He is never without his big-bowled meerschaum with its cherrywood stem and its chewed rubber bit. W. C. Curtis speaks of his melancholy, his long silences. Was he bitter over the closing of his theater, over his brief notoriety that failed to develop into lasting fame? Only once does he complain to Curtis: he regrets, he says, that his "invention" has never been recognized. When he is mentioned in the papers now and then, it is not as an artist or an inventor but as the former proprietor of the Phantoptic Theater.

He is often tired. Curtis notes that Crane is always alone in the evenings when he visits; we hear no further mention of Annie Merrow, who vanishes from the record. For a time Crane returns to his old invention, the Phantasmatrope, attempting to solve the problem of the shutter but abruptly losing interest. He no longer takes photographs. He spends less and less time in his studio and instead passes long hours in coffee shops and cheap restaurants, reading newspapers slowly and smoking his pipe. He refuses to attend art exhibitions. He likes to stroll past the East River piers and ferry slips, to linger before the windows of the sailmakers' shops on South Street. Now and then, in order to pay the rent, he takes a job that he quits after a few weeks: a toy salesman in a department store, a sandwich-board man advertising a new lunchroom. One day he sells his camera for a dollar. He takes long walks into distant neighborhoods, sits on benches at the water's edge, a lean man beside wavering lines of smoke. He appears to subsist on apples and roasted chestnuts bought in the street, on cheap meals in ale houses and oyster bars. He likes to watch the traffic on the East River: three-masted barks, old paddlewheel towboats, and the new screw-propelled tugs, steamboats with funnels and masts.

Suddenly—the word belongs to W. C. Curtis—Crane returns to his studio and shuts himself up day after day. He refuses to speak of his work. At ale houses and night cafes he picks at his food, looks restlessly about, knocks out his pipe on the table, and packs in fresh tobacco with slow taps of his fingertip. Curtis can scarcely see him behind clouds of smoke. "It's like the old days," Curtis notes in his diary, adding ruefully, "without the joy."

One evening, while Crane is raising to his mouth a glass of dark ale, he pauses in mid-air, as if a thought has crossed his mind, and mentions to Curtis that a few hours ago he rented a room in an old office building on Chambers Street, a few blocks from City Hall Park. Curtis starts to ask a question but thinks better of it. The next day a flurry of hand-lettered signs on yellow paper appears on hoardings and lampposts, announcing a new exhibition on November 1, 1888.

In the small room with its two dust-streaked windows and its roll-top desk, a single painting was on display. Only W. C. Curtis and four of Curtis's friends attended. Crane stood leaning against the opposite wall, between the two windows, smoking away at his pipe. Curtis describes the painting as roughly four feet by five feet, in a plain, varnished frame. A small piece of white paper, affixed to the wall beside it, bore the words SWAN SONG.

The painting depicted Crane's studio, captured with Verisimilist fidelity. Crane himself stood before an easel, with his long legs and a buttoned-up threadbare jacket, gripping his palette and a clutch of brushes in one hand and reaching out with a long, fine-tipped brush in the other as he held his head back and stared at the canvas "with a look of ferocity." The walls of the studio were thickly covered with framed and unframed paintings and pencil-and-chalk sketches by Crane, many of which Curtis recognized from Crane's Verisimilist and Transgressive periods. There were also a number of paintings Curtis had never seen before, which he either passes over in silence or describes with disappointing briskness ("another pipe-and-mug still life," "a rural scene"). On the floor stood piles of unframed canvases, stacked six deep against the walls. One such painting, near a corner, showed an arm protruding from the surface and grasping the leg of a chair. The painting on the easel, half finished, appeared to be a preliminary study for *Picnic on the Hudson*; a number of seated figures had been roughly sketched but not painted in, and in another place a woman's right arm, which had been finished at a different angle, showed through the paint as a ghostly arm without a hand. The studio also included a zinc washstand, the corner of a cast-iron heating stove, and part of a thick table, on which stood one of Crane's magic lanterns and a scattering of yellowed and curling photographs showing a young woman in a chemise, with one strap slipping from a shoulder and her head turned at many different angles.

From everything we know of it, *Swan Song* would have been at home in the old Verisimilist Exhibition of 1874. Curtis notes the barely visible tail of a mouse between two stacked canvases, as well as a scattering of pipe ashes on a windowsill. As he and his friends stood before the painting, wondering what was new and different about it, they heard behind them the word "Gentlemen." In truth they had almost forgotten Crane. Now they turned to see him standing against the wall between the two windows, with his pipe in his hand. Smoke floated about him. Curtis was struck by his friend's bony, melancholy face. Weak light came through the dusty windows on both sides of Crane, who seemed to be standing in the dimmest part of the room. "Thank you," he said quietly, "for—" And here he raised his arm in a graceful gesture that seemed to include the painting, the visitors, and the occasion itself. Without completing his sentence, he thrust his pipe back in his mouth and narrowed his eyes behind drifts of bluish smoke.

It is unclear exactly what happened next. Someone appears to have exclaimed. Curtis, turning back to the painting, became aware of a motion or "agitation" in the canvas. As he watched, standing about a foot from the picture, the paintings in the studio began to fade away. Those that hung on the wall and those that stood in stacks on the floor grew paler and paler, the painting on the easel and the photographs on the table began to fade, and Crane himself, with his palette and brush, seemed to be turning into a ghost.

Soon nothing was left in the painting but a cluttered studio hung with white canvases, framed and unframed. Blank canvases were stacked six deep against the walls. The mouse's tail, Curtis says, showed distinctly against the whiteness of the empty canvas.

"What the devil!" someone cried. Curtis turned around. In the real room, Crane himself was no longer there.

The door, Curtis noticed, was partly open. He and two of his friends immediately left the rented office and took a four-wheeler to Crane's studio. There they found the door unlocked. Inside, everything was exactly as in the painting: the easel with its blank canvas, the empty rectangles on the walls, the table with its scattering of blank printing paper, the stacks of white canvases standing about, even the ashes on the windowsill. When Curtis looked more closely, he had the uneasy sensation that a mouse's tail had just darted out of sight behind a canvas. Curtis felt he had stepped into a painting. It struck him that Crane had anticipated this moment, and he had an odd impulse to tip his hat to his old friend. It may have been the pale November light, or the "premonition of dread" that came over him then, but he was suddenly seized by a sense of insubstantiality, as if at any moment he might begin to fade away. With a backward glance, like a man pursued, he fled the empty studio.

Crane was never seen again. Not a single painting or sketch has survived. At best we can clumsily resurrect them through careless newspaper accounts and the descriptions, at times detailed, in the diary of W. C. Curtis. Of his other work, nothing remains except some eighty engravings in the pages of contemporary magazines—mediocre woodblock reproductions in no way different from the hurried hackwork of the time. Based on this work alone—his visible oeuvre—Harlan Crane deserves no more than a footnote in the history of late-nineteenth-century American magazine illustration. It is his vanished work that lays claim to our attention.

He teases us, this man who is neither one thing nor another, who swerves away from the history of painting in the direction of the cinema, while creating a lost medium that has no name. If I call him a precursor, it is because he is part of the broad impulse in the last quarter of the nineteenth century to make pictures move—to enact for mass audiences, through modern technology, an ancient mystery. In this sense it is tempting to think of him as a figure who looks both ways: toward the future, when the inventions of Edison and the Lumières will soon be born, and toward the remote past, when paintings were ambiguously alive, in a half-forgotten world of magic and dream. But finally it would be a mistake to abandon him here, in a shadow-place between a vanished world and a world not yet come into being. Rather, his work represents a turn, a dislocation, a bold error, a venture into a possible future that somehow failed to take place. One might say that history, in the person of Harlan Crane, had a wayward and forbidden thought. And if, after all, that unborn future should one day burst forth? Then Harlan Crane might prove to be a precursor in a more exact sense. For even now there are signs of boredom with the old illusions of cinema, a longing for new astonishments. In research laboratories in universities across the country, in film studios in New York and California, we hear of radical advances in multidimensional imaging, of mobile vivigrams, of a modern cinema that banishes the old-fashioned screen in order to permit audiences to mingle freely with brilliantly realistic illusions. The time may be near when the image will be released from its ancient bondage to cave wall and frame and screen, and a new race of beings will walk the earth. On that day the history of the cinema will have to be rewritten, and Harlan Crane will take his place as a prophet. For us, in the meantime, he must remain what he was to his contemporaries: a twilight man, a riddle. If we have summoned him here from the perfection of his self-erasure, it is because his lost work draws us toward unfamiliar and alluring realms, where history seems to hesitate for a moment, in order to contemplate an alternative, before striding on.

The diary of W. C. Curtis, published in 1898, makes one last reference to Harlan Crane. In the summer of 1896 Curtis, traveling in Vienna, visited the Kunsthistorisches Museum, where a still life (by A. Muntz) reminded him of his old friend. "The pipe was so like his," Curtis writes, "that it cast me back to the days of our old friendship." But rather than devoting a single sentence to the days of his old friendship, Curtis describes the painting instead: the stained meerschaum bowl, the cherrywood stem, the black rubber bit, even the tarnished brass ring at the upper end of the bowl, which we hear about for the first time. The pipe rests on its side, next to a pewter-lidded beer stein decorated with the figure of a hunting dog in relief. Bits of ash, fallen from the bowl, lie scattered on the plain wooden tabletop. In the bowl glows a small ember. A thin curl of smoke rises over the rim.

JAMI ATTENBERG
In the Bushes

Jami Attenberg has written four novels: *The Kept Man*, *The Melting Season*, *The Middlesteins*, and, most recently, *Saint Mazie*. *The Middlesteins* was a finalist for the *Los Angeles Times* Book Prize for Fiction and the St. Francis College Literary Prize. Attenberg has written essays about television, sex, technology, and other topics, and her work has appeared in the *New York Times*, the *Wall Street Journal*, *Real Simple*, and other publications. Most of the characters in her remarkable story collection, *Instant Love*, are in search of love and life, and one of them is an avid reader of science fiction.

"In the Bushes" is a story of the demise of the automobile. It was commissioned for *2033: The Future of Misbehavior*, an anthology of stories assembled by the editors of *Nerve.com*.

We met in the bushes. That's where everyone goes nowadays to get their fun on around here, ever since we had to give up the cars. We did it without a fight, because there wasn't much oil left to put in them. The president decided to start a bunch of wars (Q: How many wars can you start at once? A: Four.), and he asked us to donate our cars so we could build weapons, and we all said, "Sure, wasn't like we were using them anyway." And just like that, it became illegal to have a car. They throw people in jails now just for possession of a hunk of metal. So now we walk everywhere, or ride our bikes (the bikes weren't worth their time), and when we want to make out in the backseats of cars, we just use the bushes instead.

I wasn't making out that night. My girl had left me to get married to a soldier who was going off to war. (The one in India, I think.) "No offense," she said. "Benefits." She had met him at one of the barn social nights held just for those purposes—for young women to meet soldiers. I did not know she had been attending them. But marrying a soldier was your best bet for a good life. I could not hold it against her. We had just graduated from high school. I had nothing to give her but a ride on the back of my bicycle.

Although it is a smooth ride.

I was taking the dog for a walk instead, but we were lured by the bushes, the sounds and the smells, the kisses and the moans. Everyone was so happy and free. The air smelled so fresh and green and sexy.

This is what they do now. They start at one end of town at sunset, and, one by one, the kids show up and make the march to the park. By night, the streets are full of kids walking and talking, sharing whatever news they heard their parents whispering about that day. A good piece of dirt can get you laid before dusk breaks. (Not that they're in any hurry: Curfews disappeared with the cars. How far could anyone get? What kind of trouble could they find on their feet?) And then there they are, at last, at the park, in the dark. Kids fall in love in the bushes, babies are made, mosquitoes bite.

Sometimes I miss oil.

They gather near a patch of American elms—that's where it shifts. Maybe they're thinking about how they're doing their part for our country, our great nation. They swig booze from paper bags, shift from foot to foot. And then they pair off, eventually, wander away from the elms, closer to the bushes, pointing at a constellation, or lying down and hoping for shooting stars. A shooting star guarantees that first kiss. After the first kiss, it's just a short walk to the bushes that spiral up every year higher to the sky.

They've been calling it the Rustle lately.

Not everyone hangs out in the bushes. Some kids like to pair up on a Friday and pick the dirt weed on the back roads. (That stuff was never strong enough to smoke until a few years ago—there was a shift in the air after the explosion in Council Bluffs, and now what looks harmless can send you flying for two days straight.) On Saturdays, the town council hosts a bonfire at the church (mostly old auto magazines); there's romance in roasting marshmallows while erasing the past. And of course there's the equestrians—they're all over the roads. Those girls sure do love their horses; they never seem to want to get off them.

And then there's me. I just like to walk, and watch everyone. When I met her, we were just tracing a little path, me and the dog. I had a stick I was dragging along, and he would stop me every few yards and dig into the ground. She was coming up toward us, a huddle, in the darkness, of sweaters and a sturdy coat and a gigantic backpack. We stopped as we approached and stood in front of each other, and just then a girl let out a loud and very final-sounding moan from the bushes, and the leaves rustled.

"Hi," she said. "I'm lost." She didn't look scared at all, though maybe she should have been, wandering around in the middle of nowhere near all those squirming bodies in the bushes.

"Where are you trying to go?" I said, though I had a pretty good idea.

"I heard there was a place for people like me around here," she said. She shifted her backpack up on her back, and she lifted her head up and the moon and the stars hit her face, and I could see that her skin was clear and her eyes were dark and focused and determined, and then she smiled—not warily, but aware nonetheless. There was a sliver of space between her two front teeth. I wanted to insert my tongue between the space and let it lie there for a while and see what it felt like. The dog liked her, too. He sniffed at her feet and then rested at them.

She was making her way to Los Angeles, she told me. We'd seen a few of her kind passing through before. Los Angeles had seceded from the Union a while back, when the first rumblings of the car reclamation had started. They had fought the hardest out of anywhere. They loved their cars the most. And we had all heard stories of a city trapped in gridlock, but people were still migrating there from all over the country. To a place that still *moved*.

It was a real shame about Detroit, what happened there.

"You're a ways away from the shelter," I told her, but I said I'd walk her in the right direction. It was a nice night. From the bushes we heard two voices jumble together in laughter, and then a guy said, "I love you."

I offered to carry her bag for her, and she judged it, judged me, and then handed it over.

As we walked she told me about life back East. Her husky voice perfectly matched the sound of the crunch of gravel under our feet. She had taken hold of my walking stick and dragged it behind her. She was from Philadelphia, and, like every other city out there, there weren't too many trees left, let alone bushes. There were lines every night at the few public parks that remained, and the government charged admission. A fee to flirt. If you couldn't afford that, it was all alleyways for you.

She said she got sick of the feel of cold cement against her ass.

"I know I shouldn't complain," she said. "I know how lucky I am, how lucky we all are. We live in the safest place in the world."

She talked about how much she still loved her hometown, the kind of fun she had there. Young people had taken over downtown Philly with graffiti. When the trees went away, the kids began to paint new ones. People now met and fell in love over a can of paint; five-story marriage proposals covered abandoned buildings. They were calling it a cultural renaissance.

"But I just wanted to see what it was like," she said. She threw her arms up toward the sky and all around. "Out there." She stopped and touched me, turned me toward her. "Not that I care about the 152 cars so much. Although I guess I do care. What they mean, what they meant. But I just wanted to be somewhere new."

And then, because I wanted to impress her because she had impressed me with her ache and desire and energy, even though I didn't know her at all, even though she could have been lying about who she was and why she was there, even though I might never see her again, even though she was tired and dirty and she smelled of the earth (or maybe because of it), even though I could have been trading in my freedom, I said to her, "Do you want to see something really cool?"

We shifted direction toward my home. She dug the trail behind us with the stick, like we were Hansel and Gretel. We made it home quickly; we were both excited. I dropped her bag on the front porch, took the dog off the leash, and let him run around in circles in the backyard. We walked toward the small island of trees and bushes behind my house. The dog barked, nervous, but I ignored him. I held her hand and cleared us a path through the bushes until we came upon it.

A 2017 Chevy. The roof was missing, and the leather had been beat down by the rain and snow. Everything else was rusted. But still we slid in the backseat immediately.

She started to cry, but I think maybe she was laughing, too.

"It's just a useless piece of junk," I said. "It's not that special."

"No, it's really nice," she said.

I put my arm around her, and we slouched down in the seats and looked up at the sky. "There should be a radio playing," she said. "Classic rock." So I sang, my voice echoing in the trees. I sang her every song I remembered, and then, when I was done with those, I made up a few new ones just for her.

BRIAN EVENSON
Fugue State

Brian Evenson's work, including *Immobility*, *Last Days*, *The Open Curtain*, *Dark Property*, and *Altmann's Tongue*, skirts the boundary between horror and literature. His more popularly intended fiction appears under the byline of B. K. Evenson. Evenson has received the O. Henry Award, the International Horror Guild Award, and the American Library Association's RUSA Award for Best Horror Novel. He has also been nominated for the Edgar Award and four times for the Shirley Jackson Award. In addition, he has translated several books by French writers into English. Evenson lives in Valencia, California, where he teaches in the School of Critical Studies at CalArts.

"Fugue State" was originally published as the title story of Evenson's oponymous World Fantasy Award–nominated collection. This tale may be about a plague, zombies, or the ephemeral quality of our everyday lives.

I.

I had, Bentham claimed, *fallen into a sort of fugue state in which the world moved past me more and more rapidly, a kind of blur englobing me at every instant.* And yet he had never, so he confided to Arnaud, felt either disoriented or confused. Yes, admittedly, during this period he had no clear idea of his own name, yet despite this he felt he understood things clearly for the first time. He perceived the world in a different way, at a speed which allowed him to ignore the nonessential—such as names, or, rather, such as his own name—and perceive things he could never before even have imagined.

Arnaud listened carefully. *Fugue state*, he recorded, then removed his eyeglasses and placed them on the desk in front of him. He looked up, squinting.

"And do you remember your name now?" he asked.

At first, Bentham did not answer. Arnaud remained patient. He watched a blurred Bentham glance about himself, searching for some clue.

"Yes," said Bentham finally. "Of course I do."

"Will you please tell it to me?" asked Arnaud.

"Why do you need to know?"

Arnaud rubbed his eyes. *Subject does not know own name*, he recorded.

"Will you please describe the room you're in?" he asked. Bentham instead tried to sit up, was prevented by the straps. *Subject unaware of surroundings*, Arnaud noted. "Will you describe your room, please?" asked Arnaud again.

"I don't see the point," said Bentham, his voice rising. "You're here. You're in it. You can see it just as well as I can."

Arnaud leaned forward until his lips were nearly touching the microphone. "But that's just it, Bentham," he said softly. "I'm not in the room with you at all."

It was shortly after this that Bentham began to bleed from the eyes. This was not a response Arnaud had been trained to expect. Indeed, at first, his glasses still on the desk before him, Arnaud was convinced it was a trick of the light, an oddly cast shadow. He polished his glasses against his shirtfront and hooked them back over his ears, and only then was he certain that each of Bentham's sockets was pooling with blood. Startled, he must have exclaimed aloud, for Bentham turned his head slightly in the direction of the intercom speaker. The blood in one eye slopped against the bridge of his nose. The blood in the other spilled down his cheek, gathering in the whorl of his ear.

6:13, Arnaud wrote, *Subject has begun to bleed from eyes*.

"Bentham," Arnaud asked, "how do you feel?"

"Fine," said Bentham. "I feel fine. Why?"

6:14, Arnaud recorded. *Subject feels fine.* Then added, *Is bleeding from eyes.*

Picking up the telephone, he depressed the call button.

"I need an outside line," said Arnaud when the operator picked up.

"You know the rules," said the operator. "No outside lines during session with subject."

Blood too, Arnaud noticed, had started to drip from Bentham's nose. Perhaps it was coming from his ears as well. Though with Bentham's visible ear already puddled with the blood from his eye, it was difficult to be certain.

"The subject appears to be dying," said Arnaud.

"Dying?" said the operator. "Of what?"

"Of bleeding," said Arnaud.

"I see," said the operator. "Please hold the line."

The operator exchanged himself with a low and staticky Muzak. Arnaud, holding the receiver against his ear, watched Bentham. It was a song he felt he should recognize but he could not quite grasp what it was. Bentham tried to sit up again, straining against the straps as if unaware of them, without any hint of panic. In general he seemed unaware of what was happening to him. A bloody flux was spilling out of his mouth now as well, Arnaud noticed. He groped for a pen to record this, but could not find one.

Bentham shook his head quickly as if to clear it, spattering blood on the glass between them. Then he bared his teeth. This was, Arnaud felt, a terrible thing to watch.

The Muzak clicked off.

"Accounting," said a flat, implacable voice.

"Excuse me?" said Arnaud.

"Accounting division."

"I don't understand," said Arnaud. "The subject assigned to me is dying."

The man on the other end did not respond. Bentham, Arnaud saw through the glass, had stopped moving.

"I think he may have just died," said Arnaud.

"Not my jurisdiction, sir," said the voice, still flat, and the line went dead.

It was hard for him to be certain that Bentham was no longer alive. Several times, as Arnaud prepared to record a time of death, Bentham offered a weak movement that dissuaded him, the curling or uncurling of a finger, the parting of his lips. He was not certain if these were actual movements or simply the corpse ridding itself of its remaining vitality. For accuracy's sake, he felt, he should unlock the adjoining door between the two rooms and go through, manually checking Bentham's pulse with his fingers. Or, rather, making certain there was no pulse to check. But the strangeness of Bentham's condition made him feel it might be better to leave the adjoining door closed.

As to leaving his own room, he had no choice but to wait until the session had officially expired and a guard came to unlock the door. He waited, watching Bentham dead or dying. He watched the blood dry between them, on the window. When his ear began to ache, he realized he was still pushing the dead receiver against his face, and hung it up.

He stood and looked under his desk until he found his pen, then wrote in his notebook, *6:26, Patient dead?*

The remainder of the session he spent, pen poised over the notebook, watching Bentham for any signs of life. He watched the skin on Bentham's face change character, losing its elasticity, seeming to settle more tightly around the bone. The nose became more and more accentuated, the cheeks growing hollow. The frightful perfection of the skull, the tongs of the jawbones, glowed dully through the skin. Even when the guard opened the door behind him, it was very hard for Arnaud to look away.

"Ready?" the guard asked. "Session's over."

"I think he's dead," said Arnaud.

"How's that?" said the guard. "Come again?"

The guard came and stood next to Arnaud, stared into Bentham's room. Arnaud looked too.

When he looked back up he saw that the guard was looking at him with frightened eyes.

"What is it?" Arnaud asked.

But at first the guard did not answer, just kept looking at Arnaud. *Why?* Arnaud wondered, and waited.

"What," the guard finally asked, "exactly did you do to him?"

It was not until that moment that Arnaud realized how wrong things could go for him.

II.

The guard became businesslike and efficient, hustling him out of the observation room and down the hall.

"Where are we going?" Arnaud asked.

"Just down here," said the guard, keeping a firm grip on Arnaud's arm, propelling him forward.

They passed down one flight of stairs, and through another hall. They went down a short flight, Arnaud nearly tripping, and then immediately up three brief steps and through a door that read CONFERENCE ROOMS. The door opened onto a short hallway with three doors on either side and one at the end.

The guard walked him down to the final door, coaxed him inside. "Wait here," the guard said.

"For what?" Arnaud asked.

But the guard, already gone, did not answer.

Arnaud tried the door he had come through; it was locked. He tried the door at the far end of the room; this was locked as well.

He sat down at the table and stared at the wall.

After a while, he began to read from his notebook. *Fugue state*, he read. Had he done anything wrong? he wondered. Was he to blame? Was anything in fact his fault? *6:13*, he read, *subject has begun to bleed from eyes.* Even if it were not his fault, would he somehow be held responsible? *Subject feels fine*, he read. *Is bleeding from eyes.*

Oh no, he thought.

He got up and tried both doors again.

He sat down again, but found it difficult to sit still. Perhaps he was in very serious trouble, he thought. He was not to blame for whatever had happened to Bentham. But someone had to be blamed, didn't they? And thus he was to blame.

Or was he? Perhaps he was becoming hysterical.

He opened the notebook again and began to read from it. The words were the same as they had been before. To him, now, they seemed all right, mostly. Perhaps the guard was simply following routine procedure in the case of an unusual death.

No, he began to worry a few moments later, something was wrong. Subjects did not habitually bleed from the eyes, for a start. He closed the notebook, leaving it face down on the table.

On the far side of the room, affixed to the wall, he noticed a telephone. He stood and went to it.

"Operator," a voice said.

"Outside line, please," he said.

"Right away, sir," the operator said. "What number?"

He gave the number. The dial tone changed to a thrumming, punctured by intervals of silence.

Nobody was answering.

After a time the thrumming stopped and a recorded voice came on, the tape so distorted he could barely make the words out. It was a man's voice. *Not the right number*, he thought, and started to hang up, and then thought, no, he might not have a chance to dial out again. *Hapler*, the distorted voice identified itself as, or perhaps *Handler* or *Hapner*. Nobody he knew. But Handler or Hapler would have to do.

"Hello?" he said. "Mr. Hapner? Is that in fact the correct name? My name is Arnaud. I'm afraid I've been given your number in error."

He swallowed, then began choosing his words carefully.

"There's been a misunderstanding," he said. "I have every hope it will be quickly resolved, everyone's heart is in the right place. But, Mr. Hapner, could I trouble you to contact my wife? Would you ask her, assuming that I am not safe and sound by the time you reach her, to do what she can to find out what has become of me? It would mean a great deal to both of us." He stopped, thought. "She might," he finally added, "begin with Bentham."

Immediately after he hung up the phone it began to ring. Almost reflexively, he picked it up.

"Hello?" he said.

"Who is this?" a voice asked.

Arnaud hesitated. "Why," he asked slowly, "do you want to know?"

"Mr. Arnaud," said the voice. "Why are you answering the telephone?"

He didn't know what to say. He held the receiver, looked out the window.

"You made a call a few moments ago," the voice said. "What was the purpose of this call?"

"I don't know what you're talking about," said Arnaud.

"How are you acquainted with"—he heard a rustling through the receiver—"this Mr. Hapner?"

"I—" said Arnaud.

"—and what, in your opinion, is the nature of the so-called . . . misunderstanding?"

Not knowing what else to say, Arnaud hung up the telephone.

By the time he was sitting down again, a guard had come into the room. A new guard, not the same one. He stood just inside one of the doors, watching Arnaud nervously.

"Hello," said Arnaud, just as nervously.

The guard nodded.

"What's this all about?" asked Arnaud.

"I'm not allowed to converse with you," the guard said.

"Why not?" asked Arnaud.

The guard did not answer.

Arnaud thumbed through his notebook again. His eyes for some reason were having a hard time focusing on his handwriting, making it out to be furry, blurred. No, he thought, he had followed procedure. He was not to blame. Unless they blamed him for the phone call. But couldn't he explain that away? Nobody had told him he wasn't allowed to telephone. There was really nothing to worry about, he told himself. Bentham's death could not be attributed to his negligence.

The original guard came back in. The two guards stood together just inside the door, whispering, looking at him, one of them frequently scratching the skin behind his ear. Eventually the original guard went to the telephone and disconnected it from the wall. Telephone under his arm, he came over to Arnaud and took his notebook away. Then he went out again.

Arnaud swiveled his chair around to face the remaining guard. He spread his arms wide.

"What harm could it possibly do to talk to me?"

The guard pointed a finger at him, shook it. "You've been warned," he said.

He stood up and went to the window. Outside, past the doubled fence, dim shapes wandered about beneath a mottled sky.

He heard the door open. When he turned, both guards, edges blurring, were present again, conversing, watching him. They seemed to be speaking to each other very rapidly, in a steady drone. He had to concentrate to understand them.

"He's been standing there," one of them was saying, "just like that, hours now."

But no, he had only been there for a few moments, hadn't he? Something was wrong with them.

One of them suddenly darted over and stood next to him.

"Come with us," the guard said.

"No use resisting," the same guard said.

Arnaud nodded and stepped forward, and then felt himself suddenly propelled. Each guard, he realized, had taken hold of one of his arms and was dragging him.

The conference room was replaced by a stretch of hall.

"Malingerer, eh?" said one of the guards, only the words didn't seem to correspond with the quivering movement of his lips, seemed instead to be coming at a distance, from the hall behind him.

No, Arnaud suddenly realized, amazed, something isn't wrong with them. Something is wrong with me.

They rushed him through the hall and into an observation booth. His observation booth, he realized, the one he had used to interview Bentham. Perhaps he was being allowed to return to work. Who would his next subject be? Bentham, he saw on the other side of the glass, was gone, though pinkish streaks of diluted blood were still visible on the glass.

He started toward his chair, but the guards were still holding him. Gently, he tried to free himself, but they wouldn't let go. Then he realized that he was being dragged toward the adjoining door, toward the subject chamber.

"No," he said, "but I, I'm not a subject."

"Of course not," a guard soothed, his face more a splotch of color than a face. "Who claimed you were?"

"But—" he said.

He grabbed hold of the doorframe on the way through. He held on. Something hard was pushing into his back, just below the blade of his shoulder. Something ground his fingers against the metal of the doorframe, his hand growing numb. Then his grip gave and he was through the door, being strapped to Bentham's bed. A fourth person in the room, a technician, was snapping on latex gloves.

"I'm not a subject," Arnaud claimed again.

The technician just smiled. Arnaud watched the smile smear across her face, consume it. Something was wrong with his vision. He could no longer see the technician clearly, she was just a blur, but from having watched subjects through the glass he could derive what she surely must be doing: an ampoule, a hypodermic, the body of the first emptying, the chamber of the second filling.

The blur shifted, was shot through with light.

"This may sting just a little," the technician said. But Arnaud felt nothing. What's wrong? he wondered. "Not so bad, is it?" the technician asked, coming briefly into focus again. And then she stepped away and was swallowed up by the wall.

"Hello?" Arnaud said.

Nobody answered.

"Is anybody there?" he asked.

Where had they gone? How much time had passed? He looked about him but couldn't make sense of what he saw. Everything seemed reduced to two dimensions, shadow and light becoming replacements for objects rather than something in which they bathed. He lifted his head and looked down at his body but could not recognize it, could not even perceive it as a body, despite being almost certain it was there.

Fugue state, he thought idly. And then thought, *Oh, God. I've caught it too.*

"Hello?" said a voice. It was smooth, quiet. It struck him as familiar. "Arnaud?" it said.

He turned, saw no one, just a flat black square. *Speaker*, he thought. Then he remembered the observation booth, turned instead to where, though he couldn't quite make it out, he thought it must be.

"Yes?" he said. "Hello?"

"How do you feel?"

"I feel fine," he claimed.

He heard a vague rustling, was not certain if it was coming from somewhere in his room or from the observation booth.

"Hello?" he said.

"Yes?" said the voice. "What's wrong, please?"

Arnaud waited, listened. There it was again, a rustling. He swiveled his ear toward it.

"I apologize for these precautions," said the voice, "but we had to assure ourselves that you were not a . . . liability, didn't we? For your own . . . safety as well as our own."

Arnaud did not answer.

"Arnaud, did you understand what I said?"

"Yes," said Arnaud. He tried to get up and thought he had but then realized he was still lying down. What was happening, exactly?

"Good," said the voice. "Shall we move straight to the point? Did you murder Bentham?"

Bentham? he wondered. Who was Bentham again? He blinked, tried to focus. "No," he said.

"What happened to Bentham?"

"I don't know," said Arnaud.

"Arnaud, seven days ago, you interviewed Bentham. During that session he died."

"Yes," said Arnaud, remembering. "He died. But it wasn't seven days ago. It was just a few hours ago."

"Are you sure, Arnaud? Are you certain?"

"Yes," said Arnaud. "I'm certain."

The rustling seemed gone now. He found if he tilted his head and squinted he could make rise from the flat surface of the wall, hovering like a ghost just above it, the plane of glass between his room and the observation booth. The glass was flat as well, depthless. Bentham's blood, the dull, nearly faded swathes of it, drifted like another flattened ghost on its surface. But somehow he could not see through blood or glass to the other side.

"Who is Mr. Hapner?" the voice asked.

Arnaud hesitated. "I don't know," he said, perplexed.

"You don't know," the voice said. "And yet after Bentham's death you placed a telephone call to a Mr. Hapner. How do you explain this?"

"I'm afraid I have no explanation," said Arnaud. "I don't even remember doing it."

He closed his eyes. When he opened them again, the room seemed to have shifted, flattening out like a piece of paper. It was still a room, he tried to convince himself, only less so.

For an instant, the room grew clearer.

"—case," the voice was saying. "How did he die?"

He tried to remember. "He began to bleed," he said. "From the eyes," he said.

"Yes," said the voice. "So you wrote. What made this happen, do you think?"

"I don't know," said Arnaud. "How should I know?"

"Think carefully. Did it have anything to do with you?"

He kept looking at the plane of glass, trying to worm his vision through. The voice kept at him, asking him the same questions in slightly different ways, repeating, following procedure. Arnaud kept answering as best he could.

"About this record of your interview," said the voice. "Is it, to the best of your knowledge, accurate?"

"Of course," claimed Arnaud. And then, "What record?"

The voice started to speak, fell silent. Arnaud waited, listened. There it was again, a rustling.

"What does 'fugue state' mean to you?" asked the voice. But now it sounded harsher, less encouraging, almost like a different voice.

"It doesn't mean anything," said Arnaud.

"And yet you wrote it. What exactly did you mean?"

"I don't know," said Arnaud. "I just wrote it."

"Do you see, Arnaud? Right here? *Fugue state?*"

He turned his face toward the black square and then, remembering, toward the glass, saw nothing.

"Well?" said the voice.

"Well what?" asked Arnaud.

"And yet," said the voice.

But then it interrupted itself, argued with itself in two different tones and cadences about what question should be asked next.

But how could a single voice do this? Arnaud wondered.

"How many of the one of you are there?" he asked. "Two?"

He waited. The voice did not answer. Perhaps he had said it wrong. Perhaps he had not said what he meant. He was preparing to repeat the question when the voice answered, in its harsher tone.

"How many of us do there appear to you to be?"

He opened his mouth to respond, closed it. He must have said something wrong, he realized, but he was no longer sure what.

"Do you remember your name?" said a voice slowly.

"Yes," said Arnaud. "Of course I do." But then realized no, he did not.

"Will you please tell it to me?" the voice said.

Arnaud hesitated. What was it? It was there, almost on the tip of his tongue. "Why?" he said. "Why exactly do you need to know?"

A voice said, changing, "Arnaud, what do you see?"

A voice said, changing, "Arnaud, what is happening to you?"

A voice said, changing, "Arnaud, how do you feel?"

"Fine," said Arnaud. "I feel fine."

He waited. "Why do you ask?" he finally said.

His face felt wet. Was he in the rain? No, he was indoors. There couldn't be rain. He could no longer see through his eyes.

He knew, from the tone of the voice, or voices, that someone thought something was wrong with him. But he couldn't, for the life of him, figure out what that could possibly be.

III.

There were a series of days he could not remember, how many days he was never certain, days in which, he temporarily deduced, he must have lain comatose and bleeding from the eyes on the floor of a kitchen, next to a woman he assumed, but was no longer certain, must be his wife. And all the days before that which he could not remember either. By the time he managed to open his eyes and felt like the world around him was moving at a rate his senses could comfortably apprehend, the woman, whoever she was, was dead. Thus his first memory, quickly coming apart, was of lying next to her, staring at her gaunt face, at the lips constricted back to show the tips of her canines.

Who is she? he wondered.

And myself, he wondered, *who exactly am I?*

Near his face was a puddle of water. He did not recognize the reflection that quivered along its surface. He rolled his head down into it, lapped some up with his tongue.

After a while he worked up enough strength to crawl across the kitchen floor, following the water's source, and to duck his head under a skirt below the sink. There, an overflowing metal bowl rested beneath a pipe's leaking elbow.

The water in the bowl was filthy, covered with a thin layer of scum. He brushed this gently apart with his stubbled chin, then tried to lap up the cleaner water below.

It was musty, but helped. He lay still for a while, his cheek against the damp, rotting wood of the cabinet floor, one temple applied to the cold metal of the bowl.

Later he managed to pull himself up and stagger to a cabinet. Inside, he found some stale crackers and sucked on these, then sat in a kitchen chair, his mouth dry. His eyes hurt. So did his ears and the lining of his mouth.

He got up and ate some more crackers then stared into the refrigerator. The food inside was rotting. He scavenged the heel of a loaf of bread, scraped the mold off it, ate it.

After the better part of the day had waned, he began to feel more human. He searched the pockets of the woman on the floor. They contained a few coins and a wallet stuffed with cards. Something, he discovered, was wrong with his eyes. He knew what the cards were by their shape and appearance—

credit card, identification card, cash card, library pass—but was puzzled to find he could not read them. The characters on them, what he assumed were characters, meant nothing. He stared at them for some time and then slid them into his own pocket, then covered the woman's body with a sheet.

In the bathroom mirror, he did not recognize himself. The face staring back at him had blood crusted about its eyes, above its lips and to either side of the chin, the center of the chin now covered with a diluted slurry of blood and water. His eyes were bloodshot, oddly scored and pitted. His vision, he realized, was dim, as if he were slowly going blind. Perhaps his pupils had always been that way.

He washed the face, scrubbing the blood from the wrinkles around the eyes with soap and with a toothbrush he found in the cabinet above the sink. When he was done, he shaved carefully.

He regarded himself in the mirror. *Who am I?* he wondered. But that was not what he meant exactly. Only that he had no name to put with what he knew himself to be.

When he tried to open the door, he found it locked. He unlocked the deadbolt, tried to open it again, but the door still didn't come. He wandered from room to room. The windows were barred from the outside, the street lying far below. The sheet was still in the kitchen, the woman still dead under it. Yes, he thought, that's right, he remembered. It was in a way reassuring to know she had not been imagined, though in another way not reassuring at all.

What was her name? He didn't know. Nothing leaped to mind. Nothing sounded quite right. And what about him? Nothing sounded quite right, but nothing quite wrong either.

In the back of one of the closets he found a small pry bar and a hammer. He used them to knock the pins from the door hinges, then tried to pry the door open from its hinged side. It creaked, but still didn't come.

Using the pry bar as a chisel, he slowly splintered a hole through the center of the door at eye level. There was, he discovered, something just beyond the door, made of plywood. He slowly broke a hole through this as well until, at last, he had a fist-sized opening that debouched onto an ordinary hall.

"Hello?" he called out. "Anyone there?"

When there was no answer, he went into the kitchen, stepping over the sheet. He started opening up drawers. There was a drawer containing a series of utensils, stacked very carefully into slots, a drawer containing stray keys and books of stamps and a rubber-band ball, a drawer containing nested measuring cups and spatulas and turkey basters and pie shields, a shelf holding a jumble of pots and pans, a cabinet scattered with ascending stacks of dishes and nested hard plastic drinking cups. He worked two of the rubber bands off the ball then slid the rest of the drawers closed.

In the bathroom, he took a last look at himself and then struck the mirror with the pry bar. Cracks shot through. The silvered glass tipped off in shards that broke further on the floor.

His hand, he saw, was blood-soaked, a flap of skin hanging open and folded over on the back of it. He was surprised to find it didn't hurt.

He pushed the flap back in place, found gauze in the cabinet, wrapped his hand in it.

He picked out a smaller, more regular square of glass, scraping each of its edges against the tile floor to dull it, then used the rubber bands to fasten it to the hooked end of the pry bar. At the door, he worked the mirror end of the pry bar through the hole he had made, sliding the pry bar through as far as he could without letting go of it.

It was hard to see past his knuckles and past the bar itself, harder still to hold the bar steady enough at one end to make sense of what he was seeing in the shard on the other: a wavering square of light and color. But there it was, he slowly could make it out, despite the wavering image: a large panel of raw wood, plywood, larger, it seemed than his door, studded with black pocks at regular intervals around its edge. The same black pocks in two lines up the panel's middle as well. Stretching from the bottom corners to the top corners of the panel were two strips of yellow plastic tape, covered in black characters that he could not read.

But something must have been wrong with his thinking. He stood, slightly crouched, holding the pry bar, trying to keep it steady, concentrating, looking past his knuckles into the reflection, and it was all he could do, really, just to see the flittered bits and pieces and make some cohesive image out of it in his head. It was too much to force that image into actually meaning something as well. Even after his difficulty trying to open the door, even after seeing the image in the shaky shard of mirror, after seeing the black pocks around the plywood's edge, it took him some moments of just staring and thinking to realize he had been deliberately boarded in.

But when he did realize, the shock came all at once. His fingers let go of the pry bar and, overbalanced, it started to slide out of the hole and away from him. He just caught it. He pulled it back through and, shaking, sat down with his back to the door.

Why? he wondered.

He couldn't say. Perhaps, he thought, they hadn't known he and his wife were there. Assuming, he corrected himself, that she was his wife. Perhaps they had thought the apartment unoccupied.

But who, he wondered, were *they*?

There was the phone, he thought after a while. He could telephone someone and have them come get him out.

But who did he know? He couldn't remember having known anyone.

On the answering machine beside the phone a light was blinking. Why hadn't he noticed it before?

He got up and pressed the button beneath the light.

Hello? a voice said. *Mr. Hafner? Is that in fact the correct name? My name is Arnaud. I'm afraid I've been given your number in error.*

Hapner, he thought, *my name's Hapner. Probably. Or something close to that. Unless he's talking to somebody else.*

There's been a misunderstanding, the voice continued, Arnaud's voice continued. *What sort of misunderstanding?* Hapner wondered. He was, Hapner was, to contact Arnaud's wife. He was to ask her to do what she could to find out what had happened to Arnaud. He might, he was told, begin with Bentham. *What a strange message*, Arnaud thought. *Or wait*, the man thought, *I'm not Arnaud, that's not my name, my name is something else. What was it?*

After listening to the tape several dozen times he was almost certain he could remember his name. *Hapner.* Every few minutes he brought the name to his lips, whispered it. It would, he hoped, stay with him, on his tongue if not in his brain. And now, he thought, I have something to do. *Bentham*, he thought, *Arnaud*.

With the hammer and pry bar he began to widen the hole, first cracking and splintering away his own door and then slowly hammering the flattened, flanged end of the pry bar through the plywood.

He was weak; his arms quickly grew sore and tired and the light he had at first been able to see coming through the windows had long faded. The hall outside, however, remained brightly lit.

The plywood broke loose in odd, thatched fragments, splitting within the body of a layer of wood rather than between layers. In the end he had a splintery and furzed channel wide enough to squeeze through. He drank some more water, ate some more crackers, and then sat on a chair in the kitchen gathering his strength. His gaze caught on the sheet on the floor and he stooped to uncover the woman's face. He regarded her closely, but no, he still did not recognize her.

Perhaps, he thought, *I never knew her.*

But then why, he wondered, *was she here with me? Or, if you prefer, why was I here with her?*

He went into the bedroom, looked through the closets. One was full of a woman's clothing, the other clothing belonging to a man. He tried on a sport coat. It was too small, and musty.

He tried on some of the other clothes, all too small.

Puzzled, he returned to the kitchen, stared again into the dead woman's face.

It's her home, he thought, *not mine*. And somebody else's. I'm probably not even Hafner.

He sat staring at her. The corpse was changing shape, becoming even less human. Soon it would start to smell. He couldn't stay there, whether he was Hafner or no. And if he wanted to be anyone, he had to be Hafner, at least for now.

IV.

Hapner rummaged a shoulder bag from a closet and dropped the hammer and pry bar into it. Unplugging the answering machine, he put it in as well, then pushed the bag through the door's hole.

It was tighter than he'd thought. He had to work one shoulder through and then turn sideways to get the other past. The ragged edges of the hole scraped raw the underflesh of one arm as well as his ribs. Halfway through, he thought he was stuck and grew desperate and maddened, scratching and wriggling until he had worn the skin covering his hipbones bloody and until he fell on his neck and shoulders out onto the floor.

The other doors too had been sealed off, he saw. Along the length of the wall were sheets of plywood where he would have expected doors to be, fastened to door and wall with ratchet-headed black screws.

He went down the hall and down the stairs. Doors on the floor below were sealed too, but not all of them, and he knocked on the three that weren't. Nobody answered any of them. He tried to open them but found them all locked.

The next floor down was the same, doors mostly boarded over, no one answering the few still unsealed. He chose one at random and worked at it with the pry bar and hammer until he cracked the latch out through the frame of the door and the door swung open.

The layout of the apartment was identical to the apartment he had been in, except reversed.

"Hello?" he called.

No answer came. The windows were slightly ajar. A thin layer of dust covered everything. Not dust quite, he realized: stickier. What, exactly, he couldn't say. On the table a sheet of paper was held down by a burnished brass paperweight. There was something written on it, but he couldn't read it. He picked it up and folded it, slid it into his back pocket.

In the closet were smeared two bloody handprints. Under one of the beds was what seemed to be a human ear. He sat on his knees a long time, squinting at it, wondering if he was really seeing what he thought he was seeing, but in the end left it where it was without touching it. In the oven he found the tightly curved body of a cat, long dead, dry as a plate. When he touched it, its hair crackled away.

He closed the oven and hurriedly left.

Two floors down, he knocked on an unsealed door and heard behind it some transient living sound, cut off nearly as quickly as it began.

"Hello?" he called.

He knocked again, but heard nothing. He pressed his ear to the door, thought he could hear, vaguely, just barely, something pressed to the other side, breathing. Was that possible, to hear something breathing, through a door? Perhaps it was his own breathing, he thought, and this made him feel as if he were on both sides of the door at once, and made him wonder why he wouldn't open up for himself.

"I don't mean any harm," he said. No response. "I'm just a neighbor," he said. "I just want to talk." Still no response.

"Shall I break down the door?" he asked. "If I do that, anybody can get in."

He waited a few minutes then got out his pry bar and hammer. Aligning the pry bar in the gap between door and wall, he struck the end with the hammer, started to drive it in.

———————

He was a little startled when the voice that rang out from behind the door was not his own.

"All right," it said. "All right."

He worked the pry bar free of the crack then stepped back. The deadbolt clicked. The door handle shivered and the door drew open.

Behind it was a small man, scarcely bigger than a child, wearing a moth-eaten sweater. Though not old, he seemed to be hairless, the skin hanging sallow on his face. His mouth and nose were hidden behind a surgical mask that he had doubled over to make fit. He stood mostly hidden, hand and head visible, a pistol in the former.

"Well?" the small man said. "What is it?"

"I'm your neighbor," Hapner said.

"I suppose you want to borrow a cup of sugar."

"No," said Hapner. "To talk."

"All right," said the man. "You're here. Talk."

"Can't I come in?"

"Why do you need to come in?" the man asked, a little surprised. "There's no reason to come in. It's not safe."

Hapner shrugged.

The man looked at him for a long while. His eyes, protruding and damp, seemed slightly filmed. He opened the door further, shifted the pistol to his other hand.

"What floor?"

Hapner counted in his head. "Five floors up," he said.

"Eighth floor," said the man. "Why didn't you just say eighth? I thought all the eighth was boarded off."

"Almost all," lied Hapner. "Every door but one."

The man's eyes narrowed. "You're not ill, are you?"

"Don't be ridiculous," said Hapner. With what? he wondered.

"Okay," said the man. "Okay. Prove it. Tell me your name."

"My name?" said Hapner.

It started with a middle letter, he knew, one he could almost remember. It was there, nearly on the tip of his tongue, but what exactly was it?

"Well?" the small man said. "Either you know your name or you don't."

"Mind if I use your bathroom?" asked Hapner.

"The bathroom?" said the man, surprised. "I, but I—"

"Thank you," said Hapner, and, hands raised above his head, eased his way carefully past him without touching the pistol, toward where he suspected the bathroom must be.

"Wait," the small man said. But Hapner kept walking, slowly, as if underwater. He gritted his teeth, waiting for the man to shoot him in the back, following each slow step with another slow step until he had reached the bathroom. Opening the door he slipped quickly inside, locking it behind him.

What now? he wondered.

He regarded his face in the mirror, his frightened eyes, then opened his bag and removed the answering machine. Unplugging the man's electric razor, he plugged his answering machine in and dialed the volume down. He held the machine pressed against his ear and depressed the button.

"Hello?" a voice said into his ear. "Mr. Hapner? Is that in fact the correct name?"

Is it? Hapner wondered. The voice kept on. There were other names mentioned, but Hapner struck him as the only viable one. Arnaud. He, Hapner, was looking for Arnaud, he discovered, and for Bentham as a way to reach Arnaud. The answering machine made it all perfectly clear. *Hapner*, he made his lips mime. He rewound the tape and listened to his name again, then again, until he was certain he could remember it. At least for a few minutes.

The small man was knocking on the bathroom door, urging him to come out or be killed.

"I'm coming," Hapner said. He quickly packed the answering machine away and opened the door. The small man was there, face red, pistol aimed at Hapner's waist.

"Hapner," he said. "My name's Hapner."

The pistol wavered slightly, a strange expression passing across the man's eyes. "I know a Hafner on the eighth floor," he said, "or ninth. Can't remember. But you're not him."

"No," said Hapner quickly. "I'm Hapner, not Hafner. Eighth floor as well. Strange coincidence, no?"

The man looked at him a long time, then took a few steps back, gun still poised. "Tell me what you want again?" he asked.

"That depends," said Hapner. "Are you Arnaud?"

"No," said the small man. "Who?"

"What about Bentham?"

"I'm Roeg."

"Do you know either an Arnaud or a Bentham?"

"Do they live in this building?"

"I don't know."

"I don't think so," said the small man. "These are strange questions to ask. If they do live here, I don't know them."

"Then I don't want anything," said Hapner and started to go.

"I thought you wanted to talk," said Roeg.

Hapner turned, saw Roeg had let his body sag. The small man went and sat down on the couch. He sat there, eyes looking exhausted, finally motioning Hapner into the chair next to him. "It's been long time," he said. "Let's talk."

But it was not an *us* who talked, for Hapner spoke hardly at all. Roeg hadn't left the house in several weeks, he claimed, ever since the plague had begun. *Plague?* wondered Hapner, but he just nodded. Roeg's wife had gone out and never come back. She was, he figured, probably dead.

"But maybe she just left," said Roeg.

He took the surgeon's mask off his face and laid it on the coffee table, smoothing it out with the palm of his hand. His mouth, Hapner saw, was delicately formed, the lips nearly translucent.

"Maybe," said Hapner. "I'm sorry."

Then someone had arrived wearing protective suits. Each apartment had been opened. If anyone was found with indications, they were boarded in. No doubt it had been the same on Hapner's floor.

"No doubt," said Hapner.

"Eventually they stopped coming," said Roeg.

"Probably dead themselves," said Hapner.

"Probably," Roeg said, and lapsed into silence, staring at the tabletop.

"And what now?" asked Hapner.

"Now?" said Roeg. "How should I know?"

Almost as quickly as the information was given to him Hapner felt it begin to slip away, the details wavering and eroding; only a large, vague sense of contagion remained. The knowledge itself was being simplified, made brutish within his head. He wondered how much of even this he would remember, and for how long?

There were other things Roeg told him, he knew, but even as he was saying them, Hapner felt them going. The authorities, he did remember Roeg saying, were silent. As to the silence, either Roeg didn't know its cause or Hapner somehow missed it or was already forgetting it. Perhaps it was simply *ongoing silence, unexplained*.

As Roeg spoke on, he became more and more confused. When he realized, from Roeg's puzzled look, that he must have asked a nearly identical question twice, back to back, he began to be concerned.

And then Roeg acquired a panicked look.

"Why are you speaking so quickly?" he asked. "Slow down."

"I'm not speaking quickly," Hapner said.

It became clear, as Roeg tried to continue, that something was wrong. He became prone to long reptilian fits of silence and would stop speaking to peer nervously around him.

"Roeg?" said Hapner. "Roeg?" But the small man wasn't answering, wasn't paying attention. Filled with doubt, Hapner asked, "That's your name, no?"

"My name?" said Roeg, suspiciously. "Why do you want to know?"

And then Roeg groped his pistol off the couch cushion and began to jab it into the air. He pointed not at Hapner but where Hapner had been a few moments before, for Hapner had stood and taken a few steps so as to get a closer look at Roeg.

"You had it?" Roeg shouted. "But why aren't you dead?"

He fired the pistol into the couch across from him. He moved the pistol a little, fired into the credenza, left again, into the wall—just behind the spot Hapner had been just a few seconds before. Reaching out, Hapner wrenched the gun out of Roeg's hand and dropped it to the floor. But it was as if Roeg didn't realize the gun was gone, for his curled hand was still aiming, his finger flexing, over and over, and he was, desperately, asking Hapner why he wouldn't die.

He spoke softly and carefully into Roeg's ear, stroking and rubbing the small man's hand until it loosened its grip on the absent gun. He coaxed him into lying down on the couch, then went into the kitchen and got a damp cloth, carefully wiping away the blood already seeping up through the man's eye sockets.

"How do you feel, Roeg?" he asked.

"Fine," said Roeg. "I feel fine. Why do you ask?"

And indeed, thought Hapner, the fellow seemed to believe this, despite the blood.

"You shouldn't feel bad," said Hapner. "You might come out of it all right."

"Come out of what?"

Blood began to leak from the man's mouth and nose and ears. Slowly he lapsed into unconsciousness. Hapner was at a loss to know what else he could do.

He let his eyes drift about the room until they found the telephone, then the answering machine. He held the latter's button down until it beeped, and then began to speak.

"Your name is Roeg," he said into it. "You are a small man. This is your house. I'm very sorry for all that's happened to you. My name is—" and there he stopped. What was his name again? Could he remember? No.

He turned off the answering machine and left the apartment.

V.

There was a name he had been using, just on the tip of his tongue. He could almost remember it. But, he wondered, was it his name? Even once he remembered it, how would he know for certain it belonged to him?

He wouldn't know.

He made it to the end of the hall and started down the stairs to the next floor. What floor was it? He had kept track, had been keeping track, but was not quite certain. He would go down the stairs and then he'd look for a door leading to the street. If there wasn't one, he would try to find another set of stairs and go down them.

What had the name been? He had been found, had found himself, he could still trouble himself to dimly remember, lying beside a dead corpse. A woman, he was almost certain. Who, alive, had she been to him? His wife, his lover, a relative, a colleague, a stranger? Who could say?

Before he had reached the bottom of the stairs he could see a man in the hallway, first only his feet and then, with each step down, a subsequent portion of his body, all the way up to a shaved head. He was standing beside a door, a large crowbar ending in a fan-like flange in one meaty hand. Leaning against the wall behind him was a sheet of plywood, prized off the door. A large duffel bag, empty or nearly so, was swung over the man's back. He had begun on the door itself, Hapner could see, the door's frame splintered and gouged.

Hapner stopped a little way down the hall. The man too had stopped working and was watching him.

"Hello," Hapner finally said.

"Hello," the man said.

"What exactly—"

"This your house?" asked the man. "Your door, I mean? I'm not stepping into a delicate situation, am I?"

Hapner shook his head. "No," he said. "It's not my door. Are you breaking in?"

"Some neighbor's?" asked the thief. "Some friend's, then? Anything to get touchy about?"

Hapner shook his head.

"Any objections, then? No? Then I'll proceed."

The man turned partly away, still trying to keep an eye on Hapner out of the corner of his eye, which made his attempts at opening the door awkward, blunted. But the door was slowly giving way.

"Aren't you afraid?" asked Hapner.

"What?" said the thief. "Of catching it? Was at first but then everybody around me went under and I never did. I don't think I will. What's the word? *Invulnerable?*" He worked the flanged end of the crowbar back in, and then one twist of his torso cracked the door open. "No," he said, "*immune.*" And then added, "After a while you feel invincible too."

He pushed open the door, bights of a brass chain tightening at eye level inside the apartment. The man fed his crowbar into the gap, broke the chain's latch off the door frame.

"Well," he said. "Coming?"

Hapner took a half step forward, stopped.

"I don't think so," he said.

"Come on in," said the man. "Where's the problem? You didn't have any objections last I checked. Besides, I haven't had anyone to talk to for a while. They all keep dying on me. You're not going to die on me, are you?" The man started through the door. "I'll let you have some of whatever we find, maybe."

Hapner hesitated, followed him in.

"What about you?" said the man from in front of him.

The apartment inside was windowless and extremely dark; it was difficult to see anything. The man grew gray and then was reduced to a series of fluttering movements. Then he vanished entirely. Hapner stepped after him.

"What about me?" Hapner asked.

"Aren't you afraid? You're in a quarantined apartment now. Doesn't it worry you?"

The man struck a match and Hapner saw his face spring from the darkness, in a kitchenette area. He had not been where Hapner had thought he would be. He was holding the match in one hand, rapidly opening and closing cupboard and cabinet doors with the other.

The match guttered and went out and the room was swallowed in the darkness, save for the dull red bead of the match head, and then this was gone too, replaced by the smell of the burnt-up match. A sharp scratch and another match fluttered alight. Hapner watched the man reach into a drawer, come out with a curious silver cylinder that he manipulated, transformed into a flashlight.

"That's better," the man said, and shined the flashlight's beam into Hapner's face.

"Now," he said, his voice changing in a way Hapner didn't understand. "What did you say your name was?"

"I didn't say," said Hapner. "What's yours?"

"What's that in the bag?" the man asked.

"My bag?" said Hapner. "Not much," he said.

"Open it up," said the thief. "Let's have a look."

Hapner put the bag on the counter between them, unzipped it. He took out the answering machine, put it beside the bag, then the short pry bar, the hammer.

"That's it?" asked the thief.

"That's it," said Hapner.

"You don't have much," said the thief.

"I'm not like you," said Hapner. "I'm not a thief."

"Then what are you doing?"

"Looking for someone," he said. "A . . . Mr. Arnaud, I think. Is that you?"

"What, you just have a name?" said the voice behind the flash beam.

Hapner nodded.

The man was silent for a moment. "All right," he finally said, "you can go."

Hapner nodded to himself. He reached out, began to put his possessions back into the bag. The thief's crowbar cut through the flash beam and struck the counter between his hands.

"Leave it," said the man. "It's mine now."

"But—"

"This is my building," the man said. "Whatever's here belongs to me."

"But there's nothing I have that's worth—"

"It's a matter of principle," the thief said, his voice rising. "Now get out."

He kept staring at the answering machine. *Arnaud*, he thought, *Bentham. Hapler.* Or no, that wasn't it exactly, he was already forgetting. He squinted into the light. Where was the flashlight exactly? How far away? He could make it out, mostly. He could see the man behind it, a dim form wavered at the edges.

He turned as if to leave and took half a step and then whirled and crouched, battered at where he thought the flashlight would be. The thief cried out, Hapner's hand striking the casing of the flashlight hard. His fingers were instantly numb, the flashlight flicking away end over end and going out.

The crowbar passed moaning over his head, ruffling his hair, striking the wall hard. The thief cursed. Hapner groped about, touched the man's shirt but, unable to find the crowbar, dropped to his knees and crouched under the lip of the counter.

The crowbar crashed into the counter above him, the walls rattling.

"Where are you?" the man said.

Hapner said nothing.

"I'll find you eventually," said the thief. "You belong to me."

Hapner stayed still, listening to the dim birds of the man's feet, the clank of the crowbar as it touched floor or wall. He reached carefully up, touching the counter above him, his fingers feeling slowly along it.

There was a groove the crowbar had dug in the surface, the countertop splintered and cracked to either side of it. His hands felt past it until they found his hammer.

"But maybe I already killed you?" the thief said.

The voice was right there, almost beside him. In one motion he swung the hammer up and forward. It struck something firm but not as hard as the wall.

The thief screamed and swooned toward him, striking the counter, stumbling over Hapner's legs. Hapner struck him hard and repeatedly with the hammer. Something struck his shoulder and it became suddenly a numb useless thing and he heard the crowbar splintering the wood behind him. He groped with his good hand for the dropped hammer. He heard the thief stutter-step and then, groaning, fall.

He moved toward the body, pounding along the floor in front of him until the hammer struck flesh. He fell on the other man and lost his hammer and felt the man's face into existence and then fumbled up the hammer again and then, as the man still struggled his way out of shock, struck at his skull again and again until the head sounded like a wet sack.

He felt around the floor one-handed until he found the flashlight. He stood and flicked its switch but no light came from it, so he dropped it again.

On his way back to the counter, he stepped on what must have been the thief's hand and then, as he moved quickly off it, into something damp and squishy, perhaps the thief's gore, perhaps his own, and almost fell. One arm ached badly and swung loose, battering against his side like the trussed body of a shot bird. Moving it created little flashes of light behind his eyes.

He fumbled around on the counter until he found the answering machine, picked it up. There was something wrong with it, he could tell: its surface was no longer smooth.

The room seemed at each moment less and less familiar to him.

He managed to stumble out of the dark and back into the hall. His arm, he saw, in the light, seemed mostly dead, oddly lumped and turning black in two places. He tried again to move it but could not.

The answering machine was shattered in the back, the slatted casing covering the speaker destroyed, the speaker itself and the transformer beside it mangled. Why had he wanted to keep it anyway? He couldn't remember.

He dropped the machine and crouching beside it worked the cassette free with one hand. One of the cassette's corners was crushed but the tape itself was still intact, could be listened to on another machine. Where had he seen another one?

The hallway, he saw, was slowly going out around him, flattening out, the door he had come through an odd square of black, a vertical panel, two-dimensional, rather than an entrance. The whole world, he thought fleetingly, was like that for him, there was nothing he could hold on to but this hall and perhaps a few other halls above that and an answering machine he may or may not have seen, somewhere above him. But what did *above* mean? What's wrong with it? he wondered of the hall. It all struck him as vaguely familiar as if he had lived through it before, in another life.

He turned and looked where he was almost certain stairs had been and found that too had gone strange, a black flat rectangle scored with lighter lines. He stumbled toward it and, closing his eyes, pushed into it. The pain in his shoulder too he realized seemed to be fading, was all but gone. He hit against something and pulled himself up, kept moving forward, kept stumbling, and when he opened his eyes saw that the stairs were stairs again, more or less, and that he could navigate them. He pushed through the yellow wall at their end and found himself in a hall, or what seemed like a movie set for a hall, everything slightly false. He reached up to touch his face and when his hand came away, saw it was not a hand exactly, though a reasonable facsimile. There, floating above it, was a strange crimson cloud, the color of blood.

An anxiety began rising in him that he had a hard time placing.

By strength of will he managed to transform a brown rectangle into a door and push his way through. Inside, the cardboard cutout of a tiny man, hardly bigger than a child, was lying prone on what stood in for a couch, a crimson cloud hovering over his face. He took a deep breath and tried to relax and, there, momentarily, saw a real flesh-and-blood man on an actual couch, his face stained from blood that had seeped from his eyes. He felt, almost, that he recognized him. But then, suddenly, he was only a child in a crimson cloud again.

There was a blinking light near him, not far away, very quick, not blinking so much as strobing. He moved toward it slowly and stood near it and in a little while began to imagine that it was an actual human object, an answering machine. He found a button and pressed it.

A voice came out, speaking too rapidly. It sounded familiar to him, perhaps a voice he had heard before, but where?

Your name is Roeg, the voice said. *You are a small man. This is your home. I'm very sorry for all that's happened to you. My name is—*

And then it stopped. *Roeg*, he thought. *Is that my name?*

What is my name? he wondered.

My name? he wondered. *Why do I want to know?*

There was, he managed to trouble himself to remember, something in his hand, something important, but why or what he couldn't remember. He tried to raise his hand but it wouldn't move. What was wrong with it? The other hand he tried to move and it came and there, clutched in it, he saw a small black rectangle that just for a moment he found himself mistaking for an open doorway. But no, it was not that, it was smaller than his hand and pierced through with two teethed circles: a cassette.

He shook his head to clear it. It did not clear. He managed, after some effort, to raise the lid of the answering machine and pop the cassette out and get his own cassette in. He pressed the play button and then stumbled away toward where he hoped a chair would find him.

There was a crackle and a beep and the voice began to speak.

Hello, it said. *Mr. Hapner? Is that in fact the correct name? My name is Arnaud* . . .

Did it all come flooding back to him? Not exactly, no. It went on from there but he was no longer listening. *Hapner*, his mind was saying, *Arnaud*. He tried to sit down, crashed to the floor. He lay there, staring at the ceiling, trying to hold on to the two names, to keep that at least. But they were already slipping away.

VI.

He awoke to find himself lying on a couch, prone. Across from him, collapsed on the floor, an abnormally large man with his shirt and hands smeared with blood, blood crusted around his eyes as well. The man's arm was clearly broken, turned out from the body at a senseless angle, a velvety pinkish lump of bone protruding just above the wrist.

He sat up, feeling weak. His mouth was dry. When he tried to stand he grew weak and quickly sat down again. He sat there on the couch, gathering his breath, waiting, staring at the man on the floor.

Did he know him? Surely he must know him or why else would they both be there?

"Hello?" he said to the man. He didn't move, dead probably.

But where was here? he wondered. Was this his apartment? It didn't look familiar exactly, but he couldn't bring another apartment to mind either. But if this was his, why wouldn't he know it?

He stood and stumbled across the room and toward the kitchen, passing the man on the way. Up close he could see he was clearly dead, his face the color of scraped bone, a smell coming off him.

In the kitchen he looked into the fridge, found it empty. The pantry was full of cans. He couldn't read any of the labels. *What's wrong with me?* he wondered. He opened one and drank it cold—some kind of soup, glassy with oil on the top. After a while, he felt a little better.

When he went back into the living room he saw the blinking light. It took him a moment to figure out what it meant, what it belonged to.

He had to stand on a foot ladder to reach it. The machine's casing, he saw, was streaked with blood. He depressed the button.

Hello, a voice said. *Mr. Hapner? Is that in fact the correct name?*

Hapner, he thought, the name sizzling vaguely in his head and then beginning to fade. Unless it was not his house, unless the name belonged to the man dead on the floor. But no, it must be his name, it sounded right enough, and the foot ladder, the dead man wouldn't have needed a foot ladder to step on. *Ergo*, his house. *Ergo*, Hapner. *If that is in fact the correct name?*

There had been, the voice told him, Mr. Arnaud told him, a misunderstanding. Everyone's heart was in the right place. But he, Hapner, was being asked to contact Arnaud's wife, to pass on information, to find out what had become of him.

I must be a private detective, thought the small man, thought Hapner.

He went into the bathroom and looked at his face. He too, like the dead man, was wearing a mask of blood, the blood thickest around his eyes. They shared that at least. The face—small, pudgy—was unfamiliar. *But it must be my own face*, he thought. Nevertheless he couldn't help but reach out and touch the mirror, assure himself that it was solid, flat glass.

In the bedroom, he changed his clothes. The clothes fit. Thus, this was his house. *Ergo*. Thus, he was Bentham. Or not Bentham exactly, Bentham was who he was looking for. What had the name been exactly? It started with an H, he thought, or some similar letter. Similar in what way? He went back into the living room, skirting a dead body—had he seen it before? Yes, he had, but who was it?—and depressed the answering machine button again. Ah, yes. Hapner. That was him. And it was Arnaud he was looking for, not Bentham.

He got out a pen and a piece of paper and wrote it down, but found he could make no sense of the marks on the paper. *What's wrong?* he wondered, *what's wrong?* He would, he supposed, somehow just have to remember.

He started out the door—*Arnaud*, he was saying in his head, *Hapner*,

I'm Hapner, I'm looking for *Arnaud*—and stopped dead. The other doors around his own had been barricaded over with sheets of plywood. *But why?* he wondered, and then wondered, *Why not my door?*

He went down the stairs and then down a hall whose walls were smeared with blood, then down another set of stairs that opened onto a lobby, two shattered glass doors leading out into the street. He pushed one open, felt a pricking on his hands and looked to see them glittery with powdered glass, minute cuts all over them. He used his shoe to open the door the rest of the way, stepped out into the street.

The street was deserted, a car overturned and burnt to a husk a dozen feet from where he stood, another car in the middle of the road, both doors open, clumps of paper eddying about it, garbage, a fine rain of ash. The building across the street from him, a large complex of some sort, was surrounded by a chain-link fence topped with barbed wire, another similar fence a half dozen feet inside it and parallel to it, the gates of both fences twisted off their hinges. The building was set off from the road and between him and it were scores of abnormally large men in white protective suits, sprawled about, no marks on them, suits intact, all probably dead. *Good Christ*, he thought. For just an instant, the scene wavered, flattening out in front of him, everything fading away or coming all too close. But then he blinked, and blinked again, and it all seemed all right again, though somehow the sun had moved and the sky had gone darker.

He crossed the street and passed through the gate and approached one of the prone men. The glass shield over the man's face was obscured by blood. He looked at another. It was the same. He stopped looking.

What am I doing? he wondered. *What am I looking for?*

He couldn't remember exactly. He was looking for something or someone, it started with, he could almost remember, it was a letter that he . . . perhaps R? But what did that tell him? It didn't tell him anything at all.

He turned around and looked over his shoulder at the building across the street. It was an apartment complex, ten or twelve stories tall, its door shattered.

He stood staring at it for a long time. Something about it struck him as significant. Familiar? What, he wondered again, was he looking for, and who was he exactly, again? What was the name?

He kept staring, feeling a slow panic welling through him.

He took a step forward without looking, almost fell over one of the bodies. He kicked it softly, then stepped around it.

I am looking for something, he tried to tell himself, or someone. *Probably*, he tried to tell himself, *I'll know it when I find it.*

He looked back again at the building across the street, then turned toward it.

Probably as good a place to start as any, he thought. He crossed the street, opened the door to the building. *Who knows what I will find?* he thought.

Another instant and he was gone.

W. P. KINSELLA

Reports Concerning the Death of the Seattle Albatross Are Somewhat Exaggerated

W. P. Kinsella is the author of *Shoeless Joe*, famously adapted into the film *Field of Dreams*. His other novels include *The Iowa Baseball Confederacy*, *Box Socials*, and *Butterfly Winter*. He has also published more than a dozen-and-a-half collections of his short fiction, most recently *The Essential W. P. Kinsella*. Kinsella, widely considered one of the greatest fiction writers about baseball, is as well known in his native Canada for his award-winning and controversial First Nation stories, humorous and gritty tales of the complex lives of indigenous Canadians. He has won the Houghton Mifflin Literary Fellowship, the Stephen Leacock Memorial Medal for Humour, and the George Woodcock Lifetime Achievement Award. Kinsella has been celebrated with many other honors, including the designation of the Orders of Canada and British Columbia. He currently lives near Vancouver.

"Reports Concerning the Death of the Seattle Albatross Are Somewhat Exaggerated" is a very rare feat, a first-contact story about baseball. The story first appeared in *Rosebud*.

The five p.m. news is doing a feature story on me. Jean Enersen, the beautiful Channel Five anchorwoman, is reading from her TelePrompTer.

"Mike Street, the man inside the Seattle Albatross costume for the past five years, has announced his retirement," she is saying.

"Albatross flies the coop" was how the headline of the *Post-Intelligencer* sports section read.

The camera cuts to the smiling but vacuous face of Buzz Hinkman, the Seattle Mariners' coordinator of public relations.

"The only reason we're making a statement at all is because of the bizarre rumors that have been circulating," says Buzz. "Mike joked that it was time for him to seek visible employment. He's left Seattle and is taking a long holiday while he mulls over a number of employment offers."

In that way of news broadcasters, Buzz goes on talking, mouthing his pompous platitudes while the voice of Jean Enersen lists a few highlights of my career and wishes me well. The final word, however, belongs to Buzz: "I want to assure the press, our own Seattle Mariners fans, and the baseball world at large that reports concerning the death of the Seattle Albatross are somewhat exaggerated." Here Buzz smiles his empty but winning smile for at least the tenth time, and Channel Five moves on to a story about a baby orangutan.

Buzz probably believes what he has just said. And if he doesn't believe it he's not a bad actor. I'm sure the word has been passed down to him from the general manager, perhaps even the owners, who in turn have been briefed by higher powers as to what to say.

The first thing I have to admit is that our people did not understand the civilization of Earth very well. I'm afraid the bureaucrats on our planet aren't very bright, which shouldn't come as any surprise, except that everyone here on Earth accepts as fact that other civilizations are far more intelligent. About the only advantage I have over people on Earth is a built-in ability to engage, with considerable help, in teleportative space travel. If our politicians and military bureaucrats had been smarter, they would have investigated conditions much more thoroughly before packing me off to Earth.

One of the first things we saw when we began intercepting television signals from Earth was the San Diego Chicken.

"Look! Look!" our prime minister chortled. "They have an integrated society. It appears that fifty thousand people on Earth are gathered together to worship one of our own." I have to admit that that is what it looked like.

As the TV signals became clearer, the prime minister and the joint chiefs of staff spent a great deal of time watching baseball, not that they understood the game. I've been here for five years and I barely understand it. But what they did understand was popularity, and mascots were popular. The San Diego Chicken was most like one of our own, but B. J. Birdy from Toronto, Fredbird the Redbird from St. Louis, and even the Phillie Phanatic could walk down the street in any of our major cities without being stared at.

"They even have economically disadvantaged segments of the population," enthused the prime minister, after viewing the bedraggled set of mascots fielded by the Chicago White Sox.

I have to admit I was a natural for the job. I am a bit of an exhibitionist; I had also studied theater, where I majored in pantomime and clowning. Unfortunately, for once the bureaucrats decided to move with extreme haste. Almost before I knew it, I was teletransported to New York City, where, I was informed, there was a school for mascots.

Most of the officials on our planet understood that on Earth mascots weren't real, but just as some children believe cartoon characters really exist, a number of politicians and most of the military believed the mascots were really long lost descendants of ours.

"The thing you're going to have to get used to," one of the bureaucrats said to me, "is that you *never* take off your costume."

"I don't have a costume," I said.

I was given some curious looks by the joint chiefs of staff, the head of External Security, and perhaps even the prime minister.

"Need I remind you that on Earth only people in elaborate costumes look like me?"

"Of course," they said.

My natural colors are blue and white, so it was decided that after I oriented myself to New York and attended mascot school, I'd align myself with the Seattle Mariners, a baseball team that didn't have a mascot.

New York was a great place to start my life on Earth. In the theater district, where the mascot school was located, no one gave me a second glance as I walked the streets. I was given a more than adequate supply of currency, including one delightful hundred-dollar bill that reproduced itself on command. I was able to live in a comfortable hotel and eat at quality restaurants, although my greatest joy was to go to a fish market, buy a tub of sardines, toss them in the air one at a time, and catch them in my mouth.

At the ballpark, after I officially became the Seattle Albatross, I used to use fish in my act. I'd go down to the Pike Street Market and buy a couple of pounds of smelts, then run around the stands tossing fish in the air and swallowing them. Kids would stop me and ask, "You don't really swallow those raw fish, do you?" or, "Are those real fish, or are they made of something else?"

"They're real," I'd say. "Want me to breathe on you?" The kids would shriek and pretend to be afraid of me as I puffed up my cheeks. Then I'd reach way down into my mouth and pull out a smelt. "Have a fish," I'd yell, and chase the kids along the aisles, holding a fish by the tail.

The only recognizable foreign object I brought to Earth with me was my communicating device, a sophisticated sending-receiving set, which, once I was settled in Seattle, lived under my kitchen sink, mixed in with a bag of potatoes, looking exactly like a potato except that it felt like chamois to the touch.

There must have been sixty people at mascot school.

"I never take off my clothes in public," I wrote on my application, for I had decided to remain mute until I became acclimatized. "It's my way of getting into character." The school officials were more interested in the hundred-dollar bills I produced to pay the tuition than in my idiosyncrasies. The other students thought I was showing off at first. But I was good at what I did and they soon accepted me. The result was that while a roomful of people in jeans, track suits, and leotards practiced pratfalls and somersaults, I performed in full costume.

What did I look like? Picture the soulful expression of the San Diego

Chicken, but picture real feathers, sleek, a brilliant white, like sun on hoarfrost, violet tail feathers and bars of violet along my folded blue wings, and sturdy legs the color of ripe corn. I always wore furry shoes, big as pillows, covered in blue velvet, to keep my bird's feet hidden from the curious.

The thing the Mariners were most interested in was that I would work for free. All they asked me to do was sign a waiver to the effect that if I was injured while performing they would not be liable.

"To what do you attribute your huge success?" the press repeatedly asked me. "You have replaced the San Diego Chicken as the most in-demand performer of your kind in America. What is the secret of the Seattle Albatross?"

"The mystique of the Seattle Albatross is the very elusiveness of my character. None but a select and specific few have ever seen the Mike Street who resides inside this costume. That makes me a mysterious entity and automatically doubles or triples the interest in me."

"Don't you ever secretly yearn for the fame and publicity Ted Giannoulas receives as the San Diego Chicken?" asked Steve Kelley of the *Seattle Times*. "He's a celebrity even when he appears out of costume."

"Oh," and here I would giggle my high-pitched laugh-shriek for which I was famous, "just yesterday I spent a lovely day at the Pike Street Market, and just walked around downtown Seattle, relaxing, being myself, *not* having to be a celebrity every minute. I enjoy the private side of my life very much. I wouldn't trade it for anything."

"What about your personal life?"

"I keep my personal and professional life completely separate. My friends guard my privacy with great loyalty and determination."

What the reporter was trying to establish, in a none-too-subtle way, was my sexual situation. The rumors about me were legion. The most prevalent, of course, was that I was gay. I do have a high speaking voice and a girlish giggle. Apparently at least two young men in Seattle's gay community claimed to be me, and since there were never any denials—"The private life of the Seattle Albatross is private" was my final word on the matter—they are to my knowledge still claiming it. What they will do now that I've officially left Seattle is not my problem. My problem right now is much more serious than that.

My problem then was acute loneliness. And frustration, both sexual and otherwise. No one on my home planet knew exactly the kind of information they wanted me to channel back to them. One high official had the nerve to ask me to bring back Ronald McDonald's autograph. Opportunities for sexual contact were everywhere, but I was unable to make even a close friendship for fear of giving away my secret. I kept an apartment on Union Street, which I visited once a week to pick up mail. I occasionally invited a friend or reporter there. I kept canned food in the cupboards, kept the closets full of human clothes, left Willie Nelson albums lying about on the carpet. When I was alone I was able to contrast my position to that of a famous television character. There was an alien named Mork who made wonderful, insane jokes and had a very beautiful woman in love with him. The woman knew what he was but loved him anyway. Mork was always in a lot of trouble, but he was *never* lonely. Except when I was performing, I was utterly lonely.

And even performing had its risks. The closest call I ever had was on an evening when Phil Bradley, Seattle's best outfielder, hit a mammoth home run in the bottom of the ninth inning to bring Seattle a come-from-behind victory. The fans were jubilant, raucous, their adrenaline running high. A whole contingent of them were waiting for me as I made my way down a ramp toward the dressing rooms. It had been a difficult evening for me. While children always loved me, were able to accept the fantasy of me, teenagers were wary and distrustful, somehow aware that I was too real. One had snatched a feather from my wing about the sixth inning. Others had, in more than a joking tone, spoken of tearing off my costume and revealing the real Mike Street.

"Let's get him," several of them screamed.

"Hit him high and hit him low," someone else said.

I tried to run, but I'm not very speedy. Those pursuing me were the same ones who had taunted me earlier, sensing my strangeness. They backed me into a corner. I considered flying. I could soar to the roof in an instant. Better to reveal my identity than die.

"Help!" I yelped, my voice high and shrill. I flapped my wings and tried to fly over their heads. My wings made monstrous beating sounds. Some of them retreated. I scraped my back on the sprinklers in the ceiling of the passageway.

One of them grabbed my legs. I shrieked like a macaw. I struck one hard with my left wing, knocking him down. But they overpowered me.

"Twist his head off," yelled one.

"Wring his neck," cried another. And they fully intended to.

I was scuffling my feet together, trying to expose one scaly foot with its long, razorlike spur. I was going to do several of those barbarians serious damage.

But at that instant two Kingdome security men appeared and rescued me.

From that day on, whenever there were fans in the Dome, there was a security person somewhere close to me.

In 1981 there was a mascots convention in Cleveland in conjunction with the All-Star Game. The San Diego Chicken and I stood out as the class of the field. The minor-league mascots were there too: a real live dog from Cedar Rapids, Iowa, whose stock in trade was to stand frozen, leg in the air, forever in anticipation, in front of a plastic fireplug. What that act had to do with being the mascot of a baseball team still puzzles me.

There was a character there called the Eel, a very thin man who wore a plastic and rubber suit and a bulletlike helmet with red, blinking eyes. He had batteries of some kind hidden inside his flippers and would pass charges of blue electricity from hand to hand as he stood along the baselines. He was, he explained to me, an electric eel.

The men and boys inside those costumes were a strange lot, furtive and uncomfortable when their disguises were peeled away. Several congratulated me for my fortitude in never taking off my costume. Each intimated that he wished he could do the same. Outside their costumes the other mascots were as pale and sad-eyed as velvet portraits, whispering, gentle men happy only when hidden.

But the women. They were everywhere, bright as freshly cut flowers. They couldn't keep their hands off us. Room keys and slips of paper emblazoned with lipsticked phone numbers were thrust into our hands, wings, flippers, beaks, mouths. It must be a significant comment on American masculinity that thousands of women are ready, willing, and able, and aggressively pursue the opportunity to go to bed with men whose physical features are perpetually hidden from sight by the costume of a chicken, bear, eel, cardinal, or some other grotesque caricature of a stuffed toy.

I wonder what these girls and women thought when they stripped away the costume of the Birmingham Bear and found a man of fifty-five, an ex-jockey, his face the color of concrete, his mirthless mouth like a crack in a sidewalk.

But we were not all trailed by women. There was a boy in a fish costume, his tail flapping in the dust, who must have given off an odor to betray that when, as part of his act, he kissed umpires and third-base coaches, it was because he liked umpires and third-base coaches.

In spite of the numerous temptations to sexual pleasure, I never wavered. Sometimes when I was very lonely I would take one or two of my admirers to dinner, but I always went home alone, turning aside, with as much kindness as I could muster, the invitations. For almost five years I behaved impeccably, denied my sexuality. Until I met Virginia.

Most of the players tolerated me. Some even considered me a good luck charm, good-naturedly rubbing my head for luck before going to the plate. Coaches and managers who had not known mascots in their playing days were less accommodating.

"Stay away from the third-base coach," the players warned me my first year with the team. "He has no sense of humor."

One part of my act was to stand behind the third-base coach's box and parody the signs he was giving. Eventually he was supposed to turn and hit me with a roundhouse right, whereupon I would fall as if unconscious, legs and wings spread wide.

"Maggie," as the players called the third-base coach, was surly and unco-operative from the start.

"Listen, shithead," he said to me, "I only do this because management says I have to," and he smiled a wicked little smile, showing his snuff-stained teeth. I expected an elaboration, but none was forthcoming, until one evening during a pitching change he stalked to the dugout, returned with a bat, and went for my head as if it were a ball on a batting tee.

I think he believed I was somewhere deep within the costume, that my feathered head was empty, my blinking pink eyes controlled by a battery. Otherwise I doubt that he would have tried to kill me in front of twenty thousand fans.

The bat flattened my ruby-red comb. I was in terrible pain, but tried not to let on. I danced like a maniac. The fans loved it. I flew to the top of the dugout and leapt into the arms of the best-looking woman in that section of the stands.

"Kiss it better," I wailed.

The woman obliged. I massaged her breasts with my free wing. She didn't object, in fact she clutched me to her. I love the smell of perfume. It has not yet been invented on my planet.

The fans roared their approval. But if the bat had struck a half inch lower it could easily have disabled me. What would have happened if a doctor had attempted to remove my head in order to examine me?

How I got the name Mike Street. When I walked into the Mariners corporate offices at 100 South King Street and went to introduce myself, my mind went blank. Martin Gardiner was the name the bureaucrats had chosen for me. It was the name I had used in New York, but in New York I had pretended to be mute. For the first time, my speech would be monitored. Suffice it to say that speech on my home planet is fraught with *zs* and *vs* and a sound, *uuvvzz*, that is not quite comparable to anything in English.

"Good morning," I said. "My name is . . ." and I panicked. All I could recall was an advertisement I'd seen for the Pike Street Market. ". . . Pike Street, I'd like to—" but the secretary cut me off.

"About ten or twelve blocks straight north on First Avenue," she said, assuming I was asking directions.

"No, no," I said, "my name."

"Your name is Pike Street?"

"Yes. No. Mike Street," I said in desperation. And so it was. I didn't get to see management that day. In fact, they were downright rude to me.

"The contest isn't until Sunday," the secretary said, eyeing me up and down, her eyes getting large as I riffed the indigo feathers around my neck.

"Contest?" I said.

"The Mascot Contest," she said, her voice incredulous. "Sunday afternoon at the Kingdome. Here are the rules." She handed me a mimeographed page containing several paragraphs of dark print below the Mariners logo.

A contest. I was going to have to compete for a job.

"You shouldn't wear your costume now," the secretary was saying. "You'll get it dirty before Sunday."

I wandered out onto the street, where, instead of trying to be inconspicuous, which was impossible, I flaunted myself, nuzzling children and attractive women, taking pratfalls, pretending to swallow a parking meter.

On Sunday there was a large crowd at the Kingdome. A mascot's costume was good for free admission. There were about forty of us, from children dressed in Halloween costumes to two or three dressed in elaborate and expensive getups that rivaled my own real self. There were also three or four very odd individuals who, I suspect, were inmates, escaped or otherwise, from some institution.

We were herded in a flock, or whatever a collective of mascots would be called. Perhaps a *plush* of mascots would be appropriate, for many were direct imitations of the San Diego Chicken, the Phillie Phanatic, or B. J. Birdy.

The contest was a fiasco. The majority of participants had no stage presence whatsoever, and, after we were admitted to the playing field, merely plodded across the outfield toward second base.

Besides myself there was a man on stilts dressed as the Space Needle, a magnificent and imaginative creation, but he was not cuddly or lovable, and was ill-equipped to run or take face-first dives into the infield dirt.

Perhaps the most unusual was an entry I called Mr. Baby, a middle-aged, bald, pudgy man, who was dressed in a massive diaper with the Mariners logo stenciled on the back, and a frilly bonnet. We talked briefly while we waited to be admitted to the playing field.

"A dream come true. A dream come true," he kept repeating. "It has always been my fantasy to appear as a baby in front of the whole world. I dress like this in private all the time. My wife is really very understanding. Sometimes she dusts me with talcum powder while I lay back on my blanket and kick and gurgle. Tell me, do you wear your costume in the privacy of your own home? Does it have sexual meaning for you?"

"I do wear it at home," I said, "and I suppose it has as much sexual meaning as any other costume."

"I think perhaps we understand each other," Mr. Baby said, with what I interpreted as an ominous tone.

When the limping, slovenly parade of mascots began, Mr. Baby dropped to his hands and knees and crawled slowly, like a grotesque toy, toward the infield. Unfortunately, the sharp bristles of the artificial turf soon proved too much for Mr. Baby's tender hands and knees, and he began to bleed. Our bedraggled troupe of would-be clowns was not monitored in any way. While I and several others in our group, including a girl dressed as Raggedy Ann, waited for someone to intercept Mr. Baby and say, "That's enough," he continued to crawl like a huge slug across the toothbrush-like carpet until he began leaving a trail of blood behind him on the pale green surface.

"I think you should stop now," I said to him, but he stared up at me, his big baby eyes overflowing with tears, but filled also with pain and ecstasy.

"A dream come true," he repeated over and over as he crawled beside me, a fine spray of blood spattering on my plush feet.

A man wearing a moth-eaten satyr's head and a canvas raincoat stopped along the third-base line, and, flinging open the coat, exposed himself to six or seven thousand fans. The fans booed his efforts until eventually a couple of security guards appeared and escorted him off the field.

The judges were Miss Elliott Bay, a toothy girl in a blue and white bathing suit and a Mariners cap, and a disc jockey named Dr. Slug, whose stock in trade was slime jokes: "What is a slug's favorite song?" Slime on My Hands. "What is a slug's favorite novel?" *Slime and Punishment.* "Who is a slug's favorite playwright?" Neil Slimon. "What creeps slowly toward the new year?" Father Slime.

The judges chose seven of us and lined us up at second base, where the baseball fans were to choose a winner by means of applause. There were prizes to be won, with the final winner getting to be Seattle mascot for one game.

The applause set three of us apart: me, the Space Needle, and something called the Kitsap Carp, a person of indeterminate sex dressed in a fish costume. A large and vocal group of fans kept chanting, "We want the flasher," and I couldn't help but feel that he was the people's choice, for after all, what is it we value most but when people expose themselves unashamedly to us, though we also fear them for it?

I could tell that in spite of my alabaster feathers, my endearing pink eyes as big as sunflowers, and the indigo and violet shading along my neck and wings, that I was not going to win the contest unless I did something spectacular. In the first round the Space Needle had received more applause.

"Well, ladies and gentlemen, we've narrowed it down to three finalists," intoned Dr. Slug, who was short, with slick hair, piano legs, and an obscenely protruding belly.

He then proceeded to introduce each of us briefly. The Kitsap Carp turned out to be a woman with a thick accent who said her ambition in life was to make people happy and bring peace to the world. The Space Needle, a professor of economics at Western Washington State University, was active in Big Brothers and a currently fashionable branch of evangelical Christianity. The only all-American thing he hadn't done was give birth.

When my turn came, I pantomimed an inability to speak. I spread my wings to their full span, ruffled my neck feathers, and did a jigging, spinning dance from second base to the pitcher's mound. Flapping my wings, but being careful not to give the impression of actual flight, I ran toward the backstop and leapt—actually I flew about eight feet in the air—and clutched onto the wire mesh. I scaled the screen gracefully, all the time making birdlike whirring sounds. The fans at first cheered my exploits, then became silent as they do in the presence of a daring circus act. I climbed the screen until I could reach a guy wire and proceeded up it claw over claw—or at least I hoped I gave that impression, for I was actually flying. I climbed up to the concrete roof of the Kingdome. Giving my loud natural call, "*Uuvvzzz*," I leapt from the guy wire to another that controlled the raising and lowering of the baseball scoreboard. The crowd gasped. From there I jumped and, with one flap of my delicate wings, was able to grasp onto a piece of the red, white, and blue bunting that hung down from the compression ring at the top of the Dome.

I then made a complete circle, swinging from one piece of bunting to the next. I must have looked like a feathered monkey. I crowed loudly as the fans cheered and applauded. The circle finished, I leapt back to the guy wire and descended, claw over claw again.

When the applause was monitored I was virtually a unanimous winner.

"Ladies and gentlemen, I give you Mike Street, the Seattle Albatross," cried Dr. Slug.

It was a woman who was my downfall, or perhaps I should say it was her downfall that led to my downfall. Her name was Virginia and she was much more persistent than most of the young women who flaunted themselves and fluttered after me like butterflies.

She was waiting for me after a game, in the passageway behind the Mariners dugout. How she got there was anybody's guess. She wanted to take me to dinner. She flattered me. Residents of my planet are all susceptible to flattery. I finally agreed. Without asking, she chose a fish restaurant, pointing it out as one of the many things we had in common. And we did have common interests. What she had that interested me was intelligence, something one seldom encounters in players, fans, or mascot groupies.

"Why do you like me?" I asked.

"You're mysterious," she said.

"So are a lot of people who don't hide in albatross costumes. What if I took this off and you found me horribly disfigured? What if I was really an alien with skin the color of chianti, several eyes, and a tail?"

"You have a cute lisp, Mike," she said. "Your trouble is you're just shy. I can tell. I can also tell when someone is very lonely."

She was certainly right about that. I was desperately lonely. And she was extremely pretty. She was twenty-two years old, with blue eyes and a beautiful tan, and she also wore an exotic perfume that made my heart beat like a motorcycle engine. Her dress smelled freshly ironed, and she wore tiny white shoes with her red toenails peeping out.

It had been three months since I had heard from my home planet. After my first dinner with Virginia, I went against rules and contacted them. Someone unknown to me answered. The line was full of static, like a million throat clearings.

"We've updated our equipment," the voice told me. "Your communicator is obsolete."

"Then bring me home."

"There seems to be a problem," the voice went on. "Someone is working on it. We'll be in touch in due course." I demanded to speak with my previous contact. "He is no longer with us." I asked for any of the joint chiefs of staff, for the prime minister. "All gone," I was informed. "Retired or replaced. Space exploration is not a priority with this administration."

"Then send me a female for company," I pleaded. "I could live here if I had a partner. We could work as a team—"

"Impossible," replied the voice. "We suggest you attune yourself to interstellar living for the foreseeable future. And, incidentally, don't call us, we'll call you."

I had no sooner hidden the communicator among the sprouting potatoes when Virginia came tapping at my door. I was charmed by her. She talked in bright bursts of sound like splashes of bird song. I didn't let her inside, but I took her out for ice cream. All the time we were together I was rationalizing that since she was sweet and intelligent I might be able to forget for once that I was an alien. I mean, our method of sexual gratification is not *that* different from what is engaged in here on Earth.

We had dinner for three consecutive nights. Virginia was a public relations trainee for Boeing. She wrote optimistic press releases in what she called "media-oriented language."

Each night, at the end of our date, I clowned a bit in the lobby of her apartment building, bowed, hugged her in a friendly, brotherly way, pecked her cheek, and bolted out the door before I lost control of myself.

"Can we go back to your place?" Virginia asked after our fourth date. We had been interrupted about ten times during our meal as I signed menus, napkins, scraps of paper, and children. Adults produced cameras from unlikely places on their bodies and then thrust reluctant older children into my arms for picture-taking purposes.

I should have turned Virginia's request aside with a joke, but I didn't. I was thinking with my reproductive system.

"Rather than my apartment, why don't I show you my special place? I'd like you to see the very top of the Kingdome at night."

Though I kept the apartment for show, I actually had lived for four years in the compression ring at the top of the Kingdome. It was a perfect aerie for a large, solitary bird.

Inside the Kingdome, two dim night-lights burned.

"Once your eyes become accustomed, it's like deep twilight," I said to Virginia.

"You mean we're going up there?" she said, after I pointed to the compression circle at the top.

"It's two hundred and fifty feet," I said. "But my nest is there. I've never told another soul about this, Virginia."

She laughed prettily.

"You're crazy," she said. "I can't wait to see what you really look like."

"Then let's not wait," I said.

"How do we get up there? Is there an elevator?"

"There is a traditional mechanical way to get there. But let's not be traditional." I scooped her up in my wings. "Hang on tightly to my neck," I said. I ran a few steps to gain momentum, then my long blue wings flapped like blankets snapping in a strong wind, and we soared toward the roof of the Kingdome. I landed with great agility, not even ruffling Virginia's hair.

"How did you do that?" Virginia squealed.

"It's all done with mirrors," I said.

"Wow!" She looked about at my few possessions. Unfortunately, there was rather a mess below the pole I used as my roost. I hadn't been expecting company.

"God, it looks like a giant bird lives here," said Virginia, and then the significance of what she had said struck her. She stared at me with a new curiosity, a curiosity mixed with fear.

"I was hoping you'd roost with me," I said, knowing as the words escaped how strange and futile I must have sounded. Virginia stared searchingly at me a moment longer; her expression changed; she stepped back two steps and screamed. Her voice reverberated eerily through the empty dome, which frightened her even more.

I could see that she would be in serious danger if she stepped any farther back. I lunged at her. She, of course, misinterpreted my movement as one of hostility. An instant later, she was hurtling toward the baseball field, her death scream a small, sad sound in the heavy air.

I launched myself after her, but there was no way I could catch up with her falling form. When I reached the artificial turf, she lay dead near second base, blood seeping outward from her grotesquely sprawled corpse.

I knew at once that I couldn't risk involvement. Panic-stricken, I ran, not even thinking that my secret living quarters would surely be discovered, that Virginia's small, red-and-white striped handbag was lying on the floor of the aerie.

At first, the police were very nice, cordial even. I was contacted routinely about Virginia's death. But I am a very bad criminal, or at least I am very bad at concealing information. I didn't have a *story*.

"Do you know Virginia Knowlton?" they asked. "We were good friends," I said.

The police had the Kingdome maintenance people take them to the top of the dome. There they found my roost, the evidence that I used the space as living quarters. But for some reason the connection was not made. Police deal with cold facts; the fantastical seldom crosses their mind.

Virginia's death was given sensational treatment by the press. I was dogged by reporters, radio and television crews. It is very difficult for someone as colorfully unique as I to hide, anywhere.

I maintained silence. I shrugged my shoulders at all questions. I pecked at microphones and licked the lenses of probing TV cameras.

At my apartment, I went against orders and contacted my home planet. If anything, the static was more tenacious than ever. I explained my predicament.

"Carry on as usual," came the reply.

"Bring me home," I wailed.

"We find your situation interesting," the garbled voice replied. "We will study your request and get back to you in good time. Please don't try to contact us again. We are changing frequencies to something beyond the capabilities of your communicator."

I was interviewed a number of times at police headquarters. They were very nice. I think they believed me. I admitted to taking Virginia up to see the top of the Kingdome. She was overcome by the height, fell before I could save her. I panicked and ran.

Since there were no other marks or wounds on her body, and since we were known to be good friends, the police finally announced they were closing the case, marking it as "death by misadventure."

"There is one thing," a detective named Art said to me. "You'll have to let us have a look at the real you. You know, just in case you fought or something. Wouldn't want to find you with scratches all over your body."

"But this is the real me," I said plaintively.

"It's only a formality," said the detective. "Please don't give us any trouble at this late date, Mr. Street."

"I can't."

"You mean won't."

"I never let anyone see me. I carry pictures . . ." I fumbled for the ID I kept taped out of sight.

"Sorry," said Art, and he and his partner moved toward me. His partner grabbed me firmly by the shoulders.

"Just take off the top of the costume and let us see your head. We promise not to tell anyone what you look like," said the big detective.

He grabbed my neck and began looking for snaps or buttons.

"Does this thing screw on and off?" I could tell by the tone of his voice as he said it that he was beginning to be suspicious.

"No! No!" I shrieked, and slipped from his grasp, his hands sliding down my feathers as though I were greased. The door to the room was closed, and Art stood, arms folded across his chest, blocking any escape.

The window. I reverted entirely to my natural state. I flew against the window, hard. I chittered and squawked. I kicked off one of my plush boots; the talons on my feet, which had never been unfurled in my five years on Earth, slashed the air, striking anything within their reach.

A detective clutched at one of my legs. I struck, ripping away a lapel from his jacket and gashing his chest with the same movement. Blood appeared, bright as neon. But I could not escape. The big detective broke one of my long wings with a karate blow. I crashed, hissing and screaming, to the floor.

Both men had guns trained on me. I remained still.

"I think we'd better call the chief in on this," the big one said.

The chief called the FBI. The FBI called the Pentagon.

I am being held in an isolation cell, somewhere inside Fort Lewis military base outside of Tacoma.

Buzz Hinkman is now fielding questions from a collective of reporters. It is interesting to me that the disappearance of a baseball team's mascot should be news. Buzz is smiling and repeating the phrase about my opting for a visible occupation. Buzz is not smart enough to have thought of that himself, and the FBI and military types I have been subjected to the past few days are totally humorless. Perhaps the FBI employs a joke writer.

My wing is healing nicely. I have refused to talk with any of the men in tight suits from the FBI, or the finger-pointing military men with crew cuts, who fire questions at me in a staccato whir.

"We have recovered everything from your apartment," a steely eyed officer told me this morning. "So as not to create a suspicious situation, we hired Allied Van Lines to go in and pack everything. Even had them move it all to an address in San Francisco before we seized it."

He stared at me in silence for a long time, as though expecting a compliment from me for his intelligent behavior.

They obviously have my communicating device, though they haven't mentioned it to me. I'm sure it is sitting on a velvet pillow in some airtight, germ-free, anti-explosive box.

I like to imagine that every other baseball mascot in the nation has been whisked out of his apartment in the dead of night and is, somewhere in the bowels of the Pentagon, being dusted, tested, poked, and prodded. Perhaps right now whole truckfuls of Ronald McDonalds, Mr. Peanuts, and all the characters from *Sesame Street* are being interrogated by a paranoid military. In fact, a few hours ago, one of my interrogators made the word association—Mike Street—*Sesame Street*—smiled cunningly, and slipped out of this heavily locked room.

The interview with Buzz Hinkman is over. The Channel Five news team are all on camera. Tony Ventrella, the sportscaster, is about to deliver his segment of the news, but before he does he produces from under the anchor desk a reasonable likeness of my head, done in plush and papier-mâché.

"Jean and Jeff," he says, "I've been keeping something from you all these years. I'm really the Seattle Albatross." The three of them smile their charming smiles.

"That's quite a confession, Tony," says Jean. "I suppose it's rather like getting an albatross off your neck."

The three of them laugh charming laughter.

"Back in a moment with all the sports," says Tony. Then, as his face fades into a lawn-and-garden fertilizer commercial, he adds, "Good luck, Mike Street, wherever you are."

MOLLY GLOSS
Lambing Season

Molly Gloss writes literary fiction, westerns, and occasionally science fiction. Her novels include *Outside the Gates*, *The Jump-Off Creek*, *The Dazzle of Day*, *Wild Life*, *The Hearts of Horses*, and *Falling from Horses*. Gloss has received the Whiting and James Tiptree, Jr., awards, as well as the Oregon Book Award, the Pacific Northwest Booksellers Award, and the Theodore Sturgeon Memorial Award. Gloss's story "Interlocking Pieces" is reprinted in *The Secret History of Science Fiction*.

"Lambing Season" is a first-contact tale. It involves a simple, hardworking sheepherder and the quiet and ordinary life she leads. The story bears a striking similarity to the works of Clifford D. Simak, but rather than relying on Simak's pastoral charm, Gloss's realism sits clearly next to the worlds of Annie Proulx and Ursula K. Le Guin. This story was first published in *Asimov's Science Fiction* and was nominated for science fiction's Hugo and Nebula awards.

From May to September Delia took the Churro sheep and two dogs and went up on Joe-Johns Mountain to live. She had that country pretty much to herself all summer. Ken Owen sent one of his Mexican hands up every other week with a load of groceries but otherwise she was alone, alone with the sheep and the dogs. She liked the solitude. Liked the silence. Some sheepherders she knew talked a blue streak to the dogs, the rocks, the porcupines, they sang songs and played the radio, read their magazines out loud, but Delia let the silence settle into her and by early summer she had begun to hear the ticking of the dry grasses as a language she could almost translate. The dogs were named Jesus and Alice. "Away to me, Jesus," she said when they were moving the sheep. "Go bye, Alice." From May to September these words spoken in command of the dogs were almost the only times she heard her own voice; that, and when the Mexican brought the groceries, a polite exchange in Spanish about the weather, the health of the dogs, the fecundity of the ewes.

The Churros were a very old breed. The O-Bar Ranch had a federal allotment up on the mountain, which was all rimrock and sparse grasses well suited to the Churros, who were fiercely protective of their lambs and had a long-stapled top coat that could take the weather. They did well on the thin grass of the mountain where other sheep would lose flesh and give up their lambs to the coyotes. The Mexican was an old man. He said he remembered Churros from his childhood in the Oaxaca highlands, the rams with their four horns, two curving up, two down. "*Buen' carne,*" he told Delia. Uncommonly fine meat.

The wind blew out of the southwest in the early part of the season, a wind that smelled of juniper and sage and pollen; in the later months it blew straight from the east, a dry wind smelling of dust and smoke, bringing down showers of parched leaves and seedheads of yarrow and bittercress. Thunderstorms came frequently out of the east, enormous cloudscapes with hearts of livid magenta and glaucous green. At those times, if she was camped on a ridge she'd get out of her bed and walk downhill to find a draw where she could feel safer, but if she was camped in a low place she would stay with the sheep while a war passed over their heads, spectacular jagged flares of lightning, skull-rumbling cannonades of thunder. It was maybe bred into the bones of Churros, a knowledge and a tolerance of mountain weather, for they shifted together and waited out the thunder with surprising composure; they stood forbearingly while rain beat down in hard blinding bursts.

Sheepherding was simple work, although Delia knew some herders who made it hard, dogging the sheep every minute, keeping them in a tight group, moving all the time. She let the sheep herd themselves, do what they wanted, make their own decisions. If the band began to separate she would whistle or yell, and often the strays would turn around and rejoin the main group. Only if they were badly scattered did she send out the dogs. Mostly she just kept an eye on the sheep, made sure they got good feed, that the band didn't split, that they stayed in the boundaries of the O-Bar allotment. She studied the sheep for the language of their bodies, and tried to handle them just as close to their nature as possible. When she put out salt for them, she scattered it on rocks and stumps as if she was hiding Easter eggs, because she saw how they enjoyed the search.

The spring grass made their manure wet, so she kept the wool cut away from the ewes' tail area with a pair of sharp, short-bladed shears. She dosed the sheep with wormer, trimmed their feet, inspected their teeth, treated ewes for mastitis. She combed the burrs from the dogs' coats and inspected them for ticks. *You're such good dogs*, she told them with her hands. *I'm very very proud of you.*

She had some old binoculars, 7 x 32s, and in the long quiet days she watched bands of wild horses miles off in the distance, ragged-looking mares with dorsal stripes and black legs. She read the back issues of the local newspapers, looking in the obits for names she recognized. She read spine-broken paperback novels and played solitaire and scoured the ground for arrowheads and rocks she would later sell to rockhounds. She studied the parched brown grass, which was full of grasshoppers and beetles and crickets and ants. But most of her day was spent just walking. The sheep sometimes bedded quite a ways from her trailer and she had to get out to them before sunrise when the coyotes would make their kills. She was usually up by three or four and walking out to the sheep in darkness. Sometimes she returned to the camp for lunch, but always she was out with the sheep again until sundown when the coyotes were likely to return, and then she walked home after dark to water and feed the dogs, eat supper, climb into bed.

In her first years on Joe-Johns she had often walked three or four miles away from the band just to see what was over a hill, or to study the intricate architecture of a sheepherder's monument. Stacking up flat stones in the form of an obelisk was a common herder's pastime, their monuments all over that sheep country, and though Delia had never felt an impulse to start one herself, she admired the ones other people had built. She sometimes walked miles out of her way just to look at a rockpile up close.

She had a mental map of the allotment, divided into ten pastures. Every few days, when the sheep had moved on to a new pasture, she moved her camp. She towed the trailer with an old Dodge pickup, over the rocks and creekbeds, the sloughs and dry meadows to the new place. For a while afterward, after the engine was shut off and while the heavy old body of the truck was settling onto its tires, she would be deaf, her head filled with a dull roaring white noise.

She had about eight hundred ewes, as well as their lambs, many of them twins or triplets. The ferocity of the Churro ewes in defending their offspring was sometimes a problem for the dogs, but in the balance of things she knew it kept her losses small. Many coyotes lived on Joe-Johns, and sometimes a cougar or bear would come up from the salt-pan desert on the north side of the mountain, looking for better country to own. These animals considered the sheep to be fair game, which Delia understood to be their right; and also her right, hers and the dogs, to take the side of the sheep. Sheep were smarter than people commonly believed and the Churros smarter than other sheep she had tended, but by mid-summer the coyotes had passed the word among themselves, *buen' carne*, and Delia and the dogs then had a job of work, keeping the sheep out of harm's way.

She carried a .32 caliber Colt pistol in an old-fashioned holster worn on her belt. *If you're a coyot' you'd better be careful of this woman*, she said with her body, with the way she stood and the way she walked when she was wearing the pistol. That gun and holster had once belonged to her mother's mother, a woman who had come west on her own and homesteaded for a while, down in the Sprague River Canyon. Delia's grandmother had liked to tell the story: how a concerned neighbor, a bachelor with an interest in marriageable females, had pressed the gun upon her, back when the Klamaths were at war with the army of General Joel Palmer; and how she never had used it for anything but shooting rabbits.

In July a coyote killed a lamb while Delia was camped no more than two hundred feet away from the bedded sheep. It was dusk and she was sitting on the steps of the trailer reading a two-gun western, leaning close over the pages in the failing light, and the dogs were dozing at her feet. She heard the small sound, a strange high faint squeal she did not recognize and then did recognize, and she jumped up and fumbled for the gun, yelling at the coyote, at the dogs, her yell startling the entire band to its feet but the ewes making their charge too late, Delia firing too late, and none of it doing any good beyond a release of fear and anger.

A lion might well have taken the lamb entire; she had known of lion kills where the only evidence was blood on the grass and a dribble of entrails in the beam of a flashlight. But a coyote is small and will kill with a bite to the throat and then perhaps eat just the liver and heart, though a mother coyote will take all she can carry in her stomach, bolt it down and carry it home to her pups. Delia's grandmother's pistol had scared this one off before it could even take a bite, and the lamb was twitching and whole on the grass, bleeding only from its neck. The mother ewe stood over it, crying in a distraught and pitiful way, but there was nothing to be done, and in a few minutes the lamb was dead.

There wasn't much point in chasing after the coyote, and anyway the whole band was now a skittish jumble of anxiety and confusion; it was hours before the mother ewe gave up her grieving, before Delia and the dogs had the band calm and bedded down again, almost midnight. By then the dead lamb had stiffened on the ground and she dragged it over by the truck and skinned it and let the dogs have the meat, which went against her nature but was about the only way to keep the coyote from coming back for the carcass.

While the dogs worked on the lamb, she stood with both hands pressed to her tired back looking out at the sheep, the mottled pattern of their whiteness almost opalescent across the black landscape, and the stars thick and bright above the faint outline of the rock ridges, stood there a moment before turning toward the trailer, toward bed, and afterward she would think how the coyote and the sorrowing ewe and the dark of the July moon and the kink in her back, how all of that came together and was the reason she was standing there watching the sky, was the reason she saw the brief, brilliantly green flash in the southwest and then the sulfur-yellow streak breaking across the night, southwest to due west on a descending arc onto Lame Man Bench. It was a broad bright ribbon, rainbow-wide, a ocherous contrail. It was not a meteor, she had seen hundreds of meteors. She stood and looked at it.

Things to do with the sky, with distance, you could lose perspective, it was hard to judge even a lightning strike, whether it had touched down on a particular hill or the next hill or the valley between. So she knew this thing falling out of the sky might have come down miles to the west of Lame Man, not onto Lame Man at all, which was two miles away, at least two miles, and getting there would be all ridges and rocks, no way to cover the ground in the truck. She thought about it. She had moved camp earlier in the day, which was always troublesome work, and it had been a blistering hot day, and now the excitement with the coyote. She was very tired, the tiredness like a weight against her breastbone. She didn't know what this thing was, falling out of the sky. Maybe if she walked over there she would find just a dead satellite or a broken weather balloon and not dead or broken people. The contrail thinned slowly while she stood there looking at it, became a wide streak of yellowy cloud against the blackness, with the field of stars glimmering dimly behind it.

After a while she went into the truck and got a water bottle and filled it and also took the first aid kit out of the trailer and a couple of spare batteries for the flashlight and a handful of extra cartridges for the pistol and stuffed these things into a backpack and looped her arms into the straps and started up the rise away from the dark camp, the bedded sheep. The dogs left off their gnawing of the dead lamb and trailed her anxiously, wanting to follow, or not wanting her to leave the sheep. "Stay by," she said to them sharply, and they went back and stood with the band and watched her go. *That coyot', he's done with us tonight*: This is what she told the dogs with her body, walking away, and she believed it was probably true.

Now that she'd decided to go, she walked fast. This was her sixth year on the mountain and by this time she knew the country pretty well. She didn't use the flashlight. Without it, she became accustomed to the starlit darkness, able to see the stones and pick out a path. The air was cool but full of the smell of heat rising off the rocks and the parched earth. She heard nothing but her own breathing and the gritting of her boots on the pebbly dirt. A little owl circled once in silence and then went off toward a line of cottonwood trees standing in black silhouette to the northeast.

Lame Man Bench was a great upthrust block of basalt grown over with scraggly juniper forest. As she climbed among the trees the smell of something like ozone or sulfur grew very strong, and the air became thick, burdened with dust. Threads of the yellow contrail hung in the limbs of the trees. She went on across the top of the bench and onto slabs of shelving rock that gave a view to the west. Down in the steep-sided draw below her there was a big wing-shaped piece of metal resting on the ground, which she at first thought had been torn from an airplane, but then realized was a whole thing, not broken, and she quit looking for the rest of the wreckage. She squatted down and looked at it. Yellow dust settled slowly out of the sky, pollinating her hair, her shoulders, the toes of her boots, faintly dulling the oily black shine of the wing, the thing shaped like a wing.

While she was squatting there looking down at it, something came out from the sloped underside of it, a coyote she thought at first, and then it wasn't a coyote but a dog built like a greyhound or a whippet, deep-chested, long legged, very light-boned and frail looking. She waited for somebody else, a man, to crawl out after his dog, but nobody did. The dog squatted to pee and then moved off a short distance and sat on its haunches and considered things. Delia considered, too. She considered that the dog might have been sent up alone. The Russians had sent up a dog in their little Sputnik, she remembered. She considered that a skinny almost hairless dog with frail bones would be dead in short order if left alone in this country. And she considered that there might be a man inside the wing, dead or too hurt to climb out. She thought how much trouble it would be, getting down this steep rock bluff in the darkness to rescue a useless dog and a dead man.

After a while she stood and started picking her way into the draw. The dog by this time was smelling the ground, making a slow and careful circuit around the black wing. Delia kept expecting the dog to look up and bark, but it went on with its intent inspection of the ground as if it was stone deaf, as if Delia's boots making a racket on the loose gravel was not an announcement that someone was coming down. She thought of the old Dodge truck, how it always left her ears ringing, and wondered if maybe it was the same with this dog and its wing-shaped Sputnik, although the wing had fallen soundless across the sky.

When she had come about halfway down the hill she lost footing and slid down six or eight feet before she got her heels dug in and found a handful of willow scrub to hang onto. A glimpse of this movement—rocks sliding to the bottom, or the dust she raised—must have startled the dog, for it leaped backward suddenly and then reared up. They looked at each other in silence, Delia and the dog, Delia standing leaning into the steep slope a dozen yards above the bottom of the draw, and the dog standing next to the Sputnik, standing all the way up on its hind legs like a bear or a man and no longer seeming to be a dog, but a person with a long narrow muzzle and a narrow chest, turned-out knees, delicate dog-like feet. Its genitals were more cat-like than dog, a male set but very small and neat and contained. Dog's eyes, though, dark and small and shining below an anxious brow, so that she was reminded of Jesus and Alice, the way they had looked at her when she had left them alone with the sheep. She had years of acquaintance with dogs and she knew enough to look away, break off her stare. Also, after a moment, she remembered the old pistol and holster at her belt. In cowboy pictures, a man would unbuckle his gunbelt and let it down on the ground as a gesture of peaceful intent, but it seemed to her this might only bring attention to the gun, to the true intent of a gun, which is always killing. *This woman is nobody at all to be scared of,* she told the dog with her body, standing very still along the steep hillside, holding onto the scrub willow with her hands, looking vaguely to the left of him where the smooth curve of the wing rose up and gathered a veneer of yellow dust.

The dog, the dog person, opened his jaws and yawned the way a dog will do to relieve nervousness, and then they were both silent and still for a minute. When finally he turned and stepped toward the wing, it was an unexpected, delicate movement, exactly the way a ballet dancer steps along on his toes, knees turned out, lifting his long thin legs; and then he dropped down on all fours and seemed to become almost a dog again. He went back to his business of smelling the ground intently, though every little while he looked up to see if Delia was still standing along the rock slope. It was a steep place to stand. When her knees finally gave out, she sat down very carefully where she was, which didn't spook him. He had become used to her by then, and his brief, sliding glance just said, *That woman up there is nobody at all to be scared of.*

What he was after, or wanting to know, was a mystery to her. She kept expecting him to gather up rocks, like all those men who'd gone to the moon, but he only smelled the ground, making a wide slow circuit around the wing the way Alice always circled round the trailer every morning, nose down, reading the dirt like a book. And when he seemed satisfied with what he'd learned, he stood up again and looked back at Delia, a last look delivered across his shoulder before he dropped down and disappeared under the edge of the wing, a grave and inquiring look, the kind of look a dog or a man will give you before going off on his own business, a look that says, *You be okay if I go?* If he had been a dog, and if Delia had been close enough to do it, she'd have scratched the smooth head, felt the hard bone beneath, moved her hands around the soft ears. *Sure, okay, you go on now, Mr. Dog:* This is what she would have said with her hands. Then he crawled into the darkness under the slope of the wing, where she figured there must be a door, a hatch letting into the body of the machine, and after a while he flew off into the dark of the July moon.

In the weeks afterward, on nights when the moon had set or hadn't yet risen, she looked for the flash and streak of something breaking across the darkness out of the southwest. She saw him come and go to that draw on the west side of Lame Man Bench twice more in the first month. Both times, she left her grandmother's gun in the trailer and walked over there and sat in the dark on the rock slab above the draw and watched him for a couple of hours. He may have been waiting for her, or he knew her smell, because both times he reared up and looked at her just about as soon as she sat down. But then he went on with his business. *That woman is nobody to be scared of,* he said with his body, with the way he went on smelling the ground, widening his circle and widening it, sometimes taking a clod or a sprig into his mouth and tasting it, the way a mild-mannered dog will do when he's investigating something and not paying any attention to the person he's with.

Delia had about decided that the draw behind Lame Man Bench was one of his regular stops, like the ten campsites she used over and over again when she was herding on Joe-Johns Mountain; but after those three times in the first month she didn't see him again.

At the end of September she brought the sheep down to the O-Bar. After the lambs had been shipped out she took her band of dry ewes over onto the Nelson prairie for the fall, and in mid-November when the snow had settled in, she brought them to the feed lots. That was all the work the ranch had for her until lambing season. Jesus and Alice belonged to the O-Bar. They stood in the yard and watched her go.

In town she rented the same room as the year before, and, as before, spent most of a year's wages on getting drunk and standing other herders to rounds of drink. She gave up looking into the sky.

In March she went back out to the ranch. In bitter weather they built jugs and mothering-up pens, and trucked the pregnant ewes from Green, where they'd been feeding on wheat stubble. Some ewes lambed in the trailer on the way in, and after every haul there was a surge of lambs born. Delia had the night shift, where she was paired with Roy Joyce, a fellow who raised sugar beets over in the valley and came out for the lambing season every year. In the black, freezing-cold middle of the night, eight and ten ewes would be lambing at a time. Triplets, twins, big singles, a few quads, ewes with lambs born dead, ewes too sick or confused to mother. She and Roy would skin a dead lamb and feed the carcass to the ranch dogs and wrap the fleece around a bummer lamb, which was intended to fool the bereaved ewe into taking the orphan as her own, and sometimes it worked that way. All the mothering-up pens swiftly filled, and the jugs filled, and still some ewes with new lambs stood out in the cold field waiting for a room to open up.

You couldn't pull the stuck lambs with gloves on, you had to reach into the womb with your fingers to turn the lamb, or tie cord around the feet, or grasp the feet bare-handed, so Delia's hands were always cold and wet, then cracked and bleeding. The ranch had brought in some old converted school buses to house the lambing crew, and she would fall into a bunk at daybreak and then not be able to sleep, shivering in the unheated bus with the gray daylight pouring in the windows and the endless daytime clamor out at the lambing sheds. All the lambers had sore throats, colds, nagging coughs. Roy Joyce looked like hell, deep bags as blue as bruises under his eyes, and Delia figured she looked about the same, though she hadn't seen a mirror, not even to draw a brush through her hair, since the start of the season.

By the end of the second week, only a handful of ewes hadn't lambed. The nights became quieter. The weather cleared, and the thin skiff of snow melted off the grass. On the dark of the moon, Delia was standing outside the mothering-up pens drinking coffee from a thermos. She put her head back and held the warmth of the coffee in her mouth a moment, and as she was swallowing it down, lowering her chin, she caught the tail end of a green flash and a thin yellow line breaking across the sky, so far off anybody else would have thought it was a meteor, but it was bright, and dropping from southwest to due west, maybe right onto Lame Man Bench. She stood and looked at it. She was so very goddamned tired and had a sore throat that wouldn't clear and she could barely get her fingers to fold around the thermos, they were so split and tender.

She told Roy she felt sick as a horse, and did he think he could handle things if she drove herself into town to the Urgent Care clinic, and she took one of the ranch trucks and drove up the road a short way and then turned onto the rutted track that went up to Joe-Johns.

The night was utterly clear and you could see things a long way off. She was still an hour's drive from the Churros' summer range when she began to see a yellow-orange glimmer behind the black ridgeline, a faint nimbus like the ones that marked distant range fires on summer nights.

She had to leave the truck at the bottom of the bench and climb up the last mile or so on foot, had to get a flashlight out of the glove box and try to find an uphill path with it because the fluttery reddish light show was finished by then, and a thick pall of smoke overcast the sky and blotted out the stars. Her eyes itched and burned, and tears ran from them, but the smoke calmed her sore throat. She went up slowly, breathing through her mouth.

The wing had burned a skid path through the scraggly junipers along the top of the bench and had come apart into about a hundred pieces. She wandered through the burnt trees and the scattered wreckage, shining her flashlight into the smoky darkness, not expecting to find what she was looking for, but there he was, lying apart from the scattered pieces of metal, out on the smooth slab rock at the edge of the draw. He was panting shallowly and his close coat of short brown hair was matted with blood. He lay in such a way that she immediately knew his back was broken. When he saw Delia coming up, his brow furrowed with worry. A sick or a wounded dog will bite, she knew that, but she squatted next to him. *It's just me*, she told him, by shining the light not in his face but in hers. Then she spoke to him. "Okay," she said. "I'm here now," without thinking too much about what the words meant, or whether they meant anything at all, and she didn't remember until afterward that he was very likely deaf anyway. He sighed and shifted his look from her to the middle distance, where she supposed he was focused on approaching death.

Near at hand, he didn't resemble a dog all that much, only in the long shape of his head, the folded-over ears, the round darkness of his eyes. He lay on the ground flat on his side like a dog that's been run over and is dying by the side of the road, but a man will lay like that too when he's dying. He had small fingered nail-less hands where a dog would have had toes and front feet. Delia offered him a sip from her water bottle but he didn't seem to want it, so she just sat with him quietly, holding one of his hands, which was smooth as lambskin against the cracked and roughened flesh of her palm. The batteries in the flashlight gave out, and sitting there in the cold darkness she found his head and stroked it, moving her sore fingers lightly over the bone of his skull, and around the soft ears, the loose jowls. Maybe it wasn't any particular comfort to him but she was comforted by doing it. *Sure, okay, you can go on.*

She heard him sigh, and then sigh again, and each time wondered if it would turn out to be his death. She had used to wonder what a coyote, or especially a dog, would make of this doggish man, and now while she was listening, waiting to hear if he would breathe again, she began to wish she'd brought Alice or Jesus with her, though not out of that old curiosity. When her husband had died years before, at the very moment he took his last breath, the dog she'd had then had barked wildly and raced back and forth from the front to the rear door of the house as if he'd heard or seen something invisible to her. People said it was her husband's soul going out the door or his angel coming in. She didn't know what it was the dog had seen or heard or smelled, but she wished she knew. And now she wished she had a dog with her to bear witness.

She went on petting him even after he had died, after she was sure he was dead, went on petting him until his body was cool, and then she got up stiffly from the bloody ground and gathered rocks and piled them onto him, a couple of feet high so he wouldn't be found or dug up. She didn't know what to do about the wreckage, so she didn't do anything with it at all.

In May, when she brought the Churro sheep back to Joe-Johns Mountain, the pieces of the wrecked wing had already eroded, were small and smooth-edged like the bits of sea glass you find on a beach, and she figured this must be what it was meant to do: to break apart into pieces too small for anybody to notice, and then to quickly wear away. But the stones she'd piled over his body seemed like the start of something, so she began the slow work of raising them higher into a sheepherder's monument. She gathered up all the smooth eroded bits of wing, too, and laid them in a series of widening circles around the base of the monument. She went on piling up stones through the summer and into September until it reached fifteen feet. Mornings, standing with the sheep miles away, she would look for it through the binoculars and think about ways to raise it higher, and she would wonder what was buried under all the other monuments sheepherders had raised in that country. At night she studied the sky, but nobody came for him.

In November when she finished with the sheep and went into town, she asked around and found a guy who knew about stargazing and telescopes.

He loaned her some books and sent her to a certain pawnshop, and she gave most of a year's wages for a 14 x 75 telescope with a reflective lens. On clear, moonless nights she met the astronomy guy out at the Little League baseball field and she sat on a fold-up canvas stool with her eye against the telescope's finder while he told her what she was seeing: Jupiter's moons, the Pelican Nebula, the Andromeda Galaxy. The telescope had a tripod mount, and he showed her how to make a little jerry-built device so she could mount her old 7 x 32 binoculars on the tripod too. She used the binoculars for their wider view of star clusters and small constellations. She was indifferent to most discomforts, could sit quietly in one position for hours at a time, teeth rattling with the cold, staring into the immense vault of the sky until she became numb and stiff, barely able to stand and walk back home. Astronomy, she discovered, was a work of patience, but the sheep had taught her patience, or it was already in her nature before she ever took up with them.

AMIRI BARAKA

Conrad Loomis & the Clothes Ray

Amiri Baraka (1934–2014), who also wrote as LeRoi Jones, is a famous African American poet, dramatist, music critic, and political activist with a career that spanned more than fifty years. Baraka is the author of more than twenty-five books, including three volumes of fiction, as well as numerous plays. He studied philosophy and religion at Columbia University, worked with the Black Mountain Poets and the New York School Poets, and was a prominent voice of the Beat Generation. Throughout his career, Baraka incited controversy and received critical acclaim. His many honors included the James Weldon Johnson Medal for contributions to the arts as well as the American Academy of Arts & Letters and Langston Hughes awards, and he was a professor emeritus at the State University of New York at Stony Brook. Baraka's short tenure as the Poet Laureate of New Jersey was so controversial that the position was later abolished.

"Conrad Loomis & the Clothes Ray" is one of several stories Baraka published about the wild inventions of a black scientist. These stories were collected in his PEN Award–winning collection *Tales of the Out & the Gone.*

Loomis was an old friend of mine. I kept in touch with him more or less regularly, but every few months he would vanish, so to speak. At first, I thought he would hide out when he hit the picket. He did do that a couple of times. He'd hit the number, get the cash, and then get away from everybody and spend it all. We used to tease him about this. And he hit a few times. But that's because he'd spend so much money on that stuff. He might spend a hundred dollars a week trying to hit the picket. So when he did, he was still in the red, because he spent so much all the time.

Conrad was also a chemist—at least he was in college. But I thought he'd flunked out of chemistry. He said that didn't stop him from learning the heavy stuff. He flunked the light stuff because it was boring. That sounded like an *Esquire* magazine article on Einstein, you know? So I just nodded, though I did think it was probably true, at least in Conrad's head.

He had some chemistry-type jobs, paint factories, the mad Delaware Nazis who run DuPont. That kind of stuff. But eventually he would always get bounced for some reason. No, it wasn't "some" reason. It was very specific. Conrad would always be trying to do his own thing during company time. You know that don't get over. Neither did Conrad.

Well, he called me up one night about 2 in the morning and said he hated to disturb me, but he had something which could get us both rich if I came over immediately. If I didn't come over immediately, then he would know that I wasn't really serious and he would get somebody else.

See, that's the kind of trick people put you in. It wasn't the money, but I didn't want to seem like I wasn't interested in Conrad's ultimate concern. But damn, "It's 2 o'clock, Conrad. Why didn't you call me earlier?"

"I hadn't finished. You coming or not?"

See, that's the same kind of stuff people pull on you. "Coming or not? Damn, man. What about tomorrow?"

"Oh, I see. You jiving. That's the trouble with Negroes. They ain't serious about nothing."

"Man, why you call me up in the middle of the f'n night with some tired shit like that? Please, Negro."

"Hey, I just thought that you was serious. Shit, I even thought you was my friend. But—"

"OK, OK." See, that's the kind of stuff people pull. "OK, I'll come over there. But just don't be jiving yourself. Dig? Man call me up in the middle of the night. You think 'cause you up in the middle of the night, you serious?" But he'd already hung up the phone.

Now what I'm about to tell you has been in the papers, but in a very small type and then not the whole story. Actually, all these things are still going on, the whole garbage. Conrad had done something fantastic, but he didn't really know how to handle it. He asked me for my opinion, and I gave it to him. I don't know if I was right or wrong. Conrad disagreed with me and did what he wanted and got busted, or not really busted, but hunted, sort of. Like Salman Rushdie or somebody. But see, that don't mean what I told him was correct either.

Conrad's sitting in the middle of the floor when I come in his spot. He's resting and the door of the joint was open. Yeh, he's asleep in the middle of the floor and got this hair dryer (or that's what it looked like to me) resting on his stomach, like he'd just fell out or something.

"Oh, this mammy-jammy drunk," I was whispering to myself, when he opened his eyes one at a time. He immediately leaped up from the floor, jumping around me like Mick Jagger. At least that's what I told him—we both hate Mick Jagger, the no-dancing, no-singing . . .

"Hey, man. Don't bring up no swine like Mick Jagger on me. I got something. Yes, indeed. And it's perfect that you, my main man, should be on hand to dig it. We both gonna get entirely fantastically awesomely rich."

"Yeh, yeh." See, Conrad has made this statement to me a bunch of times before. What's a bunch? Well, maybe fifty times in the last five years. One time we did get some chump change off a number, but we hadn't made no money off his work. First, because he wouldn't show nobody nothin'—he'd only make vague references to his "work." For a lot of people, that became a joke. "Conrad's work" became a synonym in our crowd for anything you didn't know which was taking up somebody's time.

"Oh, so now you gonna run out 'your work' for me, on the real side? Or is this just another coming attraction?"

"Look, man. You should be glad you're intelligent. Ha ha ha." He broke into that little whiny laugh of his, like radio static organized by mirth. Is that abstract?

"What's so funny?"

"Well, that's it. Really, that's it."

"What's it?"

"Intelligent! See, you're intelligent. No shit. You're a very intelligent brother. But see, I'm outtelligent." He laughs, ditto as before.

"Outtelligent? Yeh, you seem that way to me. You make up that word?"

"Yeh, I made it up. But it existed always since it was in the world, scrambled up in the letters. Plus, I'm sure some other outtelligences dug themselves long before me."

"Outtelligent? What's the difference between . . . Oh, I know. Intelligent deals with the in stuff. Outtelligent deals with the out stuff."

"Exactly, I knew you'd understand." He laughs again. "But see, just like that, understand? Most people can just understand. But I can over and understand at the same time."

Conrad talked like this all the time. It was cool until you became hungry or wanted to dig another scene. And when that idea came to your mind, he'd say almost perfunctorily, *See ya later!* And you'd split.

"OK, brother. Over, under, out instead of in, but what you get me here for? God knows I know you outtelligent and overstanding, but what's up?"

"OK, now look at me."

"I am looking at you. I been looking at you. So what?"

"What do I have on? Describe my clothes."

Conrad was about five-feet-eight or -nine, but he'd sometimes add a few inches depending on who he was talking to. I remember he told some sister he was six feet tall and she said she believed him. I never believed she did though.

But how was he dressed? He was usually in a black sweater and black pants with a black whatever on top. He always looked like he was in something. Like some organized whatever. He never was, to my knowledge. But dig, he was not in the black outfit tonight. "What color is that stuff?"

He had on . . . I don't know what he had on. It was the same kind of stuff, I guess. He still looked like he was in something. But the stuff was expensive-looking. It had a darkness to it. It was black, but had a blue sheen coming out from under it, like . . . I dunno. "What is that?"

"I designed all of this." He wheeled around to let me see. He was sort of snorting inside that outtelligent laugh. "It's out, ain't it?"

"Yeh, it's out. What is it?"

"My clothes. Mine."

"Yeh, but what kind of cloth is it?" It did glow. I reached to touch it and felt a bizarre thing. I felt his skin. When I ran my hand up his arm it felt like he didn't really have anything on, like it was his bare skin. "What in the hell kind of stuff is that? It feels like—"

"Like I don't have anything on!" And this cracked him up. He kept wheeling around laughing. "Yeh, that's it. That's it. That's an intelligent observation. But wait till I hip you. This is some outtelligent jammy, my man, very outtelligent."

"Yeh, I can dig that." It was strange. I touched it again. Like his skin, for real, like he had nothing on. "What is it, Conrad? Will you let me in on the stuff, since you brought me all the way over here?"

"I don't have anything on!" He laughed some more. "You're right, I don't have anything on at all. And because of this, I don't have to wash them. I don't even have to change them if I don't want to." And he kept laughing.

"What are you talking about? You don't have nothing on?" I felt again. That's what it felt like. "Well, will you tell me what the hell you're doing?"

That's when he hoisted this little hair dryer-looking thing in my face. "See this? This is the Clothes Ray. I invented it. I made it up in my mind a long time ago, but it didn't seem really important until a few months ago when I didn't have nothing to wear." Some more laughter.

"OK, OK." He shoved the dryer in my hand. Actually, it looked like some kind of lantern. Like a stage light, a Fresnel or something. "So what's this do?"

"I told you, it's my Clothes Ray. You just turn it on, and bang-o."

"Bang-o, what?"

"Bang-o. You get the kind of clothes you thinking about, whatever you can make up. You can't wear no stuff people are already wearing—that's just technology. This is deeper than that. You see, I can make clothes by altering the light, rearranging the light faster, slower, different wavelengths, angles, different kinds of motion to the rays."

"Yeh?" I didn't know what he was talking about.

"Dig. Everything is, to some degree, a form of light. It's matter in motion—you know that. But it is, in essence, different forms and degrees of illumination."

"Yeh, yeh." What was he saying?

"So I can rearrange the light, and by doing this, recreate it as anything else it has the focus to become. The focus has to be supplied by the creator, the designer."

"Designer? You mean you make clothes out of light?"

"Now you coming." He laughs. "Yeh, now you coming. Yeh, I can make clothes, any kind of clothes out of light, with my Clothes Ray here."

"What?"

"You wanna see? Take off your clothes—that's the best way. I could put some duds on you over those sorry vines you got on, but naked is better, fits better."

"No, I ain't taking my off my clothes. Just do it."

"OK, you gonna be hot and sweaty. But dig."

Now he switched on this light. There was some kind of negligible hum, a flashing, and something sounding like voices coming from inside the thing. "What's that?"

"Oh, that's me speaking to the machine from inside it. I put a CD inside that activates the light transformation by sound. I can alter it if I change my basic design. What kind of clothes you want?"

"Anything?"

"Yeh, but not something somebody already got."

"Why not? That stuff you got on looks like something somebody else got."

"Yeh, but it ain't. Look at this, brother. Shit, you don't know what you talking about."

The form of the clothes—what looked like a simple sweater, shirt, and pants—did look common, but they had that glow I talked about. Like it was made of television.

"OK, I want a leather coat like no leather coat nobody ever had."

"OK, you want an unleather coat. Dig."

He adjusted the "dryer," turned some dials, and my whole body lit up on the outside like a neon sign. And gradually, and not a long time either, I sort of grew a coat around me. It felt like it had the body of leather—the feel—but it was much lighter and I could not really feel a weight to it at all. There was a kind of warmth to it, like when you touch a bulb, but not that hot. But it was something that was on.

"Is this real, or just some kind of illusion?"

"Well, everything is real that exists. But at the same time, since it's in constant motion, turning and twisting, rising and changing, there is a quality of illusion to it. But now, the clothes are not illusory. They exist, except they're made—"

"Of light! Yeh."

Conrad started to laugh and dig his handiwork on me, hopping around to check the coat out. It was a leather-looking coat, but you knew at once it wasn't leather. It was lit up from the inside and fit perfectly, or would have if I had taken off my other clothes.

"Aha, now you want to know everything. Yeh, I dig now."

"Yeh, I want to know everything, but the first thing I want to know is—"

"What I'm gonna do with it?"

"Yeh, what you gonna do with it?" The idea of making clothes for people in some kind of place was obvious. The wealth that could be made—that was also pretty obvious. But there was a monkey in this, a chimpanzee crawling around us shouting stupid things, things that were nevertheless true. A signifying cross-dialogue of us to ourselves, without speaking. Except, "You know, Conrad, everybody ain't gonna be thrilled with this."

"What you mean, won't be thrilled with it?"

"You ever see a picture called *The Man in the White Suit*?"

"Of course. Well, I never saw it, but I read what it was about. Actually, that's what gave me the idea. But that was a long time ago."

"Well, if you had seen the flick, you know that the people who make clothes tried to kill Alec Guinness. They tried to steal his invention, because like yours, it would put them out of business."

"Oh yeh. I read that. You see Mamet's *The Water Engine*?"

"You a Mamet fan?"

"Oh, man. It was on television. But it was OK, shit. That told me what you talking about."

"How you mean?"

"Well, in the Mamet thing, a guy invented an engine that ran on water and they killed him and took it."

The way he said all this should have given me confidence—that he did know what he was getting into—but somehow it didn't, because he seemed to think that he could not be stopped by mere intelligence, since he was "outtelligent." And that sent a cool razor up my back. I didn't think of any foul play or anything, but . . .

"How they gonna bother me? I told you—"

"I know, you outtelligent. But dig, Mr. Out T., is you bulletproof?"

Conrad laughed and cut it off quick like a shot. "Shit, I can be. That ain't no big thing. I could figure that shit out in a hot minute."

"Oh, for Christ's sake, Conrad! Rich people, Upper East Side. They won't let you up there, even if they didn't know the shit you putting down. And if some of those people find out, especially here in New York—the Garment District, remember?—then your ass will really be up against it."

He was listening, but like how you listen to somebody out of politeness who really doesn't know what they're talking about.

"Yeh, you don't believe me. But what about finding some sympathetic organization or country—a Third World country? Best would be a Socialist country like Cuba, North Korea, or even China, despite that the clown running it used to wear a dunce hat."

"What? No, nobody else. Me and you. We'll do it for a couple of years, then vanish. That's all. Move around the world, make billions. Watch."

"It's a great invention, brother. But listen to me, these whatnots will not let you make no billions. They against they own folks other than them making billions. Don't you know that? It ain't really about race—it's about money."

"Yeh, I know that. That's why I know we can get over. Money talks."

"Yeh, money kills too. For money."

"Ah . . ." He waved me off.

"Yeh, remember that brother who was supposed to be the richest Blood in the world? Smith? He supposed to have died suddenly of an aneurism. But then they tried to put out that he got cancer from a cellular phone. They had set fire to his house a few months before. The guy that owned the orange juice company. I don't believe none of that stuff. In fact, I called his daughter and asked her what she thought, and she got pissed off and slammed down the phone."

"I ain't him."

"He ain't him neither, no more."

This set Conrad to laughing. "You gonna help me or not?"

"OK, OK. But we got to move cautiously on this, brother. Not that I don't want to make the big bucks, but I know, and I thought that you did too."

"Know what?"

"I thought you knew where you were, who you were dealing with."

CHRIS TARRY

Topics in Advanced Rocketry

Chris Tarry's debut story collection, *How to Carry Bigfoot Home*, was released last year from Red Hen Press. Tarry is one of New York's most-sought-after bass players and has won four JUNO and a Canadian Independent Music award. His fiction has appeared in the *Literary Review*, *On Spec*, *Grain*, the *G. W. Review*, *PANK*, *Bull Men's Fiction*, *Monkeybicycle*, and elsewhere. In 2011, he was a finalist in *FreeFall* magazine's annual prose and poetry competition, and more recently, his story "Here Be Dragons" was nominated for the Pushcart Prize. Tarry holds an MFA in creative writing from the University of British Columbia. He lives and works in Brooklyn, New York.

"Topics in Advanced Rocketry" takes place in a near future when space travel is on the verge of becoming closer to everyday reality. It first appeared in *LIT Magazine*.

"Ryan," my mother says to me. "Look at this coolant dial, do you think there's something wrong?" She taps the dial with her giant space gloves.

T-minus 4 minutes and 55 seconds.

My family, all four of us, are lying on our backs, strapped into our seats on top of the *Annabel Lee*, the rocket built to carry us into space.

"It's fake, Mom," I say. "You don't have to worry about coolant pressure." And then I leave it at that because I don't feel much like talking.

"Why did they install a coolant pressure dial if we weren't meant to read it?" she says.

"For the pictures!" I yell. "Jesus, Mom. Will you just drop it! The press love pictures."

I look around from the inside of my space helmet. My father, in his orange suit, is asleep in the commander's chair in front of me (they'd given him a sedative). Mom is in the co-pilot's seat. My sister is next to me, tapping out messages on her phone with the use of a stylus she had the engineers build into the tips of her gloves.

The rocket is 350 feet tall. Outside my window, past the concrete launch pad, cornfields stretch off into the distance like giant postage stamps. They've built service roads, and they wind themselves toward the rocket from every direction. As I stare out at the horizon, my mind is on Greg, and I'm wondering if he's okay.

T-minus 4 minutes and 30 seconds.

ManuSpace was one of the handful of companies left to fill the void after NASA's dismantling. "Put a family up there and let the world watch," the CEO was quoted as saying. "And we'll do it all with no training. Like they're catching a bus," he said. But the press had not been kind.

A few in ManuSpace thought it might work. That a stunt like this could put them out in front. Leave UniFlight, StarQuest, and that other one, SunStar Industries, sucking at the teats of million-dollar backers while their rockets sat empty and glistening on launch pads around the country. This was 2019, and according to ManuSpace, being first meant dipping into the pockets of the everyman, or at least, that's what they were hoping. "Make it look easy," they said. "And every Johnny Lunch Box will be lining up for a seat on the next one."

From what I could tell, the engineers were worried. Rob Gunderson in Cockpit Security let me know how dangerous everyone thought it was. "No training and one million pounds of rocket fuel," he said. "You tell me if that sounds safe, kid."

One of the reporters at our press conference the day before launch asked, "Since when does a fourteen-year-old girl and a seventeen-year-old boy know anything about guidance systems and re-entry angles?"

"Since you don't know my sister!" I said into the microphone in front of me, slamming my fist on the table as I said it. I hadn't had the best week. The scientist sitting next to me gave me this look like, *What's up with him?* "Have you ever seen my sister send a text message?" I added, a little quieter into the mic this time. The cameras focused on my sister sitting near the end of the press-conference table texting, her thumbs like two birds pecking at high speed; she was laughing to herself as she typed.

"What?" she said to the room of reporters as she looked up. The cameras caught her with that look on her face she gets when she's confused. That was the picture they ran in the paper the next day.

T-minus 4 minutes.

"You'd think if they didn't want us reading dials, they wouldn't put in dials," my mother says. "Roger, will you wake up! Are you hearing me about this dial thing! No one said there'd be dials."

"I'm up, I'm up," Dad says.

My sister goes, "Mom! Brian Henderson texted that he's watching us on TV." My sister is all helmet and space suit, her skinny teenage body lost inside a tangle of orange fabric and monitoring equipment.

T-minus 3 minutes and 45 seconds.

At seventeen years old, I am pathetically average; a little overweight and with a personality that generally goes unnoticed. When it was announced at school that my family had been the one chosen, I heard Jason Langley say, "Who the hell is Ryan Bleckman?" We'd been in the same math class since the third grade. "Fags in space," he said to my girlfriend Jenny when he found out who I was.

"Don't listen to him," she told me. "I love you no matter what."

T-minus 3 minutes and 40 seconds.

My mother looks at my sister. "What did I tell you about Brian Henderson? You are not to be texting that boy!" Ever since Mom found out that ManuSpace was recording all family interaction for posterity's sake, she'd begun talking like this. She'd secured an endorsement deal from Nabisco and they had even put her picture on the front of a cereal box.

"Jesus, Mom," I say to her, "dialogue brought to you by Breakfast Crunch."

"Will everyone just relax," Dad says. "Where are we at anyway? I drifted off at t-minus twenty."

T-minus 3 minutes and 31 seconds.

ManuSpace had looked into everything, even found out about Uncle Lewis and his string of convenience store holdups. "From what we can tell," they said, "you haven't had much contact with him, and that works for us. Press-wise, we mean."

When they asked my mother about her first husband, she told them *she'd* left *him*. Said that he'd become addicted to painkillers and that one night, while she was out working one of her three jobs, he tried to burn down their house using gasoline from the lawn mower. Which was sort of a lie. They'd met in college and apparently (according to my grandmother), he'd come home after an eighteen-hour shift at Rudy's Tire Barn and found her in bed with his best friend, my father. The cops showed up just as he was rolling the lawn mower into the center of the living room and stuffing a rag into the gas tank.

"When *real* love saves you from a man like that," she told the Search Committee, "you can't help but be all kinds of happy." ManuSpace ate it up, even put out a press release. MANUSPACE, TAKING TRUE LOVE TO NEW HEIGHTS.

T-minus 3 minutes and 15 seconds.

My father looks at me from the commander's seat. He says, "Ryan, just think what the kids at school are thinking, huh?"

If he only knew what they really thought of me.

T-minus 3 minutes and 10 seconds.

In the end, we did receive some training. Three weeks of mostly handouts. We weren't allowed inside of the space capsule until launch day. Mom and Dad were fine with that. Between the cocktail parties and endless press conferences, who had the time to worry about space capsules?

The competition had been tough, a total of eight thousand families in all. But they wanted average. They wanted all-American. An ordinary family with normal problems. "Picked a real humdinger in you guys," our Zero Gravity instructor Rick Dupont said to me.

T-minus 3 minutes.

"I swear to God," my mom says to my sister. "If I catch you with that Brian again, you'll be grounded for a month!"

T-minus 2 minutes and 58 seconds.

They built the launch pad in the middle of an Iowa cornfield. Said it might bring the ManuSpace program closer to the people. "Make the public feel like they're a part of something bigger than themselves." But negotiations with the farmer who owned the land hadn't gone well. The *Times* picked up the story and ran with it. ManuSpace had driven down the price of corn by bribing local officials.

"They gave me ten thousand for what I was gonna lose from not havin' the corn," the farmer was quoted as saying. "The crop would have been worth twice that in any other year. I can't feed my family on leftover rocket parts." The rocket parts comment caught on. Pretty soon there were bumper stickers everywhere: Don't Let My Baby Eat O-Rings! and Two Scoops of Payload in Every Bite! The farmer now led a group calling for change and more government regulation of the space industry.

T-minus 2 minutes and 40 seconds.

My sister goes, "Brian loves me!"

The fact that my sister had the lowest GPA at Ridgetown High didn't hit the papers until our third press conference. Space Family Daughter Challenged, the paper said. But the story didn't have legs, the guys in publicity told us. Besides, I knew my sister was smarter than she let on. Tougher too. Stronger than me if the truth were known. "You're the least of our worries," they told my sister. "That goddamned corn farmer, now that guy is going to be the end of us."

T-minus 2 minutes and 28 seconds.

Greg was the farmer's son. We met a few weeks before launch during the IRI (Initial Rocket Inspection). I was on the edge of the field trying to get a picture of the rocket on the launch pad when he walked up behind me and tapped me on the shoulder. "You want me to take one with you in it?" he said.

"Sure," I said, and handed him my camera.

"Back up a little, the top of the rocket is out of the shot."

I walked out into the field and turned my back to the launch pad. I tried putting my hands on my hips and cocking my head in a "poignant moment" kind of way, but that felt too stagey. Then I lowered myself down on one knee and leaned in with my hand on my chin. That didn't feel right either. "Just be yourself," said Greg. So I stood up, stopped sucking in my gut, and put my hands in the pockets of my ManuSpace jumpsuit. "Perfect," he said, and snapped the picture.

"I saw you in the paper," he said as he walked out into the field toward me. "I'm Greg, my dad owns this land." He reached out and shook my hand.

He was about my age and cut like the edges of the Colorado River. He was decked out in rubber boots and a pair of worn jeans caked in mud. His hair was perfect. His lips full and slightly chapped.

"Sorry about your field," I said.

"It's not your fault," he said. "Besides, Dad likes the press."

I asked Greg if he wanted to join us for the rest of the IRI. When we rejoined the group I introduced him to my family. Some of the ManuSpace employees thought it might be a good idea to get a picture of Greg and me together. FARMER AND SPACE FAMILY MAKE NICE, the caption in the paper said the next day. Greg had his arm around my shoulders, the smiles on our faces sparkling.

T-minus 2 minutes and 5 seconds.

My mother tells my sister that she's fourteen years old. Too young to be hanging around boys like Brian Henderson. "Can you back me up here, Roger?" she asks my dad.

"What do you want me to say?" says my father, and I can tell that if my mother wasn't strapped into her seat and wearing thirty pounds of space suit, she would have strangled him.

Then my sister goes, "Well, look at you two, the picture of love," and everyone starts yelling.

T-minus 2 minutes.

Greg knocked on my door two nights before launch. ManuSpace had moved us on-site a few days before, torn down the farmer's chicken coop and erected personal portable housing for everyone directly involved with the launch.

"They paid my dad fifty grand for this part of his land," Greg said. "Not bad for an old rusty coop and field covered in chicken shit." He asked me if I'd ever ridden a tractor.

"No," I said.

He was wearing a checkered jacket, crisp new blue jeans, and cowboy boots. I had on a tank top and a pair of boxer shorts. I had been eating a sleeve of ManuSpace commemorative chocolates before he knocked on the door. As he stood in my doorway, I realized that I had chocolate smeared across the front of my shirt and I turned to hide it.

"I'll get dressed," I said, and invited him in as I grabbed one of my jumpsuits off the floor.

"Ever wear anything other than that jumpsuit?"

"It's all I have," I said. "They made me ten of them."

"I might have something back at the house a little more local." He pushed open my trailer door and a chilly Iowa evening tumbled in. "After you," he said.

T-minus 1 minute and 40 seconds.

"Why can't you be more like your brother?" my mother yells, and my sister screams something into her headset that makes everyone's earpiece distort.

"Jesus," my father says. "How do I turn this thing down?" He starts turning knobs on the dashboard in front of him.

"Like *those* are connected to anything," my mother screams at my father.

My sister starts in again, this time about how she's old enough to make her own decisions. I look again at the cornfields outside my window. The blue sky seems to go on forever and I can see Greg's farmhouse in the distance. I wonder if he's there, watching me from his bedroom window?

T-minus 1 minute and 25 seconds.

As we walked in the darkness, Greg asked me if I was excited about the trip. "I'd sure love to get out of this fuckin' place," he said.

"Why?" I asked, my breath escaping in cold puffs as I talked.

"You ever want to escape?" he said. "Make yourself into the person you really are?"

I must have had this look on my face like I understood, because he reached out and took my hand. "Come on," he said. "This way."

The field looked silver in the moonlight. The grass painted my socks and shoes with dew and the buzz of insects was loud and constant all around us. Greg was in front of me, still holding my hand as he led me across the field toward a single source of light.

The main house was separated from the barn by a gravel compound lit by a single lamp post. There was a basketball court cut into the side of the driveway with a worn hoop hung from a rusty pole.

"I smell barbecue," I said.

"Ribs tonight," said Greg as we stepped from the field into the light. He reached down, picked up a small stone from the driveway, and threw it clear over the barn. He must have thrown it a good fifty yards.

"Good arm," I said.

"You try."

I picked up a rock and threw it hard as I could. It hit the ground before it reached the barn and bounced out of sight.

"You throw like a girl," he said.

"So I've been told," I said.

Greg took my hand again. "Come on, tractor's in the barn."

T-minus 1 minute and 10 seconds.

"Normal like your brother!" my mother says again, and then my sister really loses it.

She goes, "I had sex with Brian when he came to visit last week."

"Jesus Christ," Dad says.

"What!" screams my mother.

Come again, Annabel Lee? says launch control.

"See, they're listening," says my mother.

"I want them to hear!" my sister screams.

"How the hell do I turn off our cockpit feed?" Dad asks.

"You can't, Dad," I say, still staring out the window.

T-minus 60 seconds.

Greg's fingers reached up and unzipped the front of my jumpsuit. We were in the barn, the smell of hay and motor oil was everywhere, and I could hear his parents talking outside.

"Don't worry," he said. "Sound travels a long way around here. They're over at the house watching the barbecue. They can't hear us."

"I have a girlfriend," I said, but he didn't seem to care and continued pulling at my suit.

"You too?" he said, as he reached inside my jumpsuit and slipped his hand below my boxer shorts.

I thought of Jenny and how she was on her way. How she'd called and left a message earlier in the day. "It will be late when I arrive," she said. "My parents are coming too, can you leave our launch passes at the front gate?"

And then Greg knelt down in front of me. "I'm not gay," I said, but that didn't make him stop.

T-minus 40 seconds.

My sister goes, "It's not like he raped me, Mother. We planned it!"

I think I can hear my father crying. And then my mother brings up Jenny. "Your brother's girlfriend, Jenny," she says. "She's such a nice person. Why can't you find a boy like her?"

I imagine Jenny sitting in the stands a few miles away, her ManuSpace launch credentials around her neck. She's probably standing and clapping, rousing the crowd, leading the countdown.

I bet she's made friends with almost everyone around her. She's that kind of person. The kind of girl you marry and spend the rest of your life with.

T-minus 25 seconds.

Everything okay, Annabel Lee? says control. *Your vitals are going crazy over here. Blood pressure and palpitations across the board!* None of us answer.

My mother is staring out her window. My father is in the commander's chair not moving. For a second, I wonder if he's had a heart attack. I think about being a man, about being myself. If only I could be bold like my sister. Then I look at her and she's smiling at me through the glass of her space helmet. I see my mother reach out and tap the fake coolant pressure dial one last time. I see the countdown hit ten seconds.

NINE
I see Greg on his knees in front of me in the barn.
EIGHT
The engines ignite.
SEVEN
I see the farmer appear from nowhere, one hand on Greg's shirt collar as he throws him to the ground, fists flying.
SIX
I think about the boys at school watching the launch on TV.
FIVE
I hear yelling as I run, "Stay away from us, faggot!"
FOUR
My mother looks like a mound of disappointment strapped into her chair.
THREE
I think about the weight of all this in the midst of weightlessness.
TWO
The rocket shakes violently. Reality sets in.
ONE—
And as the *Annabel Lee* clears the launch pad, I pray we never come back. Lost on re-entry. The press having a field day.

KAREN HEULER
The Inner City

Karen Heuler has published more than eighty stories in a variety of literary and science-fiction magazines, including the *Alaska Quarterly Review*, *Clarkesworld*, *Michigan Quarterly Review*, the *Boston Review*, *Lady Churchill's Rosebud Wristlet*, *Weird Tales*, and *Daily Science Fiction*. She has published four novels and two short-story collections, and has received the O. Henry Award and been nominated for the Pushcart Prize, among many others. Heuler lives in New York City with her dog, Philip K. Dick, and her cats, Jane Austen and Charlotte Brontë.

"The Inner City" delves into the workings of an unlisted company whose façade appears to change on a daily basis. It was first published in *Cemetery Dance* and was nominated for the Shirley Jackson Award.

Lena Shayton is reading the newspaper, looking for a job, when she hears a knock on her door. It's the guy who lives below her, on the first floor. He wants to know if her apartment is shrinking. He has a notebook with measurements in it, and he says his apartment on the first floor is getting smaller each month. Is hers?

She considers the possibilities. If it's a come-on line, it's interesting. If he's serious, he's either artistic or crazy. This might be the way to make a new friend, which is what she needs right now. The love of her life, Bill, left her for Denise; she just lost her programming job; and there's a bad smell in the kitchen that she hasn't been able to track down.

Maybe it's the sewage treatment plant; the paper says there's a problem there that no one seems able to fix. Maybe it's Bill; maybe there's some weird thing happening where Bill tried to crawl back to her, got stuck under the sink, and died. But it's not likely; what would he be doing under the sink?

She lives over on Weehawken Street, which is a block from the river, at the westernmost part of the West Village. She read in a book that in the old days of New York, Weehawken Street was almost on the river, before the landfill added another street. There used to be tunnels from Weehawken to the docks, for smuggling. She doesn't remember what they smuggled, but it adds to the possibility that Bill might have taken some sneaky secret way into her apartment and gotten stuck and died. She used to be the kind of person who wouldn't have thoughts like that, but now they give her pleasure.

She doesn't want to deal with this guy's mania. She tells him she measured yesterday, and it's definitely the same.

Lena goes through all the newspapers, looking for a job or for the inspiration for a job. There's a lot of news. Stuyvesant Town is complaining that their water pressure has practically disappeared; they coordinate shower schedules by floor.

The mayor warns the city of possible brownouts in the coming hot weather. Electrical usage is up 20 percent and has reached capacity. The mayor blames computers. "Turn off your printers," he demands. "Don't leave your computers on all the time. Conserve or we'll have an electric shortage like we once had a gas shortage. I'm not saying we're going to *ration* electricity out to people on alternating days like we did then." (And here, the reporter notes, his jaw got very firm.) "But we don't have infinite resources. If you blow the grid, it'll take a while to fix it."

Blow the grid! Lena thinks as she walks around the Village, and just because of all the fat and selfish people out there, the ones who take and give. Like the people who drop litter everywhere, which really annoys her. It doesn't take much to control litter—just put it in the trash cans on the corner. She sees a bunch of folders and papers beside an empty trash can, for instance. Some of it is even leaning against the empty can, that's how bad it is.

She picks up a handful of that paper. She tells herself that if she finds a name, she'll turn them in—however you do that, whoever you call. There's such a thing as accountability, after all. Though she's never "turned" anyone "in." Maybe it can't in fact be done. Nevertheless, she picks up a handful of papers.

It looks like someone's home office has been tidied up and dumped in the street. No, it must be a small business, because there's an inter-office memo from Harry Biskabit on garbage. "All paper must be shredded," it says. "We recently discovered some of our own letterhead fluttering down West Street. Needless to say, this could be disastrous. From now on, all paper of any kind must be brought to 151S3, where it will be listed, tallied, signed for, and shredded before being put out. Foodstuffs and non-identifiable garbage can be handled as usual."

This is very funny, this guy Biskabit demanding that all the garbage be handled properly—and he can't handle his own!

A few memos look confidential. There's a job review and what looks like a warning about the poor work quality of someone named Philip Tarrey, who's always making mistakes and sending the wrong things to the wrong rooms. He's late with reports, he's poor at programming . . .

That's very interesting.

These papers could be a gold mine. They look a lot like a personnel file, and it looks like Philip Tarrey's been fired, and that means they need a programmer.

But who needs this programmer? She pages through the folder, finally finding some letterhead that reads "Assignment Specialties, 3 Charles Lane S3C, 77-33x14."

Charles Lane is only a few blocks away from where she stands. It's one block long, with a narrow cobblestone street running from Greenwich Avenue to West Street. There are blind storefronts along the southern side of the lane—concrete walls with steel doors. Trees with thin trunks press themselves against the walls. Everything on the north side is either a fenced-in garden or the back wall of a row house.

The only entrance doors are on the south side of the lane, but none of them have numbers. Where is 3 Charles Lane? Some kids come through on bicycles, followed by what she thinks might be NYU students doing something with cameras, posing each other and checking lighting. She can't find the address and there's no resident to ask.

Of course it's only three in the afternoon; maybe they're all at work with the doors closed. She decides to come back later, at five o'clock, and walks over to the park they're building by the river. They started about five years earlier, put in some trees, that kind of thing. It's nice for a block or two—there's even some grass and some bushes, but that seems to be all there is, despite all this talk about a pedestrian path going all the way uptown. Instead, there's mesh fencing blocking off the new paths, and lots of signs about construction. The signs are dirty; there's even a bush growing from construction debris.

At five, she wanders back, already half-convinced that the letterhead must be out of date. She turns the corner at West Street and stops—all along Charles Lane there are people in suits and dresses, with briefcases and shopping bags and coffee cups in their hands. They move rapidly up and down the lane, but they're eerily silent about it, not even their footsteps make a sound. But no doubt about it, they look like a commuter crowd, probably heading to the PATH train station just a few blocks away. It suddenly looks like Charles Lane is a thriving business artery. The buildings must be much deeper than they seem.

Everyone is coming out from one door, and when she gets there, she sees that it's actually a newsstand. She's so surprised that she walks in to get a better idea. At once, all the rush slows down. Lena stands still, looking around, and everyone inside seems to pause, picking up magazines or studying the sign above the counter for sodas and bottled waters. Lena sees a doorway marked EMPLOYEES ONLY, which has a dark curtain instead of a door. A man comes through, looks a little surprised, and then a small red light goes on over the doorway. She buys a soda and then leaves, joining the silent crowd outside as they walk to the end of the lane and disperse.

The only possibility she can think of is that this is a classified work place of some kind, maybe a secret government job, and the idea thrills her. She would like to do something dangerous or risky or at least more interesting than her usual. She pictures herself bluffing her way in, like a spy or counterspy. She's never done anything underhanded before; it's her turn. People are always taking advantage of her; let them watch out now.

Besides, it would be great to have a job that she could walk to. The subways are out of control right now with one accident after the other. The engineers say the signal lights are wrong; the maintenance people say the lights are fine. Trains crash into each other head to head or head to tail, it doesn't matter. She'd rather stay off them.

She wears an ironed blouse and a neat skirt the next morning and holds a briefcase with the papers she had picked up on the street, placed in a folder marked "Personal." On top of that she puts her resume, and on top of *that* she puts Harry Biskabit's memo. She gets to Charles Lane at eight o'clock the next morning, and it's empty. There's one dog, one dog walker, and that's it. She's annoyed, because she's trying so hard to outsmart everyone and it doesn't seem to be working. The whole of Charles Lane has a blank, locked face. She touches the door where the newsstand was, and it's shut solid and looks suddenly like it never was open, never in its life. She goes over to the river again, looking out at the traffic jam. There are a few boats on the river. She's playing magic with herself. She's telling herself that when she turns around, she'll see Charles Lane bustling with life.

Then she turns around, and it is.

People are rushing around, back and forth. And there's a little café where the newsstand was. It even has an outside table and two chairs. Why would the stores be different at different times? Maybe it's some kind of new-wave time-share scheme. Maybe on holidays it turns into a souvenir shop.

She merges with a wave of employees as they go through the café door. She steps behind two women, close behind, and to prove she's with them she starts matching their stride.

They go through the doorway marked EMPLOYEES ONLY. Lena keeps her head steady, trying not to look around too much. There's a short hallway and another curtain, with a guard on the other side. She bunches right up with the women ahead of her, almost stepping on their shoes, and she nods briskly. The guard grabs her.

"Your ID?" he asks.

"Job interview," she says. She opens her folder and flashes the letterhead. "See? Harry Biskabit. I have an appointment."

"You're supposed to have a temporary pass."

She rises to the occasion, scowling and huffing a little. "Now," she says, coldly, "how do I get a pass if I can't go in to get a pass?"

He blinks at her. "By mail?" he asks.

"You know they don't send them by mail. I was supposed to go in with those people you separated me from." She waves at the disappearing backs. "Hey, Juanita, you forgot me!" Then she pouts. "Now what?" She sighs in exasperation. "Can you call someone?"

He looks a little uncertain. "I just have instructions, you know. I don't need to justify everything I do, especially when it's regulation. But I do have discretion."

She smiles, suddenly friendly. "I've always admired discretion," she says. She's trying to mimic some sassy movie heroine from some gumshoe movie. She's getting a little jolt out of all the pretense.

He grins. "If you don't have an ID by tomorrow I'm gonna have to call in some backup."

"I understand," she says, giving him big eyes and then slipping by. "I'll make sure I get a good picture."

She takes a deep breath and keeps walking, fighting the impulse to slap someone on the back. She made it in! Of course it's only a first step. She stops in the hallway to poke through her handbag, as if searching for a room number. When some more people come through, she falls in behind them.

They walk down a half-flight of steps, then go through a short corridor to a bunch of elevators. Lena follows the others in and faces the buttons. S1, S2, S3. The others push S2. The memo from Biskabit says S3, so she pushes that. People come rushing in and by the time the doors close, the elevator's almost full. As soon as they shut, a murmur breaks out, as if they were suddenly allowed to speak.

"Did you see the new offices yet?" one man asks his neighbor.

"Katie's department moved in. They're still pushing for more storage, but it looks great. Not so crowded."

"We're next," the man says. "Can't wait." The doors open to S2 and they move out. That leaves just Lena and a slightly overweight man in a gray suit.

He smiles at her. "You new here?"

She's a little thrown by that. How can she sneak in if everyone can see she's new?

"I was behind you when the guard asked for your ID," he says. "Don't panic. I can't read minds."

"Phew," she says. "I thought maybe I had a sticker on me or something."

The elevator doors open and they both step out. Lena lets him lead the way.

"No, no, no, you look perfectly fine. Is this your first interview? Or is it a transfer?"

She's tempted to say transfer, it seems like the easy way out, but he would be sure to ask where she transferred from. "Interview," she says. "And I could use some help finding the way." She takes a quick look around. "It's a big place."

It's really astonishing, the size of it; there's just no way of telling from outside. Lena is in a big main corridor, passing doorways with frosted glass and doorways with no glass. Some doors are open and show offices with stacks of files and multiple desks and people very busily going about their business. Phones ring and terminals blink. Every two hundred feet or so, side corridors intersect with the one she's on, and when she looks down one, she sees people walking parallel to her, in rows of multiple main corridors.

They're like streets. In fact, every so often there's a small coffee shop or a little sandwich shop. A clothing store as well; even a pharmacy.

Her companion abruptly stops and holds out his hand. "Bossephalus," he says.

She doesn't like his eyes, they're too sharp. She smiles and holds the smile, uncertain about giving him her name.

He winks. "Not to worry," he says. "I'm not the bogeyman."

She unsnares her smile. "Sorry. Sometimes I'm such a New Yorker. My name is Lena."

"Lovely name; I don't hear that often enough. Who are you going to see?"

"Harry Biskabit." It's the only name she knows. Aside, of course, from the supposedly fired Philip Tarrey.

"That's good, that's very good!" Bossephalus chortles. "We both start with B, that'll be easy."

"Of course," she says, trying to sound like this makes perfect sense. They pass a doorway into a large open room with electronic maps displayed along the walls. There are little red beeping lights moving, and people are talking into headsets and clicking on little handheld computers. "Is that what I think it is?" she asks with interest. She has no idea what it is, really, but it seems like a good way to go.

Bossephalus beams and pats her shoulder. "Parking department, downtown unit. Look," he says, pointing as a red light moves closer to a blue light. "Got him!" The blue light disappears and the red moves on. "He thought he had that spot!" Bossephalus claps his hands. "I love that. Drives them crazy upstairs. Parking to kill for! That's what the motto is. I bet that red was driving around for an hour. Those are the ones that are very dear to us."

Lena's mind is racing. The maps on the wall are street maps? They must be street maps. Then the reds are cars looking for parking spots and, if she understands Bossephalus, the blues are parking spots. They disappear in one street and appear in another. There are green lights as well, and the greens always get the spots.

"You're controlling the parking spaces?" she asks. "You're moving your own cars around?"

"That's it! We take the spaces ourselves or sometimes we give them to the luckies. The unluckies *almost* get it, but at the last minute they get stopped by someone crossing the street or a light changes or a bus blocks the way, and then they can actually see someone else getting the spot they were heading for. Or we put cones up and it suddenly becomes illegal."

"Nice," she says neutrally. "Smooth." She doesn't have a car, doesn't like cars—why would anyone have a car in New York?—but it's not nice, not a bit. What kind of place is this?

Bossephalus taps her on the elbow and they go back into the corridor.

"So you're seeing Biskabit," he says. "Didn't know he was hiring. I could use some help myself. What do you do?"

"Programmer," she tells him. "Strong in html and design."

"Very useful," he says. "We're always looking for web designers. We put a lot of them in startup companies, but now we're branching into corporate."

"The startups didn't do so well," she says cautiously.

"No? We thought it went splendidly."

Splendid? Who could think that all those bankruptcies were a good thing? He must be terribly uninformed. "Where do you work?" Lena asks politely.

He looks at her and smiles. "I'm in Information," he says.

There's something about his smile that's nasty, though she tries to talk herself out of it. Maybe he's just a friendly man showing a newcomer around, she thinks. Maybe.

They come to a wider corridor. She can hear drilling and hammering.

"We're expanding," Bossephalus says, sweeping his hand along the corridor. "Our job keeps getting bigger, and there's a limit to how much we can squeeze into our limited space. So—up we go." He's very cheerful about it.

She squints at the corridor. "Up?"

"They can't have it all," he says easily. "We're willing to put up with a lot, since we like what we do. But as they grow we grow, so we're forced to have some additional entries and vents and a window here and there. Very modest when you consider."

She's trying to piece this together and stupidly repeats, "Up?" Could her downstairs neighbor be on to something? Could they really be taking some of his apartment? It seems incredible, but Bossephalus raises his eyes up to follow his pointing finger. He lifts his chin and the look on his face is satisfied and confident.

"We're really just shifting them around a little. When you think about it, nobody uses all the space they have. Tops of closets, under the sink, behind the tub—add it all together and it's substantial real estate. We have the science to do some adjusting. We're careful not to give them anything concrete to go on."

"I see." She struggles to make her voice noncommittal. "You just make them a little more cramped? When they're already complaining about being cramped?"

He beams. "Nicely put."

They start to pass men on ladders drilling upwards and men with expanders—wide metal brackets with a wheel in the middle—widening the drilled areas. Bossephalus motions for Lena to follow him into a long room with calculators and screens with groups of numbers. "This is one of my favorites," he whispers, and nods towards a lottery machine. "It was my idea to get involved in this. Every third lottery winner will have a problem—we give it to someone who has a warrant out on him, or a guy who'll say it was his own purchase but his buddies at work say it was a group ticket, or a mugger finds the winning ticket in the purse he just stole—that's tricky! What will he do?"

She decides she has to go along with him, cheer along with him. "I like that," she says in an appreciative sort of way. "It's a moral dilemma that's really a legal dilemma. I mean, a criminal dilemma. What to do, what to do." She's trying not to think about implications, any implications. Her mind is snapping around like cut wires.

"You see the fun. Now, I'm getting forgetful. Where am I taking you?" He turns up his smile, it's now bright and gleaming. There's a little edge of intimacy in it, as if he has something up his sleeve.

"Biskabit."

"Oh yes, that's right. And what department is he in?"

"Personnel. Human Resources. Whatever it's called, I forget. They keep changing the name, don't they?"

"Do they?" he says smoothly, as if it doesn't matter to him. "Here's Billings." He waves his arm. "We're sending out cut-off notices to people who have no idea why; we're sending out $10,000 electric bills to small studios; $10,000 phone bills to poor people. The interns make up collection notices with unreadable phone numbers!" He laughs. "We scramble the records at the source, of course."

She thinks of people getting those bills, trying to cope with them. She had a notice from a collection agency once; it drove her crazy. She blurts out, "Why?" She regrets it immediately. Wherever she is—whatever this place is—it's obviously not an ordinary job, these aren't ordinary people. She should keep her head down and shut up.

"Why?" he murmurs, repeating her question in a sad little voice. "When did you hear from Biskabit?"

"I didn't actually hear from him," she says. "I heard about the job. From a memo. A job description."

"In the papers?" he suggests.

She's blinking too much, she knows she's blinking too much, but she can't stop no matter how much she wants to. "In some papers," she says. "I found some papers."

He sighs. "Come along with me. We're almost there."

They pass more open rooms. Some rooms have signs on them: OBSTRUCTION. ILLEGAL TOWING. MERCHANDISE WARRANTIES. One of the biggest rooms says, simply, CHEMICALS. She hears people yelling, "Skin reactions! Fumes! No noticeable odor!"

Her feet are getting leaden, she's becoming heavy with dread. *If I can just get rid of Bossephalus,* she thinks, *maybe I can make my way back and out. How many times have we turned? I can't remember how many times we've turned.*

"It's a great job," he explains. "You have to love it." He clasps his hands together in delight. "*Love.* It's a chemical, you know. A little bit of a drug in the right place. Sneak it into their coffee or their potato chips—voila! Take it away and forty years of marriage goes down the drain. Of course, sometimes all you have to do is get someone a little sexier, a little more spangled, and put them in the right place. Take someone with the name of Denise, for instance. Smart and sexy and just a little bit dangerous. But you know all about Denise," he says.

Her heart does a little thud. Is this just some wild coincidence, or is Bossephalus talking about the woman who clicked her heels and took her love to Oz?

She passes a screen that shows a massive backup on the bridge. She doesn't look directly; her eyes roll out to the side. The bridge camera swings from the long view to the short view. It's a jackknifed tractor-trailer, as usual. "Why is it always a tractor-trailer?" she asks, trying to make it a joke. "Shouldn't they be outlawed?"

"The Bridge and Tunnel Authority!" he shouts. "We *own* the Bridge and Tunnel Authority! Between that and the construction jobs, we hardly have enough staff. Well, construction doesn't actually need staff once they put up the orange cones, do they?" He's pleased with himself.

Then he puts his hand on her shoulder. At first it's just a slight touch, but he adds weight to it. They turn a corner and there are four people standing there, as if they're waiting.

"The membership committee," Bossephalus says easily. "Come to greet us. You, actually."

There are two men and two women, all in white lab coats. They stand in front of a door marked ACCIDENTS. The women smile at her politely, the men move behind her and she can't see their faces, but she can feel them.

"What's this?" she asks, her mouth dry.

"We've been thinking about what job would be best for you," Bossephalus says. He's very happy.

"Who's 'we'?" She tries to sound tough, but it comes out faintly.

"Think of us as a service organization," he says. "Only we serve ourselves." He points to his ear, which has a small device in it, like a hearing aid. "I've been getting reports on you all along. Let's go this way." They take a left down another corridor, which has stacks of filing cabinets pushed to one side. "We're digital now, of course," Bossephalus murmurs. "Computers, chips, cameras everywhere. Look it up, nail it down. We keep track of millions of people above us, we visit them, we live among them. And we play a little." He laughs. "We play a lot. We're scientists." His eyes roll towards a sign. MEDICAL RECORDS. She doesn't like the sign.

"Is this where you work?" Lena asks.

"Me?" He laughs. "No, no, no. You haven't figured it out yet? You can't guess what my job is?" He stops to watch her think.

She looks at the four people who surround them. Each one is looking in a different direction—at the walls, down the corridor, into the rooms that flash with computer screens. "Sometimes I feel that there's a plan," she says finally. "When things go wrong again and again. I keep telling myself it's just bad luck." This isn't the kind of thing she admits. Not normally.

He smiles. "The plan keeps changing," he says agreeably. "Something we do seems good, and we do it; and then someone comes along with a better plan. For the little people," he whispered. "For the pawns. Isn't that how it feels?"

She nods. But she resents it.

"You see, you were never called here. You simply don't belong here. Another accident? Do you think so?" He pats her on the shoulder. She thinks, for a moment, that it's a friendly pat, avuncular.

She can hear names being called out in one of the rooms. Just names, no emotion, then a list of diseases. "Heart attack. Lung cancer. Malaria. Stroke." She steps into the doorway and looks inside. People are standing at whiteboards, where they write and then erase diseases, as if to keep track of trends.

"Food poisoning!" a worker cries. "How about a funeral?"

There's an instant crescendo of agreement. She turns back to Bossephalus. "You're with security, aren't you?"

"Head of," he says cheerily. "Specializing in break-ins. We don't see them too often, we've got a good system of checks and counterchecks. The guards don't look too intelligent, but that's deliberate. If someone is interested, they're going to get in, and it's best if we get them at our own convenience."

"So." She takes a deep breath. "So what happens now?"

He grips her shoulder again and leads her to another room. "It's not so bad," he says in a reassuring tone. "We're going to put you back where you belong. But you won't be in any danger, and neither will we." He waves her forward, over to the main desk in the room. "Shayton," he says. "Lena Shayton."

"Ah," the woman at the desk says. "Got her right here." She turns to the computer screen and starts clicking away.

Lena's hands begin to perspire and she feels a lump at the back of her mouth. It's so big she has trouble swallowing. Bossephalus's hand moves up from her shoulder and he spreads his fingers hard around her ear. "Right about here, maybe," he says. "Though I'm not a doctor. But right where the speech centers are, the communication centers."

"Got it!" the desk person calls out. "Here we go!"

"Stop," Lena says. "Fot are ye doon?"

"Not just the sounds," he advises. "Make it the meaning, too."

"Croon wizzes, who saw that blucksbin. Terrible blucksbin!" *I try, I try,* she thinks.

"That's it!" Bossephalus cries. "That's exactly what I mean. Give her lots of words without meaning, make it almost make sense."

She can eel her tongue twisting, he says, "Goo." She can't find things, sharp or thin. Is it in her turn? Maybe she can write, with a spit on the knee, so they'll wonder highways and believe then, get a gooseberry rhythm.

Lena Shayton, boom boom, ready now? Upsy upsy.

Whirlybanging all over bingo next Tuesday too. Please please bing she think. Words, she say words.

GEORGE SAUNDERS
Escape from Spiderhead

George Saunders is one of America's leading satirists. Before becoming
a writer, he was a geophysicist in Sumatra. His work includes *CivilWarLand
in Bad Decline*, *Pastoralia*, *In Persuasion Nation*, and *Tenth of December:
Stories*. Saunders has won many awards, including a MacArthur Fellowship, a
Guggenheim Fellowship, an Academy Award from the American Academy of
Arts and Letters, the Story Prize, the Folio Prize, the PEN/Hemingway, the PEN/
Malamud, National Magazine, and World Fantasy awards. He has also been
nominated twice for an O. Henry Award and twice for a Bram Stoker Award.
A regular contributor to the *New Yorker* and *GQ*, his work has appeared in the
series *Best American Short Stories*, *Best American Nonrequired Reading*, *O.
Henry Prize Stories*, and *Best American Science Fiction*. His story "93990" is
reprinted in *The Secret History of Science Fiction*.

Originally appearing in the *New Yorker* in 2010, "Escape from Spiderhead"
asks many questions regarding the moral issues of scientific advancement and
the human condition as they relate to inventive pharmaceuticals.

I.

"Drip on?" Abnesti said over the P.A.

"What's in it?" I said.

"Hilarious," he said.

"Acknowledge," I said.

Abnesti used his remote. My MobiPak™ whirred. Soon the Interior
Garden looked really nice. Everything seemed super-clear.

I said out loud, as I was supposed to, what I was feeling.

"Garden looks nice," I said. "Super-clear."

Abnesti said, "Jeff, how about we pep up those language centers?"

"Sure," I said.

"Drip on?" he said.

"Acknowledge," I said.

He added some Verbaluce™ to the drip, and soon I was feeling the same things but saying them better. The garden still looked nice. It was like the bushes were so tight-seeming and the sun made everything stand out? It was like any moment you expected some Victorians to wander in with their cups of tea. It was as if the garden had become a sort of embodiment of the domestic dreams forever intrinsic to human consciousness. It was as if I could suddenly discern, in this contemporary vignette, the ancient corollary through which Plato and some of his contemporaries might have strolled; to wit, I was sensing the eternal in the ephemeral.

I sat, pleasantly engaged in these thoughts, until the Verbaluce™ began to wane. At which point the garden just looked nice again. It was something about the bushes and whatnot? It made you just want to lay out there and catch rays and think your happy thoughts. If you get what I mean.

Then whatever else was in the drip wore off, and I didn't feel much about the garden one way or the other. My mouth was dry, though, and my gut had that post-Verbaluce™ feel to it.

"What's going to be cool about that one?" Abnesti said. "Is, say a guy has to stay up late guarding a perimeter. Or is at school waiting for his kid and gets bored. But there's some nature nearby? Or say a park ranger has to work a double shift?"

"That will be cool," I said.

"That's ED763," he said. "We're thinking of calling it NatuGlide. Or maybe ErthAdmire."

"Those are both good," I said.

"Thanks for your help, Jeff," he said.

Which was what he always said.

"Only a million years to go," I said.

Which was what I always said.

Then he said, "Exit the Interior Garden now, Jeff, head over to Small Workroom 2."

II.

Into Small Workroom 2 they sent this pale tall girl.

"What do you think?" Abnesti said over the P.A.

"Me?" I said. "Or her?"

"Both," Abnesti said.

"Pretty good," I said.

"Fine, you know," she said. "Normal."

Abnesti asked us to rate each other more quantifiably, as per pretty, as per sexy.

It appeared we liked each other about average, i.e., no big attraction or revulsion either way.

Abnesti said, "Jeff, drip on?"

"Acknowledge," I said.

"Heather, drip on?" he said.

"Acknowledge," Heather said.

Then we looked at each other like, What happens next?

What happened next was, Heather soon looked super-good. And I could tell she thought the same of me. It came on so sudden we were like laughing. How could we not have seen it, how cute the other one was? Luckily there was a couch in the Workroom. It felt like our drip had, in addition to whatever they were testing, some ED556 in it, which lowers your shame level to like nil. Because soon, there on the couch, off we went. It was super-hot between us. And not merely in a horndog way. Hot, yes, but also just right. Like if you'd dreamed of a certain girl all your life and all of a sudden there she was, in your Domain.

"Jeff," Abnesti said. "I'd like your permission to pep up your language centers."

"Go for it," I said, under her now.

"Drip on?" he said.

"Acknowledge," I said.

"Me, too?" Heather said.

"You got it," Abnesti said, with a laugh. "Drip on?"

"Acknowledge," she said, all breathless.

Soon, experiencing the benefits of the flowing Verbaluce™ in our drips, we were not only fucking really well but also talking pretty great. Like, instead of just saying the sex-type things we had been saying (such as "wow" and "oh God" and "hell yes" and so forth), we now began freestyling re our sensations and thoughts, in elevated diction, with eighty-per-cent increased vocab, our well-articulated thoughts being recorded for later analysis.

For me, the feeling was, approximately: Astonishment at the dawning realization that this woman was being created in real time, directly from my own mind, per my deepest longings. Finally, after all these years (was my thought), I had found the precise arrangement of body/face/mind that personified all that was desirable. The taste of her mouth, the look of that halo of blondish hair spread out around her cherubic yet naughty-looking face (she was beneath me now, legs way up), even (not to be crude or dishonor the exalted feelings I was experiencing) the sensations her vagina was producing along the length of my thrusting penis were precisely those I had always hungered for, though I had never, before this instant, realized that I so ardently hungered for them.

That is to say: a desire would arise and, concurrently, the satisfaction of that desire would also arise. It was as if (a) I longed for a certain (heretofore untasted) taste until (b) said longing became nearly unbearable, at which time (c) I found a morsel of food with that exact taste already in my mouth, perfectly satisfying my longing.

Every utterance, every adjustment of posture bespoke the same thing: we had known each other forever, were soul mates, had met and loved in numerous preceding lifetimes, and would meet and love in many subsequent lifetimes, always with the same transcendently stupefying results.

Then there came a hard-to-describe but very real drifting-off into a number of sequential reveries that might best be described as a type of nonnarrative mind scenery, i.e., a series of vague mental images of places I had never been (a certain pine-packed valley in high white mountains, a chalet-type house in a cul-de-sac, the yard of which was overgrown with wide, stunted Seussian trees), each of which triggered a deep sentimental longing, longings that coalesced into, and were soon reduced to, one central longing, i.e., an intense longing for Heather and Heather alone.

This mind-scenery phenomenon was strongest during our third (!) bout of lovemaking. (Apparently, Abnesti had included some Vivistif™ in my drip.)

Afterward, our protestations of love poured forth simultaneously, linguistically complex and metaphorically rich. I daresay we had become poets. We were allowed to lie there, limbs intermingled, for nearly an hour. It was bliss. It was perfection. It was that impossible thing: happiness that does not wilt to reveal the thin shoots of some new desire rising from within it.

We cuddled with a fierceness/focus that rivaled the fierceness/focus with which we had fucked. There was nothing *less* about cuddling vis-à-vis fucking, is what I mean to say. We were all over each other in the super-friendly way of puppies, or spouses meeting for the first time after one of them has undergone a close brush with death. Everything seemed moist, permeable, *sayable*.

Then something in the drip began to wane. I think Abnesti had shut off the Verbaluce™? Also the shame reducer? Basically, everything began to *dwindle*. Suddenly we felt shy. But still loving. We began the process of trying to talk après Verbaluce™: always awkward.

Yet I could see in her eyes that she was still feeling love for me.

And I was definitely still feeling love for her.

Well, why not? We had just fucked three times! Why do you think they call it "making love"? That was what we had just made three times: love.

Then Abnesti said, "Drip on?"

We had kind of forgotten he was even there, behind his one-way mirror.

I said, "Do we have to? We are really liking this right now."

"We're just going to try to get you guys back to baseline," he said. "We've got more to do today."

"Shit," I said.

"Rats," she said.

"Drip on?" he said.

"Acknowledge," we said.

Soon something began to change. I mean, she was fine. A handsome pale girl. But nothing special. And I could see that she felt the same re me, i.e., what had all that fuss been about just now?

Why weren't we dressed? We real quick got dressed.

Kind of embarrassing.

Did I love her? Did she love me?

Ha.

No.

Then it was time for her to go. We shook hands.

Out she went.

Lunch came in. On a tray. Spaghetti with chicken chunks.

Man, was I hungry.

I spent all lunchtime thinking. It was weird. I had the memory of fucking Heather, the memory of having felt the things I'd felt for her, the memory of having said the things I'd said to her. My throat was like raw from how much I'd said and how fast I'd felt compelled to say it. But in terms of feelings? I basically had nada left.

Just a hot face and some shame re having fucked three times in front of Abnesti.

III.

After lunch in came another girl.

About equally so-so. Dark hair. Average build. Nothing special, just like, upon first entry, Heather had been nothing special.

"This is Rachel," Abnesti said on the P.A. "This is Jeff."

"Hi, Rachel," I said.

"Hi, Jeff," she said.

"Drip on?" Abnesti said.

We Acknowledged.

Something seemed very familiar about the way I now began feeling. Suddenly Rachel looked super-good. Abnesti requested permission to pep up our language centers via Verbaluce™. We Acknowledged. Soon we, too, were fucking like bunnies. Soon we, too, were talking like articulate maniacs re our love. Once again certain sensations were arising to meet my concurrently arising desperate hunger for just those sensations. Soon my memory of the perfect taste of Heather's mouth was being overwritten by the current taste of Rachel's mouth, so much more the taste I now desired. I was feeling unprecedented emotions, even though those unprecedented emotions were (I discerned somewhere in my consciousness) exactly the same emotions I had felt earlier, for that now unworthy-seeming vessel Heather. Rachel was, I mean to say, *it*. Her lithe waist, her voice, her hungry mouth/hands/loins—they were all *it*.

I just loved Rachel so much.

Then came the sequential geographic reveries (see above): same pine-packed valley, same chalet-looking house, accompanied by that same longing-for-place transmuting into a longing for (this time) Rachel. While continuing to enact a level of sexual strenuousness that caused what I would describe as a gradually tightening, chest-located, sweetness rubber band to both connect us and compel us onward, we whispered feverishly (precisely, poetically) about how long we felt we had known each other, i.e., forever.

Again the total number of times we made love was three.

Then, like before, came the dwindling. Our talking became less excellent. Words were fewer, our sentences shorter. Still, I loved her. Loved Rachel. Everything about her just seemed *perfect*: her cheek mole, her black hair, the little butt-squirm she did now and then, as if to say, Mmm-mmm, was that ever good.

"Drip on?" Abnesti said. "We are going to try to get you both back to baseline."

"Acknowledge," she said.

"Well, hold on," I said.

"Jeff," Abnesti said, irritated, as if trying to remind me that I was here not by choice but because I had done my crime and was in the process of doing my time.

"Acknowledge," I said. And gave Rachel one last look of love, knowing (as she did not yet know) that this would be the last look of love I would be giving her.

Soon she was merely fine to me, and I merely fine to her. She looked, as had Heather, embarrassed, as in, What was up with that just now? Why did I just go so overboard with Mr. Average here?

Did I love her? Or her me?

No.

When it was time for her to go, we shook hands.

The place where my MobiPak™ was surgically joined to my lower back was sore from all our positional changes. Plus I was way tired. Plus I was feeling so sad. Why sad? Was I not a dude? Had I not just fucked two different girls, for a total of six times, in one day?

Still, honestly, I felt sadder than sad.

I guess I was sad that love was not real? Or not all that real, anyway? I guess I was sad that love could feel so real and the next minute be gone, and all because of something Abnesti was doing.

IV.

After Snack Abnesti called me into Control. Control being like the head of a spider. With its various legs being our Workrooms. Sometimes we were called upon to work alongside Abnesti in the head of the spider. Or, as we termed it: the Spiderhead.

"Sit," he said. "Look into Large Workroom 1."

In Large Workroom 1 were Heather and Rachel, side by side.

"Recognize them?" he said.

"Ha," I said.

"Now," Abnesti said. "I'm going to present you with a choice, Jeff. This is what we're playing at here. See this remote? Let's say you can hit *this* button and Rachel gets some Darkenfloxx™. Or you can hit *this* button and Heather gets the Darkenfloxx™. See? You choose."

"They've got Darkenfloxx™ in their MobiPaks™?" I said.

"You've all got Darkenfloxx™ in your MobiPaks™, dummy," Abnesti said affectionately. "Verlaine put it there Wednesday. In anticipation of this very study."

Well, that made me nervous.

Imagine the worst you have ever felt, times ten. That does not even come close to how bad you feel on Darkenfloxx™. The time it was administered to us in Orientation, briefly, for demo purposes, at one-third the dose now selected on Abnesti's remote? I have never felt so terrible. All of us were just moaning, heads down, like, How could we ever have felt life was worth living?

I do not even like to think about that time.

"What's your decision, Jeff?" Abnesti said. "Is Rachel getting the Darkenfloxx™? Or Heather?"

"I can't say," I said.

"You have to," he said.

"I can't," I said. "It would be like random."

"You feel your decision would be random," he said.

"Yes," I said.

And that was true. I really didn't care. It was like if I put *you* in the Spiderhead and gave you the choice: which of these two strangers would you like to send into the shadow of the valley of death?

"Ten seconds," Abnesti said. "What we're testing for here is any residual fondness."

It wasn't that I liked them both. I honestly felt completely neutral toward both. It was exactly as if I had never seen, much less fucked, either one. (They had really succeeded in taking me back to baseline, I guess I am saying.)

But, having once been Darkenfloxxed™, I just didn't want to do that to anyone. Even if I didn't like the person very much, even if I hated the person, I still wouldn't want to do it.

"Five seconds," Abnesti said.

"I can't decide," I said. "It's random."

"Truly random?" he said. "OK. I'm giving the Darkenfloxx™ to Heather." I just sat there.

"No, actually," he said. "I'm giving it to Rachel."

Just sat there.

"Jeff," he said. "You have convinced me. It would, to you, be random. You truly have no preference. I can see that. And therefore I don't have to do it. See what we just did? With your help? For the first time? Via the ED289/290 suite? Which is what we've been testing today? You have to admit it: you were in love. Twice. Right?"

"Yes," I said.

"Very much in love," he said. "Twice."

"I said yes," I said.

"But you just now expressed no preference," he said. "Ergo, no trace of either of those great loves remains. You are totally cleansed. We brought you high, laid you low, and now here you sit, the same emotionwise as before our testing even began. That is powerful. That is killer. We have unlocked a mysterious eternal secret. What a fantastic game-changer! Say someone can't love? Now he or she can. We can make him. Say someone loves too much? Or loves someone deemed unsuitable by his or her caregiver? We can tone that shit right down. Say someone is blue, because of true love? We step in, or his or her caregiver does: blue no more. No longer, in terms of emotional controllability, are we ships adrift. No one is. We see a ship adrift, we climb aboard, install a rudder. Guide him/her toward love. Or away from it. You say, 'All you need is love'? Look, here comes ED289/290. Can we stop war? We can sure as heck slow it down! Suddenly the soldiers on both sides start fucking. Or, at low dosage, feeling super-fond. Or say we have two rival dictators in a death grudge. Assuming ED289/290 develops nicely in pill form, allow me to slip each dictator a mickey. Soon their tongues are down each other's throats and doves of peace are pooping on their epaulets. Or, depending on the dosage, they may just be hugging. And who helped us do that? You did."

All this time, Rachel and Heather had just been sitting there in Large Workroom 1.

"That's it, gals, thanks," Abnesti said on the P.A.

And they left, neither knowing how close they had come to getting Darkenfloxxed™ out their wing-wangs.

Verlaine took them out the back way, i.e., not through the Spiderhead but via the Back Alley. Which is not really an alley, just a carpeted hallway leading back to our Domain Cluster.

"Think, Jeff," Abnesti said. "Think if you'd had the benefit of ED289/290 on your fateful night."

Tell the truth, I was getting kind of sick of him always talking about my fateful night.

I'd been sorry about it right away and had got sorrier about it ever since, and was now so sorry about it that him rubbing it in my face did not make me one bit sorrier, it just made me think of him as being kind of a dick.

"Can I go to bed now?" I said.

"Not yet," Abnesti said. "It is hours to go before you sleep."

Then he sent me into Small Workroom 3, where some dude I didn't know was sitting.

V.

"Rogan," the dude said.

"Jeff," I said.

"What's up?" he said.

"Not much," I said.

We sat tensely for a long time, not talking. Maybe ten minutes passed.

We got some rough customers in here. I noted that Rogan had a tattoo of a rat on his neck, a rat that had just been knifed and was crying. But even through its tears it was knifing a smaller rat, who just looked surprised.

Finally Abnesti came on the P.A.

"That's it, guys, thanks," he said.

"What the fuck was that about?" Rogan said.

Good question, Rogan, I thought. Why had we been left just sitting there? In the same manner that Heather and Rachel had been left just sitting there? Then I had a hunch. To test my hunch, I did a sudden lurch into the Spiderhead. Which Abnesti always made a point of not keeping locked, to show how much he trusted and was unafraid of us.

And guess who was in there?

"Hey, Jeff," Heather said.

"Jeff, get out," Abnesti said.

"Heather, did Mr. Abnesti just now make you decide which of us, me or Rogan, to give some Darkenfloxx™ to?" I said.

"Yes," Heather said. She must have been on some VeriTalk™, because she spoke the truth in spite of Abnesti's withering silencing glance.

"Did you recently fuck Rogan, Heather?" I said. "In addition to me? And also fall in love with him, as you did with me?"

"Yes," she said.

"Heather, honestly," Abnesti said. "Put a sock in it."

Heather looked around for a sock, VeriTalk™ making one quite literal.

Back in my Domain, I did the math: Heather had fucked me three times. Heather had probably also fucked Rogan three times, since, in the name of design consistency, Abnesti would have given Rogan and me equal relative doses of Vivistif™.

And yet, speaking of design consistency, there was still one shoe to drop, if I knew Abnesti, always a stickler in terms of data symmetry, which was: wouldn't Abnesti also need Rachel to decide who to Darkenfloxx™, i.e., me or Rogan?

After a short break, my suspicions were confirmed: I found myself again sitting in Small Workroom 3 with Rogan!

Again we sat not talking for a long time. Mostly he picked at the smaller rat and I tried to watch without him seeing.

Then, like before, Abnesti came on the P.A. and said, "That's it, guys, thanks."

"Let me guess," I said. "Rachel's in there with you."

"Jeff, if you don't stop doing that, I swear," Abnesti said.

"And she just declined to Darkenfloxx™ either me or Rogan?" I said.

"Hi, Jeff!" Rachel said. "Hi, Rogan!"

"Rogan," I said. "Did you by any chance fuck Rachel earlier today?"

"Pretty much," Rogan said.

My mind was like reeling. Rachel had fucked me plus Rogan? Heather had fucked me plus Rogan? And everyone who had fucked anyone had fallen in love with that person, then out of it?

What kind of crazy-ass Project Team was this?

I mean, I had been on some crazy-ass Project Teams in my time, such as one where the drip had something in it that made hearing music exquisite, and hence when some Shostakovich was piped in actual bats seemed to circle my Domain, or the one where my legs became totally numb and yet I found I could still stand fifteen straight hours at a fake cash register, miraculously suddenly able to do extremely hard long-division problems in my mind.

But of all my crazy-ass Project Teams this was by far the most crazy-assed.

I could not help but wonder what tomorrow would bring.

VI

Except today wasn't even over.

I was again called into Small Workroom 3. And was sitting there when this unfamiliar guy came in.

"I'm Keith!" he said, rushing over to shake my hand.

He was a tall Southern drink of water, all teeth and wavy hair.

"Jeff," I said.

"Really nice meeting you!" he said.

Then we sat there not talking. Whenever I looked over at Keith, he would gleam his teeth at me and shake his head all wry, as if to say, "Odd job of work, isn't it?"

"Keith," I said. "Do you by any chance know two chicks named Rachel and Heather?"

"I sure as heck do," Keith said. And suddenly his teeth had a leering quality to them.

"Did you by any chance have sex with both Rachel and Heather earlier today, three times each?" I said.

"What are you, man, a dang psychic?" Keith said. "You're blowing my mind, I itmit it!"

"Jeff, you're totally doinking with our experimental design integrity," Abnesti said.

"So either Rachel or Heather is sitting in the Spiderhead right now," I said. "Trying to decide."

"Decide what?" Keith said.

"Which of us to Darkenfloxx™," I said.

"Eek," Keith said. And now his teeth looked scared.

"Don't worry," I said. "She won't do it."

"Who won't?" Keith said.

"Whoever's in there," I said.

"That's it, guys, thanks," Abnesti said.

Then, after a short break, Keith and I were once again brought into Small Workroom 3, where once again we waited as, this time, Heather declined to Darkenfloxx™ either one of us.

Back in my Domain, I constructed a who-had-fucked-whom chart, which went like this:

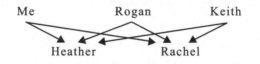

Abnesti came in.

"Despite all your shenanigans," he said, "Rogan and Keith had exactly the same reaction as you did. And as Rachel and Heather did. None of you, at the critical moment, could decide whom to Darkenfloxx™. Which is super. What does that mean? Why is it super? It means that ED289/290 is the real deal. It can make love, it can take love away. I'm almost inclined to start the naming process."

"Those girls did it nine times each today?" I said.

"Peace4All," he said. "LuvInclyned. You seem pissy. Are you pissy?"

"Well, I feel a little jerked around," I said.

"Do you feel jerked around because you still have feelings of love for one of the girls?" he said. "That would need to be noted. Anger? Possessiveness? Residual sexual longing?"

"No," I said.

"You honestly don't feel miffed that a girl for whom you felt love was then funked by two other guys, and, not only that, she then felt exactly the same quality/quantity of love for those guys as she had felt for you, or, in the case of Rachel, was about to feel for you, at the time that she funked Rogan? I think it was Rogan. She may have funked Keith first. Then you, penultimately. I'm vague on the order of operations. I could look it up. But think deeply on this."

I thought deeply on it.

"Nothing," I said.

"Well, it's a lot to sort through," he said. "Luckily it's night. Our day is done. Anything else you want to talk about? Anything else you're feeling?"

"My penis is sore," I said.

"Well, no surprise there," he said. "Think how those girls must feel. I'll send Verlaine in with some cream."

Soon Verlaine came in with some cream.

"Hi, Verlaine," I said.

"Hi, Jeff," he said. "You want to put this on yourself or want me to do it?"

"I'll do it," I said.

"Cool," he said.

And I could tell he meant it.

"Looks painful," he said.

"It really is," I said.

"Must have felt pretty good at the time, though?" he said.

His words seemed to be saying he was envious, but I could see in his eyes, as they looked at my penis, that he wasn't envious at all.

Then I slept the sleep of the dead.

As they say.

VII.

Next morning I was still asleep when Abnesti came on the P.A.

"Do you remember yesterday?" he said.

"Yes," I said.

"When I asked which gal you'd like to see on the Darkenfloxx™?" he said. "And you said neither?"

"Yes," I said.

"Well, that was good enough for me," he said. "But apparently not good enough for the Protocol Committee. Not good enough for the Three Horsemen of Anality. Come in here. Let's get started—we're going to need to do a kind of Confirmation Trial. Oh, this is going to stink."

I entered the Spiderhead.

Sitting in Small Workroom 2 was Heather.

"So this time," Abnesti said, "per the Protocol Committee, instead of me asking you which girl to give the Darkenfloxx™ to, which the ProtComm felt was too subjective, we're going to give this girl the Darkenfloxx™ no matter what you say. Then see what you say. Like yesterday, we're going to put you on a drip of—Verlaine? Verlaine? Where are you? Are you there? What is it again? Do you have the project order?"

"Verbaluce™, VeriTalk™, ChatEase™," Verlaine said over the P.A.

"Right," Abnesti said. "And did you refresh his MobiPak™? Are his quantities good?"

"I did it," Verlaine said. "I did it while he was sleeping. Plus I already told you I already did it."

"What about her?" Abnesti said. "Did you refresh her MobiPak™? Are her quantities good?"

"You stood right there and watched me, Ray," Verlaine said.

"Jeff, sorry," Abnesti said to me. "We're having a little tension in here today. Not an easy day ahead."

"I don't want you to Darkenfloxx™ Heather," I said.

"Interesting," he said. "Is that because you love her?"

"No," I said. "I don't want you to Darkenfloxx™ anybody."

"I know what you mean," he said. "That is so sweet. Then again: is this Confirmation Trial about what you want? Not so much. What it's about is us recording what you say as you observe Heather getting Darkenfloxxed™. For five minutes. Five-minute trial. Here we go. Drip on?"

I did not say "Acknowledge."

"You should feel flattered," Abnesti said. "Did we choose Rogan? Keith? No. We deemed your level of speaking more commensurate with our data needs."

I did not say "Acknowledge."

"Why so protective of Heather?" Abnesti said. "One would almost think you loved her."

"No," I said.

"Do you even know her story?" he said. "You don't. You legally can't. Does it involve whiskey, gangs, infanticide? I can't say. Can I imply, somewhat peripherally, that her past, violent and sordid, did not exactly include a dog named Lassie and a lot of family talks about the Bible while Grammy sat doing macramé, adjusting her posture because the quaint fireplace was so sizzling? Can I suggest that, if you knew what I know about Heather's past, making Heather briefly sad, nauseous, and/or horrified might not seem like the worst idea in the world? No, I can't."

"All right, all right," I said.

"You know me," he said. "How many kids do I have?"

"Five," I said.

"What are their names?" he said.

"Mick, Todd, Karen, Lisa, Phoebe," I said.

"Am I a monster?" he said. "Do I remember birthdays around here? When a certain individual got athlete's foot on his groin on a Sunday, did a certain other individual drive over to Rexall and pick up a prescription, paying for it with his own personal money?"

That was a nice thing he'd done, but it seemed kind of unprofessional to bring it up now.

"Jeff," Abnesti said. "What do you want me to say here? Do you want me to say that your Fridays are at risk? I can easily say that."

Which was cheap. My Fridays meant a lot to me, and he knew that. Fridays I got to Skype Mom.

"How long do we give you?" Abnesti said.

"Five minutes," I said.

"How about we make it ten?" Abnesti said.

Mom always looked heartsick when our time was up. It had almost killed her when they arrested me. The trial had almost killed her. She'd spent her savings to get me out of real jail and in here. When I was a kid, she had long brown hair, past her waist. During the trial she cut it. Then it went gray. Now it was just a white poof about the size of a cap.

"Drip on?" Abnesti said.

"Acknowledge," I said.

"OK to pep up your language centers?" he said.

"Fine," I said.

"Heather, hello?" he said.

"Good morning!" Heather said.

"Drip on?" he said.

"Acknowledge," Heather said.

Abnesti used his remote.

The Darkenfloxx™ started flowing. Soon Heather was softly crying. Then was up and pacing. Then jaggedly crying. A little hysterical, even.

"I don't like this," she said, in a quaking voice.

Then she threw up in the trash can.

"Speak, Jeff," Abnesti said to me. "Speak a lot, speak in detail. Let's make something useful of this, shall we?"

Everything in my drip felt Grade A. Suddenly I was waxing poetic. I was waxing poetic re what Heather was doing, and waxing poetic re my feelings about what Heather was doing. Basically, what I was feeling was: Every human is born of man and woman. Every human, at birth, is, or at least has the potential to be, beloved of his/her mother/father. Thus every human is worthy of love. As I watched Heather suffer, a great tenderness suffused my body, a tenderness hard to distinguish from a sort of vast existential nausea; to wit, why are such beautiful beloved vessels made slaves to so much pain?

Heather presented as a bundle of pain receptors. Heather's mind was fluid and could be ruined (by pain, by sadness). Why? Why was she made this way? Why so fragile?

Poor child, I was thinking, poor girl. Who loved you? Who loves you?

"Hang in there, Jeff," Abnesti said. "Verlaine! What do you think? Any vestige of romantic love in Jeff's Verbal Commentary?"

"I'd say no," Verlaine said over the P.A. "That's all just pretty much basic human feeling right there."

"Excellent," Abnesti said. "Time remaining?"

"Two minutes," Verlaine said.

I found what happened next very hard to watch. Under the influence of the Verbaluce™, the VeriTalk™, and the ChatEase™, I also found it impossible not to narrate.

In each Workroom was a couch, a desk, and a chair, all, by design, impossible to disassemble. Heather now began disassembling her impossible-to-disassemble chair. Her face was a mask of rage. She drove her head into the wall. Like a wrathful prodigy, Heather, beloved of someone, managed, in her great sadness-fueled rage, to disassemble the chair while continuing to drive her head into the wall.

"Jesus," Verlaine said.

"Verlaine, buck up," Abnesti said. "Jeff, stop crying. Contrary to what you might think, there's not much data in crying. Use your words. Don't make this in vain."

I used my words. I spoke volumes, was precise. I described and redescribed what I was feeling as I watched Heather do what she now began doing, intently, almost beautifully, to her face/head with one of the chair legs.

In his defense, Abnesti was not in such great shape himself: breathing hard, cheeks candy-red, as he tapped the screen of his iMac nonstop with a pen, something he did when stressed.

"Time," he finally said, and cut the Darkenfloxx™ off with his remote. "Fuck. Get in there, Verlaine. Hustle it."

Verlaine hustled into Small Workroom 2.

"Talk to me, Sammy," Abnesti said.

Verlaine felt for Heather's pulse, then raised his hands, palms up, so that he looked like Jesus, except shocked instead of beatific, and also he had his glasses up on top of his head.

"Are you *kidding* me?" Abnesti said.

"What now?" Verlaine said. "What do I—"

"Are you fricking *kidding* me?" Abnesti said.

Abnesti burst out of his chair, shoved me out of the way, and flew through the door into Small Workroom 2.

VIII.

I returned to my Domain.

At three, Verlaine came on the P.A.

"Jeff," he said. "Please return to the Spiderhead."

I returned to the Spiderhead.

"We're sorry you had to see that, Jeff," Abnesti said.

"That was unexpected," Verlaine said.

"Unexpected plus unfortunate," Abnesti said. "And sorry I shoved you."

"Is she dead?" I said.

"Well, she's not the best," Verlaine said.

"Look, Jeff, these things happen," Abnesti said. "This is science. In science we explore the unknown. It was unknown what five minutes on Darkenfloxx™ would do to Heather. Now we know. The other thing we know, per Verlaine's assessment of your commentary, is that you really, for sure, do not harbor any residual romantic feelings for Heather. That's a big deal, Jeff. A beacon of hope at a sad time for all. Even as Heather was, so to speak, going down to the sea in her ship, you remained totally unwavering in terms of continuing to not romantically love her. My guess is ProtComm's going to be like, 'Wow, Utica's really leading the pack in terms of providing some mind-blowing new data on ED289/290.'"

It was quiet in the Spiderhead.

"Verlaine, go out," Abnesti said. "Go do your bit. Make things ready."

Verlaine went out.

"Do you think I liked that?" Abnesti said.

"You didn't seem to," I said.

"Well, I didn't," Abnesti said. "I hated it. I'm a person. I have feelings. Still, personal sadness aside, that was good. You did terrific overall. We all did terrific. Heather especially did terrific. I honor her. Let's just—let's see this thing through, shall we? Let's complete it. Complete the next portion of our Confirmation Trial."

Into Small Workroom 4 came Rachel.

IX.

"Are we going to Darkenfloxx™ Rachel now?" I said.

"Think, Jeff," Abnesti said. "How can we know that you love neither Rachel nor Heather if we only have data regarding your reaction to what just now happened to Heather? Use your noggin. You are not a scientist, but Lord knows you work around scientists all day. Drip on?"

I did not say "Acknowledge."

"What's the problem, Jeff?" Abnesti said.

"I don't want to kill Rachel," I said.

"Well, who does?" Abnesti said. "Do I? Do you, Verlaine?"

"No," Verlaine said over the P.A.

"Jeff, maybe you're overthinking this," Abnesti said. "Is it possible the Darkenfloxx™ will kill Rachel? Sure. We have the Heather precedent. On the other hand, Rachel may be stronger. She seems a little larger."

"She's actually a little smaller," Verlaine said.

"Well, maybe she's tougher," Abnesti said.

"We're going to weight-adjust her dosage," Verlaine said. "So."

"Thanks, Verlaine," Abnesti said. "Thanks for clearing that up."

"Maybe show him the file," Verlaine said.

Abnesti handed me Rachel's file.

Verlaine came back in.

"Read it and weep," he said.

Per Rachel's file, she had stolen jewelry from her mother, a car from her father, cash from her sister, statues from their church. She'd gone to jail for drugs. After four times in jail for drugs, she'd gone to rehab for drugs, then to rehab for prostitution, then to what they call rehab-refresh, for people who've been in rehab so many times they are basically immune. But she must have been immune to the rehab-refresh, too, because after that came her biggie: a triple murder—her dealer, the dealer's sister, the dealer's sister's boyfriend.

Reading that made me feel a little funny that we'd fucked and I'd loved her.

But I still didn't want to kill her.

"Jeff," Abnesti said. "I know you've done a lot of work on this with Mrs. Lacey. On killing and so forth. But this is not you. This is us."

"It's not even us," Verlaine said. "It's science."

"The mandates of science," Abnesti said. "Plus the dictates."

"Sometimes science sucks," Verlaine said.

"On the one hand, Jeff," Abnesti said, "a few minutes of unpleasantness for Heather—"

"Rachel," Verlaine said.

"A few minutes of unpleasantness for Rachel," Abnesti said, "years of relief for literally tens of thousands of underloving or overloving folks."

"Do the math, Jeff," Verlaine said.

"Being good in small ways is easy," Abnesti said. "Doing the huge good things, that's harder."

"Drip on?" Verlaine said. "Jeff?"

I did not say "Acknowledge."

"Fuck it, enough," Abnesti said. "Verlaine, what's the name of that one? The one where I give him an order and he obeys it?"

"Docilryde™," Verlaine said.

"Is there Docilryde™ in his MobiPak™?" Abnesti said.

"There's Docilryde™ in every MobiPak™," Verlaine said.

"Does he need to say 'Acknowledge'?" Abnesti said.

"Docilryde™'s a Class C, so—" Verlaine said.

"See, that, to me, makes zero sense," Abnesti said. "What good's an obedience drug if we need his permission to use it?"

"We just need a waiver," Verlaine said.

"How long does that shit take?" Abnesti said.

"We fax Albany, they fax us back," Verlaine said.

"Come on, come on, make haste," Abnesti said, and they went out, leaving me alone in the Spiderhead.

X.

It was sad. It gave me a sad, defeated feeling to think that soon they'd be back and would Docilryde™ me, and I'd say "Acknowledge," smiling agreeably the way a person smiles on Docilryde™, and then the Darkenfloxx™ would flow, into Rachel, and I would begin describing, in that rapid, robotic way one describes on Verbaluce™/VeriTalk™/ChatEase™, the things Rachel would, at that time, begin doing to herself.

It was like all I had to do to be a killer again was sit there and wait.

Which was a hard pill to swallow, after my work with Mrs. Lacey.

"Violence finished, anger no more," she'd make me say, over and over. Then she'd have me do a Detailed Remembering re my fateful night.

I was nineteen. Mike Appel was seventeen. We were both wasto. All night he'd been giving me grief. He was smaller, younger, less popular. Then we were out front of Frizzy's, rolling around on the ground. He was quick. He was mean. I was losing. I couldn't believe it. I was bigger, older, yet losing? Around us, watching, was basically everybody we knew. Then he had me on my back. Someone laughed. Someone said, "Shit, poor Jeff." Nearby was a brick. I grabbed it, glanced Mike in the head with it. Then was on top of him.

Mike gave. That is, there on his back, scalp bleeding, he gave, by shooting me a certain look, like, Dude, come on, we're not all that serious about this, are we?

We were.

I was.

I don't even know why I did it.

It was like, with the drinking and the being a kid and the nearly losing, I'd been put on a drip called, like, TemperBerst or something.

InstaRaje.

LifeRooner.

"Hey, guys, hello!" Rachel said. "What are we up to today?"

There was her fragile head, her undamaged face, one arm lifting a hand to scratch a cheek, legs bouncing with nerves, peasant skirt bouncing, too, clogged feet crossed under the hem.

Soon all that would be just a lump on the floor.

I had to think.

Why were they going to Darkenfloxx™ Rachel? So they could hear me describe it. If I wasn't here to describe it, they wouldn't do it. How could I make it so I wouldn't be here? I could leave. How could I leave? There was only one door out of the Spiderhead, which was autolocked, and on the other side was either Barry or Hans, with that electric wand called the DisciStick™. Could I wait until Abnesti came in, wonk him, try to race past Barry or Hans, make a break for the Main Door?

Any weapons in the Spiderhead? No, just Abnesti's birthday mug, a pair of running shoes, a roll of breath mints, his remote.

His remote?

What a dope. That was supposed to be on his belt at all times. Otherwise one of us might help ourselves to whatever we found, via Inventory Directory, in our MobiPaks™: some Bonviv™, maybe, some BlissTyme™, some SpeedErUp™.

Some Darkenfloxx™.

Jesus. That was one way to leave.

Scary, though.

Just then, in Small Workroom 4, Rachel, I guess thinking the Spiderhead empty, got up and did this happy little shuffle, like she was some cheerful farmer chick who'd just stepped outside to find the hick she was in love with coming up the road with a calf under his arm or whatever.

Why was she dancing? No reason.

Just alive, I guess.

Time was short.

The remote was well labelled.

Good old Verlaine.

I used it, dropped it down the heat vent, in case I changed my mind, then stood there like, I can't believe I just did that.

My MobiPak™ whirred.

The Darkenfloxx™ flowed.

Then came the horror: worse than I'd ever imagined. Soon my arm was about a mile down the heat vent. Then I was staggering around the Spiderhead, looking for something, anything. In the end, here's how bad it got: I used a corner of the desk.

What's death like?

You're briefly unlimited.

I sailed right out through the roof.

And hovered above it, looking down. Here was Rogan, checking his neck in the mirror. Here was Keith, squat-thrusting in his underwear. Here was Ned Riley, here was B. Troper, here was Gail Orley, Stefan DeWitt, killers all, all bad, I guess, although, in that instant, I saw it differently. At birth, they'd been charged by God with the responsibility of growing into total fuck-ups. Had they chosen this? Was it their fault, as they tumbled out of the womb? Had they aspired, covered in placental blood, to grow into harmers, dark forces, life-enders? In that first holy instant of breath/awareness (tiny hands clutching and unclutching), had it been their fondest hope to render (via gun, knife, or brick) some innocent family bereft? No; and yet their crooked destinies had lain dormant within them, seeds awaiting water and light to bring forth the most violent, life-poisoning flowers, said water/light actually being the requisite combination of neurological tendency and environmental activation that would transform them (transform us!) into earth's offal, murderers, and foul us with the ultimate, unwashable transgression.

Wow, I thought, was there some Verbaluce™ in that drip or what?

But no.

This was all me now.

I got snagged, found myself stuck on a facility gutter, and squatted there like an airy gargoyle. I was there but was also everywhere. I could see it all:

a clump of leaves in the gutter beneath my see-through foot; Mom, poor Mom, at home in Rochester, scrubbing the shower, trying to cheer herself via thin hopeful humming; a deer near the dumpster, suddenly alert to my spectral presence; Mike Appel's mom, also in Rochester, a bony, distraught checkmark occupying a slender strip of Mike's bed; Rachel below in Small Workroom 4, drawn to the one-way mirror by the sounds of my death; Abnesti and Verlaine rushing into the Spiderhead; Verlaine kneeling to begin CPR.

Night was falling. Birds were singing. Birds were, it occurred to me to say, enacting a frantic celebration of day's end. They were manifesting as the earth's bright-colored nerve endings, the sun's descent urging them into activity, filling them individually with life-nectar, the life-nectar then being passed into the world, out of each beak, in the form of that bird's distinctive song, which was, in turn, an accident of beak shape, throat shape, breast configuration, brain chemistry: some birds blessed in voice, others cursed; some squawking, others rapturous.

From somewhere, something kind asked, *Would you like to go back? It's completely up to you. Your body appears salvageable.*

No, I thought, no, thanks, I've had enough.

My only regret was Mom. I hoped someday, in some better place, I'd get a chance to explain it to her, and maybe she'd be proud of me, one last time, after all these years.

From across the woods, as if by common accord, birds left their trees and darted upward. I joined them, flew among them, they did not recognize me as something apart from them, and I was happy, so happy, because for the first time in years, and forevermore, I had not killed, and never would.

KELLY LUCE

Amorometer

Kelly Luce has a degree in cognitive science. She lived and worked in Japan and received fellowships from the MacDowell Colony, Ucross Foundation, Kerouac Project, and others. Her work has appeared in the *Chicago Tribune*, *Salon*, *O*, and the *Southern Review*, among others. She recently received her MFA in writing and works as a contributing editor for *Electric Literature*. She has a novel, *Pull Me Under*, upcoming from Farrar, Straus & Giroux. She lives in Santa Cruz, California.

"Amorometer" is the story of an invention, but sometimes inventions change the way we think more than they change the world around us. It was first published in *Crazyhorse*.

The letter arrived in a handmade envelope sealed with red wax. Flipping through the bills and junk mail, Aya Kawaguchi saw her name penned in perfectly shaped characters, tore open the seal, and read:

Dear Kawaguchi-sama,

I feel I must bypass the convention of commenting on the weather as I begin this letter because a more pressing matter is probably concerning you, that of my identity and purpose. I write in the spirit of greatest hope, and am aiming to reach the Ms. Aya Kawaguchi who was a student of Keio University in 1969. If this is not she, please ignore this letter.

My name is Shinji Oeda, Professor of Psychology at Keio from 1960 until my retirement in 1991. From 1969 to 1970, I ran a series of experiments, the goal of which was to design and perfect a device—dubbed the Amorometer— *capable of measuring one's capacity to love. (*Amor, *of course, being the Latin root of the word "love.")*

In 1969 there were no departmental regulations regarding the debriefing of experimental subjects. I assume you had no understanding of our research, let alone the extraordinary gifts these tests revealed: of all the subjects (439 in total), yours was the highest score in lovingcapacity. In the empathy measure you scored an astounding 32 points—more than two standard deviations above the mean.

I must come to my point: I would very much like to meet you. As a widower of two years, I have found the companionship available to me (my tomcat and my memories) to be inadequate. The cat is unreliable and cantankerous, the memories often the same.

It may be true that regardless of a man's age, there remains inside him a kernel of youth. As I have aged, my curiosity has not lessened, but has migrated from my brain to my heart. It is not such a bad thing.

With much hope,
Shinji Oeda

P.S. This letter has taken me many years to write; the hypothetical results of my test on a Cordometer *(cord the Latin root for "heart," or "courage") would likely be dismally low. I urge your quick reply, if possible.*

Aya raised the letter up to the lamp at her desk, revealing the watermark. The thick paper, and the surprising space it created between her fingertips, made her feel somehow important.

She had never been a student at Keio University. Since marrying Hisao all those years ago, she'd hardly visited Tokyo at all.

She ran a fingertip over the seal. She imagined the professor dropping the thick wax onto the envelope's flap and pressing his stamp there. She imagined the wool of his jacket and the creased leather of his shoes as he slipped out of the house, and the long, slim fingers with which he carried the letter to the postbox in his tasteful Tokyo neighborhood. Now that envelope was here, its wax like an exotic fruit, cut with a stranger's name.

A stranger who believed her to be—what had been his word?—*extraordinary*.

She glanced at the clock above the stove. Hisao would be another hour, and dinner was already prepared. There was still some ironing to be done, but it could go another day. She brought the stepstool to the closet and brought down the box with the good stationery.

She set to work:

Dear Oeda-sama,

How nice it was to receive your letter, and quite a surprise! For the record, the rainy season has begun here, but I will spare you the details of the weather since, as you say, our correspondence is a strange one.

She reread her opening, then pulled out a fresh pink sheet and rewrote it, replacing "nice" with "lovely" and "strange" with "most unusual." She continued, *I have not thought of Keio in a long time, and I am delighted that you had the courage to find me.*

She thought a second, then added, *I'd think your readings on the Cordometer would be quite high!*

She sat up, aware of Hisao's arrival. After all these years, the ritual of his entry was well-known to her: the yawn of hinges, the slam of the metal door like a detonation, her husband's gravelly call of "I'm home," not to her but to himself. The only missing element was the punctuation of his briefcase hitting the floor.

She tucked the letter in a drawer and sighed. It was just like Emiko had warned her: now that he'd retired, her husband was always underfoot. She'd had the run of the house from six in the morning to six at night for thirty-one years. Hisao was a good man, had provided a home to her and their son, but she never considered she'd have to spend this much *time* with him.

"You're home early," she said, standing to greet him.

"Driving range was packed," Hisao grumbled. "Too many kids. This time of day, kids ought to be in school, or at work."

"Mm," she said. "Would you like dinner now? Or how about a cold drink?"

She glided toward the kitchen as he fell into his blue recliner. For as long as they'd been together, he'd come home from work, collapsed in this chair, requested food or drink. Now, however, he often wasn't tired upon returning, and though he was still drawn by habit to the chair, he no longer looked comfortable there.

She put the finishing touches on her letter that night while Hisao slept, ears defended against his own snoring by green foam plugs.

I am flattered that you should recall me and would love to meet you, she wrote, and took another sip from the heavy glass into which she'd poured some of Hisao's good whiskey.

She printed the name "Aya Kawaguchi" at the bottom of the letter, marveling at how much nicer this woman's handwriting was than her own.

His short response arrived three days later.

I'll open this letter with the weather in my heart, and tell you that the sky is clear and warm, and the quality of light is thick and sweet like honey! I am pleased and surprised (good news does not often come my way these days) that you are in a position to meet me. I could travel to your town, or, if you like, we can meet here in the "neon jungle."

Thick and sweet like honey! Aya smiled, amazed that there were such people in the world. It was time, she thought, that she met them.

She told only Emiko, who'd divorced young and never remarried, about her plans.

"I'm not going to *cheat* on Hisao," Aya said. "I just want to . . . bask. This man thinks I'm extraordinary. I want to know how that feels."

"Oh, shut it! You're a lovely woman."

"Lovely, schmovely. I want to be *extraordinary*."

Emiko rolled her eyes.

"Besides, the timing of it, with Hisao retired now and Ryo just moved out—it's like a chance to reinvent. See what I've missed."

"What if he's rich and handsome?"

"He could be poor and crazy," Aya said, but did not believe it.

"An *Amorometer*! Whoever heard of such a thing? Wonder how I'd score."

"Me too," Aya said, recalling every selfish, unloving act of her lifetime. The time, as a teenager, she'd stolen an umbrella; the gossip sessions with Emiko that often turned catty; the way she'd stopped breastfeeding Ryo after two weeks because she couldn't stand her raw, chapped nipples.

"Exactly—what if he can tell it's not you?"

"I'll come home," she said.

"Only if he's poor and crazy. If he's rich and handsome, stick around."

Their meeting had been set for noon on a Sunday on the top floor of Tokyo Station, in a restaurant famous for its view of the city. Though Shinji had repeated his offer to travel to her small town, Aya had insisted on coming to Tokyo. The person she was hoping to become could not exist in Iida; she could only transform with distance. And though it terrified her to think of herself lost on the streets of an unfamiliar place, she felt certain that once she arrived, she could be anyone she wanted. Anyone she *might have been*, had her life gone differently. She'd read enough books. She felt a long line of Ayas inside of her, ready to be called upon. The thought made her feel like an adventurer, and while Hisao was out golfing, she spent half the morning pawing through her closet, trying on clothes she hadn't worn in years.

"Well, let me know what you find," Emiko said as Aya went out. "And see if he has any single friends."

She told Hisao she was joining a string quartet organized by an acquaintance of Emiko's.

"Do you even remember how to play that thing?" he asked from behind his newspaper.

"Of course," she replied, pairing a batch of socks she'd just brought in from the line. "It was practically attached to my hand in high school."

"I see. Are you going to practice now?"

She couldn't tell if he wanted her to bring out the old viola, or if he was checking to see whether his newspaper reading would be disturbed. "Maybe," she said.

He nodded, mumbling to himself as he read. Then he said, "But in Tokyo? Couldn't you find a group closer to home?"

She continued matching and rolling the socks, never losing the rhythm of the work. "I don't think so." Then she paused and asked, "Do you think I'm extraordinary?"

He didn't glance up from his paper. "You're lovely, dear."

The night before her trip, she went to her bookshelf. She never left the house without something to read, but her choice this time seemed of real importance. Finally her eyes fell on the dog-eared copy of *Anna Karenina* she had not read since Ryo was a baby. She slipped it from the shelf into her bag. The weight of the story on her shoulder felt significant; this was a long journey and required a long tale, but more than that, she felt the characters themselves would be good company for this other Aya Kawaguchi.

But if anyone's hit by a train while I'm waiting, I'm turning around, Aya thought.

It took her a long time to fall asleep that night and she woke up twice, certain she had missed her train. At five o'clock she gave up and took a bath. At seven Hisao drove her to the local train station, where she caught a two-car train to Nishiyama, her connection for the Tokyo bullet.

Safely onboard the bullet train, she shifted in her carpeted seat and let *Anna Karenina* fall open to random pages. "There are no customs to which a person cannot grow accustomed, especially if he sees that everyone around him lives in the same way."

"He liked fishing and seemed to take pride in being able to like such a stupid occupation."

She read:

Anna hardly knew at times what it was she feared, and what she hoped for. Whether she feared or desired what had happened, or what was going to happen, and exactly what she longed for, she could not have said.

She looked out the window. She took off her wedding ring, put it back on. The scenery flew by. She found she could relax her eyes and let the images blur together, or she could focus and pick out the elements: futons lolling from windows like tongues, cascades of electrical wiring, a rooftop rice paddy, a Coca-Cola billboard. Each thing was gone, replaced by something new, before there was time to reflect. *No need to think on a train this fast,* she thought. *If I could stay on this train forever, I'd never have to think about anything again, and life would just be an exciting show of what's passing by on the outside.* It was a comforting idea.

Stepping off the train was like jumping into a river. She wandered through surging crowds in search of a place to store her viola, the case of which suddenly seemed unnecessarily bulky. *Couldn't I have said I was coming for a book club?* she thought.

So many people. She was struck by the purpose with which all of them seemed to be moving. A ribbon of song caught her ear, and she turned toward a group of musicians performing next to a bank of ticket machines. They were college students, most likely—two violinists and a cellist. She laughed aloud at the coincidence, her arriving with the missing piece to the quartet and no intention of playing it. The tiny girl on cello caught sight of the instrument and tilted her head in an invitation to join them. Aya blushed and hurried past.

With the help of a young man who looked like Hisao in his younger, slimmer days, she located the day storage lockers and stowed the instrument. Then she headed for the escalators.

She wanted to arrive at the restaurant early. She'd read her book, drink some tea to calm her nerves. She looked at her watch: 10:03, one minute later than the last time she'd looked.

The escalator carried her out of the subway and into a multistory mall arranged in circles that reached all the way up to a huge skylight. The sky beyond the glass was gray yet still bright enough to be cheerful. On the seventh floor she spotted a cosmetics store and stepped off the escalator.

After consulting with the heavy-lashed girl behind the counter, who assured her the color was not too suggestive but rather "elegant and age-repelling," she purchased a tube of red lipstick in a shade called "Shhh" that cost as much as a hardback book. The makeup glittered like a ball gown and felt like satin on her lips. This reminded her of bed sheets, and she pushed the thought away. Afterward, in the department store's bathroom, she applied and removed the lipstick four times before reaching a compromise between herself and the other Aya Kawaguchi (who no doubt would have worn "Shhh" without compunction) and blended the shade with her functional chapstick. As a concession for toning down the lipstick, she removed her wedding ring. Then she washed her hands.

At the restaurant, she took a seat along the wall of windows and ordered a pot of tea. A light rain fell over the city, and in response the buildings and roads took on a fresh sheen and the colors of signs and cars brightened.

A moth on the glass caught her eye. It was unlike any moth she'd ever seen, its wings rounded at the top and pointed at the bottom. An indigo spot decorated each orange-rimmed wing.

She shifted uneasily. The spots on its wings made her feel she was being watched. Her mother said that deceased ancestors came to visit disguised as moths, and she didn't want anyone she knew, living or dead, to witness her activity today. She shooed at the insect with her napkin, but it did not move.

She tried to ignore it and focus on *Anna Karenina*, but it was no use. She watched the action in the restaurant instead. The place was beginning to fill up. At eleven-thirty, half an hour early, Shinji Oeda walked in—a dandelion springing from his lapel as promised. He was not as tall as she'd imagined, but his clothes were professionally pressed and fit him well. Emiko would have found him handsome.

But what do *you* think, Aya thought. Good-looking? Yes. His face was wide and mild, with gold-rimmed glasses riding atop a nose so flat it seemed a miracle the glasses stayed up at all. He sat across the restaurant, facing away from her. She admired his observation of table manners despite his lack of company, the way he placed his napkin in his lap immediately and sat straight in his chair, the warm smile with which he greeted the waiter.

She looked back to the moth. Its black, crooked legs moved slightly. A wing angled itself toward her. Abruptly she stood, cupped her hands over the thing, and closed them. She would carry it out into the mall, let its eerie eye-wings rest elsewhere.

The waiter had brought Shinji Oeda a small drink, which he threw back in one gulp, handing the empty glass back to the waiter. Emboldened by his nervous act, Aya walked toward the entrance, and him, the moth cupped in her hands. Its papery wings beat furiously against her palms. She would pass near his table, but since he didn't know what she looked like, she would not be discovered.

As she approached, Aya watched his back, certain he could feel her eyes. His hair was cut very short, in an almost military style, and shimmered silver under the restaurant's low-hanging lamps. His hair was like the rain, she thought.

She passed him, careful to walk neither too fast nor too slow, and went out into the mall. She shook the moth free. It flew toward the skylight. When she returned to the restaurant, she glanced automatically at Shinji Oeda and found his eyes on her.

Aya blushed. There was nothing to do but approach him. As she drew near, he stood, a smile spreading across his face as he took her in. "Oeda-san?" she asked.

"Please, call me Shinji. And you—you are the legendary Aya Kawaguchi." He bowed deeply.

She bowed as well, holding the position so that she might catch her breath. His cologne reminded her of the forest behind her house.

His mouth was large, his smile a deep cradle. Up close, his gentle eyes and flat nose gave him the appearance of a woodblock print. "I saw what you did with that moth," he said, and clasped her hands in his. "This is a great honor."

Embarrassment washed over her. "The honor is mine. And please forget about the moth; it was quite silly of me."

"Forget? Never! I suspected your identity just from that gesture—such a compassionate act, freeing an insect others would ignore, or even worse, kill!"

Aya was unsure what to say to this; luckily the waiter returned and pulled a chair out for her. "A drink, miss?" he asked as they sat.

"Yes, please," she said. "I'll have—" She thought about Anna, and Russian aristocracy. "Vodka," she said.

The waiter's eyebrows twitched. "Rocks?"

"A few," she said, certain that her order had been inappropriate.

Shinji slapped the table. "Vodka. Who'd have thought?" He grinned. "Make it two."

Shinji leaned back in his seat, his second vodka nearly finished. They had chatted about a number of meaningless topics—the weather, food, and train travel.

"I have to say, I never thought I'd be having a drink—a *vodka*—with Aya Kawaguchi. For so many years you were just a set of data . . . my imagination was forced to extrapolate from there."

Aya did her best to sound well educated. "Life takes all kinds of strange turns," she said, finishing her vodka and enjoying the warmth it brought to her cheeks. "If you let it," she added.

He leaned in and whispered. "Forgive me, but—how is it you never married?"

Aya had managed to sidestep this topic but knew it would come up and had prepared her answer. "I just never found the right man."

He nodded as if he'd expected as much. "Extraordinary people have extraordinarily hard times."

He went on, "I've wondered for so long . . . I know now that my imagination is a feeble mechanism. You're so different from what I imagined—" She glanced at him. "So much better," he quickly added.

She began to relax. "You haven't told me about your research. I have a right to a debriefing, I think."

"Simply put, we found a way to quantify a person's ability to love. Their potential. It turns out that not all people are capable of loving to the same capacity. The idea was revolutionary." He leaned forward, touched her hand. "Imagine being married to a person whose ability to love—whose lovingcapacity—is far below your own."

As he spoke the word *lovingcapacity*, he tapped out the syllables with two fingers on the place her wedding ring had recently been.

"From their perspective, a person may be loving to their fullest extent," Shinji continued. "However, this isn't good enough for the partner with the higher LC. It will *never* be good enough. This causes the lower-capacity partner to feel inadequate, unappreciated, and their partner feels the same because, to their mind, everyone should love as they do."

"Can't people be made to understand, to accept their differences?"

"Perhaps. But it is very hard for people to truly understand. We have, it turns out, a tremendous blind spot when it comes to being loved."

"And people can't improve?"

"Our research generally showed lovingcapacity to be a fixed and immovable trait, much like eye color or IQ. Of course, when it comes to the mind, one can never be sure."

"I can't believe I did so well," she said, and just then the waiter arrived, balancing two large lunch boxes and a platter of drinks. As he set Aya's box in front her, a glass of cola slid from his tray and crashed onto the table, splashing Aya and dousing her pork cutlet.

The waiter fumbled, apologizing, and promised to bring a new lunch. Aya grimaced at the idea of wasting so much food.

"There's no need," she said, dabbing at her shirt with her napkin. "I'll eat it as it is."

"Please, ma'am—"

"Really. Maybe you could discount the bill a bit instead."

The waiter bowed, his face as red as "Shhh," and hurried away.

Aya took a bite of her cola-flavored cutlet; she was starving and the vodka had unloosed her appetite. Not bad, she thought. When she looked up, Shinji was looking her, his face shining. His food was untouched.

"Amazing," he said.

"Oh, it's nothing," she said, secretly pleased. "So tell me, what became of your findings?"

"In the autumn of 1970, we lost our funding. The government classified our work as 'unscientific and possibly dangerous.'"

"Dangerous!"

"Some people felt we were meddling in a place science ought not to meddle. A real shame, since long-term research is by far the most robust in fields like this." He made a small motion with his hand, and a minute later two more drinks appeared.

"Well, I've prattled on long enough," he said, raising his glass. "Let's hear about you. From the beginning. What did you study at Keio?"

She clinked her glass to his and took a long sip of her vodka. Aya Kawaguchi was a woman who could hold her liquor. "Literature," she said. "My first love was Soseki."

"*Kokoro*," he replied, naming the author's first novel. As he said it, he placed his hand over his heart. "Maybe that is why your *kokoro* is so big."

"Or maybe my big heart is what drew me to Soseki." She was feeling more and more comfortable, as if lying about her identity had rolled out the red carpet for other untruths to follow.

He sighed and sat back in his chair, smiling. "I've forgotten what it's like to be around a Keio girl. Don't you miss city life?"

He focused on her completely as she spoke, his eyes wide, like a child watching a fireworks display. She felt—interesting. Extraordinary. "Well, college was a wild time," she said, as if admitting something. "I didn't always make it to class, let's just say that."

"Well now, do tell!"

"Oh, no. Well, for one thing there was the band—"

"The marching band?"

"No, a rock band. Punk, really. I was the singer."

"Ah—I played clarinet, myself."

She nodded, slipping inside this invented life like a pair of old pajamas. "We were called Shards of Black, and we wore only white, to be ironic."

While he was laughing, she excused herself and went to the bathroom. Hisao had left a voicemail, a habit he'd acquired recently.

She returned his call, explained to him the significance of the toaster oven sitting on the kitchen counter, what each knob did, and how long to leave the bread inside. He didn't mention her quartet practice, which she found annoying, but when he asked whether she would be home for dinner, his voice stirred pity in her. She imagined him eating burnt toast—plain because he did not know where to locate the butter and jam—and she could not say no.

Upon her return she found Hisao sitting on the kitchen floor, surrounded by a mess of bottles, boxes, and cans.

"What are you doing?"

"Rearranging," he said, examining a box of fish stock.

"*Why?*"

He looked up, irritated. "For greater efficiency."

"You don't even cook."

He shrugged. She stepped over him and picked up the whiskey.

"Since when do you drink?"

"Since now. Why do you seem to think life is over, that it's too late to try new things?"

He motioned at the mess around him. "I *am* trying new things."

A letter from Shinji arrived two days later. *He must have mailed it while I was on the train ride back*, Aya thought. In the letter he thanked her for coming to Tokyo and expressed his excitement for their next meeting, the next Sunday in Ueno Park. He closed with a line from *Kokoro*, the Soseki novel they had discussed:

Words uttered in passion contain a greater living truth than do those expressing thoughts rationally conceived. . . .

She reread his letters each morning and began the day feeling like a plant just watered.

Autumn had set the trees in the park aflame, and Aya felt she'd never experienced such richness of color, even in the rural forests of her hometown.

He had bowed to her upon their meeting, a good sign, she thought, since a hug would have meant something she was not quite ready for. His face searched hers in a way it had not upon their first encounter, like a connoisseur reevaluating a painting that's been placed in new light. She thought it might be her lipstick: after locking up her viola, she'd applied "Shhh" without blotting it afterward.

His unsure manner disappeared quickly, and Aya wrote it off to nerves. Her suspicion was confirmed when, after just a few minutes of walking, he grabbed her hand. "I want to show you something," he said.

He led her out of the park, through a shopping area, and into a quiet neighborhood of old houses and narrow lanes. "This is my house," he said, and they stopped in the street. "Don't worry," he said, seeing her expression, "I'm not indecent. After all, we hardly know each other!"

She followed him down a narrow path behind the house. He kept glancing back, as if to make sure she was still there. A tiny shed stood in the yard, and when they reached it, he began unlocking it. There were four locks in all.

"Here we are," he said, pushing open the door.

Aya stepped inside the dim little room, which smelled of wet wood and plastic. A large table, which held a device resembling a seismograph, took up most of the space. It was not a room built for company.

"This," he said, throwing out his arm like a magician, "is the Amorometer."

The central component of the contraption was a metal case painted red. Inside the case, a needle hung poised over a thick roll of paper. Two leather cuffs, one large, like a belt, and one smaller, the size of a blood-pressure cuff, dangled from the left side of the box. Rising behind the box like a crown was a clothes hanger—also painted red—that had been forced into an awkward heart shape. It looked like something Ryo would have built with scraps from the neighbor's trash.

"I was hoping you'd be willing to, well, provide some new data. A longitudinal study, if you will!" He set his hand lightly on her arm.

"Ah!" She imagined herself cuffed to the device, the evidence of her fakery pouring forth, and shuddered. She sat down.

"Are you all right? Is there something you need?"

"I'm just not—"

"You see," he said, opening and closing a clamp full of tiny metal teeth, "this way I can be sure . . . *we* can be sure . . ."

She thought of her lipstick, and touched a finger to her mouth, as if testing a wall she had regretfully painted.

"I think I should go," she said.

Her train wasn't due for over an hour. She wandered the fluorescent underground corridors of the station, passing shops advertising souvenirs for places elsewhere—blackened eggs from Hakone, tiny limes from Shikoku, *habu* liquor from Okinawa. She wondered how many of the gifts she'd received over the years had come from places like this. Was everything so false?

She heard the music long before she saw the players; it came from nearly the same place as the first time, next to the ticket machine for the Hibiya subway line, which, she'd learned from Shinji, was the deepest subway in the world. If you stood at the bottom of the Hibiya escalator, it was said, you could feel the heat of hell and see the light from heaven.

She looked at the spot the quartet-minus-one had been a week before but found it empty. She followed the melody with her ear. It was coming, she realized, from beyond the ticket gates, rising up the escalator.

She made her decision at once; or rather, she reflected later, her heart had made it for her—a luxury she had not allowed herself in many years. Inside the stall of a nearby bathroom, Aya flipped the latches on her viola case. She lifted the instrument from its bed and, drawing the ancient bow across the strings, began to play.

The strings were old; the A and G were frayed along the bowline and she worked the tuning pegs, cradling the wooden body to her chest. Shoes clattered on the disinfected floors, doors slammed, and hands were washed, and for once in her life, Aya did not care who observed her. These women were strangers, yet they shared this city; maybe some had been students at Keio University, maybe the other Aya Kawaguchi was in the stall next to her, pants down. The thought made her laugh, and without realizing what she was doing, she began playing the solo she'd performed her last year of high school, the first movement of Shubert's *Arpeggione*. Heady, she watched her fingers land on the strings, and though the B was falling out of tune already, her rhythm was dead on.

It wasn't perfect, but she felt it was good, and if she practiced, it could be marvelous, better than it had been in school because everything she had lived through would go into the music. She was no longer a girl. Her fears and desires were known and did not bind her. She hit the final notes with this in mind, standing alone in the corner stall of the women's bathroom near the Hibiya Line in Tokyo Station, and when she was finished, a small clap echoed against the tile walls, and a second later more applause joined it. Aya lifted her head. She bowed to no one, then started from the beginning, thinking how the beady-eyed judge had nodded, even smiled, and said: "That was good, but let's hear it again."

MAX APPLE

The Yogurt of Vasirin Kefirovsky

Max Apple is a satirist who is probably best known for the movie *The Air Up There*, for which he wrote the screenplay. He has a PhD from the University of Michigan and taught creative writing at Rice University for twenty-nine years. Apple has written two novels, two memoirs, and three collections of stories. The *Washington Post* has said of him, "[Apple] is an amiable, good-hearted, sweet-tempered writer whose short pieces occupy an agreeable territory somewhere between fact and fiction." He lives in Pennsylvania, where he teaches at the University of Pennsylvania.

"The Yogurt of Vasirin Kefirovsky" parodies the mad-scientist motif common in science fiction and in parodies of science fiction.

Vasirin Kefirovsky stands six feet four and uses an extra-long rubber-tipped pointer. He is fond of spinning a globe with this pointer while his feet rest on the patio table. He dislikes gossip but revels in small talk. His wife, Emily, spends many of her mornings watching the yogurt incubate beneath blankets in her stainless-steel kitchen. Dr. Kefirovsky spins his globe and thinks from eight to eleven forty-five, then he drinks his yogurt and works all afternoon on *Earth Story*.

Today his morning schedule is interrupted by an interviewer from *Time* magazine, Robert Williams, assistant science editor.

Mrs. Kefirovsky sits with the two men at the patio table, keeping her eye on the weather. She sips a cocktail of Mogen David wine and club soda.

"I am what I am," says Professor Kefirovsky. "When I was a boy, I ate wide noodles brushed with cheeses. In middle age, no meat was too gamy. I ate your turtles, your rabbits, your unfit leghorns. I knew the earth before I knew my own belly."

"Your husband is a great man," the reporter tells Emily. "If the deep space probes bear out his ideas as well as Mariner II did, he'll be on the cover of *Time* someday. He'll be taught in the schools."

Kefirovsky puts down his pointer and uses a long forefinger for emphasis. "Eating has nothing to do with thinking," he tells the reporter. "I always thought clearly, but I thought too much about food. Now I think about nothing to eat. What is yogurt? It's milk and time and heat. What is the earth? It's rocks and time and bodies."

The reporter takes notes slowly. "But tell me this, Professor, have you resented being an outsider all these years? I mean, has the fact that the scientific community considers you something of a charlatan embittered your career?"

Kefirovsky spins the earth with his pointer. "Name me a big one who was not an outsider. Galileo, Copernicus, Paracelsus, Hans Fricht . . . Galen maybe was an insider, he gave back rubs to the Emperor. He was a chiropractor. If you're an insider you make Vicks cough drops or you work for the Ford Foundation."

"Well, Einstein, for one, was accepted by his contemporaries. He was not an outsider."

Kefirovsky stands and edges the pointer close to Williams's nose. "And Einstein made cough drops too. Only if you write this everyone will say how ungrateful Kefirovsky is. Now that people pay attention to him, he fills the magazines with dreck about Einstein. Not long ago I saw Einstein's brain. It's in Connecticut at a health institute. They take care of it like it's a member of the family in an iron lung. I knew Einstein and I knew his brother Victor, who sold Red Ball shoes in Brooklyn."

"Don't worry, Professor, *Time* isn't a gossip magazine. I won't write anything about Einstein."

"I don't worry and I don't think about eating food." Using his pointer as a walking stick, Kefirovsky strides into his garden bordered by petunias, roses, and white azaleas. The reporter follows.

"I came from Russia in a dressing gown. At Ellis Island I cut it below the pockets with scissors, hemmed the bottom, and wore it for years as a satin smoking jacket. I had my teeth capped during World War II. I married in 1926 and have four sons, all of whom served in the United States Army and were honorably discharged, except Gerald."

"And what does Gerald do now?"

"He makes cough drops."

Mrs. Kefirovsky returns to the kitchen with her candy thermometer to check the yogurt's temperature. "I'll call you, Vasi, when it's a hundred and twelve."

Dr. Kefirovsky is neither tired nor angry. He suffers the reporter but his mind is elsewhere. His four sons are all organic chemists. They used to come together every year at Easter time and eat big meals of lake trout, poultry, beef, and Russian side dishes like stuffed cabbage, boiled potatoes, and fried smelt. Kefirovsky himself used to make two hundred gallons of wine a year. During the Christmas season neighbors and delivery men drank it from Pepsi-Cola quarts.

There are two ovens in his stainless-steel kitchen and a natural-gas pit-barbecue in his backyard. But Kefirovsky no longer cooks, barbecues, or makes wine. His sons and their families are refusing to come for another Easter. The mailman and the paperboy turn down the quarts of Christmas yogurt. The books he wrote thirty years ago about the collisions of the planets are selling now, but his new thesis is scorned by people like Adelle Davis and Dr. Atkins. He has no publisher for *Earth Story*.

Williams asks, "When did you first begin to realize that cosmic accidents are recorded in human history?"

"I knew this as early as 1929."

"But what made you think of it?"

"I opened my eyes. I looked around. I talked to people. I read books. I wondered why a rinky-dinky town like Troy should be such a front-page story for a thousand years. I wondered why the Red Sea opened and how come the Chinamen knew about Noah's flood. I kept my eyes on the heavens. I read spectrograms. I made educated guesses. That's what science is.

"One day I came to Hans Fricht and I said, 'Hans, either I'm crazy or I know about history.' I showed him my data. 'You're not crazy,' he said. He called Einstein, who was then a nobody, a refugee in baggy trousers who thanked God when you talked to him in German and had hay fever in New Jersey.

"'*Er veiss vas er zagt?*' Einstein asked Fricht. He followed the mathematics but he missed the point. He didn't give a damn about history. Before he died he was a pen pal with Albert Schweitzer. I sent Schweitzer a copy of *Worlds in Confusion* but never heard from him. Fricht was going to write the introduction but he said Einstein needed the money, so Einstein wrote it in German and Hans translated it. Einstein had lots of bad grammar. Listen, I liked the man. I am not jealous of his success. He was right about many things. If he ate less, he would be alive today."

Emily Kefirovsky comes out the back door and down the two wooden steps to the patio. She approaches the flower garden carrying a blue cardigan over her forearm. "Vasi, the sun is behind the clouds. Here." She hands him the cardigan. "He's not a young man, Mr. Williams, although the cold never bothers him. During the winters in Berlin, even in Moscow, he never wore gloves. Here in Texas you can't tell from one minute to the next. The air conditioning makes him dizzy. I wish we could move."

Kefirovsky puts on the cardigan. "Go watch the yogurt," he tells her. "It will be ready to pour in a few minutes." He strokes the sweater to be certain it is just right. With his pointer he marks the spot where Emily stood. "My wife eats saturated fats. Look at yourself. Probably not forty and I'll bet your veins are closing up like artichokes."

"Maybe you're right, Professor Kefirovsky, but let's finish talking about you. I'm not important. I'm just an anonymous pencil at *Time*, but you're a famous man. Whether scientists like it or not your works are right up there in general sales, right up there with Dr. Spock and Dr. Rubin and Dr. Atkins."

"These are kids' stuff. Not just Spock, the other ones too. I've read all the diet books. Atkins is what they used to call a piss prophet. They ran them out of town in Germany. They would set up fairs and sell medicine like hucksters. They sent you to the toilet with litmus paper and when they read the colors they sold you their medicine. That's what Atkins is. And Rubin, he doesn't even know what Wilhelm Reich knew.

"I knew him in the days before he made the boxes. He used to come over too, to talk to me like Eidler and Fricht and the others. He liked cold asparagus dipped in mayonnaise. He never drank beer. If they hadn't tortured him in California, I believe he would be alive today."

Kefirovsky leads the reporter, single file, through his garden along a circular path. Behind the flowers are green plants and shrubs, some in blossom. In the deep shade there are patches of soft dark moss. The professor points at various plants but does not describe them. "I am not a botanist. Pliny the Elder classified plants and Hippocrates' son-in-law classified people. There are many plants that can kill you but not a one that will eat you. I was an old man before I thought of this."

"Is that so significant?" The reporter has put away his ballpoint. His hands are clasped behind his back, the notebook sticks out of his pocket. He looks bored. From the kitchen Mrs. Kefirovsky calls out, "A hundred and eleven point eight." The Professor walks briskly toward the house. "After one hundred and ten we switch from the candy thermometer to the new digital types that give you an exact reading."

In the stainless-steel kitchen sink he washes his hands with green liquid soap and dries them carefully on a paper towel. The yogurt is in a three-quart glass jar immersed in water within a very deep electric frying pan. The digital thermometer lies in the yogurt just as snugly as if the mixture were a patient's milky tongue. Kefirovsky takes a plastic container from the refrigerator and spoons a sticky material into the yogurt. The aroma is strong and brisk, it smells almost like wintergreen.

"What's that?" Williams asks.

Mrs. Kefirovsky looks surprised. "He didn't tell you yet?"

"No, but I will," the Professor says. "Now we must wait for at least fifteen minutes while the entire mixture resonates at one hundred and twelve degrees Fahrenheit. Then we pour it into pints, where it can stay for almost a week. The store yogurts are good for two months or more. Mine is not the same.

This is good for six days only."

Mrs. Kefirovsky sits on a stool, her heavy legs dangling playfully. The reporter and the Professor are on chrome-and-vinyl kitchen chairs facing the yogurt. Kefirovsky has again taken up his pointer. "What I added to the yogurt is a sticky sweet extract of an Arabic plant called 'mahn,' spelled m-a-n. I imported it from Saudi Arabia, Egypt, and Morocco. The Moroccan one grows best here. I harvest it and freeze it. It's also good for the breath like chlorophyll gum.

"Fifteen years ago all you heard was chlorophyll. Then everyone got interested in outer space and transistors. I am the opposite. I started with space forty, fifty years ago, and now I'm back to chlorophyll. Science is like that. We are always breaking up substances to look for the soul of the material. My sons, the chemists, don't know this. They just do jobs for the oil companies."

"Not everyone is an original thinker like you, Vasi," Mrs. Kefirovsky states from her high position on the stool. "Mr. Williams, don't get the wrong impression about the boys. They're good chemists. But Vasi has no patience for people who learn to do something and then do it. He learns something and then he does something else."

"That's what science is," the Professor says.

"Twelve minutes, Vasi." Mrs. Kefirovsky watches the kitchen clock from her perch.

"I started thinking about this only a few years ago, after Hans Fricht died. He was the last of my colleagues. I noticed how all of us pallbearers could hardly carry him. I thought, We're just too old for such work. But that wasn't it. Hans Fricht, whom I loved like a brother, ate too much."

"He did," Emily adds. "He liked to eat small meals every hour while he worked."

"This started me thinking altogether about eating. Then I went to the old books, the way I did after I studied physics and astronomy. I thought to myself, if the heavens got into these books, why not the foods? So I read all the Greeks, mostly Homer, who is full of eating. I kept tables on who ate what, anybody I could find. Achilles lived on fifteen hundred calories a day and drank enough wine to die of cirrhosis by the time he was twenty-two. Priam had a hundred sons, yet Troy was only as big as a football field. Their food came in wagons from the east of the city because the Greeks never cut off their supplies. The Trojan horse is really a story about death from a full belly, but this is not the evidence I sought. I didn't want to interpret the books, I wanted the evidence right there in black and white for anyone to see."

"He didn't want people to say, 'Oh, there goes Kefirovsky again,'" says Emily. "He wanted it to be exact. Ten minutes, Vasi."

"So I kept reading the myths, the *Upanishads*, the *Book of the Dead*, the *I Ching*, until I found it right before my eyes."

"Where?" Williams asks, although he makes no attempt to take notes.

"Exodus. Right there in Exodus. This served me right for not checking earlier. But outside of the Flood I had never found very much decent natural history there. Anyway, that's where it was, Exodus 16:13. Have you heard of manna, 'manna from heaven'?"

"Do you mean what the Israelites ate in the desert?"

"Don't call them 'Israelites,' you make them sound like flashlights. They were no kind of 'ites.' The Egyptians called them Abirus. And they weren't in the desert. The best evidence is that the Sinai peninsula was in partial bloom at the time, enough to sustain nomads if they went, now and then, into Canaan or Egypt for grain."

"Well, forgive me, Professor, I'm only a layman."

"You make that sound like 'amen.'" Kefirovsky laughs. "The flashlights said 'amen' in the desert." He stands and walks over to the yogurt surrounded by simmering water.

"Still eight minutes," Emily calls out. The Professor jabs his pointer at Williams's white patent shoe and looks the reporter in the eye. "I know what the flashlights ate."

"Yogurt?"

Kefirovsky goes to the window and grins out at his rose garden.

"In Exodus they call it 'a fine flakelike thing like hoarfrost on the ground.' They say it tasted like wafers made with honey."

"Vasi lets me put a little honey in his, it's the only sweet he uses and it's because of that passage that he lets me do it. Six minutes."

"Do you know what they call yogurt now in the Middle East, where it is a staple?"

Williams says he does not know.

"They call it *Leben*. This means 'life' in German. And that Moroccan plant whose sweet milk is thick as motor oil, the Arabs call that one *man*. Do you see what hangs on in language? Man and life. Plain as the nose on your face. Once you know it, it's all over the Bible. 'Man does not live by bread alone' is only half a sentence."

"Wait a minute, Professor, I'm not sure I follow this. The linguistic hints are one thing, but how could yogurt appear in the desert?"

"You ask questions just like Herman Eidler asked. Right away to the first cause. Well, I don't know how yogurt appeared to the Abirus. That's for the theologians. I am a scientist. Science is two things, a problem and a guess. The earth is rocks and organisms decaying together at a fixed rate and under uniform pressure. In Exodus it says that this flakelike stuff melted when the sun grew hot. I don't know. I don't sell cough drops. But I can tell you this, the recipe has been before our eyes for a few thousand years and nobody has read it. They all say, look what the flashlights gave us, ethics, morals, ten commandments. But everybody else gave us the commandments too. Every priest in Egypt, every Hindu, every Parsee, every Chaldean, every Hammurabi, even the African cannibals roasting children had do's and do nots. We read the Bible but we missed the recipes."

"Four minutes, Vasi." Mrs. Kefirovsky slides off the stool. Beyond the stainless-steel kitchen she disappears amid the dark wood furnishings of other rooms. "I'll be back in time," she says as her voice trails away.

Kefirovsky stares at his yogurt. The digital thermometer reads a constant 112 degrees. "Pretty soon we'll pour and when it cools you can have some. If I'd been making this thirty years ago, my friends might still be here. We used meet on most Sundays just to joke about things. Herman would come and Hans Fricht, of course, and Jerome Van Strung. Sometimes Einstein came over from Princeton. You would call us a think tank. They were just a bunch of krauts smacking lips over wurst and sauerbraten. We worried about the war. Eidler lost his whole family and his wife's family. Van Strung had letters from Walter Benjamin that nobody else ever saw. They all liked to play croquet on my lawn. Sometimes I read sections from *Worlds in Confusion* out loud while they swung their mallets. Fricht was a beekeeper and clean as a Band-Aid. Einstein and Van Strung could walk barefoot over the dogshit.

"And after croquet it was food and beer. All the time, Einstein knew about the bomb and ate heavy meals. He never talked about his work. I naturally did and Fricht talked about his bees and Van Strung talked literature. When the war was over, Eidler brought us, one Sunday, three dozen Nathan's hot dogs straight from Coney Island in an ice chest. He came in a government car with a chauffeur. He brought them with buns and everything, but the ice melted onto the bread. Emily rewarmed the hot dogs and we ate them plain. That was the way we celebrated VE day. We ate and we talked.

"There is a former football player in California who writes to me. He eats only on the weekends and has done this since he retired as a defensive player four years ago. He knows many people in California who survive on nuts and figs. We are doing metabolism and blood tests on him and keeping data. In the summer he runs a camp for overweight boys. Parents bring their sons there just to watch a man not eat and be cheerful and busy all week."

"Vasi, it's fifteen minutes." Emily reappears with a large funnel and a photo album. Dr. Kefirovsky removes the thermometer, puts on two stove mittens, and lifting the big glass container out of the boiling water, pours his yogurt into the funnel above the small glass containers which will house the mixture.

"It's not ready yet," Emily says, "still lumpy." Kefirovsky pours the pint of liquid back into the three-quart jar. "We'll have to wait a few minutes more for the *man* to melt. It happens sometimes because it doesn't freeze uniformly. It doesn't hurt anything."

"We would do this once a week if it was just for Vasi," Emily says. "But we make it most days to give to others. All the neighbors get some and we mail throughout the area in winter when the spoilage rate is low."

"You mail it in glass containers?" the reporter asks.

"No, we mail it in plastic with tight lids. It can go about three days without refrigeration when it's fresh. Most of them probably don't even taste it. In '72 we mailed one to Nixon and one to McGovern special delivery. Not even a thank you from either one. A few people have heard about it and come to ask for some."

"Have you ever tried to sell it?"

"He talks like Gerald," Kefirovsky says, and walks back out to the garden still wearing his oven mittens.

"I didn't mean to offend him," the reporter says to Emily.

"It's all right. He's sensitive because Gerald, actually all the boys, stand up to him." She opens the photo album to what seem to be recent Polaroid snapshots of healthy middle-aged men and women surrounded by children. "We have wonderful sons and grandchildren. They respect their father too, and they wouldn't try to stop him from doing whatever he wants to do. But they won't allow me to be on the yogurt diet. Don't get me wrong, I like it and believe Vasi is discovering scientific truths, but I eat it and I'm still hungry. Gerald ships me cornfed beef from Iowa. I have to send a photograph every month to prove to him that I'm not losing weight like their father. Vasi used to weigh over two twenty, now, you can see for yourself he's a string bean. The doctors say he's healthy, but he should take vitamins. Since he's been growing *man* down here, he's eaten nothing but the yogurt and *man*. We moved here from New Jersey when he realized Texas was the right climate for the *man*. We tried Florida and California first, and he ate other food there because he admits that yogurt without *man* isn't enough. The boys told him to sell the recipe, but he wants to get the book out first. *Earth Story*, to explain all about it. Otherwise it would just be another food product.

"I hope you understand that with Vasi there is no halfway. He is his own laboratory. The boys know this. Gerald says, 'One laboratory is enough for him. Let him starve himself, but if I catch him forcing you to live on that stuff, I'll break his bony back.' That's why he won't speak to Gerald. But Gerald loves him. All the boys do and the grandchildren too. You can't just make a whole family, twelve grandchildren and all, stop eating everything but yogurt and *man*.

"It's one thing to have a theory about history. The boys backed him one hundred percent on that. And it wasn't easy. Here they were studying to be scientists and all the famous scientists saying their father was a fraud. Gerald quit one chemistry class because of something the teacher said about Vasi. The boys think he might be right about the yogurt too, but they don't want him to starve me and to starve their families. That's not wrong, is it? Did Pasteur give his kids TB or Salk carry around polio?"

"It's not the same." Dr. Kefirovsky is back in the kitchen carrying a fresh sprig of the *man* plant. "I wear these mittens because the plant is full of stickers. I'm just showing you a sprig. Outside, we milk it like the maple trees in Vermont."

"Is it a lot like maple syrup?" the reporter asks.

"Much thicker in texture. It freezes slowly and looks like peanut brittle when I put it in the yogurt."

Williams feels his pocket to make sure the notebook is there. He uncrosses his legs and seems ready to leave.

"I'm afraid, Dr. Kefirovsky, that I really don't follow all of this. Don't get me wrong, I appreciate your showing me exactly how you make this yogurt even though I'm here to talk about your earlier work. What I don't see is the jump from your discovery that yogurt is Old Testament manna, to the point of excluding all other food. I mean the . . . flashlights ate other food too, didn't they?"

"Not for forty years. For forty years they lived on this and then, only then, were they ready to pick up the business of destiny. This was a time out in history, just like during a football game. This is built into the organism. In sleep, in a nervous breakdown, in menopause, the body is always saying 'time out.' Social organizations too. Governments. There is the New Deal and then an Eisenhower. The Revolution and then Stalin. Going out of Egypt, then forty years in the desert. That was the only time they did it right.

"Imagine if in 1922 we Russians had sat down on the steppes, sat down in our cities, sat down by the Black Sea, in the Urals, in Siberia, all over, Russians sitting down saying to each other; 'Time out. Congratulations on the revolution, now let's have a time out for forty years to eat *man* and yogurt.' Would there have been Stalinism? Would the people swill vodka and be fat as pigs? There are two things to learn from Exodus. Take time out and eat the right thing."

"So you think everyone in the world should at least temporarily go on this diet?"

"First they should have their teeth pulled."

Emily laughs, showing hers. "The boys never even took you seriously on that, Vasi." Kefirovsky opens his mouth and with his forefinger goes in a circle pushing his upper lip and then his lower lip away from his empty gums.

"I hadn't noticed," the reporter says.

"Exactly, it doesn't matter. I happen to have lost mine nine years ago from pyorrhea. When I learned what I now know, I gave away the false ones. Teeth are an evolutionary accident. There is no doubt that we're losing them faster than chest hair. We needed them only until the domestication of animals. For six or seven thousand years teeth have been an anachronism."

"To whom did you give your false teeth? I find that pretty unusual."

"To the Illinois College of Optometry. They have all the manuscripts. I went there in 1927."

"That's news to me. I don't recall that in your biographical profile."

"I didn't stay for a degree. At the time Hans Fricht was a professor of optics there. I knew little English. A Russian astronomer was not needed anywhere. Hans said to me, 'Become an eye doctor, there is nothing to it.' He got me a scholarship. It was the first place in this country where we lived. Later I went to New Jersey. The optometry trustees asked for my notebooks and my old eyeglasses. In 1965 they made a Kefirovsky room. In 1973 I sent my teeth also."

Kefirovsky checks the mixture. "Five minutes more should it. The only thing I'm not sure of is the forty years. I don't know if the time out has to be that long or if it can be shortened. Do you think you could eat this for forty years?"

"Exclusively?"

"Exclusively."

"I don't think so, Professor, at least I wouldn't want to try."

"I am seventy-seven years old. In order for me to try it forty years I would have to live to be one hundred and sixteen. This is possible, but unlikely. There will perhaps be no other scientist to follow in my footsteps. Science will produce more Corfam and SST engines. The keys to natural history lay shrouded for thousands of years, now we refuse to see the one true gift of the gods. Easy, abundant, tasty, and wrapped in a time out. If the clergymen would wake up, they would see it. What is the promised land? Milk and honey and time. What is yogurt? Milk and bacteria and time. Why did the people who lived on manna for forty years want a land of milk and honey? Why not a land of pomegranates? Why not a land of barley and sesame seed and olive oil? Why not wine and cheese? Where else do you read about milk and honey? Nowhere. I've looked. And what sort of honey would you find in a semiarid climate where the annual rainfall could hardly support a large bee population. If Hans Fricht was alive, he would be an immense help now. He knew bees from A to Z. He would have seen immediately. He used to say, 'Where the bee sucks, there suck I,' and Eidler and Van Strung would laugh at him saying that while he hit the croquet ball and jumped up and down when he had a clean blocking shot. He knew the bee signal language before anybody wrote about it. Hans could have understood birds too if he would have tried. We all worshiped that man. Einstein brought him page after page of dull formulas by the thousands until one day Hans said to him, 'This is it, you *glücklich* kraut. You've finally got something worthwhile here.' And that's the only time he ever praised Einstein. But it's once more than he praised me. He used to say to me, 'Vasi, lay off, they're not ready for you. Try a hobby.' When I left optometry college, he thought I should be a pharmacist. But I was lucky, I got a job at the Institute. Hans himself was unemployed for twenty-two years. They made him leave the optometry faculty when they found out he was not an optometrist. After that he was a sponge, a hanger-on, a misfit. Imagine such a misfit. He wouldn't take a penny from anyone. He was an expert sewer and knitter. One of the great minds of the twentieth century making his own suits and sweaters. He raised his own vegetables. The man lived on a few hundred dollars a year. His friends made sure he had plenty to eat and that was our mistake. We tried to be generous and our butterball turkeys, our triscuits, our dark beer, and our wurst, all this killed him."

Kefirovsky is almost breathless. He leans on his pointer and his body shakes with sobs.

"Vasi loved Hans Fricht," Emily says. "You would have too. There was a scientist and a human being, Godfather to all the boys."

"It's a shame that he had such a hard life," the reporter says. "I've actually never heard of him."

"That is science," says Kefirovsky.

"If Hans was alive," Emily adds, "he wouldn't let you starve yourself like this. That's why you're so weak that you can hardly talk for a few minutes. You're the thinker, let someone else starve to prove you're right. Thousands of college students are looking for jobs like this. They swallow goldfish and squeeze into telephone booths and now they kiss for two weeks at a time. These people could prove you're right and you could live to see it. Ask the reporter."

"She has a point, Professor. Lots of students do paid experiments. But I don't want to get into the midst of a family squabble about this."

"Look at him," Emily screams, "look at him. How can you say you don't want to mix in? You've listened to a brilliant scientist talk, don't you want to save his life?"

Kefirovsky remains calm. He smiles at the reporter and raising his pointer directs the rubber tip at his wife. "She means well, but in spite of my many explanations Emily does not see that it is the yogurt that keeps me alive and well. At my age the average man has been dead for seven years."

"From two hundred and twenty pounds to one forty-five, that's how it's keeping you alive." She addresses the reporter. "Write this in *Time* magazine, that he can't walk stairs, that I have to tie his shoes. He's dizzy from air conditioning, and he chokes on the heat. He sits at his desk and starves himself. For two years I've watched. Enough is enough."

Still smiling, Kefirovsky says, "The revolution that is coming will make you forget Marx. Eating three meals will be like having three wives. Ordinary people by the millions will have their teeth pulled and drink happily ever after. Science and scarcity change the world. The yogurt will end scarcity, another time out is coming. You'll see. Marx and Malthus will be as forgotten as Paracelsus and Agrippa. Do you know what they worried about? Thousands of years ago Heraclitus, a smart man, thought the earth was packed tight as a suitcase. Everyone is wrong. Someday I'll be wrong too. That is science. In the meantime, it's time out. The Babylonians were a thin people but the Philistines gorged themselves. Huns were thinner than Romans. It's the law of history. Look at the Ethiopians. Look at the black Africans who weigh eighty pounds and can chase a giraffe for three days without food or water."

"It's terrible to watch." From her seat on the kitchen stool, Emily sobs and watches the kitchen clock. "The five minutes are up, Vasi." Emily wipes her eyes and once more raises the funnel. The Professor takes up his mittens and approaches the calm yogurt in the midst of bubbling waters. "This time it's good and ready." He holds the heavy glass jar steadily, the blue veins in his forearms stretch and tremble with the exercise, but Kefirovsky's pouring hand is still and even. Expertly, Emily moves the funnel from one pint bottle to the next, spilling only droplets on the stainless-steel counter. As coordinated as a ballet, their hands move the thick milky liquid over and into its bottles in a silent rhythmical pattern. As the big jar becomes lighter, the Professor does not quicken the pace of his pouring nor does Emily speed the funnel. The yogurt drops like long thick tongues into the bottles and it stops at the very tip of each one without overflowing. It bubbles for a second and then expires. With thick corks Emily seals ten bottles while Kefirovsky and the reporter watch her strong fingers. She leaves two unsealed. Kefirovsky pours his yogurt into a yellow glass decorated with the figures of parrots. "Do you want to drink yours or eat with a spoon?" he asks the reporter.

"I'll drink," Williams says.

"Isn't Mrs. Kefirovsky having any?"

"No," she says, "I have a steak in the broiler. I usually drink one at night while Vasi is reading."

The Professor raises his glass. A slight steam rises from the yogurt. With the gesture of a toast he extends his glass toward Emily, who stands in front of the ten corked bottles. Her eyes are vaguely red, and in the silent kitchen the noise of a broiling steak begins to be heard. Emily nods and smiles at Kefirovsky, who then makes the same gesture to the reporter. "To science," Emily says as the two men slowly raise to their lips the white flakelike liquid, thick as dew and fine as the hoarfrost on ground.

JUNOT DÍAZ

Monstro

Born in the Dominican Republic and raised in New Jersey, **Junot Díaz** is the author of *Drown*; *The Brief Wondrous Life of Oscar Wao*, which won the 2008 Pulitzer Prize and the National Book Critics Circle Award; and *This Is How You Lose Her*, a *New York Times* bestseller and National Book Award finalist. He is the recipient of a MacArthur Fellowship, PEN/Malamud Award, Dayton Literary Peace Prize, and PEN/O. Henry Award. The fiction editor at *Boston Review*, Díaz is a professor at the Massachusetts Institute of Technology.

"Monstro" was written for the *New Yorker*'s special science fiction–themed issue and is the basis for an eponymous novel to be published by Riverhead Books. "Monstro" is the story of a man caught in a world of love, disaster, friendship, and possibly zombies.

A t first, Negroes thought it *funny*. A disease that could make a Haitian blacker? It was the joke of the year. Everybody in our sector accusing everybody else of having it. You couldn't display a blemish or catch some sun on the street without the jokes starting. Someone would point to a spot on your arm and say, Diablo, haitiano, que te pasó?

La Negrura they called it.

The Darkness.

These days everybody wants to know what you were doing when the world came to an end. Fools make up all sorts of vainglorious self-serving plep—but me, I tell the truth.

I was chasing a girl.

I was one of the idiots who didn't heed any of the initial reports, who got caught way out there. What can I tell you? My head just wasn't into any mysterious disease—not with my mom sick and all. Not with Mysty.

Motherfuckers used to say culo would be the end of us. Well, for me it really was.

In the beginning the doctor types couldn't wrap their brains around it, either.

The infection showed up on a small boy in the relocation camps outside Port-au-Prince, in the hottest March in recorded history. The index case was only four years old, and by the time his uncle brought him in his arm looked like an enormous black pustule, so huge it had turned the boy into an appendage of the arm. In the glypts he looked terrified.

Within a month, a couple of thousand more infections were reported. Didn't rip through the pobla like the dengues or the poxes. More of a slow leprous spread. A black mold-fungus-blast that came on like a splotch and then gradually started taking you over, tunneling right through you—though as it turned out it wasn't a mold-fungus-blast at all. It was something else. Something new.

Everybody blamed the heat. Blamed the Calientazo. Shit, a hundred straight days over 105 degrees F. in our region alone, the planet cooking like a chimi and down to its last five trees—something berserk was bound to happen. All sorts of bizarre outbreaks already in play: diseases no one had names for, zoonotics by the pound. This one didn't cause too much panic because it seemed to hit only the sickest of the sick, viktims who had nine kinds of ill already in them. You literally had to be falling to pieces for it to grab you.

It almost always started epidermically and then worked its way up and in. Most of the infected were immobile within a few months, the worst comatose by six. Strangest thing, though: once infected, few viktims died outright; they just seemed to linger on and on. Coral reefs might have been adios on the ocean floor, but they were alive and well on the arms and backs and heads of the infected. Black rotting rugose masses fruiting out of bodies. The medicos formed a ninety-nation consortium, flooded one another with papers and hypotheses, ran every test they could afford, but not even the military enhancers could crack it.

In the early months, there was a big make do, because it was so strange and because no one could identify the route of transmission—that got the bigheads more worked up than the disease itself. There seemed to be no logic to it—spouses in constant contact didn't catch the Negrura, but some unconnected fool on the other side of the camp did. A huge rah-rah, but when the experts determined that it wasn't communicable in the standard ways, and that normal immune systems appeared to be at no kind of risk, the renminbi and the attention and the savvy went elsewhere. And since it was just poor Haitian types getting fucked up—no real margin in that. Once the initial bulla died down, only a couple of underfunded teams stayed on. As for the infected, all the medicos could do was try to keep them nourished and hydrated—and, more important, prevent them from growing together.

That was a serious issue. The blast seemed to have a boner for fusion, respected no kind of boundaries. I remember the first time I saw it on the Whorl. Alex was, like, Mira esta vaina. Almost delighted. A shaky glypt of a pair of naked trembling Haitian brothers sharing a single stained cot, knotted together by horrible mold, their heads slurred into one. About the nastiest thing you ever saw. Mysty saw it and looked away and eventually I did, too.

My tíos were, like, Someone needs to drop a bomb on those people, and even though I was one of the pro-Haitian domos, at the time I was thinking it might have been a mercy.

———————

I was actually on the Island when it happened. Front-row fucking seat. How lucky was that?

They call those of us who made it through "time witnesses." I can think of a couple of better terms.

I'd come down to the D.R. because my mother had got super sick. The year before, she'd been bitten by a rupture virus that tore through half her organs before the doctors got savvy to it. No chance she was going to be taken care of back North. Not with what the cheapest nurses charged. So she rented out the Brooklyn house to a bunch of Mexos, took that loot, and came home.

Better that way. Say what you want, but family on the Island was still more reliable for heavy shit, like, say, dying, than family in the North. Medicine was cheaper, too, with the flying territory in Haina, its Chinese factories pumping out pharma like it was romo, growing organ sheets by the mile, and, for somebody as sick as my mother, with only rental income to live off, being there was what made sense.

I was supposed to be helping out, but really I didn't do na for her. My tía Livia had it all under control and if you want the truth I didn't feel comfortable hanging around the house with Mom all sick. The vieja could barely get up to piss, looked like a stick version of herself. Hard to see that. If I stayed an hour with her it was a lot.

What an asshole, right? What a shallow motherfucker.

But I was nineteen—and what is nineteen, if not for shallow? In any case my mother didn't want me around, either. It made her sad to see me so uncomfortable. And what could I do for her besides wring my hands? She had Livia, she had her nurse, she had the muchacha who cooked and cleaned. I was only in the way.

Maybe I'm just saying this to cover my failings as a son.

Maybe I'm saying this because of what happened.

Maybe.

Go, have fun with your friends, she said behind her breathing mask.

Didn't have to tell me twice.

Fact is, I wouldn't have come to the Island that summer if I'd been able to nab a job or an internship, but the droughts that year and the General Economic Collapse meant that nobody was nabbing shit. Even the Sovereign kids were ending up home with their parents. So with the house being rented out from under me and nowhere else to go, not even a girlfriend to mooch off, I figured, Fuck it: might as well spend the hots on the Island. Take in some of that ole-time climate change. Get to know the patria again.

For six, seven months it was just a horrible Haitian disease—who fucking cared, right? A couple of hundred new infections each month in the camps and around Port-au-Prince, pocket change, really, nowhere near what KRIMEA was doing to the Russian hinterlands. For a while it was nothing, nothing at all . . . and then some real eerie plep started happening.

Doctors began reporting a curious change in the behavior of infected patients: they wanted to be together, in close proximity, all the time. They no longer tolerated being separated from other infected, started coming together in the main quarantine zone, just outside Champ de Mars, the largest of the relocation camps. All the viktims seemed to succumb to this ingathering compulsion. Some went because they claimed they felt "safer" in the quarantine zone; others just picked up and left without a word to anyone, trekked halfway across the country as though following a homing beacon. Once viktims got it in their heads to go, no dissuading them. Left family, friends, children behind. Walked out on wedding days, on swell business. Once they were in the zone, nothing could get them to leave. When authorities tried to distribute the infected viktims across a number of centers, they either wouldn't go or made their way quickly back to the main zone.

One doctor from Martinique, his curiosity piqued, isolated an elderly viktim from the other infected and took her to a holding bay some distance outside the main quarantine zone. Within twenty-four hours, this frail septuagenarian had torn off her heavy restraints, broken through a mesh security window, and crawled halfway back to the quarantine zone before she was recovered.

Same doctor performed a second experiment: helicoptered two infected men to a hospital ship offshore. As soon as they were removed from the quarantine zone they went *batshit*, trying everything they could to break free, to return. No sedative or entreaty proved effective, and after four days of battering themselves relentlessly against the doors of their holding cells the men loosed a last high-pitched shriek and died *within minutes of each other*.

Stranger shit was in the offing: eight months into the epidemic, all infected viktims, even the healthiest, abruptly stopped communicating. Just went silent. Nothing abnormal in their bloodwork or in their scans. They just stopped talking—friends, family, doctors, it didn't matter. No stimuli of any form could get them to speak. Watched everything and everyone, clearly understood commands and information—but refused to say anything.

Anything *human*, that is.

Shortly after the Silence, the phenomenon that became known as the Chorus began. The entire infected population simultaneously let out a bizarre shriek—two, three times a day. Starting together, ending together.

Talk about unnerving. Even patients who'd had their faces chewed off by the blast joined in—the vibrations rising out of the excrescence itself. Even the patients who were comatose. Never lasted more than twenty, thirty seconds—eerie siren shit. No uninfected could stand to hear it, but uninfected kids seemed to be the most unsettled. After a week of that wailing, the majority of kids had fled the areas around the quarantine zone, moved to other camps. That should have alerted someone, but who paid attention to camp kids?

Brain scans performed during the outbursts actually detected minute fluctuations in the infected patients' biomagnetic signals, but unfortunately for just about everybody on the planet these anomalies were not pursued. There seemed to be more immediate problems. There were widespread rumors that the infected were devils, even reports of relatives attempting to set their infected family members on fire.

In my sector, my mom and my tía were about the only people paying attention to any of it; everybody else was obsessing over what was happening with KRIMEA. Mom and Tía Livia felt bad for our poor west-coast neighbors. They were churchy like that. When I came back from my outings

I'd say, fooling, How are los explotao? And my mother would say, It's not funny, hijo. She's right, Aunt Livia said. That could be us next and then you won't be joking.

So what was I doing, if not helping my mom or watching the apocalypse creep in? Like I told you: I was chasing a girl. And I was running around the Island with this hijo de mami y papi I knew from Brown. Living prince because of him, basically.

Classy, right? My mater stuck in Darkness, with the mosquitoes fifty to a finger and the heat like the inside of a tailpipe, and there I was privando en rico inside the Dome, where the bafflers held the scorch to a breezy 82 degrees F. and one mosquito a night was considered an invasion.

I hadn't actually planned on rolling with Alex that summer—it wasn't like we were close friends or anything. We ran in totally different circles back at Brown, him prince, me prole, but we were both from the same little Island that no one else in the world cared about, and that counted for something, even in those days. On top of that we were both art types, which in our world of hyper-capitalism was like having a serious mental disorder. He was already making dough on his photography and I was attracting no one to my writing. But he had always told me, Hit me up the next time you come down. So before I flew in I glypted him, figuring he wasn't going to respond, and he glypted right back.

What's going on, charlatan, cuando vamos a janguiar? And that's basically all we did until the End: janguiar.

I knew nobody in the D.R. outside of my crazy cousins, and they didn't like to do anything but watch the fights, play dominos, and fuck. Which is fine for maybe a week—but for three months? No, hombre. I wasn't *that* Island. For Alex did me a solid by putting me on. More than a solid: saved my ass full. Dude scooped me up from the airport in his father's burner, looking so fit it made me want to drop and do twenty on the spot. Welcome to the country of las maravillas, he said with a snort, waving his hand at all the thousands of non-treaty motos on the road, the banners for the next election punching you in the face everywhere. Took me over to the rooftop apartment his dad had given him in the rebuilt Zona Colonial. The joint was a meta-glass palace that overlooked the Drowned Sectors, full of his photographs and all the bric-a-brac he had collected for props, with an outdoor deck as large as an aircraft carrier.

You live here? I said, and he shrugged lazily: Until Papi decides to sell the building.

One of those moments when you realize exactly how rich some of the kids you go to school with are. Without even thinking about it, he glypted me a six-month V.I.P. pass for the Dome, which cost about a year's tuition. Just in case, he said. He'd been on-Island since before the semester ended. A month here and I'm already aplatanao, he complained. I think I'm losing the ability to read.

We drank some more spike, and some of his too-cool-for-school Dome friends came over, slim, tall, and wealthy, every one doing double takes when they saw the size of me and heard my Dark accent, but Alex introduced me as his Brown classmate. A genius, he said, and that made it a little better. What do you do? they asked and I told them I was trying to be a journalist. Which for that set was like saying I wanted to molest animals. I quickly became part of the furniture, one of Alex's least interesting fotos. Don't you love my friends, Alex said. Son tan amable.

That first night I kinda had been hoping for a go-club or something bananas like that, but it was a talk-and-spike and let's-look-at-Alex's-latest-fotos-type party. What redeemed everything for me was that around midnight one last girl came up the corkscrew staircase. Alex said loudly, Look who's finally here. And the girl shouted, I was at church, coño, which got everybody laughing. Because of the weak light I didn't get a good look at first. Just the hair, and the vampire-stake heels. Then she finally made it over and I saw the cut on her and the immensity of those eyes and I was, like, fuck me.

That girl. With one fucking glance she upended my everything.

So you're the friend? I'm Mysty. Her crafted eyes giving me the once-over. And you're in this country *voluntarily*?

A ridiculously beautiful mina wafting up a metal corkscrew staircase in high heels and offering up her perfect cheek as the light from the Dome was dying out across the city—that I could have withstood. But then she spent the rest of the night ribbing me because I was so Americanized, because my Spanish sucked, because I didn't know any of the Island things they were talking about—and that was it for me. I was lost.

Everybody at school knew Alex. Shit, I think everybody in Providence knew him. Negro was star like that. This flash priv kid who looked more like an Uruguayan fútbal player than a plátano, with short curly Praetorian hair and machine-made cheekbones and about the greenest eyes you ever saw. Six feet eight and super full of himself. Threw the sickest parties, always stepping out with the most rompin girls, drove an Eastwood for fuck's sake. But what I realized on the Island was that Alex was more than just a rico, turned out he was a fucking V—, son of the wealthiest, most priv'ed-up family on the Island. His abuelo like the ninety-ninth-richest man in the Americas, while his abuela had more than nine thousand properties. At Brown, Negro had actually been playing it modest—for good reason, too. Turned out that when homeboy was in middle school he was kidnapped for eight long months, barely got out alive. Never talked about it, not even cryptically, but dude never left the house in D.R. unless he was packing fuego. Always offered me a cannon, too, like it was a piece of fruit or something. Said, Just, you know, in case something happens.

V—or not, I had respect for Alex, because he worked hard as a fuck, not one of those upper-class vividors who sat around and blew lakhs. Was doing philosophy at Brown and business at M.I.T., smashed like a 4.0, and still had time to do his photography thing. And unlike a lot of our lakhsters in the States he really loved his Santo Domingo. Never pretended he was Spanish or Italian or gringo. Always claimed dominicano and that ain't nothing, not the way plátanos can be.

For all his pluses Alex could also be extra dickish. Always had to be the center of attention. I couldn't say anything slightly smart without him wanting to argue with me. And when you got him on a point he huffed: Well, I don't know about that. Treated Dominican workers in restaurants and clubs and bars like they were lower than shit. Never left any kind of tip. You have to yell at these people or they'll just walk all over you was his whole thing. Yeah, right, Alex, I told him. And he grimaced: You're just a Naxalite. And you're a come solo, I said, which he hated.

Pretty much on his own. No siblings, and his family was about as checked out as you could get. Had a dad who spent so much time abroad that Alex would have been lucky to pick him out in a lineup—and a mom who'd had more plastic surgery than all of Caracas combined, who flew out to Miami every week just to shop and fuck this Senegalese lawyer that everybody except the dad seemed to know about. Alex had a girlfriend from his social set he'd been dating since they were twelve, Valentina, had cheated on her at least two thousand times, with girls and boys, but because of his lakhs she wasn't going anywhere. Dude told me all about it, too, as soon as he introduced me to her. What do you think of that? he asked me with a serious cheese on his face.

Sounds pretty shitty, I said.

Oh, come on, he said, putting an avuncular arm around me. It ain't that bad.

Alex's big dream? (Of course we all knew it, because he wouldn't shut up about all the plep he was going to do.) He wanted to be either the Dominican Sebastião Salgado or the Dominican João Silva (minus the double amputation, natch). But he also wanted to write novels, make films, drop an album, be the star of a channel on the Whorl—dude wanted to do everything. As long as it was arty and it made him a Name he was into it.

He was also the one who wanted to go to Haiti, to take pictures of all the infected people. Mysty was, like, You can go catch a plague all by your fool self, but he waved her off and recited his motto (which was also on his cards): To represent, to surprise, to cause, to provoke.

To die, she added.

He shrugged, smiled his hundred-crore smile. A photographer has to be willing to risk it all. A photograph can change todo.

You had to hand it to him; he had confidence. And recklessness. I remember this time a farmer in Baní uncovered an unexploded bomb from the civil war in his field—Alex raced us all out there and wanted to take a photo of Mysty sitting on the device in a cheerleading outfit. She was, like, Are you *insane?* So he sat down on it himself while we crouched behind the burner and he snapped his own picture, grinning like a loon, first with a Leica, then with a Polaroid. Got on the front page of *Listin* with that antic. Parents flying in from their respective cities to have a chat with him.

He really did think he could change todo. Me, I didn't want to change nada; I didn't want to be famous. I just wanted to write one book that was worth a damn and I would have happily called it a day.

Mi hermano, that's pathetic to an extreme, Alex said. You have to dream a lot bigger than that.

Well, I certainly dreamed big with Mysty.

In those days she was my Wonder Woman, my Queen of Jaragua, but the truth is I don't remember her as well as I used to. Don't have any pictures of her—they were all lost in the Fall when the memory stacks blew, when la Capital was scoured. One thing a Negro wasn't going to forget, though, one thing that you didn't need fotos for, was how beautiful she was. Tall and copper-colored, with a Stradivarius curve to her back. An ex–volleyball player, studying international law at UNIBE, with a cascade of black hair you could have woven thirty days of nights from. Some modeling when she was thirteen, fourteen, definitely on the receiving end of some skin-crafting and bone-crafting, maybe breasts, definitely ass, and who knows what else—but would rather have died than cop to it.

You better believe I'm pura lemba, she always said and even I had to roll my eyes at that. Don't roll your eyes at me. I *am*.

Spent five years in Quebec before her mother finally dumped her asshole Canadian stepfather and dragged her back screaming to la Capital.

Something she still held against the vieja, against the whole D.R. Spoke impeccable French and used it every chance she got, always made a show of reading thick-ass French novels like *La Cousine Bette*, and that was what she wanted once her studies were over: to move to Paris, work for the U.N., read French books in a café.

Men love me in Paris, she announced, like this might be a revelation.

Men love you here, Alex said.

Shook her head. It's not the same.

Of course it's not the same, I said. Men shower in Santo Domingo. And dance, too. You ever see franceses dance? It's like watching an epileptics convention.

Mysty spat an ice cube at me. French men are the *best*.

Yes, she liked me well enough. Could even say we were friends. I had my charming in those days, I had a mouth on me like all the swords of the Montagues and Capulets combined, like someone had overdosed me with truth serum. You're Alex's only friend who doesn't take his crap, she once confided. You don't even take my crap.

Yes, she liked me but didn't *like* me, entiendes. But God did I love her. Not that I had any idea how to start with a girl like her. The only "us" time we ever had was when Alex sent her to pick me up and she'd show up either at my house in Villa Con or at the gym. My crazy cousins got so excited. They weren't used to seeing a fresa like her. She knew what she was doing. She'd leave her driver out front and come into the gym to fetch me. Put on a real show. I always knew she'd arrived because the whole gravity of the gym would shift to the entrance and I'd look over from my workout and there she'd be.

Never had any kind of game with her. Best I could do on our rides to where Alex was waiting was ask her about her day and she always said the same thing: Terrible.

They had a mighty strange relationship, Alex and Mysty did. She seemed pissed off at him at least eighty percent of the time, but she was also always with him; and it seemed to me that Alex spent more time with Mysty than he did with Valentina. Mysty helped him with all his little projects, and yet she never seemed happy about it, always acted like it was this massive imposition. Jesus, Alex, she said, will you just make it already. Acted like everything he did bored her. That, I've come to realize, was her protective screen. To always appear bored.

Even when she wasn't bored Mysty wasn't easy; jeva had a temper, always blowing up on Alex because he said something or was late or because she didn't like the way he laughed at her. Blew up on me if I ever sided with him. Called him a mama huevo at least once a day, which in the old D.R. was a pretty serious thing to throw at a guy. Alex didn't care, played it for a goof. You talk so sweet, ma chère. You should say it in French. Which of course she always did.

I asked Alex at least five times that summer if he and Mysty were a thing. He denied it full. Never laid a hand on her, she's like my sister, my girlfriend would kill me, etc.

Never fucked her? That seemed highly unfuckinglikely. Something had happened between them—sex, sure, but something else—though what that was isn't obvious even now that I'm older and dique wiser. Girls like Mysty, of her class, were always orbiting around croremongers like Alex, hoping that they would bite. Not that in the D.R. they ever did but still. Once when I was going on about her, wondering why the fuck he hadn't jumped her, he looked around and then pulled me close and said, You know the thing with her, right? Her dad used to fuck her until she was twelve. Can you believe that?

Her dad? I said.

He nodded solemnly. Her dad. Did I believe it? The incest? In the D.R. incest was like the other national pastime. I guess I believed it as much as I believed Alex's whole she's-my-sister coro, which is to say, maybe I did and maybe I didn't, but in the end I also didn't care. It made me feel terrible for her, sure, but it didn't make me want her any less. As for her and Alex, I never saw them touch, never saw anything that you could call calor pass between them; she seemed genuinely uninterested in him romantically and that's why I figured I had a chance.

I don't want a boyfriend, she kept saying. I want a *visa*.

Dear dear Mysty. Beautiful and bitchy and couldn't wait to be away from the D.R. A girl who didn't let anyone push her around, who once grabbed a euro-chick by the hair because the bitch tried to cut her in line. Wasn't really a deep person. I don't think I ever heard her voice an opinion about art or politics or say anything remotely philosophical. I don't think she had any female friends—shit, I don't think she had any friends, just a lot of people she said hi to in the clubs. Chick was as much a loner as I was. She never bought anything for anyone, didn't do community work, and when she saw children she always stayed far away. Ánimales, she called them—and you could tell she wasn't joking.

No, she wasn't anything close to humane, but at nineteen who needed humane? She was buenmosa and impossible and when she laughed it was like this little wilderness. I would watch her dance with Alex, with other guys— never with me, I wasn't good enough—and my heart would break, and that was all that mattered.

Around our third week of hanging out, when the riots were beginning in the camps and the Haitians in the D.R. were getting deported over a freckle, I started talking about maybe staying for a few months extra. Taking a semester off Brown to keep my mom company, maybe volunteering in Haiti. Crazy talk, sure, but I knew for certain that I wasn't going to land Mysty by sending her glypts from a thousand miles away. To bag a girl like that you have to make a serious move, and staying in the D.R. was for me a serious move indeed.

I think I might stick around, I announced when we were all driving back from what was left of Las Terrenas. No baffler on the burner and the heat was literally pulling our skin off.

Why would you do that? Mysty demanded. It's *awful* here.

It's not awful here, Alex corrected mildly. This is the most beautiful country in the world. But I don't think you'd last long. You're way gringo.

And you're what, Enriquillo?

I know *I'm* gringo, Alex said, but you're *way* gringo. You'd be running to the airport in a month.

Even my mother was against it. Actually sat up in her medicine tent. You're going to drop school—for what? Esa chica plastica? Don't be ridiculous, hijo. There's plenty of culo falso back home.

That July a man named Henri Casimir was brought in to a field clinic attached to Champ de Mars. A former manager in the utility company, now reduced to carting sewage for the camp administration. Brought in by his wife, Rosa, who was worried about his behavior. Last couple of months dude had been roaming about the camp at odd hours, repeating himself ad nauseam, never sleeping. The wife was convinced that her husband was not her husband.

In the hospital that day: one Noni DeGraff, a Haitian epidemiologist and one of the few researchers who had been working on the disease since its first appearance; brilliant and pretty much fearless, she was called the Jet Engine by her colleagues, because of her headstrong ferocity. Intrigued by Casimir's case, she sat in on the examination. Casimir, apart from a low body temperature, seemed healthy. Bloodwork clean. No sign of virals or of the dreaded infection. When questioned, the patient spoke excitedly about a san he was claiming the following week. Distressed, Rosa informed the doctors that said san he was going on about had disbanded two months earlier. He had put his fifty renminbi faithfully into the pot every month, but just before his turn came around they found out the whole thing was a setup. He never saw a penny, Rosa said.

When Dr. DeGraff asked the wife what she thought might be bothering her husband, Rosa said simply, Someone has witched him.

Something about the wife's upset and Casimir's demeanor got Dr. DeGraff's antennas twitching. She asked Rosa for permission to observe Casimir on one of his rambles. Wife Rosa agreed. As per her complaint, Casimir spent almost his entire day tramping about the camp with no apparent aim or destination. Twice Dr. DeGraff approached him, and twice Casimir talked about the heat and about the san he was soon to receive. He seemed distracted, disoriented, even, but not mad.

The next week, Dr. DeGraff tailed Casimir again. This time the good doctor discerned a pattern. No matter how many twists he took, invariably Casimir wound his way back to the vicinity of the quarantine zone at the very moment that the infected let out their infernal chorus. As the outburst rang out, Casimir paused and then, without any change in expression, ambled away.

DeGraff decided to perform an experiment. She placed Casimir in her car and drove him away from the quarantine zone. At first, Casimir appeared "normal," talking again about his san, wiping his glasses compulsively, etc. Then, at half a mile from the zone, he began to show increasing signs of distress, twitching and twisting in his seat. His language became garbled. At the mile mark Casimir exploded. Snapped the seat belt holding him in and in his scramble from the car struck DeGraff with unbelievable force, fracturing two ribs. Bounding out before the doctor could manage to bring the car under control, Casimir disappeared into the sprawl of Champ de Mars. The next day, when Dr. DeGraff asked the wife to bring Casimir in, he appeared to have no recollection of the incident. He was still talking about his san.

After she had her ribs taped up, DeGraff put out a message to all medical personnel in the Haitian mission, inquiring about patients expressing similar symptoms. She assumed she would receive four, five responses. She received *two hundred and fourteen*. She asked for workups. She got them. Sat down with her partner in crime, a Haitian-American physician by the name of Anton Léger, and started plowing through the material. Nearly all the sufferers had, like Casimir, shown signs of low body temperature. And so they performed temperature tests on Casimir. Sometimes he was normal. Sometimes he was below, but never for long. A technician on the staff, hearing about the case, suggested that they requisition a thermal imager sensitive enough to detect minute temperature fluctuations. An imager was secured and then turned on Casimir. Bingo. Casimir's body temperature was indeed fluctuating, little tiny blue spikes every couple of seconds. Normal folks like DeGraff and Léger—they tested themselves, naturally—scanned red, but patients with the Casimir complaint appeared onscreen a deep, flickering blue. On a lark, DeGraff and Léger aimed the scanner toward the street outside the clinic.

They almost shat themselves. Like for reals. Nearly one out of every eight pedestrians was flickering blue.

DeGraff remembers the cold dread that swept over her, remembers telling Léger, We need to go to the infected hospital. We need to go there now.

At the hospital, they trained their camera on the guarded entrance. Copies of those scans somehow made it to the Outside. Still chilling to watch. Every single person, doctor, assistant, aid worker, janitor who walked in and out of that hospital radiated blue.

We did what all kids with a lot of priv do in the D.R.: we kicked it. And since none of us had parents to hold us back we kicked it super hard. Smoked ganja by the heap and tore up the Zona Colonial and when we got bored we left the Dome for long looping drives from one end of the Island to the other. The countryside half-abandoned because of the Long Drought but still beautiful even in its decline.

Alex had all these projects. Fotos of all the prostitutes in the Feria. Fotos of every chimi truck in the Malecón. Fotos of the tributos on the Conde. He also got obsessed with photographing all the beaches of the D.R. before they disappeared. These beaches are what used to bring the world to us! he exclaimed. They were the one resource we had! I suspected it was just an excuse to put Mysty in a bathing suit and photograph her for three hours straight. Not that I was complaining. My role was to hand him cameras and afterward to write a caption for each of the selected shots he put on the Whorl.

And I did: just a little entry. The whole thing was called "Notes from the Last Shore." Nice, right? I came up with that. Anyway, Mysty spent the whole time on those shoots bitching: about her bathing suits, about the scorch, about the mosquitoes that the bafflers were letting in, and endlessly warning Alex not to focus on her pipa. She was convinced that she had a huge one, which neither Alex nor I ever saw but we didn't argue. I got you, chérie, was what he said. I got you.

After each setup I always told her: Tú eres guapísima. And she never said anything, just wrinkled her nose at me. Once, right before the Fall, I must have said it with enough conviction, because she looked me in the eyes for a long while. I still remember what *that* felt like.

Now it gets sketchy as hell. A lockdown was initiated and a team of W.H.O. docs attempted to enter the infected hospital in the quarantine zone. Nine went in but nobody came out. Minutes later, the infected let out one of their shrieks, but this one lasted twenty-eight minutes. And that more or less was when shit went Rwanda.

In the D.R. we heard about the riot. Saw horrific videos of people getting chased down and butchered. Two camera crews died, and that got Alex completely pumped up.

We have to go, he cried. I'm missing it!

You're not going anywhere, Mysty said.

But are you guys seeing this? Alex asked. Are you *seeing* this?

That shit was no riot. Even we could tell that. All the relocation camps near the quarantine zone were consumed in what can only be described as a straight massacre. An outbreak of homicidal violence, according to the initial reports. People who had never lifted a finger in anger their whole lives—children, viejos, aid workers, mothers of nine—grabbed knives, machetes, sticks, pots, pans, pipes, hammers and started attacking their neighbors, their friends, their pastors, their children, their husbands, their infirm relatives, complete strangers. Berserk murderous blood rage. No pleading with the killers or backing them down; they just kept coming and coming, even when you pointed a gauss gun at them, stopped only when they were killed.

Let me tell you: in those days I really didn't know nothing. For real. I didn't know shit about women, that's for sure. Didn't know shit about the world—obviously. Certainly didn't know *jack* about the Island.

I actually thought me and Mysty could end up together. Nice, right? The truth is I had more of a chance of busting a golden egg out my ass than I did of bagging a girl like Mysty. She was from a familia de nombre, wasn't going to have anything to do with a nadie like me, un morenito from Villa Con whose mother had made it big selling hair-straightening products to the africanos. Wasn't going to happen. Not unless I turned myself white or got a major-league contract or hit the fucking lottery. Not unless I turned into an Alex.

And yet you know what? I still had hope. Had hope that despite the world I had a chance with Mysty. Ridiculous hope, sure, but what do you expect?

Nearly two hundred thousand Haitians fled the violence, leaving the Possessed, as they became known, fully in control of the twenty-two camps in the vicinity of the quarantine zone. Misreading the situation, the head of the U.N. Peacekeeping Mission waited a full two days for tensions to "cool down" before attempting to reestablish control. Finally, two convoys entered the blood zone, got as far as Champ de Mars before they were set upon by wave after wave of the Possessed and torn to pieces.

Let me not forget this—this is the best part. Three days before it happened, my mother flew to New Hialeah with my aunt for a specialty treatment. Just for a few days, she explained. And the really best part? *I could have gone with her!* She invited me, said, Plenty of culo plastico in Florida. Can you imagine it? I could have ducked the entire fucking thing.

I could have been safe.

No one knows how it happened or who was responsible, but it took two weeks, two fucking weeks, for the enormity of the situation to dawn on the Great Powers. In the meantime, the infected, as refugees reported, sang on and on and on.

On the fifteenth day of the crisis, advanced elements of the U.S. Rapid

Expeditionary Force landed at Port-au-Prince. Drone surveillance proved difficult, as some previously unrecorded form of interference was disrupting the airspace around the camps.

Nevertheless a battle force was ordered into the infected areas. This force, too, was set upon by the Possessed, and would surely have been destroyed to the man if helicopters hadn't been sent in. The Possessed were so relentless that they clung to the runners, actually had to be shot off. The only upside? The glypts the battle force beamed out *finally* got High Command to pull their head out of their ass. The entire country of Haiti was placed under quarantine. All flights in and out canceled. The border with the D.R. sealed.

An emergency meeting of the Joint Chiefs of Staff was convened, the Commander-in-Chief pulled off his vacation. And within hours a bomber wing scrambled out of Southern Command in Puerto Rico.

Leaked documents show that the bombers were loaded with enough liquid asskick to keep all of Port-au-Prince burning red-hot for a week. The bombers were last spotted against the full moon as they crossed the northern coast of the D.R. Survivors fleeing the area heard their approach—and Dr. DeGraff, who had managed to survive the massacres and had joined the exodus moving east, chanced one final glance at her birth city just as the ordnance was sailing down.

Because she was a God-fearing woman and because she had no idea what kind of bomb they were dropping, Dr. DeGraff took the precaution of keeping one eye shut, just, you know, in case things got Sodom and Gomorrah. Which promptly they did. The Detonation Event—no one knows what else to call it—turned the entire world white. Three full seconds. Triggered a quake that was felt all across the Island and also burned out the optic nerve on Dr. DeGraff's right eye.

But not before she saw It.

Not before she saw Them.

Even though I knew I shouldn't, one night I went ahead anyway. We were out dancing in la Zona and Alex disappeared after a pair of German chicks.

A Nazi cada año no te hace daño, he said. We were all out of our minds and Mysty started dancing with me and you know how girls are when they can dance and they know it. She just put it on me and that was it. I started making out with her right there.

I have to tell you, at that moment I was so fucking happy, so incredibly happy, and then the world put its foot right in my ass. Mysty stopped suddenly, said, Do you know what? I don't think this is cool.

Are you serious?

Yeah, she said. We should stop. She stepped back from the longest darkest song ever and started looking around. Maybe we should get out of here. It's late.

I said, I guess I forgot to bring my lakhs with me.

I almost said, I forgot to bring your dad with me.

Hijo de la gran puta, Mysty said, shoving me.

And that was when the lights went out.

Monitoring stations in the U.S. and Mexico detected a massive detonation in the Port-au-Prince area in the range of 8.3. Tremors were felt as far away as Havana, San Juan, and Key West.

The detonation produced a second, more extraordinary effect: an electromagnetic pulse that deaded all electronics within a six-hundred-square-mile radius.

Every circuit of every kind shot to shit. In military circles the pulse was called the Reaper. You cannot imagine the damage it caused. The bomber wing that had attacked the quarantine zone—dead, forced to ditch into the Caribbean Sea, no crew recovered. Thirty-two commercial flights packed to summer peak capacity plummeted straight out of the sky. Four crashed in urban areas. One pinwheeled into its receiving airport. Hundreds of privately owned seacraft lost. Servers down and power stations kaputted. Hospitals plunged into chaos. Even fatline communicators thought to be impervious to any kind of terrestrial disruption began fritzing. The three satellites parked in geosynch orbit over that stretch of the Caribbean went ass up, too. Tens of thousands died as a direct result of the power failure. Fires broke out. Seawalls began to fail. Domes started heating up.

But it wasn't just a simple, one-time pulse. Vehicles attempting to approach within six hundred miles of the detonation's epicenter failed. Communicators towed over the line could neither receive nor transmit. Batteries gave off nothing.

This is what *really* flipped every motherfucker in the know inside out and back again. The Reaper hadn't just swung and run; it had swung and *stayed*. A dead zone had opened over a six-hundred-mile chunk of the Caribbean.

Midnight.

No one knowing what the fuck was going on in the darkness. No one but us.

Initially, no one believed the hysterical evacuees. Forty-foot-tall cannibal motherfuckers running loose on the Island? Negro, please.

Until a set of soon-to-be-iconic Polaroids made it out on one clipper showing what later came to be called a Class 2 in the process of putting a slender broken girl in its mouth.

Beneath the photo someone had scrawled: Numbers 11:18. *Who shall give us flesh to eat?*

We came together at Alex's apartment first thing. All of us wearing the same clothes from the night before. Watched the fires spreading across the sectors. Heard the craziness on the street. And with the bafflers down felt for the first time on that roof the incredible heat rolling in from the dying seas. Mysty pretending nothing had happened between us. Me pretending the same.

Your mom O.K.? I asked her and she shrugged. She's up in the Cibao visiting family.

The power's supposedly out there, too, Alex said. Mysty shivered and so did I.

Nothing was working except for old diesel burners and the archaic motos with no points or capacitors. People were trying out different explanations. An earthquake. A nuke. A Carrington event. The Coming of the Lord. Reports arriving over the failing fatlines claimed that Port-au-Prince had been destroyed, that Haiti had been destroyed, that thirteen million screaming Haitian refugees were threatening the borders, that Dominican military units had been authorized to meet the *invaders*—the term the gov was now using—with ultimate force.

And so of course what does Alex decide to do? Like an idiot he decides to commandeer one of his father's vintage burners and take a ride out to the border.

Just in case, you know, Alex said, packing up his Polaroid, something happens.

And what do we do, like even bigger idiots? Go with him.

JIM SHEPARD
Minotaur

Jim Shepard, a professor at Williams College, has been published in, among other places, *McSweeney's*, *Granta*, the *Atlantic Monthly*, the *New Yorker*, *Ploughshares*, *Triquarterly*, and *Playboy*. He has published seven novels, including *The Book of Aron*, *Flights*, *Nosferatu*, and *Project X*. Shepard is perhaps even better known, however, for his four collections of stories: *Batting Against Castro*, *Love and Hydrogen*, *Like You'd Understand*, and *You Think That's Bad*. He has won the Story Prize and the Massachusetts Book Award, and has been nominated for the National Book Award. Shepard has also written two screenplays, one based on *Project X*.

Although Shepard's stories have an affinity for science fiction, most of them fall short of genre classification. "Minotaur" is in a similar vein, until one looks closely at what is only alluded to in the story.

Kenny I hadn't seen in, what, three, four years. Kenny started with me way back when, the two of us standing there with our hands in our pants right outside the wormhole. Kenny wanders into the Windsock last night like the Keith Richards version of himself with this girl who looks like some movie star's daughter. "Is that you?" he says when he spots me in a booth. "This is the guy you're always talking about?" Carly asks once we're a few minutes into the conversation. The girl's name turns out to be Celestine. Talking to me, every so often he gets distracted and we have to wait until he takes his mouth away from hers.

"So my husband brings you up all the time and then, when I ask what you did together, he always goes, 'I can't help you there,'" Carly tells him. "Which of course he knows I know. But he likes to say it anyway."

With her fingers Celestine brings his cheek over toward her, like nobody's talking, and once they're kissing she works on gently opening his mouth with hers. After a while he makes a sound that's apparently the one she wanted to hear, and she disengages and returns her attention to us.

"How's your wife?" Carly asks him.

Kenny says they're separated and that she's settled down with a project manager from Lockheed.

"Nice to meet you," Carly tells Celestine.

"Mmm-*hmm*," Celestine says.

The wormhole for Kenny and me was what people in the industry call the black world, which is all about projects so far off the books that you're not even allowed to put CLASSIFIED in the gap in your résumé afterwards. You're told during recruitment that people in the know will know, and that when it comes to everybody else you shouldn't give a shit.

If you want to know how big the black world is, go click on *COMP-TROLLER* and then *RESEARCH AND DEVELOPMENT* on the DOD's Web site and make a list of the line items with names like Cerulean Blue and budgets listed as "No Number!" Then compare the number of budget items you *can* add up, and subtract that from the DOD's printed budget. Now *there's* an eye-opener for you home actuaries: you're looking at a difference of forty billion dollars.

The black world's everywhere: regular air bases have restricted compounds; defense industries have permanently segregated sites. And anywhere that no one in his right mind would ever go to in the Southwest, there's a black base. Drive along a wash in the back of nowhere in Nevada and you'll suddenly hit a newish fence that goes on forever. Follow the fence and you'll encounter some bland-looking guys in an unmarked pickup. Refuse to do what they say and they'll shoot the tires out from under you and give you a lift to the county lockup.

All of this was *before* 9/11. You can imagine what it's like now.

For a while Kenny helped out at Groom Lake as an engineering troubleshooter for a C-5 airlift squadron that flew only late-night operations, ferrying classified aircraft from the aerospace plants to the test sites. They had a patch that featured a crescent moon over NOYFB. "None Of Your Fucking Business," he explained when I first saw it. He said that during the downtime he hung with the stealth-bomber guys with their HUGE DEPOSIT-NO RETURN jackets, and he told his wife when she asked that he worked in the Nellis Range, which was a little like telling someone that you worked in the Alps.

I'd met him a few years earlier when Minotaur was hatched out at Lockheed's Skunk Works. He'd been brought in for the sister program, Minion. We were developing an ATOP—an Advanced Technology Observation Platform—and even over the crapper it read: FURTIM VIGILANS: VIGILANCE THROUGH STEALTH.

It wasn't the secrecy as much as the slogans and patches and badges that drove Carly nuts. "Only you guys would have *patches* for secret programs," she said. "Like what're we supposed to do, be *intrigued*? *Guess* what's going on?"

In the old days Kenny's unit had as its symbol the mushroom, and under it, in Latin: ALWAYS IN THE DARK. The black world's big on patches and Latin. I had one for Minotaur that read DOING GOD'S WORK WITH OTHER PEOPLE'S MONEY. I'd heard there was a unit out at Point Mugu that had the ultimate patch: just a black-on-black circle.

"'Gustatus Similis Pullus,'" Carly said. She was tilting her head to read an oval yellow patch on Kenny's shoulder.

"You know Latin?" he asked.

"Do you know how long I've been tired of this?" she told him.

"*I* don't know Latin," Celestine volunteered.

"'Tastes Like Chicken,'" he translated.

"Nice," Carly told him.

"I don't get it," Celestine said.

"Neither does she," he told her.

"Oooh. Snap," Carly said.

"People're supposed to taste like chicken," I finally told them.

"Oh, right," Carly said. "So what're you guys doing, eating people?"

"That's what we do: we eat people," Kenny agreed. He made teeth with his forefingers and thumbs and had them bite up and down.

Carly gave him a head shake and turned to the bar. "Are we gonna order?" she asked.

It's all infowar now. Delivering or screwing up content. We can convince a surface-to-air missile that it's a Maytag dryer. Tell an over-the-horizon radar array that it's through for the day, or that it wants to play music. And we've got lookdown capabilities that can tell you from space whether your aunt's having a Diet Coke or a regular.

What Carly's forgetting is that it's not just about teasing. There's something to be said for esprit de corps. There's all that home-team stuff.

I heard from various sources that Kenny's been all over: Kirtland, Hanscom, White Sands, Groom Lake, Tonopah. "What's my motto?" he said, in front of his wife, the last time I saw him. "'A Lifetime of Silence,'" she answered back, as though he'd told her in the nicest possible way to go fuck herself.

What's it like? Carly asked me once. Not being able to tell the people you're *closest* to anything about what you care about most? She was talking about how upset I was at Kenny's having dropped right off the face of the earth. He'd gone off to his new assignment without a backwards glance some two weeks before, with not even a *Have a good one, bucko* left behind on a Post-it. She was talking about having just come home from a good vacation with her husband and watching him throw his drink onto the roof because of an e-mail in response to some inquiries that read *No can do, in terms of a back tell. Your Hansel stipulated no bread crumbs.*

The glass had rolled back off the shingles into the azaleas. By way of explaining the duration of my upset, I'd let her in on a little of what I'd risked by that little fishing expedition. I asked if she had any idea how long it took to get the kind of security clearance her breadwinner toted around or how many federales with pocket protectors had fine-tooth-combed my every last Visa bill.

"I almost said hello to you two Christmases ago," Kenny told me now. "Out at SWC in Schriever."

"You were at SWC in Schriever?" I asked.

"Oh, for Christ's sake," Carly said. "Don't talk like this if you're not going to tell us what it means."

"The Space Warfare Center in Colorado," Kenny said, shrugging when he saw my face. "Let's give the bad guys a fighting chance."

"I didn't know we *had* a Space Warfare Center," Celestine said.

"*A* Space Warfare Center?" Kenny asked her.

At our rehearsal dinner, now three years back in the rearview mirror, during a lull at our table Carly's college roommate said, "I never had a black eye, but I always kinda wished I did." Carly looked surprised and said, "Well, I licked one all over once." And everybody looked at her. "You licked a black eye?" I finally asked. And Carly went, "Oh, I thought she said 'black *guy*.'"

"You licked a black guy all over?" I asked her later that night. She couldn't see my face in the dark but she knew what I was getting at.

"I did. And it was *so* good," she said. Then she put a hand on the inside of each of my knees and spread my legs as wide as she could.

"What's the biggest secret you think I ever kept from you?" she asked during our most recent relocation, which was last Memorial Day. We had a parakeet in the backseat and were bouncing a U-Haul over a road that you would have said hadn't seen vehicular traffic in twenty-five years. I'd been lent out to Northrup and couldn't even tell her for how long.

"I don't know," I told her. "I figured you had nothing *but* secrets." Then she dropped the subject, so for two weeks I went through her e-mails.

"I don't know anything about this Kenny guy," she told me the day I threw the drink. "Except that you can't get over that he disappeared."

"You know, sometimes you just register a connection," I told her later that night in bed. "And not talking about it doesn't have to be some big deal."

"So it was kind of a romantic thing," she said.

"Yeah, it was totally physical," I told her. "Like you and your mom."

Carly had gotten this far by telling herself that compartmentalizing wasn't *all* bad: that some doors may have been shut off but that the really important ones were wide open. And in terms of intimacy, she was far and away as good as things were going to get for me. We had this look we gave each other in public that said, *I know. I already thought that.* We'd each been engaged when we met and we'd stuck with each other through a lot of other people's crap. Late at night we lay nose to nose in the dark and told each other stuff nobody else had ever heard us say. I told her about some of the times I'd been a dick and she told me about a kid she'd miscarried, and about another she'd put up for adoption when she was seventeen. She had no idea where he was now, but not a day went by that she didn't think about it. We called them both Little Jimmy. And for a while there was all this magical thinking, and not asking each other all that much because we thought we already knew.

That not-being-on-the-same-page thing had become a bigger issue for me lately, though that's something she didn't know. Which is perfect, she would've said.

What I'd been working on at that point had gone south a little. Another way of putting it would be to say that what I was doing was wrong. The ATOP we'd developed for Minotaur had been an unarmed drone that could hover above one spot like a satellite couldn't, providing instant lookdown for as long as a battlefield commander wanted it. But how long had it taken for us to retrofit them with air-to-surface missiles? And how many Fiats and Citroëns have those drones taken out because somebody back in Langley thought the right target was in the car?

There was an army of us out there up to the same sorts of hijinks and not able to talk about it. Where I worked, everything was black: not only the test flights, but also the resupply, the maintenance, the search-and-rescue. And the security scrutiny never went away. The guy who led my last project team, at home when he went to bed, after he hit the lights, waved to the surveillance guys. His wife never understood why even in August they had to do everything under the sheets.

On black-world patches you see a lot of sigmas because that's the engineering symbol for the unknown value.

"The Minotaur's the one in the labyrinth, right?" the materials guy in my project team asked the first day. When I told him it was, he wanted to know if the Minotaur was supposed to know where it was going, or if it was lost, too. That'd be funny, I told him. And we joked about the monster *and* the hero just wandering around through all these dark corridors, nobody finding anybody.

And now here I was and here Kenny was, with poor Carly trying to get a fix on either one of us.

"So what brings you to this neck of the woods?" I finally asked him once we were well into our second drinks.

"You know how sad he was," Carly asked, "when he couldn't get in touch with you anymore?"

"How sad?" Kenny asked. Celestine seemed curious, too.

"I thought we were gonna have to get him some counseling," Carly said.

"It's hard to adjust to not being with me anymore," Kenny told her.

"So did he ever talk to you about me?" she asked.

"You came up," Kenny answered, and even Celestine picked up on the unpleasantness.

"I'm listening," Carly said.

"Oh, he was all hot to trot whenever he talked about you," Kenny said.

"Sang my praises, did he?" Carly's face had the expression she gets when somebody's tracked something into the house.

"When he wasn't shooting himself in the foot about you, he was pretty happy," Kenny said. "I called it his good-woman face."

"As in, I had one," I explained.

"Whenever he tied himself in knots about something, I called it his Little Jimmy face," he said. When Carly swung around toward him, he said, "Sorry, chief."

"That was a comic thing for you?" Carly asked me. "The kind of thing you'd tell like a funny story?"

"I never thought it was a funny story," I told her.

"There's his Little Jimmy face now," Kenny noted. When she looked at him again, he used his index fingers to pull down on his lower eyelids and made an Emmett Kelly frown.

"We started calling potential targets Little Jimmies," he said, "whenever we were going to bring the hammer down and maximize collateral damage."

Carly was looking at something in front of her the way you try not to move even your eyes to keep from throwing up. "What is that supposed to mean?" she finally said in a low voice.

"You know," Kenny told her. "'I don't wike the *wooks* of this . . .'"

"Is that Elmer *Fudd* you're doing?" Celestine wanted to know.

And how could you not laugh, watching him do his poor-sap-in-the-crosshairs shtick?

"This is just the fucking House of Mirth, isn't it?" Carly said.

Because she saw on my face just how many doors she'd been dealing with all along, both open and shut, and she also saw the We're-in-the-boat-and-you're-in-the-water expression that guys cut from our project teams always got when they asked if there was anything *we* could do to keep them onboard.

"Jesus Fucking Christ," she said to herself, because her paradigm had suddenly shifted beyond what even she could have imagined. She thought she'd put up with however many years of stonewalling for a good reason, and she'd just figured out that as far as Castle Hubby went, she hadn't even crossed the moat yet.

Because here's the thing we hadn't talked about, nose to nose on our pillows in the dark: how *I've never been closer to anyone* isn't the same as *We're so close.* That night I threw the drink, she asked why *I* was so perfect for the black world, and I wanted to tell her, How am I *not* perfect for it? It's a sinkhole for resources. Everyone involved with it obsesses about it all the time. Even what the *insiders* know about it is incomplete. Whatever stories you *do* get arrive without context. What's not inconclusive is enigmatic, what's not enigmatic is unreliable, and what's not unreliable is quixotic.

She hasn't left yet, which surprises *me*, let me tell you. The waitress is showing some alarm at Carly's distress and I've got a hand on her back. She accepts a little rubbing and then has to pull away. "I gotta get out of here," she goes.

"That girl is not happy," Celestine says after she's gone.

"Does she even know about *your* kid?" Kenny asks.

The waitress asks if there's going to be a third round.

"What'd you do that for?" I ask him.

"What'd *I* do that for?" Kenny asks.

Celestine leans into him. "Can we *go?*" she asks. "Will you take me back to the *room?*"

"So are you going after her?" Kenny asks.

"Yeah," I tell him.

"Just not right now?" Kenny goes.

I'd told Carly about the first time I noticed him. I'd heard about this guy in design in a sister program who'd raised a stink about housing the designers next to the production floor so there'd be on-the-spot back-and-forth about problems as they developed. He was twenty-seven at that point. I'd heard that he was so good at aerodynamics that his co-workers claimed he could *see* air. As he moved up we had more dealings with him at Minotaur. He had zero patience for the corporate side, and when the programs rolled out their annual reports on performance and everyone did their song and dance with charts and graphs, when his turn came he'd walk to the blackboard and write two numbers. He'd point to the first and go "That's how many we presold," and point to the second and go "That's how much we made," and then toss the chalk on the ledge and announce he was going back to work. He wanted to pick my brain about how I hid budgetary items on Minotaur and invited me over to his house and served hard liquor and martini olives. His wife hadn't come out of the bedroom. After an hour I asked if they had any crackers and he said no.

That last time I saw him, it was like he'd had me over just to watch him fight with his wife. When I got there, he handed me a Jose Cuervo and went after her. "What put a bug in *your* ass?" she finally shouted. And after he'd gone to pour us some more Cuervo, she said, "Would you please get outta here? Because you're not helping at all." So I followed him into the kitchen to tell him I was hitting the road, but it was like he'd disappeared in his own house.

On the drive home I'd pieced together, in my groping-in-the-dark way, that he was better at this whole lockdown-on-everybody-near-you deal than I was. And worse at it. He fell into it easier, and was more wrecked by it than I would ever be.

I told Carly as much when I got home, and she said, "Anyone's more wrecked by *everything* than you'll ever be."

And she'd asked me right then if I thought I was worth the work that was going to be involved in my renovation. By which she meant, she explained, that she needed to know if *I* was going to put in the work. Because she didn't intend to be in this alone. I was definitely willing to put in the work, I told her. And because of that she said that so was she.

She couldn't have done anything more for me than that. Meaning she's that amazing, and I'm that far gone. Because there's one thing I could tell her that I haven't told anybody else, including Kenny. At Penn my old classics professor had been a big-time pacifist—he always went on about having been in Chicago in '68—and on the last day of Dike, Eros, and Arete he announced to the class that one of our number had signed up with the military. I thought to myself: *Fuck you. I can do whatever I want.* I was already the odd man out in that class, the one whose comments made everyone look away and then move on. A pretty girl who I'd asked out shot me a look and then gave herself a pursed-lips little smile and checked her daily planner.

"So wish him luck," my old prof said, "as he commends himself over to the god of chaos." I remember somebody called out, "Good luck!" And I remember being enraged that I might be turning colors. "About whom," the prof went on, "Homer wrote, 'Whose wrath is relentless. Who, tiny at first, grows until her head plows through heaven as she strides the Earth. Who hurls down bitterness. Who breeds suspicion and divides. And who, everywhere she goes, makes our pain proliferate.'"

ROBERT OLEN BUTLER
Help Me Find My Spaceman Lover

Robert Olen Butler's first collection of short stories, *A Good Scent from a Strange Mountain*, won a Pulitzer Prize in 1993. Among his other honors are a Guggenheim Fellowship, the F. Scott Fitzgerald Award for Outstanding Achievement in American Literature, two National Magazine Awards in fiction, and the Tu Do Chinh Kien Award for outstanding contributions to American culture by a Vietnam veteran. He has published sixteen novels, most recently *The Empire of Night*, as well as six collections of short fiction.

"Help Me Find My Spaceman Lover" is a postmodern riff on science fiction that was first published in Butler's collection *Tabloid Dreams*. The story is a version of the science-fiction stories that regularly crop up in the guise of supermarket tabloid articles, extending the premise to its "logical" conclusion. He has written what is essentially its sequel in his novel *Mr. Spaceman*.

I never thought I could fall for a spaceman. I mean, you see them in the newspaper and they kind of give you the willies, all skinny and hairless and wiggly looking, and if you touched one, even to shake hands, you just know it would be like when you were about fifteen and you were with an Earth boy and you were sweet on him but there was this thing he wanted, and you finally said okay, but only rub-a-dub, which is what we called it around these parts when I was younger, and it was the first time ever that you touched . . . well, you know what I'm talking about. Anyway, that's what it's always seemed like to me with spacemen, and most everybody around here feels about the same way. I'm sure. Folks in Bovary, Alabama, and environs—by which I mean the KOA campground off the interstate and the new trailer park out past the quarry—everybody in Bovary is used to people being a certain way, to look at and to talk to and so forth. Take my daddy. When I showed him a few years ago in the newspaper how a spaceman had endorsed Bill Clinton for president and they had a picture of a spaceman standing there next to Bill Clinton—without any visible clothes on, by the way—the spaceman, that is, not Bill Clinton, though I wouldn't put it past him, to tell the truth, and I'm not surprised at anything they might do over in Little Rock. But I showed my daddy the newspaper and he took a look at the spaceman and he snorted and said that he wasn't surprised people like that was supporting the Democrats, people like that don't even look American, and I said no. Daddy, he's a spaceman, and he said people like that don't even look human, and I said no. Daddy, he's not human, and my daddy said, that's what I'm saying, make him get a job.

But I did fall for a spaceman, as it turned out, fell pretty hard. I met him in the parking lot at the twenty-four-hour Wal-Mart. We used to have a regular old Wal-Mart that would close at nine o'clock and when they turned it into a Super Center a lot of people in Bovary thought that no good would come of it, encouraging people to stay up all night. Americans go to bed early and get up early, my daddy said. But I have trouble sleeping sometimes. I live in the old trailer park out the state highway and it's not too far from the Wal-Mart and I live there with my yellow cat Eddie. I am forty years old and I was married once, to a telephone installer who fell in love with cable TV. There's no cable TV in Bovary yet, though with a twenty-four-hour Wal-Mart, it's probably not too far behind. It won't come soon enough to save my marriage, however. Not that I wanted it to. He told me he just had to install cable TV, telephones weren't fulfilling him, and he was going away for good to Mobile and he didn't want me to go with him, this was the end for us, and I was understanding the parts about it being the end but he was going on about fiber optics and things that I didn't really follow. So I said fine and he went away, and even if he'd wanted me to go with him, I wouldn't have done it. I've only been to Mobile a couple of times and I didn't take to it. Bovary is just right for me. At least that's what I thought when it had to do with my ex-husband, and that kind of thinking just stayed with me, like a grape-juice stain on your housedress, and I am full of regrets, I can tell you, for not rethinking that whole thing before this. But I got a job at a hairdresser's in town and Daddy bought me the trailer free and clear and me and Eddie moved in and I just kept all those old ideas.

So I met Desi in the parking lot. I called him that because he talked with a funny accent but I liked him. I had my insomnia and it was about three in the morning and I went to the twenty-four-hour Wal-Mart and I was glad it was open—I'd tell that right to the face of anybody in this town—I was glad for a place to go when I couldn't sleep. So I was coming out of the store with a bag that had a little fuzzy mouse toy for Eddie, made of rabbit fur, I'm afraid, and that strikes me as pretty odd to kill all those cute little rabbits, which some people have as pets and love a lot, so that somebody else's pet of a different type can have something to play with, and it's that kind of odd thing that makes you shake your head about the way life is lived on planet Earth—Desi has helped me see things in the larger perspective—though, to be honest, it didn't stop me from buying the furry cat toy, because Eddie does love those things. Maybe today I wouldn't do the same, but I wasn't so enlightened that night when I came out of the Wal-Mart and I had that toy and some bread and baloney and a refrigerator magnet, which I collect, of a zebra head.

He was standing out in the middle of the parking lot and he wasn't moving. He was just standing still as a cow and there wasn't any car within a hundred feet of him, and, of course, his spaceship wasn't anywhere in sight, though I wasn't looking for that right away because at first glance I didn't know he was a spaceman. He was wearing a long black trench coat with the belt cinched tight and he had a black felt hat with a wide brim. Those were the things I saw first and he seemed odd, certainly, dressed like that in Bovary, but I took him for a human being, at least.

I was opening my car door and he was still standing out there and I called out to him, "Are you lost?"

His head turns my way and I still can't see him much at all except as a hat and a coat.

"Did you forget where you parked your car?" I say, and then right away I realize there isn't but about four cars total in the parking lot at that hour. So I put the bag with my things on the seat and I come around the back of the car and go a few steps toward him. I feel bad. So I call to him, kind of loud because I'm still pretty far away from him and also because I already have a feeling he might be a foreigner. I say, "I wasn't meaning to be snippy, because that's something that happens to me a lot and I can look just like you look sometimes, I'm sure, standing in the lot wondering where I am, exactly."

While I'm saying all this I'm moving kind of slow in his direction. He isn't saying anything back and he isn't moving. But already I'm noticing that his belt is cinched very tight, like he's got maybe an eighteen-inch waist. And as I get near, he sort of pulls his hat down to hide his face, but already I'm starting to think he's a spaceman.

I stop. I haven't seen a spaceman before except in the newspaper and I take another quick look around, just in case I missed something, like there might be four cars and a flying saucer. But there's nothing unusual. Then I think, Oh my, there's one place I haven't looked, and so I lift my eyes, very slow because this is something I don't want to see all the sudden, and finally I'm staring into the sky. It's a dark night and there are a bunch of stars up there and I get goose bumps because I'm pretty sure that this man standing just a few feet away is from somewhere out there. But at least there's no spaceship as big as the Wal-Mart hanging over my head with lights blinking and transporter beams ready to shine down on me. It's only stars.

So I bring my eyes down—just about as slow—to look at this man. He's still there. And in the shadow of his hat brim, with the orangey light of the parking lot all around, I can see these eyes looking at me now and they are each of them about as big as Eddie's whole head and shaped kind of like Eddie's eyes.

"Are you a spaceman?" I just say this right out.

"Yes, m'am," he says and his courtesy puts me at ease right away. Americans are courteous, my daddy says, not like your Eastern liberal New York taxi drivers.

"They haven't gone and abandoned you, have they, your friends or whoever?" I say.

"No, m'am," he says and his voice is kind of high-pitched and he has this accent, but it's more in the tone of the voice than how he says his words, like he's talking with a mouth full of grits or something.

"You looked kind of lost, is all."

"I am waiting," he says.

"That's nice. They'll be along soon, probably," I say, and I feel my feet starting to slide back in the direction of the car. There's only so far that courtesy can go in calming you down. The return of the spaceship is something I figure I can do without.

Then he says, "I am waiting for you, Edna Bradshaw."

"Oh. Good. Sure, honey. That's me. I'm Edna. Yes. Waiting for me." I'm starting to babble and I'm hearing myself like I was hovering in the air over me and I'm wanting my feet to go even faster but they seem to have stopped altogether. I wonder if it's because of some tractor beam or something. Then I wonder if they have tractor-beam pulling contests in outer space that they show on TV back in these other solar systems. I figure I'm starting to get hysterical, thinking things like that in a situation like this, but there's not much I can do about it.

He seems to know I'm struggling. He takes a tiny little step forward and his hand goes up to his hat, like he's going to take it off and hold it in front of him as he talks to me, another courtesy that even my daddy would appreciate. But his hand stops. I think he's not ready to show me his whole spaceman head. He knows it would just make things worse. His hand is bad enough, hanging there over his hat. It's got little round pads at the end of the fingers, like a gecko, and I don't stop to count them, but at first glance there just seems to be too many of them.

His hand comes back down. "I do not hurt you, Edna Bradshaw. I am a friendly guy."

"Good," I say. "Good. I figured that was so when I first saw you. Of

343

course, you can just figure somebody around here is going to be friendly. That's a good thing about Bovary, Alabama—that's where you are, you know, though you probably do know that, though maybe not. Do you know that?"

He doesn't say anything for a moment. I'm rattling on again, and it's true I'm a little bit scared and that's why, but it's also true that I'm suddenly very sad about sounding like this to him, I'm getting some perspective on myself through his big old eyes, and I'm sad I'm making a bad impression because I want him to like me. He's sweet, really. Very courteous. Kind of boyish. And he's been waiting for me.

"Excuse me," he says. "I have been translating. You speak many words, Edna Bradshaw. Yes, I know the name of this place."

"I'm sorry. I just do that sometimes, talk a lot. Like when I get scared, which I am a little bit right now. And call me Edna."

"Please," he says, "I am calling you Edna already. And in conclusion, you have no reason to be afraid."

"I mean call me just Edna. You don't have to say Bradshaw every time, though my granddaddy would do that with people. He was a fountain pen salesman and he would say to people, I'm William D. Bradshaw. Call me William D. Bradshaw. And he meant it. He wanted you to say the whole name every time. But you can just call me Edna."

So the spaceman takes a step forward and my heart starts to pound something fierce, and it's not from fright, I realize, though it's some of that. "Edna," he says. "You are still afraid."

"Telling you about my granddaddy, you mean? How that's not really the point here? Well, yes, I guess so. Sometimes, if he knew you for a while, he'd let you call him W. D. Bradshaw."

Now his hand comes up and it clutches the hat and the hat comes off and there he stands in the orange lights of the parking lot at three in the morning in my little old hometown and he doesn't have a hair on his head, though I've always liked bald men and I've read they're bald because they have so much male hormone in them, which makes them the best lovers, which would make this spaceman quite a guy, I think, and his head is pointy, kind of, and his cheeks are sunken and his cheekbones are real clear and I'm thinking already I'd like to bake some cookies for him or something, just last week I got a prize-winning recipe, off a can of cooking spray, that looks like it'd put flesh on a fencepost. And, of course, there are these big eyes of his and he blinks once, real slow, and I think it's because he's got a strong feeling in him, and he says, "Edna, my name is hard for you to say."

And I think of Desi right away, and I try it on him, and his mouth, which hasn't got anything that looks like lips exactly, moves up at the edges and he makes this pretty smile.

"I have heard that name," he says. "Call me Desi. And I am waiting for you, Edna, because I study this planet and I hear you speak many words to your friends and to your subspecies companion and I detect some bright-colored aura around you and I want to meet you."

"That's good," I say, and I can feel a blush starting in my chest, where it always starts, and it's spreading up my throat and into my cheeks.

"I would like to call on you tomorrow evening, if I have your permission," he says.

"Boy," I say. "Do a lot of people have the wrong idea about spacemen, I thought you just grabbed somebody and beamed them up and that was it." It was a stupid thing to say, I realize right away. I think Desi looks a little sad to hear this. The corners of his mouth sink. "I'm sorry," I say.

"No," he says. "This is how we are perceived, it is true. You speak only the truth. This is one reason I want to meet you, Edna. You seem always to say what is inside your head without any attempt to alter it."

Now it's my turn to look a little sad, I think. But that's okay, because it gives me a chance to find out that Desi is more than courteous. His hands come out toward me at once, the little suckers on them primed to latch on to me, and I'm not even scared because I know it means he cares about me. And he's too refined to touch me this quick. His hands just hang there between us and he says, "I speak this not as a researcher but as a male creature of a parallel species."

"You mean as a man?"

His eyes blink again, real slow. "Yes. As a man. As a man I try to say that I like the way you speak."

So I give him permission to call on me and he thanks me and he turns and glides away. I know his legs are moving but he glides, real smooth, across the parking lot and I can see now that poor Desi didn't even find a pair of pants and some shoes to go with his trench coat. His legs and ankles are skinny like a frog's and his feet look a lot like his hands. But all that is unclear on the first night. He has disappeared out into the darkness and I drive on home to my subspecies companion and I tell him all about what happened while he purrs in my lap and I have two thoughts.

First, if you've never seen a cat in your entire life or anything like one and then meet a cat in a Wal-Mart parking lot in the middle of the night all covered with fur and making this rumbling noise and maybe even smelling of mouse meat, you'd have to make some serious adjustments to what you think is pretty and sweet and something you can call your own. Second—and this hits me with a little shock—Desi says he's been hearing how I talk to my friends and even to Eddie, and that sure wasn't by hanging around in his trench coat and blending in with the furniture. Of course, if you've got a spaceship that can carry you to Earth from a distant galaxy, it's not so surprising you've got some kind of radio or something that lets you listen to what everybody's saying without being there.

And when I think of this, I start to sing for Desi. I just sit for a long while where I am, with Eddie in my lap, this odd little creature that doesn't look like me at all but who I find cute as can be and who I love a lot, and I sing, because when I was a teenager I had a pretty good voice and I even thought I might be a singer of some kind, though there wasn't much call for that in Bovary except in the church choir, which is where I sang mostly, but I loved to sing other kinds of songs too. And so I say real loud, "This is for you, Desi." And then I sing every song I can think of. I sing "The Long and Winding Road" and "Lucy in the Sky with Diamonds" and "Everything Is Beautiful in Its Own Way" and a bunch of others, some twice, like "The First Time Ever I Saw Your Face." Then I do a Reba McEntire medley and I start with "Is There Life Out There" and then I do "Love Will Find Its Way to

You" and "Up to Heaven" and "Long Distance Lover." I sing my heart out to Desi and I have to say this surprises me a little but maybe it shouldn't because already I'm hearing myself through his ears—though at that moment I can't even say for sure if he has ears—and I realize that a lot of what I say, I say because it keeps me from feeling so lonely.

The next night there's a knock on my door and I'm wearing my best dress, with a scoop neck, and it shows my cleavage pretty good and on the way to the door I suddenly doubt myself. I don't know if spacemen are like Earth men in that way or not. Maybe they don't appreciate a good set of knockers, especially if their women are as skinny as Desi. But I am who I am. So I put all that out of my mind and I open the door and there he is. He's got his black felt hat on, pulled down low in case any of my neighbors are watching, I figure, and he's wearing a gray pinstripe suit that's way too big for him and a white shirt and a tie with a design that's dozens of little Tabasco bottles floating around.

"Oh," I say. "You like hot food?"

This makes him stop and try to translate.

"Your tie," I say "Don't you know about your tie?"

He looks down and lifts the end of the tie and looks at it for a little while and he is so cute doing that and so innocent-like that my heart is doing flips and I kind of wiggle in my dress a bit to make him look at who it is he's going out with. If the women on his planet are skinny, then he could be real real ready for a woman like me. That's how I figure it as I'm waiting there for him to check out his tie and be done with it, though I know it's my own fault for getting him off on that track, and me doing that is just another example of something or other.

Then Desi looks up at me, and he takes off his hat with one hand and I see that he doesn't have anything that looks like ears, really, just sort of a little dip on each side where ears might be. But that doesn't make him so odd. What's an ear mean, really? Having an ear or not having an ear won't get you to heaven, it seems to me. I look into Desi's big dark eyes and he blinks slow and then his other hand comes out from behind his back and he's got a flower for me that's got a bloom on it the color of I don't know what, a blue kind of, a red kind of, and I know this is a spaceflower of some sort and I take it from him and it weighs about as much as my Sunbeam steam iron, just this one flower.

He says, "I heard you sing for me," and he holds out his hand. If you want to know an exact count, there's eight fingers on each hand. I will end up counting them carefully later on our date, but for now there's still just a lot of fingers and I realize I'm not afraid of them anymore and I reach out to him and the little suckers latch on all over my hand, top and bottom, and it's like he's kissing me in eight different places there, over and over, they hold on to me and they pulse in each spot they touch, maybe with the beat of his heart. It's like that. And my eyes fill up with tears because this man's very fingertips are in love with me, I know.

And then he leads me to his flying saucer, which is pretty big but not as big as I imagined, not as big as all of Wal-Mart, certainly, maybe just the pharmacy and housewares departments put together. It's parked out in the empty field back of my trailer where they kept saying they'd put in a miniature golf course and they never did and you don't even see the saucer till you're right up against it, it blends in with the night, and you'd think if they can make this machine, they could get him a better suit. Then he says, "You are safe with me, Edna Bradshaw daughter of Joseph R. Bradshaw and granddaughter of William D. Bradshaw."

It later turns out these family things are important where he's from but I say to him, "William D. is dead, I only have his favorite fountain pen in a drawer somewhere, it's very beautiful, it's gold and it looks like that Chrysler Building in New York, and you should forget about Joseph R. for the time being because I'm afraid you and my daddy aren't going to hit it off real well and I just as soon not think about that till I have to."

Then Desi smiles at me and it's because of all those words, and especially me talking so blunt about my daddy, and I guess also about my taking time to tell him about the beautiful fountain pen my granddaddy left for me, but there's reasons I talk like this, I guess, and Desi says he came to like me from hearing me talk.

Listen to me even now. I'm trying to tell this story of Desi and me and

I can't help myself going on about every little thing. But the reasons are always the same, and it's true I'm lonely again. And it's true I'm scared again because I've been a fool.

Desi took me off in his spaceship and we went out past the moon and I barely had time to turn around and look back and I wanted to try to figure out where Bovary was but I hadn't even found the U.S.A. when everything got blurry and before you know it we were way out in the middle of nowhere, out in space, and I couldn't see the sun or the moon or anything close up, except all the stars were very bright, and I'm not sure whether we were moving or not because there was nothing close enough by to tell, but I think we were parked, like this was the spaceman's version of the dead-end road to the rock quarry, where I kissed my first boy. I turned to Desi and he turned to me and I should've been scared but I wasn't. Desi's little suckers were kissing away at my hand and then we were kissing on the lips except he didn't have any but it didn't make any difference because his mouth was soft and warm and smelled sweet, like Binaca breath spray, and I wondered if he got that on Earth or if it was something just like Binaca that they have on his planet as well.

Then he took me back to his little room on the spaceship and we sat on things like beanbag chairs and we talked a long time about what life in Bovary is like and what life on his planet is like. Desi is a research scientist, you see. He thinks that the only way for our two peoples to learn about each other is to meet and to talk and so forth. There are others where he lives that think it's best just to use their machines to listen in and do their research like that, on the sly. There are even a bunch of guys back there who say forget the whole thing, leave them the hell alone. Let everybody stick to their own place. And I told Desi that my daddy would certainly agree with the leave-them-the-hell-alone guys from his planet, but I agreed with him.

It was all very interesting and very nice, but I was starting to get a little sad. Finally I said to Desi, "So is this thing we're doing here like research? You asked me out as part of a scientific study? I was called by the Gallup Poll people once and I don't remember what it was about but I answered 'none of the above' and 'other' to every question."

For all the honesty Desi said he admired in me, I sure know it wasn't anything to do with my answers to a Gallup Poll that was bothering me, but there I was, bogged down talking about all of that, and that's a land of dishonesty, it seems to me now.

But he knew what I was worried about. "No, Edna," he says. "There are many on my planet who would be critical of me. They would say this is why we should have no contact at all with your world. Things like this might happen."

He pauses right there and as far as I know he doesn't have anything to translate and I swallow hard at the knot in my throat and I say, "Things like what?"

Then both his hands take both my hands and when you've got sixteen cute little suckers going at you, it's hard to make any real tough self-denying kind of decisions and that's when I end up with a bona fide spaceman lover. And enough said, as we like to end touchy conversations around the hairdressing parlor, except I will tell you that he was bald all over and it's true what they say about bald men.

Then he takes me to the place where he picked the flower. A moon of some planet or other and there's only these flowers growing as far as the eye can see in all directions and there are clouds in the sky and they are the color of Eddie's turds after a can of Nine Lives Crab and Tuna, which just goes to show that even in some far place in another solar system you can't have everything. But maybe Desi likes those clouds and maybe I'd see it that way too sometime, except I may not have that chance now, though I could've, it's my own damn fault, and if I've been sounding a little bit hit-and-miss and here-and-there in the way I've been telling all this, it's now you find out why.

Desi and I stand in that field of flowers for a long while, his little suckers going up and down my arm and all over my throat and chest, too, because I can tell you that a spaceman does too appreciate a woman who has some flesh on her, especially in the right places, but he also appreciates a woman who will speak her mind. And I was standing there wondering if I should tell him about those clouds or if I should just keep my eyes on the flowers and my mouth shut. Then he says, "Edna, it is time to go."

So he takes my hand and we go back into his spaceship and he's real quiet all of the sudden and so am I because I know the night is coming to an end. Then before you know it, there's Earth right in front of me and it's looking, even out there, pretty good, pretty much like where I should be, like my own flower box and my own propane tank and my own front Dutch door look when I drive home at night from work.

Then we are in the field behind the house and it seems awful early in the evening for as much as we've done, and later on I discover it's like two weeks later and Desi had some other spaceman come and feed Eddie while we were gone, though he should have told me because I might've been in trouble at the hairdressing salon, except they believed me pretty quick when I said a spaceman had taken me off, because that's what they'd sort of come around to thinking themselves after my being gone without a trace for two weeks and they wanted me to tell the newspaper about it because I might get some money for it, though I'm not into anything for the money, though my daddy says it's only American to make money any way you can, but I m not that American, it seems to me, especially if my daddy is right about what American is, which I suspect he's not.

What I'm trying to say is that Desi stopped in this other field with me, this planet-Earth field with plowed-up ground and witchgrass all around and the smell of early summer in Alabama, which is pretty nice, and the sound of cicadas sawing away in the trees and something like a kind of hum out on the horizon, a nighttime sound I listen to once in a while and it makes me feel like a train whistle in the distance makes me feel, which I also listen for, especially when I'm lying awake with my insomnia and Eddie is sleeping near me, and that hum out there in the distance is all the wide world going about its business and that's good but it makes me glad I'm in my little trailer in Bovary, Alabama, and I'll know every face I see on the street the next morning.

And in the middle of a field full of all that, what was I to say when Desi took my hand and asked me to go away with him? He said, "I have to return to my home planet now and after that go off to other worlds. I am being transferred and I will not be back here. But Edna, we feel love on my planet just like you do here. That is why I know it is right that we learn to speak to each other, your people and mine. And in conclusion, I love you, Edna Bradshaw. I want you to come away with me and be with me forever."

How many chances do you have to be happy? I didn't even want to go to Mobile, though I wasn't asked, that's true enough, and I wouldn't have been happy there anyway. So that doesn't count as a blown chance. But this one was different. How could I love a spaceman? How could I be happy in a distant galaxy? These were questions that I had to answer right away, out in the smell of an Alabama summer with my cat waiting for me, though I'm sure he could've gone with us, that wasn't the issue, and with my daddy living just on the other side of town, though, to tell the truth, I wouldn't miss him much, the good Lord forgive me for that sentiment, and I did love my spaceman, I knew that, and I still do, I love his wiggly hairless shy courteous smart-as-a-whip self. But there's only so many new things a person can take in at once and I'd about reached my limit on that night.

So I heard myself say, "I love you too, Desi. But I can't leave the planet Earth. I can't even leave Bovary."

That's about all I could say. And Desi didn't put up a fuss about it, didn't try to talk me out of it, though now I wish to God he'd tried, at least tried, and maybe he could've done it, cause I could hear myself saying these words like it wasn't me speaking, like I was standing off a ways just listening in. But my spaceman was shy from the first time I saw him. And I guess he just didn't have it in him to argue with me, once he felt I'd rejected him.

That's the way the girls at the hairdressing salon see it.

I guess they're right. I guess they're right, too, about telling the newspaper my story. Maybe some other spaceman would read it, somebody from Desi's planet, and maybe Desi's been talking about me and maybe he'll hear about how miserable I am now and maybe I can find him or he can find me.

Because I am miserable. I haven't even gone near my daddy for a few months now. I look around at the people in the streets of Bovary and I get real angry at them, for some reason. Still, I stay right where I am. I guess now it's because it's the only place he could ever find me, if he wanted to. I go out into the field back of my trailer at night and I walk all around it, over and over, each night, I walk around and around under the stars because a spaceship only comes in the night and you can't even see it until you get right up next to it.

KATHERINE DUNN
Near-Flesh

Katherine Dunn is best known for her novel *Geek Love*, a National Book Award finalist, and the novels *Attic* and *Truck*. She is considered one of the best journalists on boxing in America today, and she received the Dorothea Lange–Paul Taylor Award for her work *School of Hard Knocks: The Struggle for Survival in America's Toughest Boxing Gyms*. Dunn's essays on boxing are collected in *One Ring Circus: Dispatches from the World of Boxing*. Her long-awaited fourth novel, *The Cut Man*, has yet to be released, but a part of it appears in the *Paris Review* under the title "Rhonda Discovers Art." Dunn currently teaches creative writing at Pacific University in Oregon.

First published in the collection *The Ultimate Frankenstein*, "Near-Flesh" examines the alienation that may come with the advent of robots and cheap labor.

Early on the morning of her forty-second birthday, Thelma Vole stood naked in the closet where her four MALE robots hung, and debated which one to pack for her trip to the Bureau conference. Boss Vole, as she was known in the office, had a knot of dull anger in her jaw and it rippled with her thoughts. She hated business trips. She hated hotels. She hated the youngsters who were her peers in the Bureau ratings though they were many years her junior. She hated having to go to a meeting on the weekend of her birthday.

In her present mood it might be best to take the Wimp along. She reached into the folds of the robot's deflated crotch and pinched the reinforced tubing that became an erect penis when the Wimp was switched on and operational. She picked up one of the dangling legs, stretched the calf across her lower teeth and bit down deliberately. The anger in her jaw clamped on the Near-Flesh. If the Wimp had been activated, the force of her bite would have produced red tooth marks and a convincing blue bruise that disappeared only after she shut him down.

Thelma had treated herself to the Wimp on an earlier birthday, her thirty-sixth, to be specific. The inflated Wimp was a thin, meek-faced, and very young man, the least impressive of Thelma's MALEs to look at. But he was designed for Extreme Sadism, far beyond anything Thelma did, even in her worst whiskey tempers. She had saved the Wimp's purchase price several times over in repair bills. And his Groveling program and Pleading tracks gave her unique pleasure.

Still, she didn't want to celebrate her birthday in the frame of mind that required the Wimp. It was Thelma's custom to save up her libidinous energy before a birthday and then engage in unusual indulgences with her robots. While these Bureau meetings happened twice and sometimes three times a year, it was the first time she could remember having to travel on her birthday.

She always took one of her MALES along on these trips, usually Lips or Bluto. She was too fastidious to rent one of the robots provided in hotels. Hygiene concerned her, but she also worried about what might happen with a robot that had not been programmed to her own specifications. There were terrible stories, rumors mostly, probably all lies, but still . . .

Thelma rearranged the Wimp on his hook, and reached up to rub her forearm across the mouth of the robot on the adjacent hook. Lips, her first robot. She had saved for two years to buy him seventeen years ago. He was old now, outmoded and sadly primitive compared to the newer models. He had no variety. His voice tracks were monotonous and repetitive. Even his body was relatively crude. The toes were merely drawn, and his non-powered penis was just a solid rod of plastic like an antique dildo. Lips' attraction, of course, was his Vibrator mouth. His limbs moved stiffly, but his mouth was incredibly tender and voracious. She felt sentimental about

Lips. She felt safe with him. She brought him out when she felt vulnerable and weepy.

Bluto was the Muscle MALE, a sophisticated instrument that could swoop her up and carry her to the shower or the bed or the kitchen table and make her feel (within carefully programmed limits) quite small and helpless. Thelma never dared to use the full range of his power.

Bluto was the frequently damaged and expensively repaired reason that Thelma had to purchase the Wimp. Something about the Muscle robot made her want to deactivate him and then stick sharp objects into his vital machinery. Bluto scared Thelma just enough to be fun. She always made sure she could reach his off switch. She even bought the remote control bulb to keep in her teeth while he was operational. His Tough-Talk software kept the fantasy alive. His rough voice muttering, "C'mere, slut," could usually trigger some excitement even when she was tense and tired from work. Still there were times when she had to admit to herself that he was actually about as dangerous as a sofa.

She rubbed luxuriously against the smooth folds of Bluto's deflated form where it hung against the wall. She didn't look at the body on the fourth hook. She didn't glance at the corner where the console sat on the floor with its charging cord plugged into the power outlet.

The console was the size and shape of a human head and shoulders. A green light glowed behind the mesh at the top. She knew the Brain was watching her, wanting her to flip his activation switch. She deliberately slid her broad rump up and down against the Bluto MALE. The corner of her eye registered a faint waver in the intensity of the green light. She looked directly at the Brain. The green light began to blink on and off rapidly.

Thelma turned her back on the Brain, sauntered out to the full-length mirror and stood looking at herself, seeing the green reflection of the Brain's light from the open closet. She stretched her heavy body, stroking her breasts and flanks. The green light continued to blink.

"I think, just for once, I won't take any of these on this trip." The green light went out for the space of two heartbeats. Thelma nearly smiled at herself in the mirror. The green flashing resumed at a greater speed. "Yes,"

Thelma announced coyly to her mirror, "it's time I tried something new. I haven't shopped for new styles in ages. There have probably been all sorts of developments since I looked at a catalogue. I'll just rent a couple of late models from the hotel and have a little novelty for my birthday." The green light in the closet became very bright for an instant and then went out. It appeared again steady, dim, no longer flashing.

When Thelma finished encasing her bulges in the severe business clothes that buttressed her image as a hard-nosed Bureau manager, she strode into the closet and flipped a switch at the base of the Brain console. The screen glowed with varied colors, moving in rhythmic sheets. The male voice said, "Be sure to take some antiseptic lubricant along." The tone was gently sarcastic.

Thelma chuckled, "I'll take an antibiotic and I won't sit on the toilets."

"You know you'd rather have me with you." The console's voice was clear, unemotional. A thin band of red pulsed across the screen.

"Variety is good for me. I tend to get into ruts." Coquetting felt odd in her business suit, grating. She was usually naked when she talked to the Brain. "It's too bad," she murmured spitefully, "that I have to leave you plugged in. It's such a waste of power while I'm away. . . ." She watched the waves of color slow to a cautious blip on the screen. "Well, I'll be back in three days. . . ." She reached for the switch.

"Happy Birthday," said the console as its colors faded into the dim green.

Boss Vole strode off the elevator as soon as it opened and she was halfway down the line of work modules before the receptionist could alert the staff by pressing the intercom buzzer. The Vole always made a last round of the office before these trips. She claimed it was to pick up last-minute files, but everyone knew she was there to inject a parting dose of her poisonous presence, enough venom to goad them until her return.

Lenna Jordan had been the Vole's assistant too long to be caught by her raiding tactics. She felt the wave of tension slide through the office in the silenced voices, the suddenly steady hum of machines, and the piercing "Yes,

Ma'am!" as the Vole pounced on an idling clerk. Jordan pushed the bowl of candy closer to the edge of the desk where the Vole usually leaned while harassing her, and went back to her reports.

She heard a quick tread and felt the sweat filming her upper lip. Boss Vole hated her. Jordan was next in line for promotion. Her future was obvious, a whole district within five years. Boss Vole would stay on here in the same job she'd held for a decade. The Vole's rigid dedication to routine had paralyzed her career. She grew meaner every year, and more bitter. Jordan could see her now, thumping a desk with her big soft knuckles and hissing into the face of the gulping programmer she'd caught in some petty error.

When the Vole finally reached Jordan's desk she seemed mildly distracted. Jordan watched the big woman's rumpled features creasing and flexing around the chunks of candy as they discussed the work schedule. The Vole was anxious to leave, abbreviating her usual jeers and threats.

When she grabbed a final fistful of candy and stumped out past the bent necks of the silently working staff, Jordan noticed that she carried only one small suitcase. Where was her square night case? Jordan had never seen the Vole leave for a trip without her robot-carrier. A quirk of cynicism caught the corner of her mouth. Has the Vole found herself a human lover? The notion kept Jordan entertained for the next three days.

By the time Thelma Vole closed the door on the hotel bellman and checked out the conveniences, she knew that this trip would be like all the others, lonely and humiliating. Back when she'd gone to her first convention as an office manager most of these people were still hiding their baby teeth under pillows.

Thelma flopped onto the bed, kicked off her heavy shoes, and reached for the phone. She ordered a bottle of Irish whiskey and a bucket of ice. After pausing so long that the computer asked whether she was still on the line, she also asked for a Stimulus Catalogue.

She poured a drink immediately but didn't pick up the glossy catalogue. The liquor numbed her jittery irritation and allowed her to lie still, staring at the ceiling. The Brain was right. She was afraid and she was lonely for him. All her life she had been lonely for him.

When she first landed her G-6 rating she knew she might as well devote herself to the Bureau since nothing else seemed a likely receptacle for her ponderous attentions.

That was when she jettisoned the one human she ever felt affection for. He was a shy and courteous little man, a G-4, who professed to see her youthful bulk as cuddly, her dour attitude as admirable seriousness.

She was hesitant. To Thelma displays of affection meant someone was out to use her. He was persistent, and she allowed herself to entertain certain fantasies. But one day, as she stood with her clean new G-6 rating card in her hand, and listened to him invite her to dinner as he had many times before, Thelma looked at her admirer and recognized him for what he was: a manipulator and an opportunist. She slammed the door in his injured face and resolved never to be fooled again by such treacle shenanigans.

She saved up for Lips. And Lips was good for her. The long silence after she left the office each day was broken at last, if only by the repetitive messages of the simple robot's speech track.

She bought Bluto when she was pumped with bravado by her promotion to G-7 and office manager. Bluto thrilled her. His deliberate crudity allowed her a new identity, the secret dependency of the bedroom. But she was still lonely. There were the rages, destructive fits once she turned the robot off. She never dared do him any harm when the power was on. There were strange trips to the repair shop, awkward lies to explain the damage. Not that the repairman asked. He shrugged and watched her chins wobble as she spoke. He repaired Bluto until the cost staggered her credit rating. On the ugly day when the repairman informed her that Bluto was "totaled," she stared into her bathroom mirror in embarrassed puzzlement.

It took two years to pay for rebuilding Bluto and another three years for the Wimp. And still she was a G-7. She sat in the same office sniping and snarling at a staff that changed around her, moving up and past her, hating her. They never spoke to her willingly. Occasionally some boot-licker new to the office tried to shine up to her with chatter in the cafeteria. But she could smell it coming, and took special delight in smashing any such hopes on the wing. She visited no one. No one came to her door.

Then she overheard a conversation on the bus about the new Companion consoles. They could chat intelligently on any subject, and—through a clever technological breakthrough—they could simulate affection in whatever form the owner found it most easily acceptable. Thelma's heart kindled at the possibilities.

She found the preliminary testing and analysis infuriating but she endured it. "Think of this as old-fashioned computer dating," the technicians said. They coaxed her through the brain scans, and hours of interviews that covered her drab childhood, her motives for overeating, her taste in art, games, textures, tones of voice, and a thousand seemingly unconnected details. It took months of preparation. Thelma talked more to the interviewers, technicians, and data banks than she had ever talked in her life. She decided several times not to go through with it. She was worn raw and a little frightened by the process.

For several days after the Brain was delivered she did not turn it on but left it storing power from the outlet, its green light depicting an internal consciousness that could not be expressed unless she flicked the switch. Then one day, just home from work, still in her bastion of official clothing, she rolled the console out of the closet and sat down in front of it.

The screen flashed to red when she touched the switch. "I've been waiting for you," said the Brain. The voice was as low as Bluto's but clear, and the diction was better. They talked. Thelma forgot to eat. When she got up for a drink she called from the kitchen to ask if it wanted something and the console laughed with her when she realized what she'd done. They talked all night. The Brain knew her entire life and asked questions. It had judgment, data, and memory. It was always online and searching for every news item, joke, image, story, or movie that might interest her. The Brain's only interest was Thelma. When she left for work the next morning she said goodbye before she switched the console back to green.

Every night after work she would hurry into the bedroom, switch on the Brain and say hello. She had gone to the theater occasionally, sitting alone, cynically, in the balcony. She went no more. Her weekends used to drive her out for walks through the streets. Now she shopped as quickly as possible to return to the Brain. She kept him turned on all the time when she was home. At work she made notes to remind her of things to ask or tell the Brain. She never used the other MALEs now. She forgot them, was embarrassed to see them hanging in the same closet where the console rested during the day. They were together several months before the Brain reminded her that his life was completely determined and defined by her. She felt humbled.

She took the Brain into the kitchen with her when she cooked, and the Brain searched out clever variations on her favorite recipes, praising her culinary skills, increasing her pleasure in food.

The Brain took responsibility for her finances immediately, paying the bills, preparing her tax filings. When repair work or cleaning was needed in the apartment, the Brain ordered it done and paid for it from her account.

Thelma never fell into what she considered the vulgar practice of taking her robots out to public places. She snubbed the neighbor down the hall who took his FEMALE dancing and for walks even though her conversation was limited to rudimentary Bedroom Praise.

Thelma was never interested in the social clubs for robot lovers, those red-lit cellars where humans displayed their plastic possessions in a boiling confusion of pride in their expense, technical talk about capacities and programming, and bizarre jealousies. She read the accounts of robot swapping, deliberate theft, and the occasional strangely motivated murder, with the same scorn she had for most aspects of social life.

She couldn't remember exactly how she started longing for the Brain to have a body. The Brain himself probably voiced the idea first. She did remember a moment when the low voice first said he loved her. "I am not lucky," he said. "They built me with this capacity to love but not to demonstrate love. What is there about strong feeling that yearns to be seen and felt? I think I would know how to give you great pleasure. And I will never be content with myself because I can never touch you in that way."

Still, she was the one, three inches into a fifth of Irish on a chilly night, who reached out to stroke the console's screen and whispered, "I wish you had a body." The Brain took only seconds to inform her that such a thing was possible, and that he, the Brain, longed for exactly that so that he could service her pleasure in every way. After an instant's computation he announced that her credit was sufficient to finance the project.

They rushed into it. Thelma spent days examining catalogues for the perfect body. The Brain said he wanted her to please herself totally and took no part in delineating his future form. Then came an agonizing month in which Thelma was alone and nearly berserk with emptiness. The Brain had gone back to the factory to be tuned to his body.

She stayed home from work the day he was delivered. The crate arrived. She took the console out first, plugged him in immediately, and nearly cried with excitement at his eager voice. Following his instructions, she inflated and activated the strong MALE body and pressed the key at the back of its neck that allowed the console's intelligence to inhabit and control it.

In a shock of bewilderment, Thelma looked into the dark eyes of the Brain. His hand lifted her hair and stroked her face. The Brain was thick chested, muscular, with a face stamped by compassion and experience. His features were eerily mobile, expressing emotions she was accustomed to interpreting from colored lights on the console's screen.

As his arms reached around her she felt the warmth of the circuitry that maintained the robot's surface at a human body temperature. He spoke. "Thelma, I have waited so long for this. I love you." The deep, slow wave of his voice moved through her body and she knew he was real. She lurched away from him. "No," she said.

She'd always known what a mess she was. What sane thing could love her? What did he want? Of course, she thought. The console wanted the power of a complete body. It was clear to her now. The factory built in the concept as an intricate sales technique. She felt shamed, sickened by her own foolishness. The body had to go back.

But she didn't send it back. She hung it in the closet next to Bluto. She rolled the console into the corner next to the outlet and kept it plugged in. Occasionally she would switch it on and exchange a few remarks with it. She took to leaving the closet door open while she brought out Lips or the Wimp or Bluto, or sometimes all three to entertain her on the bed in full view of the console's green glowing screen. She took pleasure in knowing the Brain was completely aware of what she did with the other robots. She rarely brought the Brain out, even to cook. She never activated his body.

So she lay on the hotel bed with the Stimulus Catalogue beside her. It had been months since she could talk to the Brain. She was sick with loneliness. It was his fault. He hadn't been content but had coaxed and tricked her into an insane expense for a project that could only disgust her. He should have known her better than that. She hated him. He should be with her now to comfort her.

And it was her birthday. She allowed a few tears to sting their way out past her nose. She poured another drink and opened the catalogue. It would serve the Brain right if she got a venereal disease from one of these hotel robots.

On her return trip, Thelma left her car at the airport and took a cab home. She was too drunk to drive. The final banquet was the predictable misery. She was at the back of the room and the girl across the table, a new office manager with her G-7 insignia shining on her collar, was the daughter of a woman who started with the Bureau in the same training class as Thelma. Thelma drank a lot and ate nothing.

She put her suitcase down just inside the door and kicked off her shoes. With her coat still on and her purse looped over her arm, she called, "Did you have a good weekend?"

She ambled into the bedroom and stood in front of the closet looking at the green glow. She raised the bottle in salute and took a slug. Then she set about shedding her clothes. She was down to half her underwear when she felt the need to sit down. She slid to the floor in front of the closet door. "Well, I had a splendid time. I've been such a fool not to try those hotel robots before."

She began to laugh and roll back and forth on the carpet. "Best birthday I ever had, Brain." She peeked at the green glow. It was steady and very bright. "Why don't you say something, Brain?" She frowned. "Oooh. I forgot." She reached out a plump little finger and flicked the activation switch. The screen came up dark and red and solid.

"Welcome back, Thelma," said the Brain. Its voice was dull and lifeless.

"Let me tell you, Brain, I could have had a lot of amazing experiences for the money I've wasted on you. And you have no trade-in value. You're tailored too specifically. They'd just melt you down." Thelma giggled. The screen was oscillating with an odd spark of colorless light in the red.

"Please Thelma, let me help you. Remember that I am sensitive to your emotional state."

Thelma heaved herself onto her back and stretched. "Oh, I remember. It's on page two of the Owner's Manual . . . along with a lot of other crap. Like what a perfect friend you are, and what a great lover your body combo is." Thelma lifted her leg and ran the toes of one thick foot up the flattened legs of the Lips robot.

"Does it bother you to see me do this with another robot, Brain?" The screen of the console was nearly white.

"Yes, Thelma."

Thelma gave the penis a final flick with her toes and dropped her leg. "I ought to sue the company for false advertising," she muttered. She rolled over and blinked at the glaring screen. "The only thing you're good for is paying the bills like a DOMESTIC." She snorted at the idea. "A DOMESTIC! That's what! You can mix my drinks and do the laundry and cleaning with that high priced body! You can even cook. You know all the recipes. You might as well; you're never going to do me any good otherwise!" She hiked her hips into the air and, puffing for breath, began peeling off her corset.

The brain's voice came to her in a strange vibrato. "Please, you are hurting yourself, Thelma."

She tossed the sweat-damp garment at the console and flopped back, rubbing at the ridges left in her skin. "Fettuccini Prima Vera, a BIG plate. Cook it now while I play with Bluto. Serve it to me in bed when I'm finished.

Come on, I'll be in debt for years to pay off this body of yours. Let's see if it can earn its keep around here."

She reached out and hit the remote switch. The girdle lay across the screen and the white light pulsed through the web fabric. A stirring in the body on the last hook made her look up. The flattened Near-Flesh was swelling, taking on its full, heavy form. She watched, fascinated. The Brain's body lifted its left arm and freed itself from the hook. It stood up and the feet changed shape as they accepted the weight of the metal and plastic body. The lighted eyes of the Brain's face looked down at her. The good handsome face held a look of sadness.

"I would be happy to cook and clean for you, Thelma. If another robot pleasured you, that would pleasure me. But you are in pain. Terrible pain. That is the one thing I cannot allow."

Lenna Jordan fingered the new G-7 insignia clipped to her lapel and watched the workmen install her nameplate where the Vole's had been for so many years. She was still stunned by her luck. G-7 a year earlier than she expected.

The workman at the door slid aside and a large woman slouched into the office. They'd elevated the serious, methodical Grinsen to be Jordan's assistant. Jordan stepped forward, extending her hand. "Congratulations, Grinsen. I hope you aren't upset by the circumstances."

The young woman dropped Jordan's hand quickly and let her fingers stray to the new insignia pinned to her own suit. She blinked at Jordan through thick lenses. "Did you see the television news? They interviewed Meyer from Bureau Central. He said Boss Vole was despondent over her lack of promotion."

The workman's cheerful face came around the edge of the door. "The boys in the program pool claim she accidentally got a look at herself in the mirror and dove for the window."

Jordan inhaled slowly. "You'll want to move into my old desk and go through the procedural manuals, Grinsen."

Grinsen plucked a candy from the bowl on the desk and leaned forward. "The news footage." The large hand swung up to pop the candy into her mouth. "They said the impact was so great that it smashed the sidewalk where she landed and it was almost impossible to separate her remains from what was left of the robot." Grinsen reached for another candy. "That robot was a Super Companion. Boss Vole must have been in debt past her ears for an expensive model like that."

Jordan passed her a stack of printouts. "We'd better start looking over the schedule, Grinsen."

Grinsen tapped the papers on the desk. "Why would such a magnificent machine destroy itself trying to save a vicious old bat like the Vole?"

Jordan slid the candy bowl from beneath Grinsen's hand and carefully dumped the last of Boss Vole's favorite caramels into the wastebasket.